W9-BRI-275

"I recommend anything by Sarah MacLean." LISA KLEYPAS

Escape in haste—
seduce at leisure...

"*I* vowed you would not die on my watch, and I mean to keep the promise." His attention fell to the place where his fingers painted honey across the nearly-healed wound on her shoulder, the stickiness of the salve nothing compared to the softness of her skin.

He cast about for a safe topic—their destination. Her destination. "You plan for a bookshop."

She nodded, the movement stilted. "I shall have a bookshop."

He imagined her disheveled and covered with dust, surrounded by books, and he liked it far too much.

He lifted his hand and looked down at it, glistening with honey. She looked, as well. "You should wash."

He should. Instead, he lifted his hand to his mouth and licked the honey from his fingers, meeting her gaze.

Her eyes widened, but did not waver. It was then that he knew.

If he kissed her, she would not stop him.

And if he kissed her, he would not stop.

SARAH MacLEAN

The Rogue
Not Taken

SCANDAL & SCOUNDREL, BOOK 1

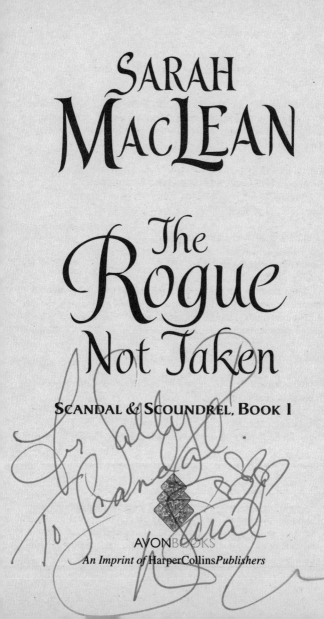

AVONBOOKS
An Imprint of HarperCollinsPublishers

This book is a work of fiction. The characters, incidents, and dialogue are drawn from the author's imagination and are not to be construed as real. Any resemblance to actual events or persons, living or dead, is entirely coincidental.

AVON BOOKS
An Imprint of HarperCollinsPublishers
195 Broadway
New York, New York 10007

Copyright © 2015 by Sarah Trabucchi
ISBN 978-0-06-237941-2
www.avonromance.com

First Avon Books mass market printing: January 2016

Avon Trademark Reg. U.S. Pat. Off. and in Other Countries, Marca Registrada, Hecho en U.S.A.
Avon, Avon Books, and the Avon logo are trademarks of Harper-Collins Publishers.
HarperCollins® is a registered trademark of HarperCollins Publishers.

Printed in the U.S.A.

10 9 8 7 6 5 4 3 2 1

For Dr. Howard Riina
and the wife he loves.
With endless gratitude.

Scandal & SCOUNDREL

Vol 1 / Iss 1   *Sunday, 10 June 1833*

DUKE AT DEATH'S DOOR?

WORD HAS IT that *notorious recluse*, the
Duke of Lyne, is nearing his end. What's more, a
confidential source tells **Scandal & SCOUNDREL**
that *his heir* (the RAPSCALLION and Riveting
"Royal Rogue") has been *summoned north* for a
FINAL face-to-face with his *frail father*. Will
Eversley extricate himself from the *embrace* of his
latest lady love to hasten HOME? Signs suggest
so, indicating *inheritance trumps inamorata*.

MORE TO COME.

Chapter 1

SOPHIE'S SOCIETY SPLASH

London
June 1833

If only the Countess of Liverpool hadn't been such an admirer of aquatic creatures, perhaps things would have turned out differently.

Perhaps no one would have witnessed the events of the thirteenth of June, the final, legendary garden party of the 1833 season. Perhaps London would have happily packed itself into myriad coaches that would have spread like beetles across the British countryside into summer idyll.

Perhaps.

But one year earlier, the Countess of Liverpool had received a gift of a half-dozen pretty orange-and-white fish that were said to be direct descendants of those beloved of the Shogun of Japan. Sophie thought the tale wholly unbelievable—Japan being notoriously insulated from the rest of the world—but Lady Liverpool was exceedingly proud of her pets, caring for the things with near-fanatical passion. Six had turned into two dozen, and the overlarge bowl in which the creatures were delivered had been traded for a container that could only be described as pondlike.

The fish had sparked the countess's imagination however, and the Liverpool Summer Soiree was oddly China-themed, despite the Countess of Liverpool knowing even less about China than she did of Japan. Indeed, when Lady Liverpool had greeted them in an elaborate white and orange diaphanous silk clearly intended to evoke her prized fish, she'd explained the disconnect. "No one knows a thing about Japan, you see. It's terribly private, which makes for no fun when it comes to a theme. And China is so very close . . . it's practically the same."

When Sophie had told the Countess that it was, in fact, not the same at all, the Countess had tittered with laughter and waved one arm replete with silk fins. "Don't fret, Lady Sophie, China has fish as well, I'm sure."

Sophie had cut her mother a look at the ignorant words, but received no acknowledgement. For weeks, she'd insisted that China and Japan were not one in the same but no one had been inclined to listen—her mother far too grateful for the invitation to such an elaborate affair. The Talbot sisters, after all, were exceptional at being elaborate.

They, along with the rest of the aristocracy, had turned out in an array of reds and golds, brocades each more intricate than the last, and topped with outrageous hats that had no doubt kept the milliners of London working night and day since the invitations had arrived.

Sophie, however, had resisted her mother's insistence that she participate in the farce and, to her family's dismay, arrived in ordinary pale yellow.

And so it was that on that lovely day in the middle of June, Lady Liverpool took pity on poor, uninteresting Sophie—the Talbot daughter who was neither the prettiest, nor the most diverting, nor the one who played the best pianoforte—and suggested that the young fish-out-of-water might like to visit with fish in their proper environment.

Sophie happily accepted the offer, grateful to exit the party of tittering aristocrats and their combined gaze—one that carefully avoided her and her family. There was, after all, never a stare so blatant as the one that carefully evaded its object. This was particularly true when the objects in question were so impossible to ignore.

The stares had followed the young ladies Talbot since they'd had their comings out—five in four years—each less welcome in Society than the last, the invitations growing fewer and fewer as the years progressed.

Sophie had always rather wished that her mother would give up on the dream of making her daughters Society darlings, but that would never happen. As a consequence, Sophie was here, alternately hiding in the topiary of the Liverpool estate and pretending not to hear the insults so regularly whispered about her sisters that they were barely whispered anymore.

So it was with no small amount of relief that Sophie followed her hostess's directions into the legendary Liverpool greenhouse, enormous and glass-enclosed, filled with a stunning array of flora and promising no gossip.

She searched for the fishpond, weaving her way between potted lemon trees and impressive ferns, until she heard the sound—a cry of sorts, rhythmic and unsettling, as though some poor creature was being tortured among the rhododendrons.

As she was not without conscience, and the creature in question clearly required assistance, Sophie investigated. Unfortunately, when she found the source of the noise, it became very clear that the woman did not require assistance.

She was already receiving assistance.

From Sophie's brother-in-law.

It bears noting that the woman was not Sophie's sister. Which was why, upon recovering from her initial shock, Sophie felt perfectly within her rights to interrupt. "Your Grace," she said, not at all quietly, the words filled with her contempt for this moment, this man, and this world that had given him so much power.

The pair stilled. A pretty blond head popped out from behind his arm, topped with a towering red silk pagoda, gold tassels hanging from its multitude of corners, swinging at her ears. Large blue eyes blinked.

The Duke of Haven did not deign to look at Sophie. "Leave us."

There was nothing in the world Sophie hated more than the aristocracy.

"Sophie? Mother is looking for you . . . She's waylaid Captain Culberth on the croquet field, poor man, and she's swatting him with that enormous fan she insisted on bringing. You should rescue the poor man."

Sophie closed her eyes at the words, willing them away. Willing their speaker away with them. She whirled around to stop her sister's advance. "No, Sera—"

"Oh." Seraphina, Duchess of Haven, née Talbot, came up short as she turned the corner into the copse of potted plants, taking in the scene, her hands flying to her ever-so-slightly-protruding stomach, where the future Duke of Haven grew. "Oh." Sophie saw shock flash in her sister's eyes as she took in the scene, followed quickly by sadness, and then cool calm. "Oh," the Duchess of Haven repeated.

The duke did not move. Did not look at his wife, the mother of his future child. Instead, he pushed one hand into those blond curls and spoke to the crook of his paramour's neck. "I said, *leave us*."

Sophie looked to Seraphina, tall and strong and hiding all the emotions that she must have been feeling. That Sophie couldn't help but feel with her. She willed her sister to speak. To stand for herself. For her unborn child.

Seraphina turned away.

Sophie couldn't help herself. "Sera! Will you not say something?" The eldest Talbot sister shook her head, and the resignation in the movement sent anger and indignation rioting through Sophie. She turned on her brother-in-law. "If she won't, I certainly will. You are disgusting. Pompous, hateful, and loathsome."

The duke turned a disdainful gaze on her.

"Shall I go on?" Sophie prompted.

The blond in his arms gasped. "Really! Speaking to a duke that way. It's terribly disrespectful."

Sophie resisted the urge to tear the stupid hat from the woman's head and club them both with it. "You're right. *I* am the disrespectful one in this situation."

"Sophie," Seraphina said softly, and Sophie heard the urgency in the word, the way it urged her away from the scene.

The duke heaved a long-suffering sigh, extricating himself from the lady in question, lowering her skirts and lifting her down from the table where she was perched. "Run along."

"But—"

"I said, go."

The woman knew when she was forgotten and she did as she was told, straightening her tassels and smoothing her skirts before taking her leave.

The duke turned, still buttoning the falls of his trousers. His duchess looked away. Sophie did not, moving in front of her sister, as though she could protect Seraphina from this horrible man she'd married. "If you think to frighten us off with your crassness, it won't work."

He raised a brow. "Of course it won't. Your family thrives on crassness."

The words were meant to sting, and they did.

The Talbot family was the scandal of the aristocracy. Sophie's father was a newly minted earl, having received his title a decade earlier from the then King. Though her father had never confirmed the gossip, it was generally accepted that Jack Talbot's fortune—made in coal—had purchased his title. Some said it was won in a round of faro; some said it was payment for the earl assuming a particularly embarrassing debt belonging to the King.

Sophie did not know, and she did not much care. After all, her father's title had nothing to do with her, and this aristocratic world was not one she would have chosen for herself.

Indeed, she would have chosen any world but this one, where people so misjudged and mistreated her sisters. She lifted her chin and faced her brother-in-law. "You don't seem to mind spending our money."

"Sophie," her sister said again, and this time, she heard the censure in the word.

She turned on Seraphina. "You cannot mean to protect him. It's true, isn't it? Before you, he was impoverished. What good is a dukedom if it's in shambles? He should be on his knees in gratitude that you came along and saved his name."

"Saved my name, did she?" The duke straightened one coat sleeve. "You're addled if you think that's how it happened. I landed your father every aristocratic investor he has. He exists because of my goodwill. And I spend the money with pleasure," he spat, "because being trapped into marriage by *your whore of a sister* has made me a laughingstock."

Sophie bit back her gasp at the insult. She knew the stories about her sister landing the duke, knew that her mother had crowed far and wide when her eldest had become a duchess. But it did not make his insults fair. "She's to bear your child."

"So she says." He pushed past them, making for the exit of the greenhouse.

"You doubt she increases?" she called after him, shocked, turning wide eyes on Seraphina, looking down at her hands clasped over the swell of her growing body. As though she could keep her child from the knowledge that his father was a monster of a man.

And then Sophie realized what he really meant. She chased after the duke. "You cannot doubt that it is *your* child?"

He swung around, gaze cold and filled with disdain. He did not look at Sophie, though. Instead, he looked at his wife. "I doubt every word that drips from her lying lips." He turned away, and Sophie looked to her sister, tall and proud and filled with cool reserve. Except for the single tear that spilled down her cheek as she watched her husband leave.

And in that moment, Sophie could no longer bear it, this world of rules and hierarchy and disdain. This world into which she had not been born. This world she had never chosen.

This world she hated.

She followed her brother-in-law, wanting nothing more than to avenge her sister.

He turned, possibly because he heard the desperation with which her sister called her name, or possibly because the sound of a woman running toward him was strange enough to surprise, or possibly because Sophie couldn't help but voice her frustration, the sound echoing loud and nearly feral in the glass enclosure.

She pushed him as hard as she could.

If he hadn't been turning, already off balance . . .

If she hadn't had momentum on her side . . .

If the ground beneath him hadn't been slick from the gardeners' thorough attention to their duties earlier in the day . . .

If the Countess of Liverpool hadn't had such a fondness for her fish . . .

"You little shrew!" the duke cried from the spot where he landed, at the center of the fishpond, knees drawn up, dark hair plastered to his head, eyes full of fury, making a promise he did not have to voice, but did nonetheless. "I shall destroy you!"

Sophie took a deep breath—knowing with utter certainty that, in this case, in for a penny was most definitely in for a pound—and stood, arms akimbo, at the edge of the pool, staring down on her usually imposing brother-in-law.

Not so imposing, now.

She grinned, unable to help herself. "I should like to see you try."

"Sophie," her sister said, and she heard the dismay and regret and sorrow in her name.

"Oh, Sera," she said, turning her smile on her sister, ignoring the dulcet tones of her brother-in-law's sputtering. "Tell me you didn't thoroughly enjoy that."

Sophie hadn't had such a pleasing moment in all her time in London.

"I did," her sister allowed quietly, "But I am, unfortunately, not the only one."

The duchess pointed over Sophie's shoulder, and she turned, dread pooling, to find the entirety of London staring at her through the enormous glass wall of the greenhouse.

The shaming came almost immediately.

It did not matter that her brother-in-law had deserved every bit of wet clothing, ruined boots, and embarrassment. It did not matter that any man who flaunted his sexual escapades before his increasing wife and her unmarried sister was the worst kind of beast. It did not matter that the scandal should have belonged wholly and exclusively to him.

Scandal did not stick to dukes.

To the young ladies Talbot, however, it stuck like honey on horsehair.

Once Jack Talbot had become the Earl of Wight and all of London had directed its attention and its disdain at the coarse, unrefined, supremely unaristocratic family, it had stuck, and it had stayed. That the newly minted earl's fortune had come from coal made the jests easy—the sisters were called the Soiled S's, which Sophie assumed was considered clever because the Talbot sisters were named, in order, Seraphina, Sesily, Seleste, Seline, and Sophie.

Though Sophie would prefer the Soiled S's to the other, less flattering moniker—whispered in ballrooms and tearooms and especially gentlemen's clubs, she had no doubt. A warning, ever since Seraphina had famously trapped her perfect duke into marriage. The meaning was clear; money might have purchased the earldom, the home in Mayfair, the beautiful—if extravagant—clothes, the perfect horseflesh, the overly gilded carriages, but it could never purchase a proper bloodline, and the girls might do anything necessary to marry into long-standing aristocratic circles.

The Dangerous Daughters.

The label was borne out by her three unmarried older sisters, each of whom was in the midst of an extravagant courtship with an equally extravagant suitor—courtships that bordered on the scandalous, and were at constant risk of remaining unfulfilled. Sesily was widely known to be the muse of Derek Hawkins, renowned artist and proprietor and star of the Hawkins Theater. Hawkins did not boast a title, but he boasted in every other imaginable way, and that was enough to win Sesily's heart—though Sophie couldn't for the life of her understand what her sister, or anyone else in Society, saw in the insufferable man.

Seleste was in a deeply emotional, exceedingly public back-and-forth with the wickedly handsome and unfortunately impoverished Earl of Clare. They were the most dramatic pair Sophie could imagine, arguing in front of entire ballrooms as often as they swooned into each other's arms. Seline, the second youngest sister, was courted by Mark Landry, owner of Landry's Bloodstock, which was giving Tattersall's a run for its money. Landry was crass and loud and hadn't a drop of blue blood, but if he married Seline—and Sophie thought he might—she would be the wealthiest of the sisters by far.

The courtships drew constant public attention and commentary, and the young ladies Talbot adored the scrutiny, each doing her best to tempt the scandal sheets—much to their mother's dismay. The sisters flourished under Society's censure, every tut behind a doyenne's fan driving them to more outrageous behavior.

All the sisters but Sophie, that was. At twenty-one, Sophie had always been the daughter whom scandal had avoided. She'd always assumed it was because she cared little for Society and their dictates and opinions, and somehow, Society seemed to understand that.

But now that the Duke of Haven was doused in water from the fishpond, with several pieces of freshwater flora stuck to his previously impeccably turned out trousers, it seemed that Society was no longer interested in leaving Sophie Talbot—widely considered to be "the quiet one" of the Dangerous Daughters—alone.

Sophie's cheeks blazed as she held her head high and exited the greenhouse, pausing in the doorway, eyes scanning the crowd. They were all there. Duchesses and marchionesses and countesses, staring from behind fluttering fans, their whispers like cicadas in the suddenly cloying summer air. It was not the ladies' response to her actions that was shocking, however. She had witnessed ladies gossip and feed upon scandal for years.

It was the men.

In her experience, the gentlemen of London cared little for gossip—leaving it in the purview of their wives as they turned their thoughts to other, more manly diversions. But apparently that was not the case when one of their own was maligned. They stared as well—the earls and marquesses and dukes—each title more venerable than the last. And in their eyes, in the force of their multitude, Sophie saw more than censure.

Loathing was so often described as cold; today, it felt hot as the sun. She lifted her hand without thinking, as though she could block the glowering heat.

"Sophie!" Her mother came rushing forward, her smile broad, her voice loud enough to carry through the throngs of whispering partygoers. The countess wore a gown of deep scarlet, which would have been scandalous enough if it were not topped with a ridiculous construction in the same hue that towered above her petite face, dwarfing her beauty in what she had been assured was "the height of Chinese fashion."

Right now, however, Lady Wight was not interested in her hat. Instead, she bore down on her youngest daughter, eyes filled with what could only be described as panic, Sophie's three middle sisters following like extravagantly dressed ducklings.

"Sophie!" the countess said. "What a scene you've made!"

"One might even think you were one of us," Sesily said dryly, her impressive décolletage threatening to burst from the seams of her outrageous gown—exceedingly tight and bordering on garish. Of course, Sesily had the temperament to wear such a thing and appear temptation herself. "Haven looked as though he wished to murder you."

I shall destroy you.

"I think he would have if we weren't so very public," Sophie replied.

"So *unfortunately* public," her mother hissed.

Sesily raised a brow and brushed an invisible speck from her bosom. "And if he weren't so very wet."

"You needn't point out your breasts, Sesily. We all have them," Seleste said dryly through a gossamer veil of gold thread, cascading down her face and neck from a crownlike contraption.

Seline snickered.

"Girls!" the countess hissed.

"It really was magnificent, Sophie," Seline said. "Whoever thought you had it in you?"

Sophie turned a scathing gaze on her next oldest sister. "What does that mean?"

"This is not the time, girls," their mother interjected. "Do you not see that this might ruin us all?"

"Nonsense," Sesily said. "How many threats of ruination must we face before you see we're like cats?"

"Even cats have a limit on their lives. We must repair this damage. Immediately," the Countess of Wight said before remembering where they were, on full view in front of all of London, and said, loud enough for all of London to hear, "We all saw what happened! His Poor Grace!"

Sophie stilled, the words surprising her. "*Poor?*"

"Yes of course!" Impossibly, the countess's voice rose an octave.

Sophie blinked.

"You'd better go along with it," Seline said casually as they crowded around her like great, gilded cormorants, all flapping fans and swinging tassels, "Or Mother will go mad with fear of exile."

"I wouldn't worry," Seleste said. "It's not as though any of them would *really* exile us. They can barely keep up with us."

Sesily nodded. "Precisely. They adore our wicked scenes. What would they do with themselves if they did not have us?"

It was not untrue.

"And we shall rise farther than any of them. Look at Seraphina."

"Except Seraphina is married to a proper ass," Sophie pointed out.

"Sophie! Language!" Her mother sounded as though she might faint from panic.

Her sisters nodded.

"We shall have to avoid that bit," Sesily said.

"It's clear that he slipped and toppled into the pond!" the countess shouted quite desperately, her wide blue eyes growing wide enough for Sophie to wonder if it were possible for them to pop right out of their sockets. A vision flashed, of her mother groping around on the perfectly manicured grass for her eyeballs, odd hat toppling from her head, unable to bear its own weight.

What a scene.

It was her turn to snicker.

"Sophie!" the countess hissed through her teeth. "Don't you dare!"

The snicker turned into a snort.

The Countess of Wight continued, hand to her chest. "Poor, poor Haven!"

It was all Sophie could take. The laugh never came, because it was so stifled by anger. Her family hadn't been the same since the title had arrived, making her mother a countess and her sisters not simply exceedingly wealthy, but exceedingly wealthy *ladies*, giving Society no choice but to acknowledge their presence. And suddenly, these women, whom she'd never thought cared much for the trappings of name and money, had cared very much.

They had never seen the truth—that the Talbot family could marry into royalty, and they'd never be welcome in Society. That Society suffered their presence because they couldn't risk losing the advice and intelligence of the new earl, or the funds that came with each of the daughters. Marriage was, after all, the most critical business in Britain.

Sophie's family knew it better than anyone.

And they adored the game. Its machinations.

But Sophie wanted none of it. She never had. For the first decade of her young life, she'd lived in the idyll that came from money without title. She'd played in the green hills of Mossband. She'd learned to make pasties from her grandmother in the kitchens of the Talbot family home, because they were her father's favorite luncheon treat.

She'd ridden her horse to town to fetch beef from the butcher and cheese from the cheesemonger. She'd never dreamed of a titled husband. She'd planned for a sound, reasonable future, married to the baker's son.

And then her father was made an earl. And everything changed. She hadn't been to Mossband in ten years, when her mother had closed up the house and happily taken up residence in Mayfair. Her grandmother was gone, died not a year after they'd left the house. Pasties had been deemed too common for earls. The butcher and the cheesemonger now delivered their wares to the back entrance of their impressive Mayfair town house. And the baker's son . . . he was a distant, foggy memory.

No one else in the family seemed to have any trouble at all adjusting to this world that Sophie had never wanted. For which she'd never asked.

No one else in the family seemed to care that Sophie hated it.

And so it was that there, in the gardens of the Liverpool estate, with all of London looking on, Sophie grew tired of pretending that she was one of these people. That she belonged in this place. That she needed its acceptance.

She had money. And she had legs to carry her.

She looked to her sisters, each beautifully appointed, each certain that she would one day rule this world. And Sophie knew she'd never be them. She'd never enjoy the scandal. She'd never want this world and its trappings.

So why defer to it?

It wasn't as though the *ton* would welcome her after today; why not take her scandal and speak the truth for once?

In for a penny, in for a pound, as her father always said.

She turned her gaze on the group of them. "Of course.

It is a travesty that poor His Grace so degraded our sister that I had no choice but to play the hero and avenge her honor, as none of the rest of these so-called gentlemen have been willing to do so," she said, loud enough for all of London to hear. "Poor His Grace, indeed, that he was raised in this world that has deluded both itself and him into thinking that a title makes anything close to a gentleman, when he—along with most of his brethren, if one is honest—is a boor. And something much worse. That rhymes with boor."

Her mother's eyes went wide. "Sophie! Ladies do not say such things!"

How many times had she been admonished for not being ladylike enough? How many times had she been molded into the perfect image of this aristocratic world that would never accept her? That would never accept any of them, if not for its need of their money? "I wouldn't worry," she replied in front of all of London. "It's not as though they think us ladies as it is."

Her sisters stilled.

"Sophie," Seline said, the word filled with disbelief and not a small amount of respect.

"Well. That was unexpected," Sesily said.

The countess lowered her voice to a barely-there whisper. "What have I told you about having opinions? You'll destroy yourself! And your sisters with you! Do not do something that you will regret!"

Sophie did not lower her voice when she said, "My only regret is that the pool was not deeper. And filled with sharks."

Sophie did not know what it was that she'd expected from the moment. Gasps, perhaps. Or whispers. Or high-pitched ladies' cries. Or even loud, masculine harrumphs.

She wouldn't have minded a swoon or two.

But she didn't expect silence.

She didn't expect cool, exacting disinterest, or the way the entire garden party simply turned from her and began again, as though she'd never spoken. As though she wasn't there.

As though she'd never been there to begin with.

Which made it fairly easy to turn her own back, and walk away.

Chapter 2

EVERSLEY ESCAPES;
ILLICIT EXIT INFURIATES EARL

Sophie soon discovered that there was a flaw in turning one's back on the aristocracy at a garden party in front of all the aristocracy.

Leaving aside the obvious—that is, the actual ruination—there was a much more immediate concern. That is, that once one had roundly rejected the attendees of said party, one could not linger. Indeed, one must find one's way home, under one's own steam, as hiding out in the family carriage would dampen the force of one's exit, truth be told.

That, and she wasn't certain her mother wouldn't commit filicide if she came upon Sophie in the family carriage. She needed an escape route that did not involve Talbots. At least until she was ready to apologize.

If she was ever ready to apologize.

She hated this world, these people, and their snide references to the Talbot crassness, to the Talbot money, to her father's purchased title, to her sister's allegedly stolen one. She hated every one of their smug faces, the way they sneered at her family and the way they lived. The way they lived their lives as though the rest of the world revolved around them.

She hated them slightly more than she hated the fact that her family didn't seem to mind any of it.

Indeed, they reveled in it.

No, she was not ready to apologize for telling the truth. And she was not ready for the gleeful defense of the aristocracy that came whenever she mentioned her concerns to her sisters.

So it was that Sophie was hiding out not in the family carriage, but on the far edge of Liverpool House, considering her next step, when she narrowly missed being hit on the head by a great, black boot.

She looked up with enough time to avoid the next Hessian projectile, and watched with surprise and not a small amount of wonder as a charcoal grey topcoat and a long linen cravat followed the footwear out of the second-story window, the latter of which became entangled in the rose climbing the trellis on the side of the house.

And all that was before the man made an appearance.

Sophie's eyes widened as one long, trousered leg exited the house, a stockinged foot finding purchase on the trellis before the rest of the man appeared, clad in a linen shirt. He straddled the windowsill, and Sophie found herself gazing up at a classically formed thigh topped by the curved strength of something else that, though equally classically impressive, she knew she should not be noticing.

To be honest, however, when a man descended a rose trellis two stories above one's head, it was best one notice. For one's personal safety.

It was not her fault that the part of him she noticed was inappropriate for noticing.

And then a matching, equally well-formed leg was

over the sill and the man was climbing down the trellis as though he were highly skilled at such a thing. Considering the look of him, Sophie imagined this was not the first time he'd traveled via rose trellis.

He dropped to the ground in front of her, back to her, and crouched to gather his discarded clothing as a second man popped his head over the windowsill. Sophie's eyes widened as she stared up at the Earl of Newsom.

"You goddamn bastard! I shall have your head!"

"You shan't and you know it," the earthbound man said smartly, coming to his full, impressive height, clothes and one boot in hand, reaching up to extricate his cravat from the trellis. "But I suppose you had to say it anyway."

The man above sputtered and spewed unintelligible noises before he disappeared.

"Coward," Sophie's now-companion muttered, shaking his head and turning his attention to the ground in a search for his second boot.

She beat him to it, leaning down to rescue the discarded item from its place at her feet. When she straightened, it was to find him facing her, his expression part curiosity, part amusement.

She inhaled sharply.

Of course, the man escaping the upper chambers of Liverpool House was the Marquess of Eversley. The man was not called the Royal Rogue for nothing, apparently.

Later, she would attribute her blunt "It's you," to the emotional turbulence of the day.

And she would attribute his wide grin, elaborate bow, and subsequent "So it is," to his notorious, long-standing arrogance.

She clutched his boot closer to her chest. "What did you do?" She lifted her chin to the second floor of the house. "To deserve defenestration?"

His brows rose. "To deserve what?"

She sighed. "Defenestration. The tossing of an object from a window."

He began to tie his cravat expertly, the long linen strips weaving to and fro. For a moment she was distracted by the fact that he did not seem to require a valet or a looking glass. And then he spoke. "First, I wasn't tossed. I left of my own volition. And second, any woman who uses a word like *defenestration* is surely intelligent enough to divine what I was doing before I exited the building."

He was everything he was purported to be. Scandalous. Sinful. An utter scoundrel. Everything Society vilified, even as it celebrated it. Just like her brother-in-law. And any number of other men and women of the British aristocracy. A fine example of the worst of this world into which he'd been born. And into which she'd been dragged.

She loathed him instantly.

He reached for the boot. She stepped backward, out of reach. "So, what the gossip pages say about you is true."

He tilted his head. "I make every effort not to read the gossip pages, but I guarantee that whatever they say about me is not true."

"They say you revel in ruining marriages."

He straightened his sleeves. "False. I don't touch married women."

At that moment, a lady's coiffed head popped out of the window above. "He's headed down!"

The warning that his opponent was coming to face him spurred the marquess to motion. "'Tis my cue." He extended one hand to Sophie. "As lovely as this has been, my lady, I require my boot."

Sophie clutched the boot closer to her chest, staring up at the lady. "That's Marcella Latham."

The Earl of Newsom's fiancée—now former fiancée, Sophie would wager—waved happily. "Thank you, Eversley!"

He turned up and winked. "My pleasure, darling. Enjoy."

"I hope you don't mind my telling my friends?"

"I look forward to hearing from them."

Lady Marcella disappeared into the window. Sophie thought the entire exchange rather bizarre and . . . collegial . . . for two people caught in a compromising situation by her rich, titled future husband.

"My lady," the Marquess of Eversley prompted.

Sophie looked to him. "You ended their marriage."

"Their engagement, really." He extended his hand. "I require footwear, poppet. Please."

She ignored the gesture. "So, you only touch betrothed women."

"Precisely."

"Very different, I suppose." Was there not a single member of the aristocracy worthy of knowing? "You're a scoundrel."

"So I am told."

"A rogue."

"That's what they say," he said, watching over her shoulder intently.

"Unscrupulous in every way."

An idea began to form.

He focused on her, seeming to notice her for the first time. His brows rose. "You look as though you've come nose to antennae with a large insect."

She became aware of her wrinkled nose. Consciously unwrinkled it. "Apologies," she lied.

"Think nothing of it."

And there, as she considered him, dressed in his summer finery, missing a boot, she realized that, horrid or not, in that moment, he was precisely what she required. If she could stomach him for the three quarters of an hour it would take to get home. "You are going to have to leave here rather quickly if you don't want a run-in with Lord Newsom."

"I'm so happy that you understand. If you'd give me my boot, I could make some haste." He reached for the footwear. She stepped backward once more, remaining out of reach. "My lady," he said firmly.

"It seems that you are in a particular position." She paused. "Or, perhaps it is *I* who am in a particular position."

His gaze narrowed. "And what position is that?"

"A position to negotiate." He was her transport home.

A shout came from around the corner of the house, and his attention slid past her, to where his enemy was no doubt about to appear. She took the opportunity to escape, boot in hand, toward the back of the house, where a line of trees and underbrush hid a low stone wall and, beyond it, a line of carriages waiting for their owners to leave the revelry and head home.

He followed her. He had to. After all, she had his boot.

And he had a carriage.

It was an ideal trade. Once protected from view by the trees, she turned to him. "I have a proposition for you, Lord Eversley."

His brows rose. "I'm afraid I'm through with propositions for the day, Lady Sophie. And even I know better than to engage in a public assignation with one of the Dangerous Daughters."

He knew who she was. She blushed at the words, anger and embarrassment warring on her cheeks. Anger won out. "You realize that if *you* were female, you would have been exiled from Society years ago."

He lifted one shoulder. Dropped it. "Ah, but I am not female. And thank God for that."

"Yes, well, some of us are not so lucky. Some of us don't have your freedom."

He met her gaze, suddenly very serious. "You don't know the first thing about freedom."

She did not back down. "I know you have more of it than I will ever be allowed. And I know that without it, I must resort to—" She searched for the word.

"Nefariousness?" he supplied, his seriousness gone once more, so quickly that Sophie almost paused to consider it. Until she remembered that he was far too irritating for thoughtful speculation.

"There is nothing nefarious about this."

"We are together in a secluded area, my lady. If you intend for it to end in the same manner your sister's assignation with her former lover and now husband famously ended, it's quite nefarious."

Of all the infuriating things the man could say. She stamped her foot on the thick spread of ground cover. "I am really quite tired of hearing about poor maligned Haven and how my sister trapped him into marriage."

"He didn't sign up for marrying your sister," Eversley said.

"Then he should not have been fiddling about with her ink!" she pronounced.

When he laughed, Sophie changed her mind about him being infuriating.

The man was horrible.

"You think it amusing?"

He pressed a hand to his chest. "I apologize." The snicker became a laugh again. "Fiddling about with her ink!"

She scowled. "It was your figure of speech."

"But you made it really, tremendously perfect. I assure you, if you understood the double entendre inherent in the metaphor, you would, as well."

"I doubt that."

"Oh, for your sake, I hope I'm right. I'd hate to think you're no fun."

"I'm perfectly fun!" she said.

"Really? You're Sophie, the youngest of Talbot girls, aren't you?"

"I am."

"The unfun one."

She rocked back at the description. Was that what people said about her? She hated the little flare of sadness that came at the words. The hesitation. The tiny glimmer of fear that he might actually be correct. "*Unfun* isn't a word."

"Until five minutes ago, *defenestration* wasn't one, either."

"Of course it was!" she announced.

He rocked back on his heels. "So you say."

"It's a word," she declared imperiously before recognizing the teasing gleam in his eye. "Oh. I see."

He spread his hands wide, as though proving his point. "Unfun."

"I'm perfectly fun," she said, without conviction.

"I don't think so," he said smartly. "Look at you. Not a nod to the Orient to be found."

She scowled. "It's a ridiculous theme for a garden party attended by people with no knowledge of and even less interest in the country of China."

He smirked. "Be careful. Lady Liverpool might hear you."

She straightened her shoulders. "As Lady Liverpool is dressed as a *Japanese fish*, I don't imagine she would care about my views."

His brows rose. "Is that a jest, Lady Sophie?"

"It is an observation."

He tutted. "So. Unfun after all."

"Well, I think you are *unpleasant*. Which *is* a word," she said.

"You'd be the first woman to think that."

"Surely I cannot be the first woman of sound mind you've ever encountered."

He chuckled, the sound warm and . . . strangely inviting. Pleasing. A sound of approval.

She pushed the thought away. She didn't care if he approved her. She didn't care what he thought of her. Or what the rest of his silly, vapid, horrible world thought of her. Honestly, if all of Society thought her *unfun*—she grimaced inwardly at the word—why should she care? He was a means to an end.

"I've had enough," she said, returning to the situation at hand. She'd watched her father negotiate enough over her lifetime that she knew when it was time to speak frankly and get a deal done. "I assume you are leaving the party?"

The question caught Eversley by surprise. "As a matter of fact, I am."

"Take me with you."

He barked a single expression of shock. "Ah. No."

"Why not?"

"So many reasons, poppet. Not the least of which is this—I've no intention of being saddled with one of the Soiled S's."

She stiffened at the moniker. Most people did not call them such to their faces. She supposed she should expect nothing less from this horrible man. "I do not intend to ensnare you, Lord Eversley. I assure you, even if I had *had* such an idea, this interaction"—she waved a hand back and forth between them—"would have cured me of such an affliction." She took a deep breath. "I require escape. Surely you understand that. As you seem to re-quire the same."

He focused on her. "What happened?"

She looked away, remembering the cold gaze of Soci-ety. Its wicked cut. "It is not important."

His brows rose. "If you're in the woods with me, love, I'd say it is quite important."

"This is a strip of trees. Not 'the woods.'"

"You're very contrary for someone who needs me."

"I don't need you."

"Then give me my boot and I'll be on my way."

She tightened her grip on the boot. "I need your car-riage. That's a different thing altogether."

"My carriage is about to be otherwise engaged," he said.

"I simply need conveyance home."

"You've four sisters, a mother, and a father. Ride with them."

"I can't."

"Why not?"

Pride.

Well, she certainly wasn't going to tell him *that*.

"You shall just have to trust me."

"Again, the ladies of your family don't exactly have reputations that engender trust."

She did not pretend to misunderstand. "Oh, and you are the very portrait of respectability."

He grinned. "I don't trade on respectability, love."

She was beginning to hate him.

She nodded. "Fine. You leave me no choice but to resort to extreme measures." His brows rose. "Take me, or lose your boot."

He watched her for a long moment, and she willed her-self to remain still under his consideration. She attempted to convince herself not to notice the beautiful green of his eyes; the long, straight line of his aristocratic nose; the handsome curve of his lips.

She should not be noticing his lips.

She swallowed at the thought, and his gaze flickered to the place where her throat betrayed the movement. His lips twitched. "Keep the boot."

It took a moment for her to remember what it was they had been talking about.

Before she could think of a retort, he was through the trees and over the wall, headed for his carriage on one stockinged foot.

By the time she reached the wall, he was at the front of a large, smart-looking black carriage, fussing about with the horses. Sophie watched him for long moments, wishing he would step on something uncomfortable. It appeared he was rehitching all the horses, checking harnesses and straps, but that would be silly, as he no doubt had a stableful of servants to do just that.

Once he'd inspected each of the six horses, he entered the coach, and Sophie watched as a young, liveried outrider closed the door with a snap and ran ahead to help make way for the carriage to exit through the crush of conveyances.

She sighed.

The Marquess of Eversley had no idea of how lucky he was to be blessed with the freedom that came with funds and masculinity. She imagined he was already stretched across the seat of that luxurious carriage, the portrait of aristocratic idleness, considering a nap to recover from his exertion earlier in the afternoon.

Lazy and immovable.

She had no doubt that he'd already forgotten her. She didn't imagine he spared much room for remembering most people—there wasn't much point, after all, with the constant stream of ladies in his life.

She doubted he even remembered his servants.

Her gaze flickered to the footman, not nearly old enough to be a footman. Likely more of a page. The boy stood on the edge of the stream of carriages, watching as drivers slowly returned to their seats and began to shift and move their charges to release the Eversley conveyance.

Her reticule grew heavy in her hand, its weight the result of the money inside. *Never leave the house without enough blunt to win you a fight.* Her father's words had been drilled into the minds of all the Talbot sisters—not that aristocratic ladies often found themselves requiring assistance to escape fisticuffs.

But Sophie was no fool, and she knew that the interaction with Society she'd just had was the closest thing to a fight she was likely to ever experience. She had no doubt that her father would deem the funds in her reticule well spent on escape.

Decision made, she approached the footman.

"Excuse me, sir?"

The servant turned, surprised, no doubt, to find a young lady at his elbow, holding a gentleman's boot. He bowed quickly. "M-my lady?"

He was as young as he'd looked. Younger than she was. Sophie sent a quick prayer of thanks to her maker. "How long before the carriage is free to leave?" she asked in a tone that she hoped was all casualness.

He seemed grateful for a question he could answer. "No more than a quarter of an hour, my lady."

She had to work quickly, then. "And tell me, do you work for the marquess?"

He nodded, his gaze flickering to the boot in her hands. "Today."

She shoved the boot behind her back, unable to keep the surprise from her voice. "Not for long?"

The boy shook his head. "I am headed to a new position. In the North Country."

A shadow crossed his face—sadness, perhaps. Regret? She grasped at it, an idea forming before she could consider it from all angles. "But you wish to stay in London?"

He seemed to realize then that he absolutely should not be speaking with an aristocratic lady. He lowered his head. "I am pleased to serve the marquess however he requires, my lady."

She nodded quickly. Underservants were shuttled from one holding to another with unfortunate regularity. She had no doubt that Eversley had never thought twice about the fact that his employees might not wish to be moved about at his whim. He did not seem the type to think of others at all.

And so it was that Sophie felt no guilt whatsoever when she put her plan in motion. "I wonder, though, if you might be willing to serve an earl?"

His wide gaze snapped to hers. "My lady?"

"My father is the Earl of Wight."

The young man blinked.

"Here. In London."

The boy seemed confused by the offer and, if she was honest, Sophie was not surprised. It was not every day, she imagined, that pages received employment opportunities at garden parties.

She pressed on. "He began his life in the coalfields. Like his father and his father's father before him. He's not an ordinary aristocrat." Still nothing. Sophie spoke frankly. "He pays servants very well. He'll pay you double what the marquess pays." She paused. Increased the offer. "More."

The boy tilted his head.

"And you can stay in London," Sophie added.

His brow knit. "Why me?"

She smiled. "What is your name?"

"Matthew, my lady."

"Well, Matthew, someone's lucky star should shine today, don't you think?"

The boy remained skeptical, but she could tell he was considering the offer when he looked over her shoulder to the Marquess of Eversley's carriage and said, "Double, you say?"

She nodded.

"I've 'eard the servants' quarters at Wight Manor are the nicest in London," he said, and Sophie knew she had him.

She leaned in. "You can see for yourself. Tonight."

He narrowed his gaze.

"You come round this afternoon, after the party disbands. Ask to speak to Mr. Grimes—my father's secretary. Tell him I sent you. I shall vouch for you when you arrive." She reached into her reticule and extracted a piece of paper and a pencil, and scribbled the direction of her family's home in Mayfair and a quick note to ensure him entry to the house. She reached back into her purse and pulled out two coins. Handing the coins and the letter to the boy, she added, "That's two crowns."

The boy gaped at her. "That's a month's worth of blunt!"

She ignored the crass reference to the money. After all, she'd been banking on such crassness. "And my father will pay you more than that. I promise."

His lips pressed flat together.

"You don't believe me," she said.

"I'm to believe a girl?"

She ignored the insult in the words, instead meeting his gaze. "How much would it take for you to believe me?"

His brows knit together and he said, more question than statement, "A quid?"

It was an enormous amount, but Sophie understood the power of money and the things it could buy—trust included—better than most. She reached back into her purse and extracted the rest of the money she carried. She didn't hesitate in paying the boy, knowing she would replenish her stash the moment she returned home.

The boy's hand curled around the coins tightly, and Sophie knew she'd won. "There is only one other thing," she said slowly, a little twinge of guilt threading through her.

Her father's newest and most loyal servant did not hesitate. "Anything you require, my lady."

"Anything?" she asked, unable to keep the hope from her tone.

He nodded. "Anything."

She took a deep breath, knowing that once she put this plan into motion, it would be impossible to turn back. Knowing, too, that if she were caught, she would be flatly ruined.

She looked behind her, Liverpool House rising like the gates of hell above the trees. Frustration and sadness and anger warred within her as she remembered the gardens. The party. The greenhouse. Her pig of a brother-in-law. The way all of London rallied in his support. Against her. The way they shunned her. Shamed her.

She had to leave this place. Now. Before they realized how much that shaming stung.

And there was only one way to do it.

She turned back to Matthew. "I require your livery."

Chapter 3

SOPHIE'S FROCK FOUND!
FOUL PLAY FEARED!

*I*t took longer than it should have for Sophie to realize that the carriage was not headed for Mayfair.

Had she realized this prior to clandestinely squeezing into Matthew's livery and tucking her hair up under his cap, she might have had the presence of mind to turn back. She most certainly would have taken the calculated risk to sit up on the block next to the coachman instead of refusing his invitation.

Unfortunately, she did not realize it—despite the coachman's raised brows and skeptical "Suit yourself"—instead taking her place as an outrider at the back of the coach, standing tall on the back step of the coach, clinging tightly, and quite happily, to its handles.

Nor did she realize it when the coach reached the end of the long drive of Liverpool House and turned left instead of right.

Nor did she realize it when the passing landscape became more pastoral. Instead, she took several deep breaths of what her father would call "fine fettled air," and felt—for the first time since she and her sisters had been packed up and transported to London—rather free.

And decidedly *fun*.

Take that, odious Royal Rogue.

Thinking of the unknowing Marquess of Eversley, inside the very carriage upon which she stowed away, she laughed. So much for his thinking she wouldn't get that for which she'd asked. She almost regretted that he wouldn't know it when she leapt from the carriage and sallied home.

She'd pay good money to see his smug expression turned to shock.

She chuckled to herself, watching blue sky and green farmland pass, dotted with flocks of sheep, copses of trees, and bales of hay. And gloried in the fact that she had escaped without the aid or the attention of the aristocracy. She could never tell anyone this story, sadly. Within moments of her return to the Talbot house on Berkeley Square, she would have to dispose of Matthew's exceedingly helpful—if ill-fitting—clothing and concoct a new tale of her return. And swear her father's new young footman to secrecy.

But for now, until the rooftops of London appeared in the distance and reminded her that the afternoon—and her public and no doubt long-term shaming—were inescapable, she would enjoy her triumph.

And she did enjoy it, cheeks aching from the pull of her grin, until she became aware of other aches, in her legs and arms.

At first, she ignored them. She was strong enough to manage for the few miles back to Mayfair. The streets of London would require stops and starts and slow going, and all she had to do was keep her head down and hold fast, and she'd be home within the hour.

And then her feet started in, still in their silken slippers, as Matthew's boots had been too small for her always-too-long "flippers," as her father referred to them, refusing to accept the fact that the comparison to water creatures was not at all complimentary.

Silk slippers, it turned out, were not made for outriding.

Nor, it turned out, was Sophie.

Indeed, within half an hour, she was having a difficult time of it, her hands now aching as well, under the too-tight grip she had on the back of the carriage. She hadn't expected her role as outrider to be quite so taxing.

She gritted her teeth, reminding herself that there were more difficult situations than this one in the world. Men had built bridges. Families had fled to the Colonies. She was daughter to a coal miner. Granddaughter to one.

Sophie Talbot could hang on to a carriage for the two miles it took to get home.

The carriage increased its speed, as though the universe itself had heard her words and desired to underscore her idiocy. She looked down and considered leaping to the ground and walking the rest of the way. Watching the road tear past, she unconsidered it.

She'd wished to leave a garden party, not the earth.

"Oh, bollocks."

Sophie. Language. She heard her mother's admonition in the minuscule part of her brain that was not currently panicking, but she had no doubt that if there was ever a time for cursing, it was this one—dressed as a servant, clinging to a carriage, certain she was going to die.

And then the coach passed a mail coach laden with people, a small child hanging off the top of it, grinning down at her.

That's when Sophie realized that, wherever this carriage and the man inside were headed, it was not London.

"Oh, bollocks," she repeated. Louder.

The child waved.

Sophie did not dare release her grip to return the gesture. Instead, she tightened her hold, pressed her forehead to the cool wood of the carriage, and chanted her litany.

"Bollocksbollocksbollocks," she said.

As though punishing her for her crassness, a wheel hit a rut in the road, and the vehicle bounced, jarring her spine and nearly tossing her from the back of the coach. She cried out in fear and desperation. Clinging tightly, the ache in her hands sharp now.

There was only one option. She had to get off this carriage. Immediately. It was only two or three miles to the Talbot home. She could walk if she exited this ridiculous situation immediately.

The coachmen called back, "I told you to sit with me!"

Sophie closed her eyes. "When do we stop?"

She waited long seconds for the terrifying reply. "It's good weather, so I'd say we'll make it in three hours. Maybe four!"

She groaned, the sound coming on a word far worse than *bollocks*. Leaping from the carriage was suddenly an entirely viable possibility.

"I suppose you're changing your mind about riding on the block?" called the coachman.

Of course she was changing her mind. She never should have gone through with such a terrible plan. If she hadn't vowed to run from the silly garden party, she'd be home now. And not here—minutes away from falling to her death.

"Shall I stop so you can join me?"

She barely heard the part of the question that came after the word *stop*.

Dear God. Yes. Please stop.

"Yes, please!"

The carriage began to slow, and relief flooded her, replacing everything else, making her forget her panic and pain for a fleeting moment. A very fleeting moment.

"I thought it odd, that you would want to ride on the back of the coach all afternoon."

Well, the coachman could have said as much. Then they wouldn't be in this predicament. As Sophie wouldn't have set foot on the coach if she had known that there was even a hint of possibility that the Marquess of Eversley wasn't headed to Mayfair. But she was not about to waste time dwelling on her mistake, when she could be spending time rectifying it. She released her grip, shoulders straight and head high, taking a deep breath, preparing to descend from the carriage and announce that Matthew was not joining them for the ride to wherever they were headed. And neither was she.

Freedom was a wonderful thing.

She was half looking forward to the marquess's shock when he discovered that she'd stowed away. He could do with a surprise now and then to offset his arrogant existence, and she was thrilled to be able to give it to him.

Right up until her legs gave way and she collapsed to the ground in an ungraceful, inglorious heap.

"Bollocks." It was becoming her very favorite word.

The coachman's eyes widened from high above, and she couldn't blame him, as she felt certain that outriders had one, single responsibility—to refrain from falling off the carriage.

"On your feet, you clumsy git," the coachman called, no doubt thinking he sounded charmingly teasing. "I haven't all day to wait for you!"

Gone was her triumph.

Gone was her freedom.

She pushed up onto her hands and knees, muscles aching after the strain of hanging on to the carriage along the bumpy roads. She stood slowly, keeping her back to the carriage as she straightened her spine and rolled her shoulders back. "I'm afraid you shall have to wait," she said, "as I require an audience with the marquess."

There was a beat as the words settled with the driver, along with a fair amount of shock, no doubt, that a footman would deign to demand to speak with his master.

Wouldn't he be surprised when he realized that the Marquess of Eversley was not her master after all. And that she was not his footman.

She felt a slight twinge of remorse when she considered that the coachman would have to retrace their path to London once she revealed herself—his body was no doubt protesting their travels as much as hers was.

"Are you mad?" he asked, all incredulity.

She looked up at him. "Not at all." She approached the carriage and banged on the door. "Open, my lord."

There was no movement from inside the vehicle. The door remained firmly shut.

"You are mad!" the coachman announced.

"I swear to you, I am not," she said. "Eversley!" she called, ignoring the twinge of pain that came as she rapped smartly on the great black coach. He was probably asleep, as one would expect from a lazy aristocrat. "Open this door!"

He was going to be furious when he saw her, but she did not care. Indeed, Sophie had a keen, unyielding desire to teach the outrageous, unbearable aristocrat a lesson. She was certain that no one had ever done such a thing—no one had ever crossed the Marquess of Eversley, known in private conversations as King. As though he weren't pompous enough, he assumed the highest title in Britain as his name.

And all of London simply accepted it. They called him

by the ridiculous moniker. Or the other one—the Royal Rogue—as though it were a compliment and not complete blasphemy.

And she'd been exiled for telling the truth about a duke.

Anger flared, threaded with something else—something she did not enjoy and which she would not name.

Sophie scowled at the carriage, as though it were the manifestation of the man inside. Of the world that created him, empty and aristocratic, imperious and infuriating.

As though nothing ever defied him.

Until now. Until her.

"He's not in there."

She looked up to the coachman. "What did you say?"

He was exasperated—that much was clear—becoming less and less forgiving of her perceived madness. "The marquess isn't inside and the ride has addled you. Get up on the block. We're miles from anywhere, and you're wasting the daylight, you mad git."

She looked to the door, refusing to believe the words. "What do you mean, he isn't inside?"

The coachman stared down at her, unamused. "He. Ain't. Inside. Which part of it is confusing?"

"I saw him get in!"

The driver spoke as though she was a child. "We're to meet him there."

She blinked. "Where?"

Exasperation won the day, and the driver turned back to the road with a sigh. "I told them not to saddle me with a boy I didn't know. Suit yourself. I haven't the time to wait for your senses to return from wherever they've run off."

With a flick of his wrists, the horses were moving, along with the carriage.

Leaving her stranded on the road.

Alone.

To be set upon by whomever happened by.

Bollocks.

She cried out, "No! Wait!"

The carriage stopped, barely long enough for her to scramble up onto the driver's block before it moved again.

For a moment, she considered telling the coachman everything. Revealing herself. Throwing herself at his mercy and hoping that he would take her home.

Home. A vision flashed, lush green land that ran for miles, hills and dales and wild northern sunsets. Not London. Certainly not Mayfair, where the only thing lush were the silk skirts she was forced to wear every day, in case someone came for tea.

And her father had enough money that someone always came for tea.

London wasn't home. It never had been—not for a decade. Not in all the time that she'd lived in that perfect Mayfair town house that her mother and sisters adored, as though they didn't miss the past. As though they'd hated the life they'd lived all those years ago. As though they would forget it if they needed to. As though they had forgotten it.

Tears came, surprising and unbidden, and she blinked them away, blaming the summer wind and the speed of the carriage.

She was alone on the driving block of a carriage, dressed as a footman, headed God knew where.

And somehow, it was the thought of returning to London that made her sad.

So she stayed quiet, knowing it was mad, willing the coachman not to notice her, listening to the sound of the wheels and the horses' hooves as the coach moved north.

Hours later, when the sun had set, it had become clear

that Sophie was out of her element. She'd thought that wearing a footman's livery, masquerading as a boy, and riding on the outside of a coach would be the most difficult parts of the charade, only to realize that those bits were, in fact, nothing in comparison to the arrival at the posting inn.

She watched from the driver's block as the coachman climbed down to arrange space in the stables for the horses and, ostensibly, for storage of the carriage itself.

The thought gave her pause. Where *did* carriages go when they weren't in use? It was a question she'd never had cause to consider.

"Are you going to sit up there like a lord? Or are you planning to come down and do some work?"

The words startled her from her thoughts, and she looked down to find the coachman staring up at her, his earlier exasperation edging into something else entirely. Suspicion.

Well. She couldn't have that. Not now, at least, before she'd decided the next steps of her plan.

Plan was something of a misnomer for this outrageous situation. *Disaster* was a better descriptor.

"Where are we?" she asked, deliberately lowering the tenor of her voice—she couldn't have him realizing that she was a woman now—and scurrying down from the carriage, willing to wager that, while she did not know what a footman did at this exact moment, descending to earth was an excellent first step. Once on the ground, she bowed her head and just barely caught herself before she sank into a curtsy. Footmen did not curtsy. That part, she knew.

"All that matters is that we are here before the marquess."

"Where is he?" The question was out before she could

stop it. She did not require the cold, critical gaze of the coachman to know that she had overstepped her bounds, but he provided it nonetheless.

"I don't know what is wrong with you, boy," he said, "but you had better set yourself straight. Servants don't question their masters' whereabouts, nor do they ask questions to which they don't need answers. Servants serve."

That was just the problem, of course. Sophie had no idea how to begin doing such a thing. "Yes, sir. I shall do just that."

He nodded and turned away, tossing over his shoulder, "See that you do."

She had no choice but to call after him, "That said . . . what . . . what shall I do?"

He stilled, then turned around slowly. Blinked at her. Then spoke as though she was a child. "Begin with your job."

That wasn't helpful.

She took a deep breath as he turned back to the horses, considering all the things she'd witnessed footmen doing in the past.

Her gaze flickered to the great black coach, empty. Except, it would not be empty. Eversley wouldn't have traveled such a distance without having prepared for it. There would be bags. Luggage.

And footmen collected luggage.

With renewed purpose, she opened the door and climbed into the carriage, prepared to collect whatever items the marquess had left for his servants to shuttle into his rooms, before she stilled in the darkness, the sounds of the bustling inn from outside muffled as she considered the inside of the massive coach. Massive, indeed. It was one of the largest private coaches she'd ever seen— bordering on conspicuously enormous—one that might boast three rows of seats without effort. But it didn't. There was a single row of seats at the back of the conveyance, leaving a great, yawning chasm of space inside, large enough for a man to lie flat. For several men to lie flat.

There were no men in the space, however. Instead, it was filled with great wooden wheels. There were ten of them, perhaps twelve. She couldn't take an exact count in the dark space, but she paused nonetheless, considering the cargo. Why was the Marquess of Eversley shuttling carriage wheels? Did they lack wheelwrights north of London?

Indeed, the only evidence of the Marquess of Eversley was a pile of formalwear—clothing that she'd watched float down from up on high when he escaped his pursuing earl.

Where had he gone?

"Boy!"

Sophie let out an exasperated sigh. The coachman was quickly becoming an unwelcome companion. Through gritted teeth she called back, "Yes, sir?"

"You're no more useful inside the coach then you were atop it!"

And then, shockingly, a hand came to her bottom, grasping the waistband of her trousers and yanking her, bodily, from the carriage. She let out a wild squeak as the coachman stood her on her feet and closed the door with a perfunctory click. After all, it was not every day that she was manhandled quite so . . . well . . . handily.

When the coachman rounded on her, she knew she was done for. Indeed, it was best that Matthew was to be employed by her father, as she felt certain that the house of Eversley was about to sack him. Also handily. "Have you lost your—"

The man's assessment of her mental faculties—or lack thereof—was cut off by the noise—a near-deafening clattering, punctuated by wild hoofbeats, the heavy breathing of horses, and exuberant male shouts. She turned just in time to see the first of the curricles bearing down on her with speed that would break both axles and necks, as though they were on a long stretch of clear road instead of a crowded posting inn drive.

With a cry, Sophie leapt backward, pressing herself to the outer wall of the coach, eyes wide, as the lead curricle tipped on one wheel, dangerously close to toppling before it slammed down, one wheel spoke flying across the yard as the driver executed a perfect half turn to face the vehicles following behind. The driver stood tall on legs that should have been tired, but instead seemed incredibly strong, towering over horse and vehicle, arms akimbo as he faced his no-doubt maniacal comrades. Much of his face was obscured by the low brim of his hat, but the light from the inn was drawn, nonetheless, to his wide, wicked grin.

Sophie found that she was oddly drawn to that grin herself.

"Looks as though I won, lads." The others were stopped now, and a chorus of groans rose from myriad curricles when he added, "Again."

As this was the first time Sophie had been outside a posting inn after dark, she had to imagine that this was an ordinary occurrence—but she'd certainly never thought that men raced their curricles up the Great North Road for fun.

Fun.

The word echoed, reminding her of her earlier conversation with Eversley, in which he'd called her unfun.

Irritation flared. She was perfectly fun.

After all, she was here, wasn't she? Dressed as a boy in a courtyard filled with men who appeared to have a keen knowledge of fun.

Her thoughts were interrupted by the man's movement as he leapt down from the carriage and headed to his horses to give the great, matching beasts praise for their work. He swaggered to the animals that huffed and sighed, great ribs heaving from their long run, even as they leaned into the weighty caress of their master.

Sophie was transfixed by him—by the group he seemed to lead. She'd never seen anything like them, clad all in black, and with great informality—black coats over black linen, and not a cravat to be seen among them. Their trousers gleamed in the light from the lanterns posted around the drive—she considered the attire. Was it . . . leather? How odd. And how fascinating.

Her gaze flickered to the leader, and the long curve of this thigh, hugged tightly by the attire. She had considered the line of that muscle for longer than was appropriate.

He was an exceedingly well-made man. Empirically so.

The second she had noticed in a single day.

She coughed at the thought, heat spreading across her cheeks, and the noise brought his attention, his head immediately turning to her. Though his eyes remained obscured, Sophie had never felt so well inspected, and she found herself immensely grateful for Matthew's livery, hiding the truth of her—that she had never been in such a situation, that she did not belong here.

She dropped her gaze to his boots, eager to disappear.

That's when she noticed that he was not wearing boots.

At least, he was not wearing two of them.

Bollocks.

The Marquess of Eversley had arrived.

And from the way he came toward her—the swagger she'd identified earlier likely due to his lacking one boot—he was about to discover that she had done the same. She did not look up at him, keeping her gaze firmly affixed on his feet, hoping he would ignore her.

It did not work. "Boy," he drawled, coming entirely too close. Unsettlingly close.

She shifted from one foot to the other, willing him away.

That did not work, either.

"Did you hear me?" he prompted.

She moved, dropping a half inch before she stopped herself from curtsying. Even if she weren't dressed as a man, he didn't deserve politeness of any kind, this ruiner of women who represented everything she loathed about the Society that had so roundly turned its back upon her. This man who had turned *his* back upon her. If only he'd been willing to help her, she wouldn't be in this ridiculous situation.

"Are you able to hear?" he fairly barked the last.

Straightening, she coughed and pressed her chin tighter to her chest, lowering her voice. "Yes, my lord." The honorific was strangled in her throat.

She was saved from whatever he was about to say by the arrival of one of his comrades. "Goddammit, King, you're fucking fearless. I thought you were going to kill yourself on the last turn."

She inhaled, not because of the unexpected foul language—a childhood around coal miners made one immune to profanity—but because of the unexpected voice, thick with a Scottish brogue. Her gaze snapped up, and she found herself face-to-face with the Duke of Warnick, a legendary scoundrel in his own right—an uncultured Scotsman who unexpectedly ascended to a dukedom, sending all of London into a panic. The duke was rarely seen in London and even more rarely *welcome* in London, but here he stood, half a yard from her, laughing and clapping the Marquess of Eversley on the shoulder to congratulate him for what Sophie could only imagine was not killing himself in the process of arriving at the inn.

Eversley matched the duke's wide grin, all arrogance and awfulness. "Broke two spokes on my right wheel," he boasted, the words explaining why the man traveled with a carriage full of curricle wheels. "But fearlessness begets victory, it seems."

Warnick laughed. "I had a half a mind to run you off the road in that last quarter mile."

"Even if you could have caught me," King boasted, "you're too much a coward to have done it."

Sophie rather thought that not killing a man was more honorable than cowardly, but she refrained from pointing it out, instead easing away from the duo, eager to escape discovery by the marquess in this open space, where he could thoroughly ruin her in front of what she now realized was a collection of men who might easily recognize a Talbot sister.

The duke stepped closer to Eversley, lowering his voice to a menacing pitch. "Did you just call me a coward?"

"I did, indeed. When was the last time you were in London?" Eversley asked pointedly before he noticed her moving. "Stay right there," he said, one finger staying her even as he did not take his gaze from the duke, leaving her no choice but to freeze in place until they finished their conversation.

She had never quite realized how rude aristocrats could be to their servants. After all, she had work to do. She wasn't certain what kind of work, specifically, but she was sure it had little to do with staring at these two cabbageheads.

The duke tilted his head. "You would know about avoiding unpleasant locales."

Eversley grinned at that. "I am an expert at it."

At that, Warnick reached into his open coat and extracted a coin. "Your winnings."

He tossed the coin and Eversley snatched it from the air, pocketing it. "I do enjoy taking your money."

"Money," the duke scoffed. "You don't care about the ha'penny. You care about the win."

Sophie resisted the urge to roll her eyes. Of course he only cared about the win. She had no doubt that the Marquess of Eversley cared for nothing but winning.

She should like to ensure that this man lost, and roundly.

Before she could enjoy her private fantasy of the marquess's loss, however, the duke lobbed his final barb. "Not that it will get you anywhere near the cost of your missing boot. Tell me you left it as a souvenir at the site of your latest assignation."

Sophie's heart began to pound at the words, at the reminder of Eversley's reputation, at the reminder of her own idiocy in turning up here, wherever they were, far from home, and with no plan to speak of.

What came next?

She was going to have to rely upon the kindness of someone in the inn to get herself home. She was going to have to beg a journey to London, which would not be easy. She would have to promise someone the funds upon arrival, and she knew how difficult that would be.

"I think the boot will be easily recovered."

The words pulled her from her thoughts, their meaning sending her gaze flying to find his, shrouded by the brim of his cap. Was it possible he recognized her?

"Perhaps I'll send the boy to fetch it."

She stilled, even her breath caught in her lungs.

He recognized her.

The duke laughed, unaware of what had happened before his eyes, and returned to his curricle, tossing back, "The boy might get an eyeful stealing into the lady's boudoir."

Sophie couldn't help her little huff of indignation. Of course, Marcella was criticized for her actions as the marquess was lauded by his brawny, boorish brethren.

Eversley cut her a look at the sound. "I hope my boot is inside that carriage."

She resisted the urge to tell him precisely what he could do with the boot in question, instead playing the perfect servant. "Unfortunately not, my lord."

He raised a brow. "No?"

She wished she could meet his gaze. Granted, his brilliant green eyes were unsettling in the extreme, but at least if she could see them, she would be able to glean something of his thoughts on the situation. Instead, she soldiered on, lifting her chin, and he noted the defiance in the gesture. "No."

He lowered his voice. "Where is it, then?"

She lowered her voice to match his. "I imagine it is where I left it. In the Liverpool hedge."

She rather enjoyed the way his throat worked in the moment of silence following her announcement. "You left my Hessian in a hedge."

"You left *me* in a hedge," she pointed out.

"I had no use for you."

"Well, I had no use for your boot."

He considered her for a long moment, and changed the topic. "You look ridiculous."

Of course she did. She lifted one shoulder, let it drop. "It's *your* livery."

"It's for a footman! Not some spoiled girl looking for a lark."

Anger flared at the words. "You know nothing about me. I am not spoiled. And it was not a lark."

"Oh? I suppose you have a perfectly reasonable explanation for why you stole my footman's livery and stowed away in my carriage."

"I do, as a matter of fact. And I was not in your carriage. I was on it."

"Along with my blind coachman, it seems. Why were you up there?"

She smirked. "Footmen don't ride inside carriages, my lord. And even if they did, the carriage in question is filled with wheels. Why is that?"

"In case I need a replacement," he said without hesitation. "Where is my footman, anyway? Did you knock him unconscious and leave him naked in the hedge alongside my boot?"

"Of course I didn't. Matthew is perfectly well."

"Is he wearing your dress?"

She blushed. "No. He bought a set of clothes from one of the Liverpool stableboys."

He did not pause in his questions. "And you? Did you strip in front of all London?"

"Of course not!" She was growing indignant. "I'm not mad."

"Oh, no," he said, "Of course not."

"I'm not!" she insisted, hissing the words so as not to draw attention to them. "I changed clothes in my family's carriage. And I paid Matthew for his livery before sending him to my father for another position."

He stilled. "You stole my footman."

"It wasn't stealing."

"I had a footman this morning. And now I don't have one. How is that not stealing?"

"It was not stealing," she insisted. "It's not as though you owned him."

"I paid him!"

"It seems I paid him better."

He went quiet, and she could see the frustration in his gaze before he offered a single, perfunctory nod and said, "Fair enough."

He turned away.

Well. That was unexpected. And not at all ideal, as she had no money, and he was the only person in the place who might be inclined to help her get home, assuming it meant that she was gone from his life.

She ignored the fact that stowing away on his carriage might have worked against her.

Sophie sighed. He was insufferable, but she was intelligent enough to know when she needed someone. "Wait!" she called, drawing the attention of the coachman and several of his companions from earlier in the evening, but not the man in question.

He was ignoring her. Deliberately.

She scurried after him, ignoring the pain of the gravel on her slippered feet. "My lord," she called, all nervousness. "There is one more thing." He stopped and turned to face her. She drew close to him, suddenly keenly aware of his height, of the way her forehead aligned with his firm, straight, unyielding lips.

"It doesn't fit you."

She blinked. "I beg your pardon?"

"The livery. It's too tight."

First he described her as unfun and now as plump. She knew it of course, but he didn't have to point out the fact that she wasn't the most lithe of women. She swallowed around the tightness in her throat and brazened on. "Excuse me, Lord Perfection, I did not have time to visit a modiste on the way." He did not apologize for his rudeness—not that she was surprised—but neither did he leave, so she pressed on. "I require conveyance home."

"Yes, you said as much this afternoon."

When he'd refused to help and landed her in this mess.

He wasn't alone in landing you in this mess. She ignored the thought. "Yes, well, it remains the case."

"And, as was the case this afternoon, it is not my problem."

The words surprised her. "But . . ." She trailed off, not quite knowing what to say. "But I . . ."

He did not wait for her to find words. "You've stolen my boot and my footman in what I can only assume is a misguided attempt to gain my attention and my title, if the former actions of your family are any indication. I'm sure you'll understand if I am less than amenable to providing you aid." He paused, and when she did not speak, he added, "To put it plainly, you may be a *colossal* problem, Lady Sophie, but you are not *my* problem."

The words stung quite harshly, and the way he turned his back on her, as though she were nothing, worth nothing—not even thought—delivered an unexpected blow, harsher than it might have been on another day, when all of Society and her family hadn't turned their backs upon her in a similar fashion.

A memory flashed of the events of the afternoon, the aristocracy, en masse, disowning her, choosing their precious duke over the truth. Over the right.

Tears came, unbidden. Unwelcome.

She would not cry.

She sucked in a breath to keep them at bay.

Not in front of him.

They stung at the bridge of her nose, and she sniffed, all unladylike.

He turned back sharply. "If you are attempting to prey upon my kindness, don't. I haven't much of it."

"Do not worry," she replied. "I would never dream of thinking you kind."

He watched her for a long, silent moment before the coachman spoke from above, where he was disconnecting the reins from the driving block. "My lord, is the boy bothering you?"

The marquess did not take his eyes from her. "He is, rather."

The other man scowled at her. "Get to the stables and find the horses some food and water. That should be something you cannot muck up."

"I—"

Eversley interrupted her. "I should do as John Coachman says," he cut her off. "You don't want to suffer his wrath."

Her wide eyes flickered from one man to the other.

"After you're done with that, find your bed, boy," the coachman said. "Perhaps a good sleep will return the brain to your head."

"My bed," she repeated, looking to the marquess, hating the way his lips twitched.

"They've space in the hayloft." The coachman's exasperation was unmistakable as he spoke to her—as though she were an imbecile—before returning to his four-legged charges, leaping down and unhitching them to bring them to the stables, leaving Sophie and Eversley in the center of the quickly emptying courtyard.

"The hayloft sounds quite cozy," the marquess said.

Sophie wondered if the marquess would find a blow to the side of his head cozy, but she refrained from asking.

"So cozy," he continued, "that I think I shall find my own bed. It seems that one of my feet is quite cold. I should like to go in and warm it up by the fire."

Her feet were also cold and aching. Silk slippers were not designed for coach-top rides through Britain or the work of footmen, after all. She thought of the warm fire that was no doubt burning inside the inn.

She wasn't certain what would be in the hayloft, but if she had to imagine, she'd say hay . . . and that meant there wouldn't be a warm fire there.

She could reveal herself. Now was the time. She could take off her hat and point out her own ridiculous footwear. She could announce herself Lady Sophie Talbot, rely upon the kindness of one of the other men who had barreled into the Fox and Falcon atop their strange-looking curricles, and beg for conveyance home.

Eversley seemed to understand her intentions even before they were fully formed. "An excellent idea. Saddle yourself to another. Warnick is a duke."

She did not pretend to misunderstand. "I wouldn't marry you if you were the last man in Christendom."

"You only say that because I've thwarted your idiot plan."

"This was never my plan."

"Of course not, why would I think it from a Dangerous Daughter?" he scoffed, and she hated him then. Hated him for invoking the ridiculous moniker. For being just like all the others. For believing that she wanted the life into which she'd been thrust.

For believing that life worth something. Worth more than the life she'd been born into. For refusing to see— just as the rest of London refused to see—that Sophie was different. And that she had been perfectly happy before. Before titles and town houses and teas and trappings of the *ton*.

Before those trappings had trapped her.

She swallowed back her frustration. "I thought you were heading to Mayfair," she said, hating the smallness in her voice.

He pointed to the road without hesitation. "Thirty miles to the south. Perhaps you'll be lucky and a mail coach will happen by."

The words reminded her of her current circumstances. "I haven't any money for a mail coach."

"It is unfortunate, then, that you gave it all to my footman."

"Not unfortunate for the boy, I imagine," she replied, unable to keep the tartness from her voice. "After all, I saved him from having to serve you for the rest of his days."

He smirked. "It looks like you've quite a walk ahead of you, then. If you start now, you'll be there by tomorrow evening."

He was horrible. Not that she'd been the most genteel of characters, but still. He was worse. "What they say about you is right."

"Which part?"

"You are no gentleman."

His gaze raked down her body, taking in her ill-fitting, too-tight livery, reminding her with every lingering inch that she'd made a terrible mistake. "Forgive me, love, but you don't seem much a lady tonight."

And he disappeared into the inn, leaving her considering her next action—the stables, or the road.

The frying pan, or the fire.

Chapter 4

SOILED S STOLEN!
SCOUNDREL SUSPECTED!

Several hours later, after the inn had gone dark and quiet, Kingscote, Marquess of Eversley, future Duke of Lyne, notorious rogue who took great pride in his reputation as a scoundrel, lay in bed, awake.

Awake, and very, very irritated.

She'd ruined his win.

And of all the things in the world that King enjoyed, there was nothing he enjoyed so very much as winning. It did not matter what he won—women, fights, road races, cards. It mattered only that the win was his.

It was not a simple thing, King's relationship with victory. It was not for mere pleasure, though many thought it such. It had little to do with diversion, or recreation. Where other men enjoyed winning, King required it. The thrill of victory was as essential as food and air to him. In victory, he was most free.

In the win, he forgot what he had lost.

And he had won the curricle race, roundly beating the half-dozen other men, each a better driver than the next, careening up the Great North Road with breathless speed, horses tearing up the hard pack of the road, exhilaration and thrill coursing through him, clearing his mind of this northward journey's purpose. Of what would greet him when he reached his final destination.

Of the past.

The win had been hard-fought. The other men had driven with impressive skill, threatening his victory, teasing him with the possibility of loss. But King had won, and it had been sweet and deeply satisfying. It was the taste of freedom, elusive and fleeting.

As he'd caught his breath high atop the curricle that would require new wheels before he started again the next day, he had experienced the keen pleasure of knowing that he'd sleep well that evening, before the light of day reminded him of truth and duty.

Except he did not get the evening.

He did not even get the hour.

Because the first thing he'd seen after coming to a stop in the drive of the Fox and Falcon was Lady Sophie Talbot, pressed up against his coach, looking ridiculous in Eversley livery.

And, like that, she'd ruined his win.

At first, he told himself it couldn't be. After all, of all the outrageously foolish things he'd seen women do in his life, this one had to be the most foolish. But he knew better. He knew how desperate girls could get. The lengths to which they would go for what they wanted.

He knew it better than anyone.

So, of course, it was she. Lady Sophie, youngest of the Soiled S's, to whom he had expressly refused conveyance, had refused to leave well enough alone.

And she'd stowed away.

As she was dressed as a footman, he imagined that she

had not ridden inside the carriage, where she would have been safest. Instead, she'd likely ridden atop the vehicle, next to the driver. Christ. She could have fallen off.

She could have been killed, and it would have been on his head.

He closed his eyes, and an image flashed, a girl, broken and lifeless, flaxen hair spread out in a halo against the packed dirt of the road.

Except, it wasn't Sophie Talbot he saw lifeless and broken. It was another girl, another time.

He cursed, low and dark in the quiet room, and threw the heavy duvet back, coming to his feet and crossing the room to find something to drink, to push the memory away. He poured his scotch, ignoring the tremor in his hands, and drank deep, turning to the window, looking down at the inn's courtyard, empty.

Unlike earlier, when he'd found his footman missing and Sophie Talbot in his place, eyes wide, shocked that he'd recognized her. He'd have to be dead not to recognize her.

Christ. How had no one else recognized her?

And where had she gone?

He didn't care. Sophie Talbot wasn't his problem. He'd told her as much.

And she'd cried.

He ignored the thought. The way the tears had somehow made the blue of her eyes, lined with those thick, sooty lashes, even more blue in the yellow lantern light outside the inn. She'd done it to manipulate him. After all, wasn't that what the Talbot sisters did? Trap unsuspecting aristocrats into marriage?

It had made a duchess of the eldest, why not a future duchess of the youngest?

Well, she had chosen the wrong mark.

She'd landed herself here, buying off a footman, surviving the carriage ride. Sophie Talbot was no simpering wallflower, whatever her reputation. He knew little about the girl—only that she was the most serious of the five Talbot sisters—not a difficult task considering the tittering vanity and disdain for propriety that marked the others in the family.

Her actions did not bear out her seriousness, however. Indeed, they made her seem positively foolish.

Well. She might be a fool, but he wasn't.

He wasn't getting anywhere near her.

She wasn't his problem.

She'd found her way here; she could find her way home.

He had other things to worry about. Like finding his way back to Cumbria before his father made good on his promise and died. King drank again, unable to wrap his head around the idea of his father dying. Dying was for creatures with beating hearts, after all, and the Duke of Lyne was too stern and unmoving to have blood in his veins. Surely.

Come quickly. Your father ails.

A simple missive, in the neat script of Agnes Graycote, housekeeper of Lyne Castle since King was a child. The woman had served the duke for decades without hesitation. She'd stayed on after King left, after the duke had stopped traveling to London, after he'd given up his attempts to reconcile with King.

As though reconciliation might ever be possible. As though he hadn't ruined King's life with his bitter aristocratic pride. As though King hadn't replied to every request for audience with the same five words—the only honest punishment he could mete out.

King almost hadn't heeded Agnes's call.

Almost.

But here he was, at an inn on the Great North Road, thirty miles from London, headed to the Scottish border, to look his dying father in the eye and say the words aloud.

The line ends with me.

He cursed again in the darkness before finishing the scotch, setting the glass on the windowsill and returning to bed, closing his eyes and willing himself to sleep. Instead of heavy slumber; however, King found the cacophony of his mind. He resisted thoughts of his childhood and his father, knowing that they would take him down a dark path he had no interest in exploring, and instead turned to a safer memory. The day. The race. His win. And the ruination of that win.

No.

He tried not to think of her. Of her request earlier in the day, of her appearance. Of the way she filled out the livery in all the wrong ways—trousers too tight, the buttons on her jacket pulling tight across her ample breasts, and the lovely swell of her midriff. Christ. She was still wearing silk slippers.

His footman's boots hadn't been included in his price, clearly.

He rolled to his back, one large hand coming to rest on his bare chest. Why hadn't she been wearing proper footwear? And how was it that his coachman hadn't noticed the ridiculous yellow slippers?

His coachman was a fool as well, obviously.

Not that King cared about the improper footwear. Indeed, she deserved that, didn't she? She was the one who had left him with only one boot.

Her feet must hurt.

Her feet, like the woman herself, were not his problem.

Neither was the bed where she slept.

Not his problem.

If she was sleeping. In a hayloft. Surrounded by all manner of men, at least some of who would notice immediately that their companion was decidedly not a man.

If *the men* were sleeping.

Emotion threaded through him, sharp and unwelcome. Guilt. Fear. *Panic.*

"Goddammit." He came to his feet, reaching for his leather breeches before the echo of the curse disappeared from the room.

She might not be his problem, but he couldn't stand by and allow her to suffer God knew what at the hands of God knew whom. He pulled his shirt on, leaving the hem untucked and the laces untied as he tore open the door to the chamber and went searching for the girl.

The inn was quiet, kitchens dark, taps dry, fires in the main room banked. His gaze fell on a clock at the far end of the room. Two in the morning—an hour that brought nothing but trouble for those awake to witness it.

He exited the inn, the eerie silence of the English countryside at night unsettling him as he made his way to the nearby stables, imagining all the ways the hour could be bringing trouble down upon Sophie Talbot.

He entered the building at a near run when he heard the men. A half dozen of them, if the myriad voices were any indication, laughter and shouting and jeers—he stopped just beyond a fall of golden light, listening, attempting to get his bearings and make out the words.

As though the universe knew just what he was listening for, he heard her first, the words clear and curious over the cacophony of sound. "I just, take it down?"

King went utterly still as a man replied. "Exactly."

"It doesn't look like it would taste very good."

Christ.

"You'd be surprised," the man coaxed. "Take all of it. All at once. You'll like it."

"If you say so," she said, and the skepticism in her voice was drowned out by a chorus of raucous cheers that set King in motion, no longer caring that one-on-six were terrible odds, particularly when the six in question were drunk and sex-starved.

"Step away from the lady," he instructed, all menacing, as he stepped into the main room of the stables, shocking the hell out of not only the group of drunk but hardly nefarious-looking men sitting at a table at the center of the long corridor between the stalls, but also the lady in question, who was still wearing her livery.

At least, he assumed it was shock that made her choke on the pint of ale she was in the process of drinking in one long series of gulps. She pulled the mug from her lips, sloshing ale down her front as she set it to the table with enough force to knock it over and spill the rest of the drink across the tabletop, where piles of playing cards were spread out, as though a round of faro had just been finished.

She stood quickly, two other men shooting out of their chairs to avoid the liquid as a small glass rolled out of the mug and fell off the table, miraculously not breaking as it continued on its journey along the boards of the stable floor to stop, quite theatrically, at King's foot.

He looked up from the glass, her earlier words echoing through him. *It doesn't seem like it would taste very good.*

They'd been teaching her how to drink—a shot of whiskey in a mug of ale—the drink of men who wished to sleep well, and quickly.

It hadn't been the other thing at all.

King cleared his throat.

"I'm sure we didn't hear you correctly, King," the Duke of Warnick rumbled in his Scottish brogue. "I could have sworn you called the boy a lady."

Of course Warnick was in the stables. The man had spent a lifetime away from polite company. If ever there were someone for whom a title was a burden, it was the duke. But, disdainful of Society or no, a duke was not the ideal witness of Lady Sophie's mad disguise and misguided plan.

Why in hell hadn't she found her bed as soon as she realized the duke was in the stables?

Sophie's gaze snapped to his, cheeks already flush from her alcoholic experience turning red with obvious embarrassment. He could read the pleading in her wide blue eyes and ignored it. He'd had enough of this woman and her trouble. He wanted her far, far away from him. "You didn't mishear. She's a woman. Anyone with eyes can see it."

From the jaws gaping around the table, it seemed that anyone with eyes could not, in fact, see such a thing.

But they heard it, he had no doubt, when she opened her mouth and tore into him. "How could you?" she said, frustration edging into fury as her hands fisted at her sides and she faced him, stiff as a board. "You've ruined everything!"

"*I've* ruined everything?" he repeated, more than a bit outraged himself. "You're the one who thought you could get away with this idiocy."

"Wait. He's a girl?" one of the other men at the table asked.

"Good that you're catching up," the duke drawled, all amusement.

"But he's wearing livery," the drunken man insisted.

"Indeed he is," Warnick said with a lingering inspection. "However, now that I take a good long look . . ."

"Enough!" Sophie cried, lifting a burlap bag from the floor, slinging it over her shoulder, and storming past King to the exit.

King turned to the duke. "No more long looks."

"But I've only had the one."

"You've had hours to look. You didn't even realize she wasn't wearing boots."

The duke's brows shot up as the other men in the stable offered a chorus of disbelief.

"We would have noticed that!" one of them said with a laugh.

"Clearly not," King pointed out. "It seems you lot see what you wish to see." Though he couldn't for the life of him imagine how they'd missed the fact that Lady Sophie Talbot was just that . . . a lady.

"Who is she?" Warnick asked.

King wasn't about to tell him. "She's no one of consequence."

The duke smirked. "I doubt that."

"Well, you shall have to accept it as fact nonetheless." King didn't have time for verbal sparring with a Scot. He turned on his heel and left the stables, heading in search of the girl.

He caught up with her on the road, a dozen yards from the entrance to the inn. She did not hesitate in her march, shoulders straight, head high. "Go away."

"It's the dead of night. Where do you think you're going?"

"I should think it would be obvious," she said. "Away from you."

"And you're going to walk there?"

"My feet are in fine working order."

"They shan't be after a quarter of an hour on this road. Why didn't you take the boots, too?"

She did not reply.

"Not enough money?"

"I had enough money," she grumbled.

"So?"

He would not discover the answer, as she chose that moment to step on a rock and gasp her discomfort.

"You see?" he said, unable to keep the smugness from his tone. Or, perhaps, uninterested in doing so.

Either way, she turned on him then. "In the span of twelve hours, you've called me unintelligent and insane, suggested that I am trying to trap you into marriage, declared me uninteresting, and pointed out the flaws of my physique."

What? "I never pointed out your flaws."

She crossed her arms. "The livery, my lord. It doesn't fit."

He blinked. "It *doesn't* fit."

She let out a frustrated sound and slashed a hand in the air. "It doesn't matter. All of that said, I cannot imagine why it is you feel it necessary to follow me as I do the one thing you've been asking me to do from the beginning of our acquaintance—leave you."

Honestly, he couldn't imagine why it was necessary, either. But it was, somehow. "Also, I never declared you uninteresting."

"No. I believe you used the term *unfun*, which is even more unflattering, as it appears that I am so deeply boring that I require a word that, prior to today, did not exist."

"It's not the same thing at all." He was hard-pressed to think of an adjective less suited to Lady Sophie Talbot than uninteresting.

"And we're back to my being unintelligent, I see."

She turned her back on him and continued her walk. He noticed that she was limping, which was unsurprising—the roads were barely conducive to carriage wheels and horseshoes.

The limp bothered him, a sliver of weakness that left him aware of her in a way he preferred not to be, making it impossible to leave her to the wolves here on the road. No matter how much he had sworn to himself that she was not his problem.

He'd pack her into the next stagecoach home the moment the sun rose. Surely there was a frock to be purchased from a maid at the inn. He'd have to pay handsomely, no doubt, but it would be worth it to send the troublesome woman back to London.

"Come back to the inn," he said. "We'll find you a bed, and tomorrow we'll get you home."

"I can find my own way home," she said. "You needn't worry about me."

He sighed, letting his exasperation show in the sound. "You could be gracious and accept my offer of help."

"Forgive me if I am not in the mood to scrape and bow because an aristocrat has condescended to tolerate me only after his reputation is at risk."

He'd struck an interesting chord, it seemed. He plucked at it again, unable to resist. "Someone has to take responsibility for you. You can't be trusted not to cause a scene."

She stopped at that. Turned to him. "I don't cause scenes."

His brows shot up. "All you do is cause scenes, love."

"I'm not your love," she said, her hands fisted at her sides.

"You most certainly are not," he agreed without thinking. "I am drawn to more feminine specimens."

Her shoulders drooped for a moment—barely long

enough to be called such—and King wanted to take the words back. They weren't accurate. She was perfectly feminine. Indeed, as she accepted the blow of his words, there was something exceedingly feminine about her, something that one did not immediately notice.

Not that he cared. He wasn't interested in her femininity.

She was obstinate as hell and more trouble than she was worth. And if there was one thing he did not care for, it was women who were troublesome.

But he'd hurt her feelings. And it was unsettling, as she didn't seem the type whose feelings were easily hurt. Indeed, she was walking again, all straight spine and stiff shoulders, guard up.

It was a ruse. Designed to keep him from seeing the truth.

He knew it, because he'd used a similar one himself.

There was nothing at all uninteresting about her.

He called after her. "You can't walk all the way back to London."

"That shows what you know," she said without breaking her stride. "I'm not going back to London. I'm headed north."

"Not if you're walking in this direction, you're not," he said, before the full meaning of her words sank in. "Wait. North? Why?"

She stopped. "This *is* north."

"No," he said. "It's south."

She peered down the dark road. "You're certain?"

"Quite. Why are you heading north?"

She pivoted and began her march in the opposite direction. "Because I'm going home."

She was perhaps the most frustrating woman he'd ever met. "London is south."

"Yes. I do have a general knowledge of geography."

"Well, you lack a knowledge of direction, it appears, so one does wonder." She did not waver from her purpose. They walked for several minutes in silence, until they were once more in the lights of the Fox and Falcon.

King couldn't help himself. "If not London, where is home?"

"Cumbria."

He stilled. What was she playing at? *He* was headed to Cumbria. To *his* home.

The Dangerous Daughters.

The nickname whispered through him with a keen awareness of the rumors about the Talbot daughters— rich, but not nearly quality. They'd need to purchase their aristocratic marriages or steal them, and the fastest way to steal a title was to ruin oneself in the arms of a peer.

A carriage ride to Cumbria would easily result in ruination.

Dangerous, indeed.

Christ. He'd been right earlier that evening. The girl was after him. The guilt he'd felt at leaving her to the men in the stables disappeared, replaced by hot anger. "So it was a plan. To trap me."

Her brows snapped together. "I beg your pardon?"

"How did you know I was headed to Cumbria? Did the footman give up that information as well?"

"You're headed to Cumbria?" she asked, all surprise.

He narrowed his gaze on her. "Coy isn't attractive on you, Sophie." He deliberately left the title she was due off her name.

"And I am so very desperate for you to find me attractive."

He raised a brow. "Tell me the truth."

"It's quite simple. I'm headed to Cumbria. I spent the first ten years of my life in Mossband."

He laughed without humor. "I've never in my life heard such a terrible lie."

"It's true. Not that I can understand why you would care."

"Fine. I shall play," he spat. "Because I spent my childhood in Longwood. But you knew that."

She shook her head. "There's no Eversley estate there."

He smirked. "No. But there is Lyne Castle."

She was doing an excellent job of looking surprised. "What's that to do with the price of wheat?"

"A pity you're leaving London. You should try the theater." He paused, then said, "Is this the bit where I tell you my father is the Duke of Lyne?"

"What?" She really was excellent at feigned ignorance.

"Yes. What a surprise," he drawled. He'd had enough of her. "You think I'm stupid enough to believe that a Dangerous Daughter doesn't know that the Marquess of Eversley is a courtesy title?"

"Stupid or no, it's the truth. I had no idea that you were to be a duke."

"Every unmarried lady in London knows I'm to be a duke."

"I guarantee that's only true of the unmarried ladies who give a fig."

He ignored her sharp retort. "I'm widely believed to be the *ton*'s best catch."

She snorted a laugh. "No doubt, what with your minuscule sense of self-importance. Let me assure you, my lord, you're a horrid catch."

"And you're a horrid liar. I assume your pronouncement of your North Country destination was intended to spur me to offer you passage, as we are both headed in that direction?

"Your assumption is incorrect."

"Don't play the innocent with me," he said, waving a finger in her face. "I see right through your outlandish plans. You were fully intending for us to play."

She blinked. "Play? At what?"

He smirked. "I'm sure you can put it together. The women in your family seem more than willing."

Understanding dawned. "As though I would let you near me. I don't even like you."

"Who said anything about liking one another?" He stayed the vision of how they might pass the time on the journey north. "No matter. I don't care for the destination you have in mind. You shan't trap me into marriage. I'm smarter than the rest of the men in London, darling. And you're not nearly as tempting as your sisters."

The words hung in the late-night air, the only indication that she'd heard them a slight straightening of her spine.

He exhaled harshly and resisted the urge to curse roundly. The last bit was cruel. He knew it the moment the words were out of his mouth. She was the plainest of the Talbot sisters, yes. And that made her the least mar-riageable. She had fortune, and nothing else.

And the surprise of it was . . . she didn't seem at all plain right now, dressed in ill-fitting livery and ridiculous footwear, standing on the Great North Road, moonlight in her hair.

There was a long silence, during which King grew more and more uncomfortable, the words echoing through his head. He should apologize before she did something horrible, like cry.

He should have known better. Because Lady Sophie Talbot did not cry there, on the Great North Road in the dead of night, miles from anywhere or anyone who would help her, faced with a man who disliked her and an insult she did not deserve.

Instead, she laughed.

Uproariously.

King blinked. Well. That was unexpected.

He did not care for the edge of disdain in the laughter, and cared for it even less when she said, "The only thing I have ever wished from you was transport to Mayfair," she said, slowly, as though she were speaking to a child. "But since you refused me that, I had to take matters into my own hands, which I appreciate"—she raised her voice slightly to stop him from interjecting—"did not work in my favor for much of the day. But things are looking up now, no thanks to you. I've a plan now. A plan that does not include you, your assistance, or your kindness. Thankfully, as you haven't offered assistance and I have seen no evidence of your kindness."

He opened his mouth to reply, and she stayed him again. "Let me be very clear. I am headed north to escape everything you are, and everything you represent. You are all I loathe about the aristocracy—arrogant, vapid, without purpose, and altogether too reliant on your title and your fortune, which you have come by without any effort of your own. You haven't a thought in your head worth thinking—as all of your intelligence is used up in planning seductions and winning silly carriage races. In case you have not noticed, I was perfectly fine in the stables until you came along and revealed me to be a woman. And when I left, with every intention of finding my own way north, it was *you* who followed *me*! And somehow I am looking to trap you into marriage?" She paused. "I do not know how I can put it more plainly. Go away."

He knew his reputation. He'd worked hard to cultivate it—the Royal Rogue, with altogether too much charm and not nearly enough ambition, a man who thrived on scandal and brought gossip with him wherever he went.

It made it easier to keep his distance from women whom he could never promise more than a night, as he had no intention of ever marrying.

Even so, as he stood there, in the drive of a posting inn, and listened to Sophie Talbot rail against his carefully constructed legend, the words stung more than they should.

He should not care what this plain, unimportant girl thought of him.

He did not care.

Indeed, it was best if they went their separate ways, and never met again. He had a dying father to worry about. A future heaped with responsibilities he did not want. A past he'd hoped never to have to face. He should leave her here. Forget they'd ever met. And he would, just as soon as he had the last word. "You're damn lucky I came after you, or you'd be walking south all night."

She narrowed her gaze on him. "Oh, yes. You've been a glorious gift of good luck from the moment you nearly dropped a boot on my head."

If he weren't so furious, he might have found the words—spoken in a tone dry as sand—amusing. Instead, he raked one long look down her body, his gaze lingering on her feet. "You will wish that you had accepted my help when I was in the mood to offer it."

"I wouldn't accept your help if I were starving to death and you happened by with a cartful of tea and cakes."

He turned on his heel then, leaving the damn woman alone on the damn road to her own damn devices. She wasn't his problem. How many times did he have to remind himself of that? If she wanted to be left behind, he would leave her behind. With pleasure.

With no money.

With no clothes.

With no damn shoes.

He hesitated, hating himself as he did. Hating himself even more as he turned back to the ungrateful woman and, without pausing, said, "How are you getting there?"

"I imagine the ordinary way," she replied, all calm. "Coach."

"Then you've forgotten that you require funds to procure passage by coach?" She'd have to ask him for the money. And he'd give it to her. But not before he made her grovel.

Instead of surprise or disappointment, however, Lady Sophie Talbot smiled, teeth flashing white in the moonlight. "I require no such thing."

The smile unsettled him. He blinked. "Six hours ago, you hadn't a ha'penny to your name."

She shrugged. "Things change."

Dread whispered through him. "What did you do?"

"I might not be as tempting as my sisters, my lord," she replied, and he did not miss the echo of his earlier insult. "But I make do."

What in hell did that mean?

She lifted her chin in the direction of the posting inn. "Sleep well."

He washed his hands of her then, leaving her for good, telling himself for one, final time that she was not his problem.

It was not until the following morning that King discovered just how much of a problem she was, when he exited the inn, frustrated and unrested, and headed past the half-dozen other racers, seeing to their curricles in preparation for the day's race. His plan was simple: replace his broken wheel, hitch his horses, and hie north, away from this place, the night he had spent here, and the woman who had somehow worked her way under his skin like an unseen bramble.

When he opened the coach door, however, he did not find the pile of spare curricle wheels he'd expected. Instead, he found a wide, yawning, empty space. Every one of the wheels gone.

Dread pooling in his stomach, he turned back to find the Duke of Warnick across the yard, leaning against his own, pristine curricle, a wide grin on his face. "Missing something, Eversley?"

King narrowed his gaze on the Scot. "Where are they?"

The duke feigned ignorance. "Where are what?"

"You know what, you highland imbecile. What did you do with my wheels?"

"I believe you mean *my* wheels." Warnick smiled. "I bought them."

"That's impossible, as I didn't sell them."

"That's not what your footman said." The duke paused. "Do we call her a footman? Or something else? Footwoman doesn't seem right." Another pause and a wicked smile. "Seems filthy, if you ask me."

Goddammit.

"You don't call her anything," he said, fury rising in his throat. "Give me the wheels."

The duke shook his head. "No. I paid for them. A pretty penny."

"Enough to get her on the next mail coach out, I imagine."

Warnick laughed. "Enough to get her on the next hundred mail coaches out. The woman drove a hard bargain."

King shook his head. "They weren't the lady's to sell and you know it."

"Lady, is she?" King felt a keen desire to hit something as the duke climbed into his curricle seat. "Either way, it seems as though it is your problem, Eversley. Not mine. I exchanged coin for carriage wheels, and that is where the transaction begins and ends for me."

"You can't even use them," King argued. "They are custom to my curricle." Every inch of the damn carriage was made to his exact specifications. Warnick couldn't do a thing with the wheels without the whole vehicle.

"That's incidental, really. Indeed, we'll call it money well spent to keep you out of the race," Warnick replied before turning to look at the other riders. "All right, lads?"

A chorus of approval sounded.

"You aren't seriously going to leave me here without wheels."

"Oh, but I am," The duke nodded and gathered his reins. "You've a lovely coach that will get you to the next posting inn."

Dread pooled in King's stomach at the words. At the thought of the dark, cavernous coach. He blustered. "You're afraid I'll win again. That's why you refuse to help me."

Warnick shrugged one large shoulder. "No one ever said we were required to play fair." And with a mighty "Hyah!" he was in motion, leaving the posting inn like a shot, a half-dozen other racers following him, leaving King in a cloud of dust. With nothing but a broken-down curricle, an empty carriage, and a seething desire for revenge.

Turning on one heel, King went looking for his coachman.

As it turned out, he was not through with Lady Sophie Talbot.

Chapter 5

MISTREATMENT BY MAIL:
NORTH ROAD? OR NORTH RUDE?

*M*ail coaches were decidedly uncomfortable.

Sophie shifted in her seat, doing her best to avoid eye contact with the legions of others piled around her in the once massive, now all-too-small conveyance. Unfortunately, there was very little room to shift, and even less to avoid eye contact.

The space was filled with women and children, none of whom seemed particularly interested in making conversation, despite the close quarters. Sophie met the gaze of a young woman across the small space between the benches of the coach. The woman looked down at her lap instantly.

"Oi!" a boy cried out as Sophie accidentally elbowed him, extracting a watch from the inside pocket of her livery.

"I do apologize," she said.

He blinked up at her, then down at her watch. "Wot's that?"

She looked down at him, surprised. "It's a timepiece."

"Wot's it for?"

She wasn't quite certain how to answer. "To tell the time?"

"Why?" This was from a small girl on the floor by Sophie's feet. She craned to look at the watch face.

"To know how long it's been since we left."

"Why?"

Sophie returned her attention to the boy. "To know how close we are to our destination."

The girl on the floor looked perplexed. "But won't we get there when we get there?"

"Aye," the boy said, crossing his arms and leaning back in his seat. "Seems a waste of time to think about how long it will take."

Sophie had never met two more fatalistic children in her life.

Though, she had to admit, she wasn't exactly telling the truth. She wasn't simply curious about when they might arrive at the next stop along the mail coach's route—she was calculating the distance between her and the Marquess of Eversley, who would no doubt be furious when he discovered that she'd sold his carriage wheels for coach fare north.

She highly doubted that he would believe that he deserved it.

Nor would he care that it was not theft, per se. She fully intended to pay him back.

But she had to get north, first.

North.

The decision had been made in the dead of the previous night, as she'd tried to sleep in the too-bright hayloft, beneath old newsprint that had been left for a makeshift blanket. Unable to find slumber, she'd sat up to find that the newspaper was a scandal sheet from several months earlier. *DANGEROUS DAUGHTER DISCOVERED WITH DRURY'S DEREK* shouted one headline, the story recounting a particularly scandalous moment in which Sesily was speculated to have been in the rafters at Derek Hawkins's theater. *SESILY SECRETLY SCANDALIZING STAR OF THE STAGE?* questioned a second story. As though there were enough to say about the afternoon.

Which there wasn't.

Sesily had been doing nothing scandalous that day. Sophie knew it, because she had been there as chaperone, listening to Derek Hawkins's endless droning about his unparalleled talent, alternating between declaring himself "the greatest artist of our time" and "a genius for the ages." At one point, the awful man had actually suggested he might be well considered for the role of Prime Minister. And he'd been serious.

The most brazen thing Sesily had done was to ask if Hawkins considered her his muse. To which he'd replied that he was beyond need of a muse; indeed, his muse came from within. He was his own odious, insufferable muse.

If there had been scandal that afternoon, Sophie might have found the whole experience more palatable.

But the gossip columns didn't care for truth. They cared for *TALBOT TATTLING*, as the papers referred to the headlines about her sisters. And her sisters adored it. She recalled Sesily reading this particular article aloud.

Sophie, however, did not adore it. Instead, she had crumpled the paper with fervor and considered the options that lay before her. Not options. Option. Singular. Because the truth was that women in Britain in 1833 did not have options. They had the path upon which they tread. Upon which they were forced to tread. Upon which they were made to feel grateful they were forced to tread.

There she had stood in the pebbled drive of the Fox and Falcon, watching the Marquess of Eversley, portrait of superciliousness, march away from her, somehow impeccable even while missing a boot. And that man—a man so arrogant he called himself King—had made her decision for her.

She wasn't returning to that path. She was forging her own.

North.

To the place where she had never been judged, where she had lived far from the threat of insult or injury or ruination. To the place she'd been allowed to be herself, not the plainest, least interesting, *unfun* Talbot sister, but simply Sophie, a little girl with dreams of being the proprietress of a bookshop.

She'd live out her days far from the glitter and gossip of London's ballrooms, far from the scandal sheets, far from the aristocracy. And she would do so happily. Without men like the odious Marquess of Eversley setting the standard of right and proper.

She'd apprise her family of the decision and settle in Cumbria. Happily. Her father would send her funds and she'd begin her life, free from Society.

Happily.

She leaned back against a particularly uncomfortable case, the corner of which gouged into the back of her neck. Not that she cared. She was too busy imagining this new, fresh life. Away from the cold, uncaring eyes of Society.

She'd rent the rooms above one of the shops on the high road in Mossband. They would remember her there—they'd welcome her home. The haberdasher, the butcher, the baker. She wondered if Mr. and Mrs. Lander were still at the bakery—he with his wide smile and she with her wide hips—and if they still made breakfast buns laden with cinnamon and honey.

She wondered if Robbie was still there.

The baker's son had been long and lean, with a winning smile and a teasing gleam in his eye. He'd been two years older than she, and her playmate in the afternoons, when he'd stolen away from the bakery with one of those buns, sticky and sweet, and they'd licked sugar from their fingers and whiled away the hours until supper with plans for the future.

They would marry, Robbie had promised her when they were too young to understand the meaning in the word. One day, he would be the Mossband baker, and she the woman who ran the bookshop. And they would rise before the sun and work a full, happy day, the smell of those buns clinging to hair and clothes and books.

It had taken Sophie no time to decide that without the yoke of London and the *ton*, she would have that bookshop. Her father would send her funds, and she would make Mossband the most lettered town in the North Country. There wasn't a bookshop for miles—books had arrived by post from London when she was a child, or had been purchased in bulk when her father traveled to Newcastle to negotiate coal prices. He'd always remembered "his girlies," as he liked to refer to his daughters, and he'd returned with gifts for them all—hair ribbons for Seraphina, elaborate clothes for Seleste's dolls, silk threads in every possible color for Sesily, sweets for Seline. But for Sophie, it was books.

Her father wasn't a reader—he'd never learned how, despite having an uncanny head for numbers—so the crate of books he brought home with him was always eclectic: texts on animal husbandry, economic dissertations, travelogues, hunting manuals, four separate versions of the Book of Common Prayer. Once, he'd come home with an obscure collection of etchings from India that her governess had promptly snatched away and never returned.

To any other young girl, her father's boxes would have been boring. But to Sophie, they'd been magic. The books had been leather-bound adventures, pages and pages of distant worlds and remarkable people and learning. And simple, unadulterated happiness. They'd piled up in her bedchamber, first on shelves, and then on the floor, and then, finally, in the armoires her mother had installed so the books could be hidden. But the book shipments had never stopped, so Sophie had always imagined that her mother hadn't minded her opinions so very much. Until the Liverpool summer soiree, when her mother had been horrified by her opinions. Just as the rest of London had been.

Cold memory pooled inside her—London's most powerful members simply turning their backs on her, as though she didn't exist. Exiling her. Worse. Disappearing her.

She couldn't go back; so she would go forward. And she would forge her own future by returning to the dearest memories of her past.

And if Robbie was still there, perhaps he'd make good on that long-ago promise. Perhaps he'd marry her. An ache began in her chest at the thought—at the idea of being married. Of being loved. Robbie had had a lovely smile. And he'd always listened when she told him about her books and her ideas.

If they married—well, there were worse things than marrying an old friend.

And if they didn't—she'd have her bookshop. And there were much worse things than that.

She opened her eyes, meeting the gaze of the young mother in the seat opposite. Instead of looking away in embarrassment this time, however, the young woman tilted her head slightly, revealing her curiosity. The woman's gaze slid down Sophie's face and throat, stilling on the place where her coat buttons strained against her breasts, and Sophie couldn't help but look down as well, following the perusal.

Discovering the button that had come undone, revealing a white chambray shirt and a swell that was decidedly unfootmanlike.

Sophie snatched the coat together, fastening the button once more, and met the woman's eyes again. She nodded in the direction of Sophie's cap. "You're coming loose."

Sophie reached up to find a long brown curl escaped from its moorings.

Sophie opened her mouth to explain, then closed it when she could not find the words. She shrugged.

The woman smiled, let in on her secret, then leaned forward to whisper, "I wondered why a fancy servant was riding by mail."

It hadn't occurred to her that the livery might draw attention to her in this world, when it made her so invisible in the world from which she'd come. "I suppose it's obvious that I'm not a servant."

"Only to someone who is looking. Most people don't look," the young woman said, before looking at the boy on the seat next to Sophie. "Give it back, John."

Sophie looked down at the boy, who was grinning up at her, dangling her watch from his fingers. "I weren't really going to take it."

"No one knew that," the woman said. "And you promised no more pocketing."

"Yer not my mum, you know."

The woman scowled at him. "Just the closest thing you've got to one."

The boy returned the watch.

"Thank you," Sophie said, belatedly realizing that she

really shouldn't be grateful for the return of her rightful possession.

"You're welcome," John responded with a smile before leaning forward and adding, "If I were going to steal something, I'd vie for your satchel."

Sophie reached down and lifted the satchel between her feet to her lap. "Thank you for the warning."

John tipped his cap.

The woman across the coach pushed one of her curls back behind her ear and laughed, the sound short and barely there, reminding Sophie that there wasn't much humor to be had in a crowded mail coach. Meeting Sophie's gaze, the other woman said, "I'm called Mary." She extended her chin at the girl on the floor. "That's Bess." Bess smiled, and Mary indicated the boy. "And you've met John."

Sophie nodded and opened her mouth to introduce herself before the other woman raised a hand and said, "And you're a fancy servant."

It was a reminder that to the rest of the coach, she looked the part of a footman. Sophie nodded. "Matthew," she said, with a silent apology to the footman whose identity she was quietly appropriating.

Mary leaned back against her seat. "Pleased to meet you."

Smell and crowd aside, the mail coach was not so bad as she'd imagined. *Perhaps things would go smoothly, after all.*

The moment the thought floated through her mind, the carriage began to slow. The girl at her feet sat up. "We're there!"

"You don't even know where 'there' is," John snapped.

She scowled. "I know that if we're stopping, we must be *somewhere*," the girl said smartly.

"Shush, both of you," Mary whispered, craning to look over the two sleeping women obstructing the view out the carriage window. Sophie followed her gaze, the trees at the edge of the road coming to a stop. "We're nowhere."

A muffled conversation came from outside as the other woman checked the opposite window before turning to Sophie. "Is it possible someone is looking for you?"

Considering she'd borrowed a significant sum from him without his knowing, Sophie imagined that the Marquess of Eversley would, indeed, be looking. She sat forward. "I hope not."

"Out of the carriage!" a man's voice boomed.

"Christ," the other woman muttered.

"I know you can hear me!"

Dread pooled in Sophie's chest. Eversley had found her. And once he had his hands on her, he would collect his money and march her back to London without hesitation. If he was feeling magnanimous there would be marching to London, she realized. If he was furious, he could easily leave her on the side of the road to fend for herself. Again.

And he hadn't seemed overly magnanimous at their last meeting.

Of course, she had called him arrogant, vapid, and unintelligent. That did not engender magnanimity, to be honest.

"Let's go, girl! We haven't got all day!"

Sophie thought the "girl" was rather rude and unnecessary, but Eversley didn't exactly eschew rudeness, in her experience.

Around the coach, women and children were stirring, asking questions about who was outside and what was happening. There would be no hiding for Sophie. She might as well not be a coward about the whole thing. Squaring her shoulders, she came off the seat, stepping gingerly around the little girl on the floor and reaching for the door handle.

"Wait!" Mary called out.

Sophie turned back. "There's nothing to be done. He's here for me."

"Don't open that door," the young woman said ominously. "Once it's open, it can't be shut."

Sophie nodded, sadness creeping through her at the thought that this woman, whom she'd known for no more than a quarter of an hour, was attempting to protect her. "I understand that. But I wronged him. Several times. And he wants his revenge."

And then she opened the door to reveal Eversley.

Except the man outside wasn't Eversley.

The *men* outside weren't Eversley.

Relief was quickly replaced by trepidation. While the trio were not her pursuer, these men were decidedly less well dressed than the marquess, and decidedly more nefarious-looking than he. She blinked. "Who are you?"

"I'll be askin' the questions, boy," the one farthest away announced. "It's nice you're willing to be all hero-like, but just step aside and give us what we want."

Understanding dawned. "You're highwaymen."

"Not exactly," he said.

"You stopped a mail coach on its journey north with the intent of robbing us and, I can only imagine, leaving us for dead," she pointed out, ignoring the gasps and shrieks that came from inside the conveyance at the words. "You're highwaymen." She looked up at the driving block. "What have you done with the driver?"

"He ran like the coward drivers always are."

Oh, dear. That was not ideal.

"Don't let them kill us!" came a little cry from inside the coach.

The leader stepped forward. "I didn't have plans to kill you. But now you're irritatin' me. And I don't like being irritated." He met her gaze, his eyes cruel and ice blue. "I ain't lettin' some nob's errand boy stand between me and what I want. Get out of the way before I decide to kill you to get to it."

Sophie did not know where her bravery came from. "What is it you want?"

"He wants me." The answer came from inside the coach, from Mary. She looked past Sophie to the man outside, her voice even as she said, "Don't hurt anyone, Bear." But Sophie saw the fear in the woman's eyes.

"I don't want you," the man called Bear said, disgust in his voice. "I want the boy."

John.

Sophie's gaze flickered past the woman to where the child had been. The seat next to hers was now empty— the boy nowhere to be found. Mary descended from the carriage. "He's not here."

"Bullshit," Bear spat, and Sophie inhaled deeply at the foul language. "You took him. And I'm still using him. He's my best drunk blade."

"I'm telling you, he's not with me."

The man got close. "But the little one is."

Sophie heard the threat in the words, the cool implication that if he did not get what he wanted, he was not above hurting Bess. She descended the carriage, coming to stand next to Mary and face the monster. "I suggest you step back."

He turned to Sophie, eyes wide. "Or what?"

Sophie was in over her head, but her father's voice echoed through her—*Bluster until it's real.* She squared her shoulders. "Or else you shall regret it."

Bear smiled, looking up and away before he turned

back, all anger. "I think you shall be the one who regrets it."

The blow came fast and furious and unexpected, stars and pain exploding at her temple. She was flat on the ground before she could think. Mary retreated, pressing herself against the open doorway of the carriage. "Dammit, Bear, I said don't hurt anyone."

"Next time, find a protector who's strong enough to take a punch," came the reply. "I told you. I'll be havin' my cutpurse."

Sophie opened her eyes at that, her location making it impossible to miss the little body curled beneath the coach. *John.* His eyes were wide and full of fear and tears, his gaze locked on Mary's feet.

"And I told you," Mary said, "he's not here."

Sophie heard the blow Bear delivered; it landed with a wicked crack against Mary's cheek, and though the young woman cried out in pain, she did not lose her footing. Bess screamed from inside the coach, and John closed his eyes at the sound. "I told you, you bastard," Mary repeated, protecting the boy. "He's not here."

The beast called Bear hit Mary again, harder, and this time, she did fall.

At the edge of Sophie's vision, John moved, and she knew what he was up to. He was going to show himself, to turn himself in to save Mary. Sophie wasn't about to allow that. "Wait!" she called out.

John stopped. Thankfully.

Sophie pushed herself up to her feet before the man could climb over Mary to search the carriage.

He turned back to her. "Stop playing the hero, boy. You won't win."

She approached, putting herself between the villain and the unconscious Mary, arms akimbo, not knowing

how she would stop him, knowing only that she couldn't
let him hurt another. "I shall stop playing the hero when
you stop playing the monster." She paused, lifting her
chin. "But that won't happen anytime soon, will it?"

He laughed again. "You've a death wish, it seems."

She allowed her hatred into her gaze. "Only if it is your
death of which we speak."

He turned away from her, arms spread wide, meeting
the gazes of his two companions with a quiet chuckle
before reaching into his waistband to extract his pistol
and returning his attention to her.

Sophie went utterly still.

"I've had enough of you," he said before raising his
arm and taking perfect aim at her head.

She closed her eyes, expecting terror to overpower her.
But the terror never came. Instead, she was flooded with
a single, calm thought.

*If only the Countess of Liverpool hadn't liked fish so
much.*

There was nothing in the world that King loathed more
than coaches.

He tugged at his cravat, desperate for air in the en-
closed space, and added this ride to the long list of things
for which Lady Sophie Talbot should be punished. As
it was, she had thrown a serious complication into his
plan—a race to Cumbria with his curricle-driving mates,
followed by a short, final audience with the father who
had ruined his life. He had visions of approaching the
duke's deathbed, of leaning down and taking the final
victory in their decade-long battle. *The line ends with me.*

And he would bury his demons. Finally.

Instead, thanks to Lady Sophie Talbot, troublesome
scandal and thief, he was not racing north. He was inside

a massive, empty coach that had a distinctly coffinlike feel. If it weren't for the clattering of wheels on the terrible road, King might not have been able to hold the panic at bay.

Instead, he leaned back against the plush cushion of the carriage and released a long breath, hating the way the small space closed in on him.

He should have saddled a horse and ridden. Yes, he would have had to change horses constantly, and risked the English weather, but at least he would have had fresh air. Growing more uncomfortable by the minute, King shucked his coat and removed his cravat altogether. Closing his eyes, he took several deep breaths, leaning into the sway of the vehicle. "It's a carriage, you idiot," he muttered into the darkness. "It's moving."

For a heartbeat, he thought it might work, thought that if he kept his eyes closed, he might be able to keep his sanity. And then the coach hit a particularly deep rut in the road, and he was tossed to one side, and his eyes opened to a small, dim space.

It was going to crash.

She was going to die.

And it would be his fault.

Panic consumed him and he moved to bang on the roof, unable to stop himself. Before he could make contact, however, the carriage slowed, as though the great, hulking mass of wood and metal understood his madness.

He had the door open and was on the ground before it stopped.

The coachman looked down at him, curiosity turning quickly to surprise, and King hated the wash of warmth that flooded his cheeks. He didn't want the man witnessing his discomfort and panic. "Why are we stopped?" he snapped, eager to redirect any attention from his madness.

The driver did not flinch. "There's someone in the road, m'lord."

King turned in the direction of the coachman's gaze to find a man, out of breath and waving his hands madly in the air. "My lord, please! We've been set upon by highwaymen!"

King hesitated at the words—knowing that this precise turn of events had fleeced any number of travelers on this road. Trick a man with a false sense of heroism into hieing off to save the day, and empty his carriage of his belongings. Not that there was anything in King's carriage worth stealing. Sophie Talbot had made sure of that.

Either way, the man in front of him was either a tremendous actor, or legitimately concerned. "The mail coach is filled with women and children," he panted. "They'll be hurt. Worse."

The mail coach.

Christ.

Even if he could have ignored the impending doom of a collection of women and children, he'd be willing to wager half his fortune that Sophie Talbot was on that exact mail coach. He met the heaving man's eyes. "Is there a servant riding with you? Wearing livery?"

Surprise flared. "As a matter of fact—"

King was in motion before the driver could finish his sentence. She had annoyed the hell out of him, that much was true, but he couldn't leave her to the nefarious doings of highwaymen on the Great North Road. Dammit, she was a lady of breeding. Of questionable breeding, certainly, but ladies of any kind of breeding did not take well to highwaymen, he imagined. She had probably begun shrieking like a lunatic the moment the coach had been stopped. That was if she hadn't fainted dead away from the shock of the situation.

With any luck, she'd fainted.

That would keep her out of trouble.

Criminals were less likely to murder unconscious females than they were to murder difficult, meddling ones.

But if any woman was skilled at being difficult and meddling . . .

King began to run faster.

He'd get to her, he promised himself. He'd get to her, and he'd get her to safety. And once he got her out of there, she'd be begging him to return her to London. He supposed that was the silver lining in this damn inconvenient cloud.

When he rounded the bend in the road to find the mail coach stopped dead in its center, however, it was to find that there were no silver linings whatsoever. Indeed, the cloud became a hurricane.

Lady Sophie Talbot was neither unconscious inside the northbound mail coach, nor a source of shrieking from within. She wasn't inside the mail coach at all.

Lady Sophie Talbot stood at the center of a criminal tableau, wearing Eversley livery and her ridiculous yellow slippers, hands on her hips as though it was a perfectly ordinary afternoon.

As though a man was not calmly lifting a pistol and pointing it at her head.

Goddammit.

King increased his speed, no thought in his head save one—he had to get to her.

"No!" he shouted, hoping for nothing other than to distract the villain long enough for Sophie to escape, but before the man with the weapon could turn to face him, a small creature launched itself from under the coach toward Sophie.

King thought he heard a child's "No!" echoing his

own, but he would never be certain, as it was difficult to hear much over the pounding of his heart and the rushing of blood in his ears.

It was also possible that he heard Sophie's "No!" as she immediately turned, ignoring the fact that *there was a pistol pointed at her head*, and captured the living projectile, turning to put herself between the little thing and the weapon, as though she were impermeable to bullets.

King's exclamation became an incoherent roar as he pushed himself closer. Faster. But he couldn't get there in time. He knew as much the moment the barrel of the gun tracked her to the ground. Things slowed, and he would imagine later that he could see the hammer on the weapon cock, move in slow motion over what would seem like minutes or hours before the pistol's report sounded, tearing through the English countryside and taking the air with it.

And still, he could not reach her.

Someone screamed. Perhaps more than one person. He'd never know, as he arrived at the scene of the crime a heartbeat too late, tackling the large man to the ground with a mighty roar, coming down on top of him with several quick blows to the face before rendering him unconscious.

Standing up, he turned on his victim's compatriots, making quick work of one before the other turned tail. King considered going after him, wanting nothing more than to brutalize each of the three men for what they had done. Threatening women and children. Shooting at them.

Dear God.

Shooting them.

Had she been shot? King turned back to the scene playing out at the foot of the carriage, ignoring the half-dozen faces peering out the door now that the immediate danger had passed. He raced toward the collection of bodies there—a prone female who appeared to be regaining consciousness and two additional figures fully entangled.

Sophie crouched low at the base of the conveyance, clutching what King now recognized as a young boy who could not be more than seven or eight. "Are you hurt?" he heard her ask as he closed in on them, and Sophie's words—the fact that Sophie could speak words—was enough to send relief threading through him with staggering power. Relief was quickly replaced by fury.

He paused, attempting to control the irrational anger that coursed through him as she ran her hands along the boy's arms and legs. "Are you certain? He did not shoot you?"

The boy shook his head.

"You aren't hurt?" she repeated, and King understood why. He was repeating a similar litany in his own mind. She was worried for the boy, which meant she hadn't been shot, either.

Breathing restored, King made quick work of instructing his coachman and the driver of the mail coach to tie up the two men he'd rendered unconscious before turning back to Sophie as her charge squirmed in her arms, embarrassed by the attention. "Stop!" the boy cried, pulling away from her touch. "I'm unharmed!"

"Don't you dare take a tone, Jonathan Morton," the woman on the ground said smartly, sitting up. "She saved your life."

The boy blinked up at Sophie. "She?"

Sophie smiled. "You saved my life, too. Now that we are friends, I suppose it is only fair that you know my secret."

The boy's brow furrowed. "You're a girl."

She nodded. "I am, indeed."

Respect chased away confusion. "You stood up to Bear," he said, looking to the still unconscious man on the ground by King. "To protect us."

She followed the direction of his attention, until she found King's boots and looked up to meet his gaze. The skin around her right eye was swelling, already turning black and blue, already forcing her eye closed. She'd been struck. Fury came again, this time directed at another. He wanted to knock the blighter unconscious again.

He took a step toward her. She turned from him, returning her focus to the boy. "I suppose I did."

"But you don't even know us."

"You didn't know me, and you tried to save me, did you not?" Sophie looked at him for a long while. "We don't need to know a person to know how to do right by them."

That seemed to make sense to the boy, and after a pause, he nodded and rose, going to help the young woman who appeared to have received a terrible blow to the head.

King could no longer hold himself back. He stepped forward and said the first thing that came to mind, words fueled by panic and fury. "That was an incredibly stupid thing to do."

Sophie pushed herself to her feet slowly. "I was feeling nostalgic for your insults." He ignored the guilt that came unbidden at the words. After a long moment, she sighed. "I suppose you came for your money."

I came to save you, you madwoman, he suddenly, irrationally wanted to say. *I came to keep you safe.*

But it wasn't true. He'd come to get his money back. To exact his revenge for her childish behavior the night before.

He'd come thinking that she was not his problem.

And, thankfully, she was unharmed and remained not his problem. "Among other things."

She shook her head. "I can't give it all to you. I need some of it. To get me north. To keep me until my father can send more." She paused. "I shall pay you back. With interest."

He crossed his arms. "You shall pay me back right now. And I will pay your passage back to London. Today. No mail coaches. I want you safe in a carriage and I don't want you setting foot on terra firma until you reach the city limits. Far from me."

She lifted her chin. "No."

He shook his head. "You don't have a choice. You stole from me. We're going to have to call the magistrate for these idiots," he said, indicating the men tied up at his feet. "We'll kill three birds with a single stone, if we need to." He leaned forward and whispered, "I wonder what they do to thieves out here in the middle of nowhere?"

She stiffened. "You wouldn't."

He narrowed his gaze. "Try me."

"You're ruining my plans."

He spread his arms wide, enjoying the way she paled at his threat. "It's what I do, darling."

She stumbled then, and he noticed that she was not simply pale. She was white. Dread pooled as he stepped forward to catch her as her gaze lost focus for a long moment, then returned to him. "Sophie?"

She shook her head. "I haven't given you . . . permission . . . to be so familiar."

"You're definitely not going to like what comes next, then," He held her in one arm and opened the buttons on her liveried coat.

She batted his hands away. "Are you mad?"

He ignored her, pushing the fabric aside. "Shit."

"And now you are cursing in front of me." She closed her eyes again. "I don't feel well."

"I imagine you don't, as you've been shot."

"What? No I haven't." She struggled as he guided her to the ground and worked her coat off. She clasped his hand firmly, forcing him to meet her insistent gaze. "I haven't been shot."

"All right," he said, returning his attention to his work. "You haven't been shot."

"I would know if I'd been shot."

"I'm sure you would." He clasped both edges of the linen shirt beneath, rending the fabric in two to get to the wound.

"Stop!" she shrieked, her hands coming to cover her bare skin. "Scoundrel! You cannot simply access women's bosoms whenever you please!"

He would have laughed at the words if he hadn't been so worried. "I assure you that I rarely have to resort to tearing clothing in order to access women's bosoms."

She looked down. Paused. "I'm bleeding."

"That's because you've been shot," he said, extracting a clean handkerchief from his pocket and pressing it firmly to the wound in her shoulder. He pulled her forward to look at the back of her. "The bullet is still inside. We have to get you to a surgeon."

She didn't reply, and he looked up to find her unconscious. "Shit," he said again. "Goddammit. Sophie." He tapped her good cheek with his hand. "Sophie. Wake up."

She opened her eyes for a moment, then let them fall closed.

Goddammit.

"No!" cried the other woman. "She can't be hurt! She was fine! She was talking!"

There was a great deal of blood for someone who was fine.

Christ.

This was his problem.

She was his problem.

"She can't die!" the girl cried.

She would not die.

"She's not dying," King said, pulling her into his arms, gathering her to him, marching her back to his coach, calculating the distance to the nearest town. The nearest surgeon.

"Oi!" the young woman called after him. He did not look back. She followed, her footsteps audible on the packed dirt road. "Where are you taking her?"

"She needs a doctor."

"She's our friend. We'll take her."

He turned to look at the girl, who had caught up with him at this point. "You don't know this woman."

"I know her well enough to know that she saved John's life. Mine, too."

"Don't worry, I'm going to keep her safe."

"How do we know she's safe with you?"

There was no time to be offended by the suggestion that he was a criminal. That he was not to be trusted. Sophie required medical attention. "She's safe with me."

"Yes. But how do we know?"

He looked down at the unconscious woman in his arms, who had been trouble since the moment he'd met her, and said the only thing he knew would end the conversation. The only thing that would pacify them. It didn't matter that it was a lie, or that it would come back to destroy them both.

"Because she's my wife."

Chapter 6

SOPHIE SHOT.
SEARCH FOR SURGEON STARTS

She woke half naked in a carriage careening hell-for-leather down what had to have been the worst road in Christendom.

The coach hit a particularly unpleasant patch in the road, and the whole thing bounced, sending a wicked pain through her shoulder. She opened her eyes, a squeak of discomfort turning quickly into one of shock.

She was in the Marquess of Eversley's arms. In his lap. In a dark carriage.

She scrambled to sit up.

He held her with arms of steel. "Don't move."

She tried to move again. "This isn't exactly . . ." Another pain hit, and she gasped the rest of the sentence. ". . . proper."

He cursed in the dim light. "I told you not to move." He pressed a bottle to her lips. "Drink."

She drank the water without hesitation, until she realized it wasn't water. She spat out the liquid that threatened to set her throat aflame. "It's spirits."

"It's the finest scotch in Britain," he said. "Stop wasting it."

She shook her head. "I don't want it."

"You'll be grateful for it when the surgeon is digging about in your shoulder in search of a bullet."

The words brought memory with them. The mail coach. The children. The brute who came looking for them. The pistol. Eversley, tearing her clothes from her.

She looked down to find his hand against the bare skin of her shoulder, covered in blood.

Oh, dear.

She took the bottle and drank deep until he removed it from her grasp.

"Am I dying?"

"No." There was no hesitation in the word. Not a breath of doubt.

She returned her attention to the place where his hand stayed firm, covered in her blood. "It looks as though I am dying."

"You're not dying." She read the words on his lips as they echoed around her in the enormous carriage. Everything about him underscored their certainty. Squared jaw, firm lips, unyielding touch. As though she wouldn't dare die because he had willed it.

"Just because you call yourself King does not make you my ruler."

"In this, I'm your ruler," he said.

"You're so arrogant. I have half a mind to die just to prove you wrong."

He met her gaze then, his green eyes snapping to hers in surprise and what one might define as horror. He watched her for a long moment before replying, soft and threatening, "If you're trying to prove that you don't require a ruler, you're not doing a very good job of it."

The carriage fell silent, and she considered her future. Possibly short. Possibly long. She might not see her sisters again. She might die, here, in the carriage, in the arms of this man, who did not care for her.

At least he hadn't left her alone.

Tears threatened to spill over, and she sniffed, hoping to keep them at bay.

"What's north?" he said, clearly attempting to distract her.

It took a moment for her to focus. "North?"

"Yes. Why are you headed to Cumbria?"

A future. Far from her past. "London doesn't wish to have me any longer."

He looked out the window. "I don't believe that."

"I don't wish to have London any longer."

"That sounds much more likely," he said. "Is there a reason for your rather urgent timing?"

She imagined that it didn't matter if she confessed the events of the garden party to him, as she was likely to die anyway. "I called the Duke of Haven a whore. In front of the entire assembly."

He did not reply with the grave concern she expected. Instead, he laughed, the sound rumbling beneath her. "Oh, I imagine he was furious."

She considered telling him about the rest of the events of the afternoon, but the universe intervened, sending the carriage into a tremendous rut, launching it into the air for a moment before crashing back onto the road. Wicked pain shot through her—bright and sharp enough for her to cry out. Eversley cursed in the darkness and gathered her to him, pulling her tight against him. "We're nearly there," he promised through clenched teeth, as though he were in pain himself, and their conversation was over, reality returned.

"Nearly where?" she asked after the pain had passed enough to find words.

"Sprotbrough."

She had no idea what Sprotbrough was, but it didn't seem to matter. They fell silent again, and she searched for something to discuss, to keep her mind from her certain death. "Is it true you deflowered Lady Grace Masterston in a carriage?"

He cut her a look. "I thought you did not read the scandal sheets."

"I have sisters," she said. "They keep me apprised."

"If I remember correctly, Lady Grace Masterson is now Lady Grace, Marchioness of Wile."

"Yes," she said. "But she was to be Lady Grace, Duchess of North."

"The Duke of North is old enough to be the woman's grandfather."

"And the Marquess of Wile is poor as a church mouse."

He tilted his head and considered her for a long moment. "She cared for him nonetheless."

"I don't think her father cared for his lack of funds."

"I don't think her father should have a say in the matter."

Several seconds passed, and Sophie said, "You ruined her for the duke."

"Isn't it possible that I ruined her for the marquess?" There was something in the words that she should understand, but the pain in her shoulder kept her from it. She tried to sit up, putting a hand to his thigh, momentarily distracted by the leather that encased it.

She looked down at the slick fabric. "Your breeches." His brows rose and she blushed. "I'm sorry. I'm not supposed to notice breeches."

"No?"

"It's not proper."

He cut her a look. "You're in my lap, bleeding from

a gunshot wound. Let's dispense with propriety for the moment."

"They're leather," she said.

"Indeed they are."

"That seems scandalous."

"In all the best ways, darling," he drawled, the words eliciting a blush as he continued. "You need boots."

Her head spun with the change of topic. "I—"

He reached for her slippered feet, running his fingers over the ruined, threadbare silk. "You shouldn't have left without boots. You should have taken the footman's."

She shook her head, looking down at the dirty yellow silk slippers. "I didn't fit. My feet. They're too big."

He pulled her tighter to him. "We'll find you a pair when we get there."

"Did you find one for yourself?"

"Luckily, my valet is exceedingly conscientious."

"Why isn't he here?"

He looked out the window. "I don't like traveling companions. He was to meet us at the next inn."

"Oh." She supposed he quite disliked this, then. "Where is Sprotbrough?"

He took her change of topic in stride. "The middle of nowhere."

"It sounds just the place to find a team of qualified surgeons languishing."

He looked down at her, and at another time, she might have been proud of herself at the surprise on his face. "Has anyone ever told you that you have a sharp tongue?"

She offered a little smile. "Not so boring after all, am I?"

He was all seriousness. "No. I wouldn't call you boring. At all."

Something flickered in her chest, something aside

from the pain of the bullet lodged deep in her shoulder, something aside from the fear that—despite his brash assurances—she might, in fact, die. Something she did not understand.

"What would you call me?"

Time seemed to slow in the carriage, a path of red-gold sunlight casting his face into brightness and shadow, and suddenly, Sophie wanted desperately to hear his answer. His lips pressed into a straight line as he considered his reply. When he finally spoke, the word was firm and unyielding. "Stupid."

She gasped. She hadn't known what to expect, but it certainly hadn't been that. "I beg your pardon. That horrible man was going to take that boy and do God knows what to him. I did what was right."

"I did not say you were not also exceedingly brave," he said.

The words warmed her as exhaustion came on an unexpected wave. She took a deep breath, finding it difficult to fill her lungs. She couldn't stop herself from resting her head on his shoulder, where it had been before she'd regained consciousness. "Do I detect a note of respect?"

His chest rose and fell in a tempting rhythm before he said, softly. "A very, very soft note of it. Perhaps."

Darkness had fallen before the carriage arrived in Sprotbrough, which could barely be called a town considering it consisted of a half-dozen clapboard buildings and a town square that was smaller than the kitchens in his Mayfair town house.

They would have a surgeon, though. If he had to summon the man from nothingness, this ridiculous, barely there town would have a damn surgeon.

He cursed, the word harsh and ragged in the blackness

as he threw open the door and tossed the step out of the conveyance. John Coachman materialized in the space, lantern in hand, the yellow light revealing Sophie's utterly still, unsettlingly pale figure.

"I still don't believe she's a girl."

King had held her for more than an hour, staying the blood from her wound, staring down at her long lashes and full lips and the curves and valleys of her body. He couldn't believe anyone wouldn't see that she was a girl immediately. But he said nothing, rearranging her on his lap for the next leg of their journey.

"Is she—" the coachman continued, hesitating on the word they both knew finished the sentence.

King wouldn't hear it spoken. "No."

He'd promised her she wouldn't die. And this time, it would be the truth. He would not have another girl die in the dark, on his watch, because he wasn't able to save her. Because he was too reckless with her.

Because he couldn't protect her.

He gathered her close and moved to exit the coach, her weight putting him slightly off balance. The coachman reached to help him. To take her from his arms. "No," he said again. He didn't want anyone touching her. He couldn't risk it. "I have her."

Once on the ground, he straightened, finding the curious gaze of a young man several yards away, no doubt surprised that anyone had found this place, let alone a peer and an unconscious lady. "We require a surgeon," he said.

The boy nodded once and pointed down the row. "Round the corner. Thatched cottage on the left."

They had a surgeon. King was moving before the directions were finished, not hesitating as he looked to the coachman. "Find an inn. Let rooms."

"Rooms?" the servant repeated.

King did not mistake the question. The other man doubted that a second room would be necessary. He doubted Sophie would survive the night. King shot him a look. "Rooms. Two of them."

And then he was turning the corner and putting everything out of his mind—everything but getting the woman in his arms to a doctor.

Sophie made knocking impossible, so he announced his arrival with his booted foot—kicking the door of the cottage, not caring that the movement was loud and crass and utterly inappropriate considering he was looking to secure the help of the doctor. Money would make amends. It always did.

When no one replied to his knocking, he tried again, harder this time, and by the third kick, his anger and frustration brought enough force to do what such blows were often intended to do—the door came out of its moorings, collapsing into the house.

King added the damage to his bill and stepped through the now-open doorway as a tall, bespectacled man came into view. The man was younger than King would have imagined, barely five and twenty, if he had to guess. And exceedingly handsome.

"I require the doctor."

Wasting precious time, the young man removed his spectacles and cleaned them. "You've broken my door."

He wasn't old enough to have hair on his face, let alone save lives.

"I shall pay for it," King replied, moving closer. "She's hurt."

The doctor barely looked at her. "I'd rather you'd not broken it in the first place." He indicated the wooden dining table in the next room. "Put her there."

King did as he was told, ignoring the twinge of discomfort he felt when he released Sophie from his grasp. Ignoring the fact that as he moved down the table, from her head to her feet to give the other man access to her wound, he couldn't help but trail his fingers along her leg, as though, somehow, touching her could keep her alive.

The doctor replaced his spectacles and leaned over her. "There's a great deal of blood. What happened?"

"She was shot."

The surgeon nodded, rolling Sophie to one side, inspecting her back. When he returned her to the table, Sophie's head lolled. "The bullet remains inside." He moved to a large leather bag nearby and extracted a bottle and a long, thin instrument that King did not like the look of. "I don't like that she's unconscious."

"Neither do I," King replied, watching as the doctor peeled away the fabric to inspect the wound.

The young man waved a hand to a nearby cupboard. "There's a collection of linen in there. And a bowl of water on top. Fetch it. She's going to bleed quite a bit when I've extracted the bullet."

King didn't like the sound of that. He retrieved the cloth and the basin and, once he returned, asked, "Are you the only doctor in the town?"

The man looked up at that. "I'm the only doctor for twenty miles."

King scowled. "Where did you learn your trade?"

"You broke down my door, sir. I don't believe you are in a position to question my skills."

King swallowed, knowing the man was correct. "You're very young."

"Not too young to know that your . . ." He paused, his gaze tracing Sophie's outrageous clothing. "Footman?"

"Wife," King said without hesitation.

"Of course." The doctor pushed his spectacles up his nose. "—that your *wife* has a bullet lodged in her shoulder that needs to come out. Would you like to wait outside for a more seasoned doctor to happen by?"

The point did not require a response.

"Will she die?" He hated the question and the edge of uncertainty in his tone when he spoke it. She would not die. *Would she?*

"The shoulder is not a vital locale," the doctor said. "She's lucky in that regard."

"Then she won't die," King said.

"Not from the gunshot. But as I said, I don't like that she's unconscious." The doctor raised the bottle over Sophie's shoulder, "This should help."

"What is it?"

"Gin."

King stepped forward. "What in hell kind of medicine is that?"

"The kind that hurts like a son of a bitch." Before King could stop him, the doctor poured half the liquid in the bottle onto Sophie's shoulder.

Her eyes shot open and she sat straight up on the table with a wild scream. "Bollocks!"

The doctor smiled at that. "Well. That is quite a greeting."

Sophie's eyes were wild and unfocused. "It stings."

"Indeed it does," the doctor said. "But you are with us. Which makes me rather happy."

"Who are you?" she asked.

"He's the surgeon." King replied.

She looked to him. "He does not look like a surgeon."

"I'm not certain of his skill."

She returned her attention to the doctor. "Do try not to kill me, sir."

The other man nodded. "I shall do my best."

"And is it entirely necessary to pour that on my wounds?" she added, "I didn't care for it."

"There is some speculation that the alcohol helps with infection," the doctor replied. "I do hope that's the case, as I would like to think that I haven't wasted a half a bottle of gin."

Neither Sophie nor King found the jest amusing. The doctor did not seem to mind, choosing that moment to raise his strange device and say to King, "Please hold her down," before saying to Sophie, "I'm afraid this is also going to sting."

King's hands were barely on her when the doctor began the bullet extraction, Sophie screaming, blood oozing, and King feeling a thousand times the ass for allowing this entire situation to happen. She protested his grip, writhing beneath him, and it took all King's residual energy to hold her still rather than pull the doctor from her and end her pain.

"Finished," the doctor said eventually, removing the forceps and showing the bullet to King before mopping up the river of blood that he'd summoned and moving to his bag once more.

King was riveted to Sophie, who had returned to the table, eyes closed, with a sigh that became a low whimper, and the sound nearly broke him. He resisted the urge to strangle the handsome man-child who called himself a surgeon. And he might have, had the doctor not returned with needle and thread. "Madam, would you like a drink before I stitch you up? It might well dull the pain."

Sophie, already pale, blanched further and nodded. The doctor thrust his chin in the direction of the sideboard. "There is whiskey there."

That, King could manage. He grasped the bottle and

uncorked it. "As this is for business rather than pleasure, I'm not going to put it in a glass," he said, putting the bottle to her lips. She tilted her head back and drank deep. "Good girl," he said quietly before she coughed, the alcohol no doubt stinging down her throat.

She shook her head. "Bollocks!"

He smiled at that. "You say that word like it is second nature."

She looked at the needle. "More coal miner's daughter than Society lady."

He laughed, but the sound was cut off by her gasp of pain as the doctor began stitching. King did his best to distract her. "Do you miss it?"

Her blue gaze found his. "Life before London?" He nodded, and she turned away, watching the needle do its work. "I do. I've never felt quite right there." She smiled. "Now I can't go back. They'll never have me with a bullet wound."

He smiled at that, imagining that if Sophie Talbot decided to return to London, she could make them take her back. "What happened at the Liverpool party?"

She met his eyes. "I shall tell you what happened to me if you tell me what happened to you."

His brows rose. "You know what happened to me."

"Before that."

"I imagine you can guess," he hedged.

"I suppose I can," she said, and there was something soft in her tone. Censure. Disappointment.

It wasn't as though King hadn't been on the receiving end of such disdain before; he had. He'd just never cared. He made his reputation on it. But somehow, this woman made him feel like an insect, despite having done nothing at all wrong.

"Excellent," said the doctor, seemingly unaware of the discussion around him, snipping the string on his perfect row of stitches and halting King's thoughts as he produced a pot of honey.

"What is that for?" King asked.

"For her wound," the man said, simply, spreading the golden stuff over the wound as though it was perfectly normal.

"She's not toast."

"The ancient Egyptians used it to stave off infection."

"I suppose I'm to think that's a good enough reason to do it now?"

"Do you have a better idea?"

King did not like this man. "Does it work?"

The doctor shrugged. "It can't hurt."

King blinked. "You're mad."

"The Royal College of Surgeons certainly thinks so."

"What do they know about you?"

"My membership was rescinded last year. Why do you think I'm in Sprotbrough?"

"I see now that it's because you're as foolish as the name of this place." King grabbed the man by the neck. "Let me be clear. She shan't die."

"Killing me won't help with that," the doctor said, utterly calm.

Goddammit. King released him. Spoke again. "She shan't die."

"Not from the gunshot," the doctor said.

King heard the repetition. "Not from the gunshot. You keep saying that."

"It's the truth. She will not die from the gunshot."

"But?"

There was a long silence while the doctor dressed the wound. Once finished, he turned away to wash his hands in a nearby basin and said, "I can't guarantee she won't die of what comes next."

Sophie opened her eyes and focused on the doctor, a small smile on her face. "He won't like that."

The doctor looked down at her with a smile. "I gather not."

She blinked. "You're very handsome for a surgeon."

The man laughed. "Thank you, madam. Of course, I would have preferred that compliment without the 'for a surgeon.'"

She inspected him for a long moment before she nodded. "Fair enough. You're very handsome. Full stop."

King wanted to break something when the doctor laughed. "Much better."

It was nonsense, obviously. King didn't care if she flirted with the damn doctor. She could live here forever if she wanted. It would make everything easier for him. He could leave her and head north and live a life without her troublesome—

The doctor put his hand to Sophie's forehead, and King could not help but want to hurt someone. Someone specific. "Is it necessary that you touch her so much?"

Unruffled, the doctor said, "If I'm to judge if she has a fever, I'm afraid so."

"Does she?"

"No." The doctor turned and exited the room without further comment.

It was not every day that King was dismissed so easily, and he had half a mind to follow the young man and tell him precisely whom he was disrespecting. But then he looked down at Sophie. And everything changed.

She was watching him, her blue eyes seeing everything. Her lips twitched in a little half smile. "You see? The universe does not bend to your every whim after all. I might, in fact, die."

"Of course you're smug about that."

"Better smug than the other."

He shouldn't ask. Later, he would wonder just what it was that made him ask. "The other?"

The emotion in her eyes was clear and unsettling. "Afraid."

The word struck at his core, and he was reminded of another time. Another girl. Equally afraid, standing before him, begging him to save her. But he'd been a boy then, not a man. And while she had died, Sophie wouldn't. "You won't—"

She shook her head, interrupting the insistent assurance. "You don't know that."

"I—"

Her gaze found his again, full of certainty. "No. You don't. I've seen fevers, my lord."

He remained silent, his gaze flickering to the bandage on her shoulder, to the blood dried on her clothes, on her skin—that smooth, unsettlingly soft skin. It shouldn't be bloodstained. She was young and wealthy, the daughter of an earl. She should be clean and unscathed. She should be laughing with her sisters somewhere far from here.

Far from him.

He turned his attention from her, hating the guilt that flared, dipping a long length of linen in the basin of water, now pink with her blood. Wringing it out, he began to tend to her stained skin.

At the first touch of the cloth, she started, and he imagined she would have pulled away at the sensation if she'd had the strength. Or the room. Instead she lifted her good arm and captured his wrist, her fingers cool and stronger than he would have imagined, considering the events of the last several hours. "What are you doing?"

"You're covered in blood," he pointed out. "I'm washing you."

"I can wash myself."

"Not without moving, you can't."

They stared at each other for a long moment, and he wondered if she would let him help her. He bit back the words that he was somehow desperate to speak. *Let me take care of you.*

She wouldn't like them. Hell. He didn't like them.

But damned if he didn't want to say them.

Damned if he didn't want to beg her to let him tend to her.

Thankfully, he didn't have to. She let go. And he began to wash her in careful strokes, clearing her arm and chest of dried blood, wishing he could will it back into her. Wishing he could reverse time. Wishing he could change this course.

"You should go," she said quietly.

His gaze snapped to hers. "What did you say?"

"You should leave me here. You have a life to lead. You were on a journey before I made a hash of it."

"A journey that brought me here."

"I'm simply saying that I can make my own way," she argued. "I am not your problem."

The words stung—how many times had he said them to himself? How many times had he said them to her? "I'm not leaving you alone."

"The doctor seems kind," she said. "I'm sure he will allow me to stay until—"

Over his rotting corpse. "You are not staying with the doctor."

She took a deep breath, and he heard the exhaustion in it. "I don't have your money."

"What does that mean?"

"If that's why you're staying. It was in a bag. I left it in the coach. It's gone now."

He didn't care about the money.

"That's why you followed me, isn't it? For the money."

"No," he corrected her. "I followed you on principle. You can't simply sell a man's curricle wheels. He might need them."

"Why did you have so many?"

"In case I broke a wheel saving an unsuspecting female from highwaymen."

She gave a small laugh at that, one that ended in a gasp when the movement forced her shoulder to make itself known. He reached for her, immediately wishing that he could stop what had to be a beast of a pain. "Sophie—"

She turned away from him. "You should go."

He shook his head. "I'm not leaving you."

"Why not? You don't even like me."

She'd been a thorn in his side since the moment he'd met her and she'd stolen his boot. She'd lost him his carriage wheels, a half-dozen races, and a large portion of his sanity. Yesterday, he'd begged her to leave him alone.

But today . . .

"I'm not leaving you."

The doctor chose that moment to return with a cup in one hand and a pouch in the other. "The fact that you do not have a fever now does not mean you won't develop one," he said to Sophie, as though King were not in the room. He held up the pouch. "These herbs might keep it at bay."

"Might?" King asked. "Why exactly were you tossed out of the Royal College?"

"I share an unpopular belief that creatures invisible to the eye cause infection." King raised a brow and the doctor smiled. "It's too late for you to refuse my help. She's already bulletless." He reached to help Sophie sit up. "The herbs might help to kill them and keep you well.

Add them to hot water three times, daily." He helped her to sit up. "Here is your first dose." She drank from the steaming mug, and he turned to King then. "Even a sane doctor would suggest you stay here for several days."

King nodded, looking to Sophie. "I was just telling your patient that I planned to stay."

She deliberately did not look at him, instead focusing on the doctor, who nodded. "Excellent. You'll need a room."

King nodded. "Already secured."

That got her attention. Even more so when the doctor said, "Your husband is an exceedingly competent man, madam."

Sophie sputtered her herbal swill. "My . . . what?"

It wasn't King's preferred way of her discovering his lie. But the universe was on his side, as the doctor did not have the opportunity to repeat himself.

"Mrs. Matthew?"

The name echoed through the small cottage, bellowed from the now permanently open doorway by a young boy, who materialized on the heels of the sound, followed by a girl not much younger than he was.

"John, we don't wander into people's homes," admonished a young woman who brought up the rear. King recognized them instantly as the children who'd nearly seen Sophie killed on the road. The woman's gaze fell on the doctor and her eyes went wide. "Cor," she said. "You're handsome."

Did everyone have to notice the damn doctor?

The surgeon smiled. "Thank you."

"You're welcome," replied the stupefied female.

"The door was open," John said.

"The door wasn't even there," said the doctor, dryly. "I take it you are here to see the patient?"

"Mrs. Matthew!" the boy repeated when he saw Sophie. "You're alive!"

Who in hell was Mrs. Matthew?

Sophie smiled at the child. "I am, indeed, John. Thanks in large part to you and this fine doctor."

"We thought yous was dead," said the smaller girl, pressing her face right up against Sophie's. "There was oodles o' blood."

"As you see, I am not dead," Sophie assured her.

"You still could be," John pointed out, coming closer, pushing a surprised King aside.

"John!" said the woman with them. "That's not very heartening."

"It's true, Mary," John insisted, turning to explain to Sophie. "My mum died of a fever after being knifed. It happens. Ain't it, Doctor?"

"It can do."

Good God. King had to gain control of this circus. "How did you find us?" he cut in, stepping toward the children.

"Easy," Mary said. "She was hurt, and you went barreling off in search of a surgeon. This is the nearest town."

"So 'ere we are!" John announced, all pride.

"Lovely," Sophie said, passing her now-empty cup to the doctor and returning to the tabletop.

"Why?" King couldn't help but ask.

Mary looked from him to Sophie to the doctor. "Because we were worried about your wife."

"His what?" Sophie asked, her gaze sliding to his.

"My wife," King said simply, quickly changing the subject. "No need to worry about her, though, as the doctor has managed it."

The doctor chimed in. "I've removed the bullet and

dressed the wound. Mr. and Mrs. Matthew will be staying here for several days so I can monitor the injury."

Mary nodded. "That's excellent. We shall stay, as well."

"No," King said.

"Oh, *darling*," Sophie replied, looking to King. "I think it would be lovely if they stayed." To an outsider, Sophie's gaze no doubt appeared wide-eyed and sweet as treacle. Only King could see the irritation in her blue eyes as she continued. "Mary, you must let my *husband* pay for your room."

Even shot in the shoulder, she was angling to fleece him.

"We couldn't," Mary said.

"Oh, you must. He's very wealthy. And you did play an instrumental role in saving the life of his *wife*."

Dammit.

"Yes," he said, over a barrel. "I'll pay for it. Of course."

"Excellent," Sophie said, quietly, the word barely a sound as she slipped into sleep; King would have called the smile on her face smug if he weren't so surprised by her slumber. He turned worried eyes on the doctor.

"There's something in the herbs to help her sleep, as well," he said. "Do you need assistance carrying her round to the inn?"

"No." King's response was clipped. He could carry his own imposter wife himself, dammit. And he wanted away from this mad surgeon as soon as possible. "Tell me, Doctor, how much for today's services?"

The doctor did not answer, now entirely focused on Mary. "You've a terrible bruise at the side of your head, Miss."

The woman raised her hand to the spot, her cheeks turning pink. "It's nothing."

The doctor turned away and opened a drawer. "It most

certainly is not nothing." He turned back with a small pot, opening it and reaching for her. She flinched away from him, and he paused, his voice lowering. "I shan't hurt you."

Pink cheeks turned red, and King had the strange feeling that he should look away as the doctor spread a white cream across the bruise on Mary's face.

King cleared his throat and reached for his purse to pay the doctor . . . only to find it gone. He looked down at his belt, where the coin had been not an hour earlier.

"Are you missing your purse, m'lord?" John asked, rocking back on his heels.

"John," Mary said, stepping away from the doctor's touch quickly, sounding somewhat breathless. "It is kind of you to honor your wife's wishes, Mr. Matthew," she added, the words sounding through the shock of King's discovery that his money was gone. "I hope you remain willing to do so once you discover that John has picked your pocket."

John extended his purse. "I weren't goin' to keep it."

A mad doctor and a school of thieves. Of course she'd saddled him with this merry band. Sophie Talbot brought trouble with her wherever she went. And how many times had he heard her called the boring Dangerous Daughter?

She was dangerous, all right. But he didn't worry for his reputation. He worried for his well-being.

King raised a brow at the boy. "You're the first pickpocket I've met who has no intention of keeping his spoils."

The boy looked down at his shoes. "It's a habit."

"It's a bad one," King said.

John looked to the doctor and offered a long gold chain. " 'Ere's your fob."

The doctor's hand went to his waistcoat pocket. "I didn't even feel it."

John grinned. "I'm the best there is in London. It's too bad I'm reforming."

King was not impressed. "Reform harder."

He turned several coins into his palm and paid the doctor before pocketing his purse and reaching for Sophie, pulling her gently into his arms.

The others in the room moved aside, but the young girl watched carefully, taking that moment to speak. "She's like Briar Rose."

King looked down, taking in Sophie's closed eyes and pale skin. He imagined she did look like the sleeping beauty from the fairy tales. For a moment, he considered the implications of the comparison. She might be a princess, but he was no prince.

"Unlike Miss Rose, this lady will wake," he vowed, more to himself than to the child.

"'Course she will," came the reply. "All you have to do is kiss her."

Were he not so tired of this motley crew, he might have laughed. He wasn't going to kiss Sophie Talbot. That way lay danger of an entirely different sort.

Chapter 7

——— ✒ ———

SLEEPING BEAUTY WAKES; NO NUZZLING NECESSARY

*S*ophie woke the next day, the late-afternoon sun streaking through the mottled glass windows, dust dancing in the light, and a somewhat unsettling smell underscoring the not-so-cleanliness of the rooms above the Warbling Wren pub.

"She wakes." The words came from a chair at the far end of the room, set back in the shadows so she could not see their speaker. She didn't need to see him, though. She knew precisely who it was.

He'd stayed with her.

She ignored the comfort that came with the thought. She didn't want him to stay with her. She didn't need him to stay with her. He was a rake and a scoundrel. And if not for him, she wouldn't be here.

But he'd stayed, nonetheless.

She pushed herself up without thinking, pain shooting through her shoulder and causing her to cry out. One hand flew to her bandage, a mistake, as the lightest touch seemed to send fire through her.

The Marquess of Eversley was beside her in an instant.

"Dammit, woman. Are you simply unable to be cautious?" He put an arm behind her back. "Lie down."

She brushed away his assistance. "I was being cautious. When a lady awakes to find a scoundrel in her chamber, she removes herself from the bed."

His reply was dry as sand. "In my experience, the exact opposite is true."

"Yes, well, I question the company you keep." Her shoulder began to throb. "How long have I been asleep?"

"Eighteen hours, give or take," he said. "Do you remember waking for your tea?"

A hazy memory came. Mary leaning over her with a teacup. "Vaguely."

"And the pain?"

She shifted and hid her wince. "Bearable."

"Interesting. I would have wagered that it hurts like a bastard."

It did, but she wasn't about to admit it. "You shouldn't use that word in front of a lady."

"No? You realize you've an affinity for certain foul language yourself."

She blushed. "One word."

"One is all you require." She looked to her lap as he said, "Does it hurt?"

Like a bastard. "Women are known for their ability to endure pain."

"Mmm. And to think you are considered the weaker sex."

She cut him a look. "A label no doubt assigned by a man who never witnessed a childbirth."

One side of his mouth kicked up in a small smile. "You're feeling better, I see." Something about the warmth in the words sent a little thread of pleasure straight through her. She was grateful for the time to collect herself when he stood and went to the door, opening it and speaking to someone out of view before closing the door and turning back to her. "I've sent for the mad doctor, against my better judgment. And for more tea."

She thought of the surgeon. "He didn't seem mad to me."

"He doused you in gin and slathered you with honey. While I wouldn't turn away a cake that had received such a treatment, it seems a bit odd for medicinal purposes." He came closer. "Now that you're awake, let me have a better look at that shoulder."

She turned her head and sniffed delicately. *Gin and honey.*

The inn was not responsible for the strange odor.

Oh, dear.

She scuttled back from his approach and held up a hand. "No!"

Eversley stilled, his eyes widening at the words. "I beg your pardon?"

He was going to smell her. "Don't come any closer!"

"Why not?"

"It's not appropriate."

"What isn't?"

"You. Being here. So near. While I am abed."

One black brow rose. "I assure you, my lady, I've no intention of debauching you."

She had no doubt of that, considering her current situation, but she couldn't well tell him the truth. "Nevertheless, I must insist on the utmost propriety."

"Who do you think nursemaided you for the last day?"

Bollocks. He was right. He'd been close. He'd had to have noticed her odor. But it didn't mean he had to any longer. She straightened her shoulders, ignoring the twinge in the left. "My reputation, you see."

He blinked. "You were shot on the Great North Road while wearing stolen livery—"

"How many times must I tell you that I paid for that livery?"

"Fine. You were shot on the Great North Road while wearing purchased livery from a stolen footman, after stowing away in an unmarried gentleman's carriage."

"Gentleman is a stretch, don't you think?"

He ignored the comment. "How, precisely, is your reputation not in already in tatters?"

Her reputation was already in tatters for any number of the events of the last four days, but she wasn't about to bring that up. Instead, she raised a hand once more, wondering how she might procure a bath without anyone inhaling in her vicinity. "That's all *perceived* damage. Not actual damage."

Those brows rose again. "You've lived in London for how long?"

"A decade."

"And you still believe there is a difference between truth and lies when it comes to scandal. Isn't that charming."

She scowled at his dry tone. "The point is, my lord, I'd appreciate you keeping your distance."

He looked as though he might argue, but instead said, more to himself than to her, "The doctor will be here in minutes, anyway."

As though Eversley summoned the man himself, the doctor took that moment to arrive, thankfully, Mary on his heels with a steaming cup of tea.

It was only then that Sophie recalled that the doctor was also handsome. Of course. Because when it rained it poured, and Sophie—who'd never held a handsome gentleman's attention for longer than the half second it took for him to realize she was not the lady he sought—was bedridden and unwashed when saddled with two of them. She was doomed.

"Mrs. Matthew!" the surgeon said, all jolly humor. "I trust you had a good rest."

She'd forgotten that they'd christened her with the name. "I seem to have, Doctor . . ." She paused. "I'm sorry, I've forgotten your name, sir."

"I never gave it," the doctor said simply, taking the tea from Mary with a dazzling smile. "Thank you."

Mary blushed. "Of course, Doctor."

Eversley snorted his irritation. Or was it something else? Could it be jealousy of the doctor's effect on women? No. Eversley was exceedingly attractive himself.

Not that she noticed.

She'd have to like him to notice.

And she did *not* like him.

The doctor approached the bed and handed Sophie the cup of herbed tea. He waited for her to take a long drink before asking, "How do you feel?"

Vaguely, Sophie realized that the man still hadn't shared his name. No one else in the room seemed to mind, however, so Sophie answered the question, keenly aware of the Marquess of Eversley's watchful gaze. "Quite well."

"Well. I'm sure that's not true." The doctor took the teacup from her and passed it back to Mary before seating himself on the bed and donning his spectacles. "So let's have a look."

She shrank back against the pillows, unable to think of anything but her odor. "I'd rather—"

He ignored her and put a hand to her forehead. "Excellent. No fever." Before Sophie could enjoy the pronounce-ment, the surgeon added, "I've smelled worse, madam, I assure you." He did not lower his voice, and the words boomed through the room.

Sophie went scarlet as Eversley looked to the ceiling in frustration. "Is that why you wouldn't let me near you?"

"You're the one who pointed out that I'd been doused in gin and honey," she defended herself.

"To underscore *his* madness, not *your* stench!"

Mary's mouth fell open.

Sophie imagined hers might have also, if she weren't so angry. "My *stench*?" She glared at him.

He rocked back on his heels, as though considering his next move. "I did not mean—"

She'd had enough. "Of all the ungentlemanly things you've said to me, my lord—and there have been many—that might be the worst of the lot."

He looked as though he wanted to say something, but refrained. Thankfully, because the doctor chose that pre-cise moment to peel away the bandage, and Sophie yelped in pain.

Eversley stepped forward. "You hurt her."

"Yes. I sensed that," the doctor said without looking up from his work. "No signs of infection, however."

Relief flooded Sophie. "Then I shall live?"

The doctor met her gaze. "For today."

"Christ," muttered Eversley. "You're a comforting bas-tard, aren't you?"

The doctor turned to him. "I tell the truth. No fever and no infection a day after the injury is positive. But medicine is more art than science. She might still die." He returned his attention to Sophie. "You might still die."

She did not know what to say, so she settled on "Oh."

He extracted more tea from his bag and set it on the

bedside table. "I wasn't sure if you'd need more than a few days' worth. But I'm feeling more hopeful."

Sophie imagined that should make her feel more certain of her future. But on the heels of his other statement, she wasn't entirely sure.

The doctor went on. "Continue with the tea—this blend will keep you more awake than the last—and be certain to keep the wound clean." He set a pot of honey on the table next to the herbs and turned to Eversley. "The honey is essential. Apply after every bath."

She might have argued that the assignment was given to the man who had become a rather prickly thorn in her side, but she was distracted by another, far more tempting word. "I may bathe?"

The doctor turned back to her. "Of course. Preferably daily, in clean, hot water. And summon me immediately if you begin to feel ill or if the wound changes appearance."

That sounded as though they could not leave. "When can we leave?" Everyone looked to her, each person more shocked than the next.

"You are in possession of free will, Mrs. Matthew," the doctor said. "However, I would hope to keep you nearby for at least a week."

"A week," she groaned. She had planned to be north within the week. Beginning her future.

"You do not care for our little town?"

Her gaze settled on Eversley. He had to get north, too. "A week is a long time to linger," she said. "My husband"—she ignored the warning in his eyes—"and I have much to attend to in Cumbria."

The doctor shrugged one lanky shoulder. "Then leave."

"Not until she is healthy." Eversley cut in. "When will we know she's healthy again?"

The doctor stood, gathering his things. "When the wound heals and she's not dead."

Eversley appeared to want to strangle the surgeon. Sophie smiled. "Thank you, Doctor."

He returned the kindness. "I trust that, whenever you leave, I will see you again, Mrs. Matthew." He moved to leave, stopping to nod once at Eversley. "Mr. Matthew."

"I shall see you out," Mary said, doe-eyed, following the handsome man's heels.

Sophie watched as the door closed. "Well. I have never met a man who makes one feel so very grateful to be alive in the moment."

Eversley scowled at her. "Why do they call us Matthew?"

"For my footman." The last word was lost in a yawn that she hurried to hide.

Eversley blinked. "You mean *my* footman."

She waved a hand in the air. "Whichever. His name is Matthew. I used it in the mail coach."

"And I pronounced us married."

"Which was a silly thing to do."

"Yes, I'm realizing that now that I've been named for a footman."

"A good one," she said, yawning again. Exhaustion seemed to be taking hold.

"A terrible one," he said, approaching her and helping her lie back against the pillows. "If he were any good, he would have told you he didn't speak to ladies of station and returned to his work. I've a fair mind to seek him out and put a bullet in *his* shoulder, as without him, you would be intact."

Was he concerned for her? "I am intact," she said softly, ignoring the pleasure that threaded through her at the idea. Ignoring the idea itself. "If in need of a bath, apparently."

"Christ," he muttered. "I didn't mean that you stink."

She closed her eyes and sighed. "Be careful, my lord. There are only two ways for that to go. The first way, you offend me. The other way, you are a liar."

There was a pause as she drifted into slumber, when she was awake enough to hear him. "Why do you travel north? What's there?"

"My bookshop," she replied, thoughts barely taking hold before they poured from her lips. "Mossband . . . sticky buns . . . Robbie."

"Robbie?"

"Hmm?" It was difficult to keep up with the conversation.

"Who is Robbie?"

Memory came, hazy and welcome, blond hair and ruddy cheeks. Her friend. The only friend she'd ever really had. "We'll marry," he'd promised once long ago.

She smiled. It would be nice to marry a friend. Perhaps he'd love her. It would be nice to be loved. Perhaps they'd marry. Perhaps they'd be happy.

After all, they'd promised it all those years ago. She'd said it, too. "We'll marry."

She repeated the words now, aloud, the Marquess of Eversley watching over her.

Chapter 8

SOILED S SCHEDULE:
WAKE . . . WASH . . . WOO?

*N*ight fell, and King let her sleep for several hours before summoning a bathtub and cold water, and then, once she grew restless beneath the sheets, hot water. Once steam rose from the copper tub and the women who'd carried the pails had been paid, he waited for Sophie to wake.

He watched her from his place leaning against the wall of the small room, his focus on her face in the candlelight as she came out of her deep sleep, the comfort of slumber giving way to the pain of her shoulder. The pain of reality.

He wondered if his father was dead yet.

Agnes's missive had been urgent. It was possible King was already the Duke of Lyne. Possible that he'd lost his final chance to have the last, punishing word with the man who had so roundly punished him.

Who had ruined his chance for family. For happiness. For love.

A memory came, unbidden, King in the Lyne hedge maze, his father behind him, revealing its code. "Two lefts and a right, then one left and a right. Until the center," the duke had said, urging him forward. "Go on then. To the center."

King had led the way, and at the center, his father had told him the story of Theseus and the Minotaur. "Who are we?" King had asked.

"Theseus, of course!" the duke had crowed. "Great heroes."

King came off the wall at the memory.

Heroes. What a fucking lie.

He moved to stand over Sophie. He could not spare time for this girl, who was turning out to be a cyclone of scandal. London called her the plain, boring Talbot girl. He huffed a little laugh at the thought. If they could see her now, bullet wound in her shoulder, sleeping under an assumed identity in a pub in the middle of nowhere.

There was nothing boring about Sophie Talbot.

She was to be married.

Why in hell hadn't she told him that from the beginning?

King knew about women who wished to marry for love.

He'd been the love in question, once.

Who was Sophie's love? If she was escaping London in exile, with specific plans for a future with this Robbie fellow—though King questioned the precise manliness of a grown man who used the name Robbie—why hadn't she said so?

Robert was a better name for her husband. More forthright. More likely to care for her.

Not that King minded one way or the other.

At the thought, her brow furrowed and her breath quickened. She would wake soon, and she would hate what consciousness brought with it.

King sat beside her on the bed. Telling himself he was checking for fever, he placed the back of his hand on her cool forehead, relief spreading through him at the temperature. The furrow deepened and, unable to stop himself, he smoothed his thumb over the little ridge between her brows.

She settled at the touch, and he ignored the pride that threaded through him as he moved to cup her cheek. He did not wish to be her comfort. She was trouble, and he had enough of that without her.

But he did not remove his hand.

"Sophie," he said her name softly, telling himself he was waking her for the bath she'd seemed to desperately want, and not to see her deep blue eyes.

She sighed and turned into his touch, but did not wake.

"Sophie," he repeated, ignoring the fact that he liked the sound of the name on his lips, ignoring the fact that he should not continue the caress, even as he did just that. Instead, he marveled over the softness of her skin, the silky threads of her eyebrows, the dark wash of her lashes against her pale cheeks, the pink of her lips—

He lifted his hand as though it had been burned, and shot to his feet.

The color of her lips was not for him to notice.

She'd asked for a bath, and he'd fetched her one. That was the extent of their interaction in this moment. He'd keep his hands—and his observations—to himself. "Sophie," he said more firmly, louder.

Her eyes flew open, finding him instantly.

"Your bath," he said.

Her gaze flew to the other end of the room as she clutched the bedclothes to her chin. "They brought it in while I slept?"

"They did."

Her voice lowered to a whisper. "Did they see me?"

He smiled at that. "Would it matter?"

Her eyes went wide. "Of course!"

"They did not. I set the dressing screen by the bed."

She nodded. "Thank you."

"But I saw you," he said, unable to resist teasing her. "Doesn't that bother you?"

"You don't count," she replied.

The words did not sit well. "I beg your pardon?"

"You don't like me."

"I don't?"

She shook her head. "No. You've more than enumerated the reasons why." She pushed herself to a seated position, wincing. "But you've endeavored to eliminate the most offensive one, thankfully."

"I like you fine."

"And a ringing endorsement that is."

He liked her fine when she was not infuriating, that was. He changed the subject. "I found you a frock, as well."

Her gaze fell to the simple grey dress that hung over the dressing screen. She nodded. "Could you summon Mary?"

"Why?"

"I need assistance."

"I can assist you."

Sophie shook her head. "Not in this."

"Which is?"

She flushed. "My lord, I cannot bathe with you."

She didn't mean for the words to tempt him. Christ, she was covered in remnants of her adventure—blood and gin and dirt and God knew what else. And of course baths required a lack of clothing. But for some reason, the quiet implication of her nudity had him hard and unsettled in an instant.

She was to be married, dammit.

"I can help you," he snapped, knowing he was being unnecessarily coarse.

She shook her head. "No."

"Why not?"

She looked at him as though he was an imbecile. "You are a man."

"I thought I didn't count."

She rolled her eyes at that. "You count in this."

He should do as she asked. Go get the girl and leave the two of them to it. But the past days had him feeling contrary. "She's not available."

Sophie blinked. "Where is she?"

"In the room I have paid for, at your request."

"You deserved that for pronouncing us married without my permission."

"I was to wait for you to regain consciousness before defining our relationship?"

"You could have told the truth," she said.

"Really?" he asked, "You think that would have helped your situation?"

She sighed, and he knew he had won. "It's the middle of the night and the girl is caring for two other children," he said, matter-of-factly. "If you want a bath, you'll have to accept my help."

She pursed her lips at that, her gaze settling longingly on the steaming bath. "You mustn't look."

"I wouldn't dream of it." It might have been the most obvious lie he'd ever told.

Somehow, she believed it, nodding and throwing back the coverlet to step out of the bed. She came to her feet, the top of her head at his chin, and he resisted the urge to help her across the room. "How do you feel?" he asked, hearing the gravel in his words. He cleared his throat.

"As though I've been shot, I'd imagine."

He raised a brow. "Clever."

She smiled. "My shoulder is sore, and I feel as though I've been asleep for a week."

He moved to the fire burning beside the bathtub and hung a kettle over the flames. "More tea when you've bathed," he said, returning to her. "There's food as well." The words summoned a low growl from her, and her hands flew to her stomach. Her cheeks turned red, and he smiled. "I take it you are hungry."

"It seems so," she said.

"Food after the bath. And then tea. And then sleep."

She met his gaze. "You're very domineering."

"It's a particular talent."

"What with you being called King."

"Name is destiny."

She ignored that, moving past him to the high copper bathtub. She turned back. "Thank you."

He resumed his place against the wall, arms crossed, watching her carefully. "You're welcome."

She reached down, her long fingers trailing in the hot water as she sighed her anticipation. The sound was like gunfire in the room—pure, unadulterated pleasure. It was delicious.

King stiffened. He was not interested in the lady's pleasure.

If only someone would tell his body that.

If only someone would tell it that it was not interested in the way the borrowed nightrail pulled across her breasts, the way it bunched above her hips and clung to the curves of her hips and thighs. Nor did it have any interest in where else those fingers might find purchase.

King dragged his gaze up to find her staring at him.

He coughed. "Aren't you going to bathe?"

She raised her brows. "As soon as you turn your back, yes."

He didn't want to turn his back. "What if you need assistance into the bath?"

She shook her head. "I won't."

He narrowed his gaze. "You might."

"Then you shall be mere feet away. Ready to act as my savior, despite your better judgment."

He scowled at that and did as he was told. Watching her undress would have been the highest form of masochism, after all, as he had no intention of touching Sophie Talbot. Turning his back was best.

Except it wasn't.

It was sheer torture.

He sensed his mistake immediately, the moment she began to remove the shift, the sound of fabric sliding over skin, the quickening of her breath as she navigated her wound, the little, nearly inaudible sound she made as she must have moved her arm in an uncomfortable way.

"Do you require assistance?" he asked, the words harsh in the quiet room.

She was silent for a moment before the soft reply came. "No."

He cleared his throat. "Be careful of your arm."

"I have been."

Past tense. Christ. Her shoulders were bare.

The moment the thought came, he heard proof of it, the hiss of fabric as she pushed it over her hips, the sound rhythmic enough to make him think she was moving them to ease passage. Undulating.

He clenched his fists and leaned against the wall, his imagination running wild.

Her breath came slightly faster, but not nearly as fast as his. Not nearly as fast as his heart was beating.

Not nearly as fast as other parts of him throbbed.

And then he heard the scrape of the wooden bath stool against the floor as she positioned it, and the soft pad of her feet as she climbed it and sank into the water with a stunning, glorious sigh, as though she sank into pure, unadulterated pleasure.

This was, by far, one of the worst nights of his life.

It took all his power not to turn around. Not to go to her. Not to stare into that damn tub and take in the long length of her, flushed and pink from the heat. From his gaze.

Christ.

He did not want her.

But he did.

She was to be married.

To a bumpkin called Robbie.

Where the hell had she met him? How was she planning to marry someone in Cumbria? He shoved his hands in his pockets. He didn't care.

She was plain and proper and uninteresting.

Liar.

And then she began to wash herself, and he resisted roaring his frustration at the sound of water against her skin, against the bathtub, sloshing and sluicing as she cleaned herself. He imagined arms and legs peeping over the edge of the tub as wet cloth slid down perfect, pale skin. Her head tipped back as she washed her neck and chest, her hands moving slowly, with infinite pleasure, across her body, above and then below the water, over curves and valleys, down, down, until the cloth disappeared and it was nothing but her hand, those long fingers dipping into moisture of a different kind—

"Why do they call you King?"

He nearly leapt from his skin at the words.

He closed his eyes, clenched his fists, and somehow found words. "It's my name."

The water shifted. "Your parents christened you King?"

He exhaled, not wishing to prolong her bath. "Kingscote."

"Ah," she said, and was quiet for a long moment, still, too. "What an extravagant name."

"My family prides itself on extravagance."

"I was on the grounds of Lyne Castle once." The reminder of his childhood home was unwelcome. He did not reply, but she spoke anyway. "The duke opened them to visitors for some reason. There was a labyrinth there." He could hear the smile in her memory of the place he'd just been remembering himself. "My sisters and I spent half the day lost inside—I found the heart of it and spent an hour or two reading at the center. They never found me."

"It's considered one of the most difficult labyrinths in Britain," he said. "I'm impressed you found your way through. You were how old?"

"Seven? Eight? It's magical. You must have adored living with it as a child."

It had been there for generations, perfectly groomed and rarely used, and King had spent countless afternoons exploring the twists and turns of the maze, losing his governesses and tutors and nurses without any difficulty. The only person who could ever find him there was his father.

He cleared his throat. "It was my favorite place on the estate."

"I imagine that it was. It was magical."

There was reverence in the words and, though he did not wish to, he was soon thinking of her there, at the fountain at the heart of the labyrinth, the marble statue of the Minotaur rising above her like fury. It occurred to him that if he had her at the center of that labyrinth right now, she wouldn't be reading.

He shoved a hand through his hair at the thought. He'd never have her there.

Not ever.

Once she was well, he'd be rid of her.

Finally.

"Do you travel home often?"

Why did she have to make conversation? It made it very difficult to hear the lap of water against her.

He gritted his teeth. "No."

"Oh," she said, obviously hoping that he would have said more. "When was the last time you were home?"

"Fifteen years ago."

"Oh," she repeated, the word softer, more surprised. "Why now?"

"You really don't read gossip columns, do you?" he asked. Wasn't that what ladies in London did between embroidery and tea?

"A truth that makes my mother quite anxious," she answered, and he could hear the smile in her voice. He wanted to look to see if she was, in fact, smiling. "But I don't like the way they speak of my sisters."

"You're very loyal."

She looked away. "It shouldn't bother me so much. My sisters adore *TALBOT TATTLING*. They're in constant competition for the most scandalous of tidbits."

"Who is winning?"

There was a pause as the sloshing water indicated she shifted in the bath. "These days, it is Seline. The one betrothed to Mark Landry. Do you know him?"

"I do."

"Well, *The Scandal Sheet* reported several weeks ago that Mr. Landry taught Seline to ride on a stunning black mare and then gifted her with the same horse, prompting my father to insist they marry."

"Because of an extravagant gift?"

"Because the horse is named Godiva. The implication

being that Seline allegedly learned in the nude in the private stables at Landry's estate."

"That sounds false."

There was a smile in her words when she replied, "It sounds uncomfortable."

He laughed.

"Needless to say," she added, laughing herself, "Seline adored the ridiculous story. Mr. Landry, too."

"Never let it be said that Mark Landry doesn't have a taste for the brazen."

"Likely why he and my sister are such a match," she replied. "You've bought horses from him, I imagine."

"That, and we share a club."

"I find it difficult to believe that Landry is welcome in White's," she said dryly. "I've never heard him speak a sentence that didn't include something shocking."

"It's not White's," King said. "We frequent the same gaming hell."

"Oh," she said quietly. "I've never thought much about gaming hells."

"You'd like it there," he said. "Filled with gossip and scandal and not entirely safe from gunfire."

She laughed. "I wouldn't be welcome, I'm sure. As we've established, I don't know enough about gossip to hold my own." There was a pause before she said, "Which returns us to, why do you return to Lyne Castle?"

Levity disappeared from the room with her question, and for a long moment he did not answer, not wishing to lose the moment. It was gone nonetheless. "My father is dying."

She stopped moving in the bath. Silence stretched around them, heavy and deafening. "Oh," she said again. "I am sorry."

He straightened at the honesty in the words. "I'm not."

Why was it so easy to tell her the truth?

She was silent for long minutes, the water quiet around her. "You're not?"

"No. My father is a bastard."

"And you return home anyway?"

He considered the words and the question in them, and then thought of his father, the man who had ruined his future all those years ago. Who had taken the one thing King had wanted and destroyed it. Who had made King's entire life about reciprocating—destroying the only thing the duke had wanted.

Later, he would not understand why he told her. "He summoned me. And I have something to tell him."

More silence. And finally a soft "I am through."

Thank God.

He did not turn as she lifted herself up in the tub, not even as he heard the water slosh around her when she returned to the bath with a little squeak. Not when it happened a second time. He amassed tremendous amounts of credit for his gentlemanly decorum.

Instead, he asked, "Is there a problem?"

"No," she said, and the sound repeated itself.

He risked a look over his shoulder.

Mistake.

He could see only her head over the lip of the deep copper tub, but if her cheeks were any indication, she was clean and pink and perfect.

"Don't look!" she cried.

"What is the problem?"

"I . . ." She hesitated. "I can't get out."

What did that mean? "Why not?"

"It's too slippery," she said, the words despondent. "And my shoulder—I can't put pressure on my arm."

Of course. Surely he was being punished by the universe.

He turned, already shucking his coat.

"Don't turn around!" she cried, sinking below the lip of the tub.

He ignored the words and walked toward her, frustration manifesting itself as irritation as he rolled up his shirtsleeves. "I assure you, my lady, I don't wish to help any more than you wish to be helped."

It was true, if slightly disingenuous.

She peeked over the rim of the bathtub. "Well. You needn't be rude."

Another man might have felt a pang of remorse at the fact she took the words as an insult and not as self-preservation.

Though her hands were placed in critical positions to hide her most inappropriate parts, it did not have the intended effect. Indeed, it drew his attention to the long, errant strand of her hair that curved, dark and tempting, down her shoulder to tease at the water, and made him desire, quite thoroughly, to move it. And replace it with his lips.

This was madness.

King kept his gaze on her face—he had to, in order to retain his sanity. "I'm going to lift you out."

Her eyes went wide. "But I am—"

"I am quite aware of your situation, my lady." Perhaps if he used the honorific, he wouldn't be so inclined to join her in the damn tub.

"Close your eyes," she said.

"No."

"Why not?"

"Because I don't want to drop you on your head. If you want eyes closed, I suggest you close yours."

Before she could argue, he leaned down and lifted her, water pouring off her, soaking his shirtfront and trousers on its way to the puddle on the floor of the room.

She squeaked as he raised her, and she did close her eyes, her hands moving to clutch his shoulders and steady her imbalance. It was a natural reaction to being hauled about, King had no doubt, but it was a mistake, nevertheless, as with her hands at his shoulders, the rest of her lacked cover.

The soft, pink rest of her.

He wasn't looking at her face anymore.

She opened her eyes and noticed, her already pink skin turning close to crimson. "Put me down!" He did, as though she were aflame, and she immediately wrapped herself in a towel. "You said you wouldn't look!"

"No," King said, "I said I didn't wish to look."

She stalked away from him, putting herself on the other side of the bed. Clearly unthinkingly, as the memory of her flushed skin in combination with a bed did not exactly dissuade him from his thoughts.

Not that he would act on them.

He did not want Lady Sophie Talbot, dammit.

Well, he wanted her. But he did not want to want her.

"That's a semantic argument."

Had he spoken aloud? No. She meant the looking.

"Madam," he said in his most serious tone. "No man in his right mind would honor that promise."

She pulled the towel more tightly around herself. "A gentleman would."

He laughed, frustration making the sound hoarse. "I assure you, he wouldn't. Not even the most pious of priests."

Her lips flattened into a thin line. "You are wet. I suggest you find yourself some dry clothes."

He'd been dismissed. By a haughty miss in nothing but a strip of linen.

A lesser man would take his leave. And Lord knew King should. He should give her time to dress and climb beneath the covers. Allow her a few moments to enjoy her cleanliness. Fetch her food. Get decent.

A gentleman would.

But King was no gentleman. As if it weren't bad enough that he'd had to suffer the temptation of the sounds of her bath, he then had to hold her, quite nude, and pretend to be unmoved by the experience when he was, in fact, very moved, as his soaking trousers did little to conceal.

He hadn't asked for this.

For her.

She riled him. And now, even as he knew he shouldn't, he wanted to rile her in return.

"Dry clothes it is," he said, enjoying the way she nodded, victory in her blue eyes right up until he untucked his shirt and pulled it over his head, and victory dissolved into shock.

"What are you doing?" she fairly shrieked.

"Donning dry clothes."

"It might work better if you did so in your own chamber!"

He pointed to the small trunk at the wall. "This is my chamber."

Her eyes went wide. "You have been sharing my room?"

"More than that," he goaded her. "There's only one bed."

She scowled at him. "You didn't."

"I didn't," he conceded. "The stench, remember?" It was a lie. He'd been too worried that she might not wake to even consider sleeping. But she need not know that.

She was too irritating for him to tell her. Instead, he

reached for the fall of his trousers, enjoying the way her gaze followed his hands. "A lady wouldn't look, Sophie." She immediately snapped her attention to his face, her cheeks blazing crimson. If he weren't so damn frustrated with her, he'd be positively gleeful. "I believe it's time for you to turn around."

She did not turn around, and it occurred to King that she was stronger than she seemed, this girl who was supposed to be plain and uninteresting. She narrowed her gaze on him. "I shall do no such thing, you horrible, arrogant scoundrel. This is my bedchamber, in which you take such rapscallionesque liberties."

He raised a brow. "*Rapscallionesque* isn't a word."

She did not hesitate. "I'm certain that those who invent words need only to meet you to see that it should be. As I imagine I would inspire them to commit *unfun* to the dictionary." She paused, pulling herself up to her full height. "I suggest you find another chamber, my lord. You are not welcome here."

Anger became her, this strange, unexpected woman. She stood before him, wet and wounded, and somehow a warrior nonetheless.

He wanted her.

And that was altogether too dangerous. For both of them.

He was here to keep her alive. And that was it.

He moved to the fireplace and poured her tea, letting silence stretch between them before he approached her, coming around the bed and closing the distance between them as she stood her ground, shoulders square, knuckles white in the fist that held the linen taut around her. He reached past her, exchanging the cup of steaming liquid with the pot of honey on the bedside table, his bare chest nearly grazing her.

It was a feat of great strength that he kept from touching her.

But in the moment, she did not back away, even as he knew her heart must have pounded as his did. She lifted her chin, but did not speak, despite the emotion in her gaze. Mistrust. Irritation. And something else he did not dare name.

"Sit," he said, the word harsh, echoing through the chamber.

She looked askance at the bed. "Why?"

"Because I vowed you would not die on my watch." He lifted the pot. "And I mean to keep the promise." His attention fell to the wound on her shoulder, which still showed no signs of infection, thankfully. The mad doctor was either quite lucky or quite intelligent.

"I'm quite able to manage, my lord."

He ignored the words. "Sit."

She sat, the linen clutched around her as he coated his fingers in honey. Silence fell, and they both watched his fingers work, the stickiness of the honey nothing compared to the softness of her skin. King supposed he'd used enough of the salve, but he could not stop touching her, spreading it smoother and smoother across her shoulder.

Wishing it was not only her shoulder. Wishing it were the rest of her as well, on all that pristine, pretty, pink, unbearably soft skin.

The moment was getting away from him and he cast about for a safe topic. "Who is Robbie?"

There was a pause. "Robbie?"

He didn't want to talk about the man, honestly. Not when she was here, clean and naked and fresh from a bath, smelling like summer. "Yes. Robbie. Your betrothed."

Her gaze snapped to his at the words. Was it confusion he saw there? It was gone before he could be sure. "Of course. Robbie. We've known each other since we were children," she said, the words perfunctory.

"Who is he?" he pressed.

"He is the baker in Mossband."

A baker. Likely short in the leg and weak in the chin.

"And you will run a bookshop." He was finished. He should stop.

She nodded, the movement stilted. "I will run a bookshop."

It was the perfect life for her. Married with a bookshop. He imagined her disheveled and covered with dust, and he liked it far too much.

He lifted his fingers and looked down at them, glistening with honey. She looked, as well. "You should wash them," she said quietly.

He should. There was a bathtub full of water mere feet away. And a washbasin and fresh water even closer. But he did not go to either. Instead, he lifted his hand to his mouth and licked the honey from his fingers, meeting her eyes. Willing her to look away.

Her eyes widened. Darkened. But did not waver. It was then that he knew.

If he kissed her, she would not stop him.

And if he kissed her, he would not stop.

Dangerous Daughter, indeed.

"There's a dress for you," he said.

"I—I beg your pardon?"

"A dress," he repeated, turning on his heel and tossing his shirt over his head before adding, "and boots." He tore open the door. "Wear the damn boots."

And he left the room.

Chapter 9

SPOTTED IN SPROTBROUGH?

*T*he pub at the Warbling Wren was fuller than one might imagine it would be at the breakfast hour, Sophie discovered as she descended from her rooms abovestairs three mornings later, dressed in the simple grey dress the Marquess of Eversley had procured for her before he'd disappeared.

She hadn't seen him since the evening that included what she now referred to as "the bath debacle." If she did not know better, she would have imagined that he'd left her, as she'd suggested he do, and headed north to his father. According to Mary and the doctor, however, who had been to check on his patient at the crack of dawn both ensuing days, the Marquess remained in town despite having no interest in Sophie's recovery, evidently.

Which suited Sophie perfectly well.

She ignored the small pang of disappointment that threaded through her at the thought. In fact, she denied that it was disappointment at all. She was simply feeling better, and her empty stomach was awakening as it did every morning.

She entered the pub proper to discover him at the far end of the room, breaking his fast by the window. He did not look up at her arrival and she pointedly looked away. They were not friends, after all. They were barely acquaintances.

He saved your life.

Sophie stiffened at the thought. He did not seem to care about such a thing, so why should she?

You wanted him to kiss you.

She shuttered the traitorous thought. That particular desire had been born of exhaustion and gratitude for the bath. She was fully recovered from it now.

She barely noticed him.

She barely noticed his shirtsleeves, rolled up to the elbow, and the lovely tan of his forearms, all strength and sinew, and the way his dark locks fell across his forehead. The way his green eyes saw everything beyond the window of the pub.

Why, he was practically invisible to her.

She resumed her direction with new purpose. Approaching a portly gentleman manning the pub's taps, she said, "I beg your pardon, sir, but I am searching for a messenger to carry a missive to London."

The barkeep grunted.

She was not swayed. "I am able to pay quite handsomely."

Mary had returned her purse yesterday, full to the brim with untouched funds. John had snatched it before the coach had been stopped. Thank heavens for the boy's inappropriate habit, else Sophie would be without all her money.

Not her money. His money.

Guilt flared and she could not stop herself from looking to him across the room. He had opened a newspaper and was reading, as though she weren't there. As though they'd never met. She quashed the guilt, vowing to reimburse every cent she used.

But desperate times and all that.

She returned to her barely-a-conversation with the barkeep. Lowered her voice. "Sirrah. I shall pay you and the messenger handsomely."

He did not look at her, but replied. "Two quid."

She blinked. "That's an enormous amount of money."

The barkeep shrugged one shoulder. "That's what it costs."

She waited for a moment, and then said, "I want a seat for the mail coach as well. North."

He grunted. "Of course."

"Gratis," she said.

He blinked.

"Free," she clarified.

He nodded. "Free."

Well. At least there was that. She placed the coin on the bar, along with the sealed envelope. "And for two pounds, I expect the letter to arrive tomorrow."

The man looked affronted. "Of course."

She raised a brow. "I do apologize, sir. I should never have suggested that you might misappropriate my funds, as you seem very reliable and aboveboard."

He did not hear the sarcasm in her words. "I am that."

"Of course you are. When is the next coach to arrive?"

"There's one due tomorrow."

Excellent. She had no reason not to be on it.

She ignored the twinge in her shoulder, nearly as irritating as the knowledge that the man across the room cared not a bit for her presence. "I shall take a seat on it."

The man reached beneath the counter and set a ticket on the bar. She pocketed the slip of paper and considered her next course of action.

"I've three questions." The words came low and soft at her ear, sending a thrill through her.

She resisted the urge to lean into him. To look at him. "Oh. Hello, my lord."

He raised a brow. "Hello."

"You've decided to acknowledge my presence."

"My lady, I assure you, were I not aware of you, I would most definitely not be lingering in Sprotbrough."

Her lips flattened into a straight line. She was nothing more than a difficulty for him. Obviously. "What are your questions?"

"Why are you exchanging funds with the barkeep?"

She pushed past him to fetch a hard biscuit and a cup of tea from the sideboard, grateful that he wasn't asking more questions about Robbie, who had somehow become her betrothed in the days since her being shot.

She should have told King the truth about Robbie. But damned if she didn't want him to think her spoken for. To think her purposeful.

To think her desired.

To desire her himself.

She resisted the thought the moment it came. Good Lord. She did not wish him to desire her. She was not mad. She did not even enjoy his company. And he certainly did not enjoy hers.

She collected her plate and cup and turned to find him there, ready to guide her by the elbow to the table he had claimed, appointed with his own breakfast and what she had to imagine was a weeks-old newspaper. "Well?" he prompted when she sat. "The barkeep's money?"

"Why do you care to know?"

"Husbandly curiosity."

She sipped her tea. "Luckily for both of us, you have no claim on my business dealings, my lord."

"No?" he asked casually, leaning back in his own chair. "With what money did you pay him?"

Sophie's cheeks warmed. "Is that your second question?"

"Yes, but let's call it rhetorical. I assume our pickpocketing young hero returned your purse and my funds?"

The already dry biscuit was like sand in her mouth. She swallowed and placed the purse on the table between them. "There are a few pounds missing," she whispered, "I shall repay you."

He did not touch the bag. "With what funds? My money is all you have."

She leaned forward. "Not for long. The barkeep is sending a letter home to my father, apprising him of my situation and asking for funds."

He leaned forward himself. "You think your father does not already seek you?"

"I cannot imagine why he would."

Dark brows rose. "You cannot."

She shook her head. "I'm not my sisters."

"What does that mean?" If she didn't know better, she'd think he was irritated.

"Only that they're much more interesting than I. They'll all marry well and make beautiful, wealthy children who will climb aristocratic trellises like wisteria." She looked out the window. A team of oxen hauled a massive cart past, revealing a pair of dusty men hitching their horses on the opposite side of the street. "I am not a climber." He watched her for a long moment, silent, until she felt she needed to add, "You see? I told you I wasn't angling to marry you."

"If I remember correctly, you told me you wouldn't marry me if I were the last man in Christendom."

"Harsh, but true, I'm afraid."

"I'd ask why, but I'm afraid your honesty might wound me." He sat back. "Care for a wager?"

"What kind of wager?"

"I wager your father seeks you already."

She smiled. "I'm certain it's not true. Matthew saw me into your carriage. My father knows I am well."

King raised a brow. "At best, your father thinks I've ruined you."

She shook her head. "Don't worry about that. He's a reasonable man who will understand everything when I explain it. You shan't be saddled with a wife."

"Oh, I don't worry about being saddled with a wife."

She considered the words. "I suppose you wouldn't be. You've avoided marriage after ruination before."

"It's less avoiding than eschewing. I shall never marry. Angry fathers be damned."

"Why not?" She couldn't resist the question, but when his face darkened in reply, she instantly regretted it. "Never mind. I shouldn't have asked that."

After a pause, he said. "Your father seeks you already, my lady. That's the wager."

Triumph flared. Even if her father was looking for her, he would receive her missive tomorrow, and call off any search. She could not lose. She smiled, allowing herself to enjoy the moment. "I assure you, he does not. What do you forfeit when I win?"

"What would you like?"

"My bookshop. On the Mossband High Street."

"Done. And *when* I win, I get a forfeit of my choosing."

Her brows snapped together. "That seems a high price."

"Higher than the cost of a bookshop?"

She tilted her head to one side. "I suppose not. All right. I agree."

He smirked and reached over to steal a bit of her biscuit. "I will simply say, you're a fool if you think your father hasn't hired two dozen men to comb the English countryside and get you home."

"I *am* going home," she said.

"Home to London."

"That's just it. London isn't my home."

"And Mossband is?"

"Yes." It must be. It was her only chance.

"You don't remember it."

"I remember it perfectly," she insisted. "I remember the town square and the baker and the haberdasher and the livery. I remember the Maypole, festooned with ribbons, and the way that the summer days lingered as the sun set over the hills and the river. I remember that it was more beautiful and more interesting and more . . ." She searched for the word. ". . . *honest* than anything in London."

"How romantic. Do you speak of the town? Or your betrothed?"

She narrowed her gaze, hating the way he mocked her and made her defensive, as though she didn't know what she was doing or why.

As though she were being terribly rash.

As though she had a choice.

"In comparison to you and London, both."

It wasn't rashness that had her heading home. She had no choice. London would never have her. It never wanted her to begin with. She had to hope that Mossband would.

He finished his tea. "You know, considering you are whiling away your days in comfort abovestairs thanks to my largesse, Lady Sophie, one would think that you would be significantly better behaved in my presence."

She faked a smile. "Sadly, my lord, I am not like the women with whom you typically consort."

He reached for his newspaper. "You shan't have an argument from me on that."

He was odious. She huffed her irritation. "What's the third?"

He looked up. "The third?"

"You said you had three questions."

"Ah," he said, looking back to the paper. "I do."

"Well?"

"What the hell did you do to the Duke of Haven?"

Oh, dear. "How did you—" she began before realizing that the question acknowledged her actions. She changed tack. "I told you."

He shook his head. "No. You told me you insulted him in front of the entire assembly."

"I did," she said.

He tossed the newspaper on top of her unpleasant biscuit. "What did you do before that, Sophie?"

She looked down at the paper, her gaze falling to a line of large, bold type. DANGEROUS DAUGHTER DUNKS DUKE!

It was not, as she had expected, an old newspaper. "That newspaper was printed and delivered with uncanny expediency to Sprotbrough."

"Who would have imagined it was such a metropolis?" he replied.

"The exclamation point seems unnecessary," she said quietly.

"You should write a letter of complaint to the editor. What did you do?"

She lifted the newspaper and offered it back to him. "I'm certain you can read all about it."

"It says you nearly drowned him. There's speculation that you wished to kill him."

She rolled her eyes. "Oh, for heaven's sake. He was backside first in two feet of fishpond."

He laughed at that. A warm, rolling laugh that surprised her with its honesty. It made her wish he laughed more. It made her forget what they were discussing, until he recovered his words and asked, incredulous, "At your doing?"

"He deserved it, if that's worth anything," she grumbled.

"I have no doubt he did, the pompous ass," Eversley said. "What did he do to you?"

"It wasn't me," she said. "I wouldn't have done it if it were me."

He watched her carefully. "For whom, then?"

"He was hidden away in the greenhouse. With a woman."

"And?"

He was going to make her elaborate. "The woman was not my sister."

"Ah," he said.

And that was it. There was no judgment in the word. And at the same time, there was no understanding. "You don't think he deserved it, after all."

"I did not say that."

"You did not *not* say it, either." When he did not reply, irritation flared. "I suppose you're all in some secret club, anyway."

"We all?" he asked.

She narrowed her gaze on his. "Lotharios who don't mind ruining marriages."

"I told you, I don't dally with married ladies."

"Only soon-to-be-married ones."

"There's a difference."

Every time she thought he was fairly decent, he reminded her of the truth. She tossed the paper at him. "No. There isn't." She paused, then added, "Lady Elizabeth, daughter of the Marquess of Twillery."

"Sounds familiar."

"She should. You ruined her planned marriage to the Earl of Exeter."

"Ah. Yes. It's coming back to me," he said, relaxing into his chair.

"She married her father's stable master."

"Happily, if I recall."

"She didn't have a choice after you ended her engagement."

"Love conquered. Isn't that what is important?" He remained unruffled.

"Of course you can be flip about it," she said. "You're a man."

"What does that have to do with it?"

"Your reputation is only enhanced by your actions. Poor Lady Elizabeth is ruined forever."

"Lady Elizabeth might disagree with that assessment of the situation." He returned his attention to the article in the paper about her altercation with Haven. "You are rather ruined yourself, it appears."

"Those assembled were not amused."

He smirked. "I don't imagine they were. So, now we know."

She looked to him in confusion. "What do we know?"

"What you're running from."

"I'm not running," she insisted. "Either way, you needn't trouble yourself with it; I have purchased a ticket on the mail coach tomorrow. I look forward to being rid of you, and I'm sure you feel the same."

"You're not going anywhere on a mail coach," he said simply, as though she were asking his permission.

She shot him a look. "You're acting like your name gives you some sort of special power over me. Again. I do not care for it."

The words were punctuated by the door to the street opening behind her, Eversley's gaze flickering over her shoulder to consider the newcomers as he turned the newspaper over. He tracked their movement for so long that she had to resist the desire to turn and look.

Instead, she leaned forward. "Don't tell me it's the *real* King?"

He cut her a look. "I suppose you think it's amusing to mock my name?"

She smirked. "I do, rather."

"You should not bite the hand that feeds you," he said.

"Are you calling me a dog?"

"No," he replied, "Hounds are more docile and obedient than you could ever be."

She was about to tell him precisely which of them was houndlike when he reached for her hand across the tabletop as though it were the most normal thing in the world, looked deep into her eyes, and smiled.

Sophie's breath caught. Good Lord, he was a beautiful man, all strength and power and that smile—it was no wonder that he was known for being a proper rake. It was almost enough to have Sophie forgetting that she disliked him and instead allowing him all sorts of liberties. Like holding her hand, for example. Her pulse quickened at the feeling of his warm skin against hers, and she at once regretted and rejoiced in the lack of gloves between them. She instantly attempted to remove her hand from his, keenly aware that even if they were married, the touch was inappropriate.

He held her like steel the moment she tried to move, and he spoke, the words loud enough for half the pub to hear. "I win, darling."

Her brow furrowed. He won what? *Darling?* She leaned in. "Are you addled, sir?"

He smiled again, the expression full of privacy and promise, as though the two of them not only liked each other, but shared a lifetime of secrets. He lifted her hand to his lips, kissing the knuckles in succession. Sophie opened her mouth, then closed it, heart pounding, attention riveted to the place where his kisses rained.

What was happening?

"Apologies for the interruption."

For a moment, she did not even hear the words, too focused on the strange, seductive man across the table. But Eversley heard enough for both of them, replying without moving his gaze from hers. "What is it?"

"We are looking for a missing girl."

They were there for her.

Eversley's grasp did not shift, and it was that firm, steady grip that kept her from gasping her surprise. She watched his eyes, read the question in them. Knew that he was leaving her the opportunity to reveal herself. She looked up at them, discovering the pair of dusty riders she'd noticed earlier. "A missing girl," she said, clutching Eversley's hand as though it were a port in the storm. "How terrible."

Perhaps it wasn't she.

The thought had barely formed before the man said, "Lady Sophie Talbot."

She was found.

Her plans were thwarted. Eversley was right—her father had sent men to find her. They would ferret her back to London, to the bosom of her family, where she would be primped and preened and sent into Society at her great, mortal embarrassment.

She would have to become Sophie, the *unfun* Dangerous Daughter.

Days ago, that might have been fine . . . but now she knew there was another possibility. There was freedom. There was Mossband. There was even the possibility of Robbie, who might make good on his promise once he discovered that she was there, and marriageable. Perhaps he had been waiting for her all these years. Perhaps he had despaired for want of her.

Perhaps not.

There was Eversley.

Her gaze flickered to his and dropped away. With whom would she spar if these men took her into custody? Would she ever see him again?

Would she mind?

The answer whispered through her, and she hated even the thought of giving it voice. But there was no turning back. She'd had her chance for proper escape. For a simple, happy life, far from London and the future for which she'd never asked.

And it had been ruined.

Know when you've been bested, her father had schooled her again and again. *Cut your losses. Shake hands. And return to destroy them another day.*

The thought echoing through her, Sophie was quiet, gathering her courage. Ignoring the constant litany of *Do not make me return* that echoed in her head as the newcomer added, "She is believed to be traveling with the Marquess of Eversley."

She paused at that. How could they know?

Matthew.

The footman would have arrived at the Talbot house and produced a letter from Sophie—and her father would have immediately had the poor boy questioned. She resisted the urge to ask if Matthew was well.

"Oh?" Eversley asked calmly, as though he had no concern whatsoever. "Are they eloping?"

"Not if we have anything to do with it." The man leaned down and said, "What are your names? If you don't mind my asking?"

Eversley's grip tightened as her gaze flew to his face, where he watched the other man. Willed him to lie. To protect her, even as she knew he was in no way beholden to her. *She was not his problem.* How many times had he told her that?

It did not matter that she rather wished she *was* his problem.

And then he replied. "Matthew," he said, with utter calm. "Mr. and Mrs." He turned his glittering smile on their visitor. "Newlyweds."

The man watched them for a long moment before Sophie settled her free hand on their entwined ones and smiled her warmest smile.

She did not know why, but he was saving her. Again.

And worse, she was beginning to like him.

She had a beautiful smile.

It was the wrong time to notice it, but the entire morning he'd been noticing her—from the moment she'd walked into the pub in what had to be a years-old dress procured from the pub owner's wife. There was nothing attractive about the frock, and still he could not keep his attention from her.

Then she'd argued with him—no surprise, as arguing seemed to be what they did together. And it was more exciting than anything he'd done with a woman in a very long time.

When the men had arrived, he'd known, without question, that they were looking for her. And he'd been about to turn her over—to explain that Lady Sophie Talbot was nothing more than a nuisance, and be rid of the woman and her troublesome life, when he'd made the mistake of looking at her.

She'd looked crushed, her blue eyes full of sadness and

resignation. And the smallest, most devastating sliver of hope.

Hope that he might help her out of this mess.

So he had. Like a fool, perpetuating the myth of their marriage, locking them together for more time, until the bounty hunters left. It was idiocy, of course, considering the fact that she'd just sent a messenger to her father, apprising him, no doubt, of the entire situation. Of her plans, which the Earl of Wight would never allow, no matter how much his youngest daughter believed herself plain or boring or irrelevant.

She thought too little of herself, and King had suddenly wished very much to change her mind. As insane as that sounded.

He blamed her beautiful smile.

Which he'd noticed at the exact wrong time, of course. Dammit.

He came to his feet the moment the man left their table and sat at the bar, knowing that they hadn't entirely convinced him that they were simple newlyweds smitten with each other. Knowing that he was about to pay the barkeep for information on them. Knowing that Sophie had just paid for an urgent delivery to London. He swore under his breath and, refusing to release Sophie's hand, pulled her from her chair to her feet, leaning down to whisper at her ear, "They are not certain of us. Feign love."

She turned to look at him, blinking. "How do I feign something like that?"

She was so damn innocent. It slayed him. He leaned back in, pressing his lips to her ear, enjoying the way she curled into the touch. "Pretend I'm your Robbie."

Confusion washed through her eyes, and he knew the truth, a thread of relief twisting through him. She did not love Robbie.

Not that he cared one way or another.

He pulled her from the room, instead, using his strength to keep her closer than was proper. Once they were through the back entrance of the pub, he drew her into the dark hallway just beyond the door, hesitating at the foot of the stairway that led to the rooms above.

He imagined they didn't have much time, so he was not gentle when he set her against the wall. "How is your shoulder?" he asked, realizing he hadn't asked her before. Though he'd spoken to Mary and to the mad doctor every day, he hadn't seen Sophie in three days. And he should have asked after her wound.

He should have asked after her, period.

She was confused by the question, but answered nonetheless. "It is fine, thank you. Stiff, but it remains uninfected."

He nodded. "Excellent."

"You knew they were here." She hissed. "That's why you wagered."

He hadn't, but he did not correct her. "You shouldn't have agreed to bet me."

"Because you're a scoundrel?"

"Because I do not lose." A stool scraped against wood in the pub. The man approached. King pressed closer to her, his hands encircling her waist. She squeaked her surprise as he leaned in. There was no time to prepare her. No time to change his plan. No time for anything but a quick, low "Time for my forfeit. Make it look real, Mrs. Matthew." And he set his lips to hers

For a moment, she froze beneath him, her lips pressed together in a flat line, her hands up at his shoulders, pushing at him, a little sound of protest caught in her throat. He lifted one hand to her neck, his thumb brushing along the line of her jaw, his fingers threading into the hair at the nape of her neck, massaging there until she relaxed, sighing her pleasure at the sensation.

He didn't intend to like kissing Sophie Talbot.

He didn't intend for anything more than the most perfunctory of caresses—long enough to convince her pursuers, and mechanical enough to get the job done.

But the sigh did him in. He caught it with his lips, readjusting the angle, pulling her tighter against him and pouring all his expertise into the touch—instinctively knowing that if she'd ever kissed another, it had been nothing like this. For, if there was anything in the world King enjoyed, it was kissing. He adored the privacy of it. The magnificent way it tested and teased and tempted and ultimately told, foreshadowing a greater, more intense act.

Her mouth was open, her full lips on his, and he took what she likely didn't even know she'd offered, worrying her beautiful bottom lip with his teeth before soothing it with his tongue and stroking deep, tasting her, the tang of bergamot from her tea and something sweeter, more delicious than he would have imagined.

She sighed again, and he pulled her closer, loving the way she gasped at the movement before giving in to it, wrapping her hands around his neck and threading her fingers in his hair. Christ. It felt good.

She felt good.

Even better when her tongue met his.

She was an excellent student.

And this kiss was getting out of control.

He broke it off, lifting his lips from hers, ready to stop the moment before it ran away with them both. But her eyes remained closed and her hands remained fisted in his hair, and he found that releasing her was not in the cards. Instead, he returned his lips to her skin, tracing her cheekbone, her jaw, running his teeth down the column of her neck to linger in the space where it met her shoulder. He kissed her there, licking delicately before he sucked just enough to elicit a lovely little cry.

A cry punctuated with his own growl.

Her grasp tightened, and she whispered his name. Not his title—the name she'd mocked again and again. "King."

The word gave him great pleasure, and he smiled against her skin. "What did you call me?"

She opened her eyes then—liquid blue and filled with desire. It took a moment for her to understand the question. The teasing in it. "Don't get ideas."

"Too late for that." His ideas were legion. And he liked every single one of them. He slid one hand down her back, over the swell of her behind, to grab her thigh and lift it, pulling her tighter to him.

She gasped at the movement, but did not pull away. Indeed, she arched into him with a low, humming moan. Sophie Talbot more than made up for her lack of experience with her glorious excitement. King could happily sequester them both in a room upstairs and spend a week exploring all the things that made her gasp and arch and sigh and moan.

But there was a man mere feet away who was searching for her. And this was neither the place nor the time for King to be intrigued by the lady. A point that was validated by the appearance of the man who'd questioned them, who stepped into the dimly lit space and did not hesitate in taking a long look at them.

King turned to keep her from view, suddenly caring very much that her current state be for his view alone. "You ask for trouble," he growled at the newcomer, who did not move for a long moment—too long for King's liking.

He turned around to face the man. "Did you misunderstand me?"

"Not at all," said the other man. "It's only that your wife has the look of Lady Sophie."

"My wife is Mrs. Louis Matthew. I made that clear. And your attention is irritating me more than I think you'd care for me to be irritated."

The man's gaze lingered on Sophie, who, for the first time in her life, stayed where she was put. Thankfully. He then tipped his hat. "Mrs. Matthew, I do apologize for the interruption."

"Thank you," Sophie said quietly.

The man looked at King. "You might choose a less public place. Newlywed or not."

King had never in his life wanted to hit a man more. He should receive a special prize for not doing so. "I appreciate your advice," King said, his tone indicating anything but appreciation.

Once the man returned to the pub, King grabbed Sophie by the hand and pulled her up the stairs and into her chamber, wanting her away from the scoundrel.

She pressed herself against the wall, her arms crossed tightly over her chest. "He knows."

King ran a hand over his face. "I imagine he does, yes."

She looked up at him. "Why didn't you tell him the truth?"

"That we are merely traveling companions who don't much care for one another?" She paused at that, and he felt like an ass for having said it with the taste of her on his lips. "Sophie—"

"No," she said, waving his words away. "It's true. And he wouldn't believe it."

It wasn't true, but he didn't push her. "No, he wouldn't."

She nodded. "Thank you. I shall only presume for another day. Until the mail coach arrives."

He looked to the ceiling. "You're not taking the mail coach, dammit. Especially not now."

"Why not? They shan't be looking for me there."

It was likely the truth, but he'd had enough of this woman and the carelessness with which she lived her life. "Because you have a habit of getting shot on mail coaches."

"It wasn't *on* the coach."

"Now who is arguing semantics?" She closed her mouth. "I shall see you to Mossband." He couldn't help the rest of the words now that he knew, almost certainly, that she'd been lying to him from the start. "Right into your baker's doughy arms."

"Aren't you clever."

"I am, rather."

He would wager his entire fortune that there was no baker. Which meant she was running, and he was the only person who could help her. Just as he'd been for another girl an eternity ago.

And he'd be damned if he was going to let this one down, too.

A short rap sounded on the door to the room and he opened it to find Mary, John, and Bess. They stepped inside without being invited. Mary spoke quickly. "There's a man downstairs asking questions about a missing girl."

"Yes, we met him," King said.

Mary looked to Sophie. "He says her name is Sophie. And she's a nob."

Sophie watched her carefully, but did not say anything.

Mary looked to King. "They say she's with another nob."

He did not reply.

John added, "We think it's you."

King spoke then. "Did you tell the man your suspicions?"

"No," John said. "We's loyal to our friends' secrets."

Sophie nodded. "Thank you."

"Wot'd you do to deserve a man hunting you?"

Sophie smiled, small and somewhat sad, and King resisted the urge to go to her and gather her in his arms. "I ran from a life I did not want."

"We cannot pretend we don't understand that," Mary said, putting her hand on Bess's shoulder and pulling the girl close.

Christ. He was going to have to take care of these three. He couldn't leave them here to their own devices. Mary was young and the other two were children.

Smart, savvy, thieving children, but children nonetheless.

"You must go," Mary said. "And quickly."

He reached into his pocket and extracted his purse, extending a handful of coins to Mary. "You'll follow. In my coach."

Her brows rose. "Why?"

He knew pride when he saw it in the young girl's eyes. Knew she would not accept charity in any sense. He'd had to badger her into accepting the room Sophie had insisted he pay for. "Because we're going to hire another carriage. And those men shall think that you three are us. In my coach. Hieing north to Scotland."

"To elope!" Bess spoke for the first time.

Sophie looked to the young girl. "What do you know of eloping?"

"I don't," Bess said, honestly. "But I know people do it in Scotland."

"As a matter of fact," King said to the little girl. "I think they just might believe we are eloping."

"Are you?" Mary asked.

"No!" Sophie said without hesitation.

He turned to her. "Another man would take offense at how quickly you discount my eligibility."

She raised her brows at him. "Another man might be less of a cad than you are, my lord."

He thought of the events in the public hallway downstairs and refrained from argument.

"Where will you go?" Mary asked.

"North. And quickly."

Mary worried her lip, considering them both. "I don't know that it's proper for you to leave without chaperone, my lady."

King was certain he hadn't heard the girl correctly.

Sophie shook her head. "I preferred Mrs. Matthew."

"But you're not Mrs. Matthew. You're an earl's daughter. You should have a companion."

"I have the marquess."

Mary cut him a look. "I'm no highborn lady, but even I know he's not an acceptable chaperone."

If the girl only knew half of it.

"He'll do fine," Sophie said. "The marquess doesn't even care for me."

Mary looked from Sophie to King, and he had the distinct impression that she did not believe the words. "My lord, you understand that we feel quite possessive of the lady. What with her saving our lives."

He nodded once. "I do."

"Then you understand, also, that if you hurt her, I shall have to gut you."

He blinked, grateful that the girl didn't know half of it. Because she clearly meant the threat, and King wasn't certain she did not have the guts and skill to do it. "I do."

Satisfied, Mary nodded. "What shall we do?"

"Stay here. Try to throw them off our scent for a few hours to let us get away. Stay a few days, if you like." He gave her a handful of coin from his purse. "That will keep you weeks if you need it. When you're ready, my coachman will bring you and my luggage to my country seat."

Mary was uncertain. "We were headed to Yorkshire. There's a place there. I hear we'll be safe."

King shook his head. "There's a place for you in Cumbria, as well. Or Wales. Or any number of other places. For John and Bess, as well. You shall all be under the protection of the Duke of Lyne."

"Cor!" John said.

"A duke!" Mary said.

Someday soon. And he'd try his damnedest to protect those who couldn't protect themselves. Perhaps, finally, he could do it.

Sophie looked to King. "Thank you."

"Thank me when we're off," he said, pushing her toward his nearby chest. "You must dress. You're leaving the pub the same way you came in."

"Shot and passed out?" John asked.

King lifted the stained-but-clean livery that sat atop the luggage and handed it to Sophie. "As a footman."

Chapter 10

~~~

QUININE: THE CURE
FOR CARRIAGE QUEASINESS

Sophie and King were on the road in less than an hour, Mary and John doing their best to distract the men who searched for them as Sophie clung to the back of the hired carriage, grateful for her prior experience.

Minutes up the road, the carriage stopped, and she scrambled inside, King rapping sharply on the roof to set them once more in motion. "We won't stop until we reach Cumbria," he said, "except to change horses. And you will stay hidden. At best, you have a few days before your father's men find you. If they think you're with me, they're already headed to Lyne Castle."

She shook her head. "My father will receive notice of my plans for Mossband tomorrow. He shan't bother you after that."

King raised his brows. "Your father will want my hide, I'm guessing. Doubly so when he discovers you've been shot on my watch."

"That's nonsense. You weren't there. You weren't watching."

"I should have been," he said, leaning back in the seat,

but before she could consider the words, he said, "Did you pack your tea?"

She nodded. "Yes."

"And the honey?"

"I did."

"And fresh bandages?"

"I am not a child, my lord. I understand the concept of leaving a place with important possessions."

He looked away, out the window, and she leaned back in the seat across from him, and attempted not to think of the day. Any of it.

But she couldn't help herself. "You rescued me again."

"It wasn't rescue."

"It was. You knew I did not wish to return to London."

He did not reply for long minutes. And then he said, "Someday, I'll learn to leave you to your own devices."

But not today.

Today, he'd saved her from being hauled back to her life in London. Today, he'd given her a chance at freedom.

Today, he'd kissed her. In the dark hallway behind a taproom, her father's bounty hunters on her heels. It wasn't precisely what she'd expected for her first kiss.

Despite being magnificent.

She ignored the thought.

He seemed utterly unmoved by the kiss, so shouldn't she be the same? He'd clearly only allowed it because they were being followed. Suspected. Nearly found out. He'd kissed her to ensure the charade appeared legitimate.

It certainly *felt* legitimate.

Not that it mattered.

It was best she never think of it again.

She sneaked a look at him, eyes closed, arms crossed, long legs stretched across the carriage in an arrogant sprawl, crowding her into the corner of her seat. As though the limits of space should defer to him.

She rearranged herself, pressing into the small space he'd left for her.

It would be easy to forget the kiss if he carried on this way.

He opened one eye. "Are you uncomfortable?"

"No," she said, making a show of folding her legs tightly against the box of the seat.

He watched her for a moment, then said, "All right," and closed his eyes once more.

She coughed.

He opened his eyes again, and she noticed the irritation in them. "I am sorry, my lord," she said, all sweetness. "Am I bothering you?"

"No," he said, the word clipped, and closed his eyes once more. She heard the lie. What was she to do? Disappear? She'd offered to travel by mail. He'd been the one who had insisted on this wild plan.

Instead, she lifted her legs and pulled them up, stretching out along the slippery wooden seat. The carriage chose that exact moment to hit a tremendous rut, and she had to grab the edges of the conveyance in order to hold her position.

"For God's sake, Sophie. Find a spot and stay in it." He did not open his eyes this time.

Her incredulous gaze met his. "You do realize that this carriage is not the behemoth in which you traditionally travel? As you have taken the low ground, my lord, I have no choice but to claim the high. And, as you may recall, I have an unhealed bullet wound in my shoulder, so the threat of the drop from seat to floor of the carriage is . . . unsettling to say the least."

He cut her a look. "I asked if you were uncomfortable. You said no."

She scowled at him. "I lied."

He sat up, just as the vehicle went round a corner. "Christ," he muttered, putting his hand to his head.

He was turning green.

She let her feet drop to the floor. "Are you ill?"

He shook his head, but put one hand on the side of the rocking carriage.

"Do carriages make you ill?" she asked. When he did not reply, she added, "My sister Sesily is ill in carriages."

"Which one is that?" If he hadn't looked so unsettled, she would have argued that her sisters were not all the same and it should not be too much trouble to tell them apart.

Instead, she clarified, "She is second eldest." She paused, then added, "As the rake you are, I'm sure you've heard what they call her when she is not in the room."

"What's that?"

"You needn't pretend you haven't. I've heard it, so I know you must have."

He cut her a look. "Have I made a practice of lying to you?"

Well. She certainly wasn't going to tell him. She blushed. "Never mind."

"You must tell me, now."

She shook her head. "It's unkind."

"I've no doubt it is, if they don't use it to her face."

She looked out the window. "Her name is Sesily."

"Yes. You said that."

She watched him pointedly. "*Ses*-ily."

He raised a brow, but did not speak.

"You wish me to say it aloud."

He closed his eyes. "I'm beginning to care less and less about it, frankly."

"Sexily," she said flatly. "They call her Lady Sexily. Behind her back."

For a moment, he did not reply. Did not move. And then he opened his eyes, skewering her with a furious look. "Anyone who calls her that is an epic ass. And anyone who calls her that in front of you deserves a fist to the face." He leaned forward. "Who said that in front of you?"

Surprised, she replied, "It's not important."

"I assure you it is," he said. "You should be treated with more respect."

Respect. What a foreign concept. She looked away. "The Dangerous Daughters do not garner respect, my lord. You know that better than anyone."

He cursed in the silence. "I am sorry for the things I said."

"You are?"

"You needn't sound so shocked."

"It's just that—my sisters don't mind the treatment, so the *ton* never seems to stop saying such things."

"But you do mind it."

She lifted one shoulder. "As we've established, I don't value the gossip pages."

He watched her for a long moment before he said, "That's not why you mind it."

"No," she said, "I mind it because it devalues us. They're my sisters. We are people. With feelings. We exist. And it seems that the world fails to see that. Fails to see them."

"Fails to see you," he said.

Yes.

"I don't wish to be seen," she lied. "I just wish to be free of it."

His green gaze consumed her. "I see you, Sophie."

She caught her breath at the words. They weren't true, of course. But how she wished they were.

She shook her head, returning to safer, less discomfiting ground. "It was a group of men talking about her. I stumbled upon them at a ball. They didn't see me. They were too busy seeing her." She lifted her good shoulder. Let it drop. "Sesily's shape is . . . Well, men notice it. And because our blood does not run blue, men like you—" She stopped. Reconsidered. "Men who think themselves above us . . . they do not hesitate to comment on it. I suppose they think they are clever. And perhaps they are. But it doesn't feel clever." She looked up at him. "It feels horrid."

"I'd like to make each one of them feel horrid." For a moment, she thought he was telling the truth. Of course, that couldn't be the case. He wanted nothing to do with her. He paused. "Who's her scandal?"

Her brow furrowed. "I don't understand."

"You each have an inappropriate man attached to you. Who is hers?"

Of course, it was the suitor who defined the Soiled S. "Derek Hawkins."

"He's a proper ass," he said, before closing his eyes and leaning back against the seat. "And the fact that he hasn't married your sister and murdered anyone who notices her shape proves it."

Though she agreed, she ignored the words. "I don't have an inappropriate man attached to me."

He met her gaze pointedly. "You do now."

Her cheeks warmed, the words summoning the memory of his kiss. She did not know what to say, so she returned to the original subject. "At any rate, Sesily's predicament makes long drives quite difficult." She looked about for somewhere to catch his sick, should there be any. Collecting his hat from the seat next to him, she turned it over and held it beneath his chin. "If you're going to be ill, use this."

He opened one eye. "You want me to vomit in my hat."

"I realize that it's not the best option," she said, "but desperate times and all that?"

He shook his head and put the hat back on the seat next to him. "I'm not going to be sick. Carriages don't make me ill. They make me wish I was not inside carriages."

She shook her head. "I don't understand."

"I am . . . uncomfortable . . . in them."

"So you don't travel?"

He raised a brow. "Of course I travel, as you can see."

"Yes. But long journeys must be difficult."

There was a pause. "I don't wish to be difficult."

She chuckled at that. "You think your aversion to carriages is what makes you difficult?"

He smiled at her jest, a tiny quirk in his otherwise flat mouth. "I think you are what makes me difficult, these days."

"Surely not," she teased. "I am easy as church on Sunday."

He grunted and closed his eyes. "I do not attend church."

"Shall I pray for your eternal soul, then?"

"Not if you're looking for someone to listen to you. I'm a lost cause, scoundrel that I am."

They rode in silence for a long while, King growing progressively more fidgety and unhappy. Finally, Sophie said, "Would you like to ride on the block with the coachman?"

King shook his head. "I'm fine here."

"Except you made it clear that you dislike traveling companions. You said as much when we were on the road to Sprotbrough."

"Perhaps I've changed my mind." The carriage bounced and she slid across the seat, knocking her shoulder against the wall of the coach and gasping in pain.

He swore harshly; he reached for her, lifting and turning her as though she weighed nothing, and settled her on the seat next to him. She was caged by his body and his legs before she could even consider what had happened.

She snapped her head around to his, where his eyes remained closed. "Let me go."

He kept his eyes closed and ignored her, resuming his relaxed position. "Stop moving. It's bad for your shoulder and for my sanity."

Well, being so close to him was not good for *her* sanity.

Not that he seemed to mind.

She closed her own eyes and put him out of her thoughts. It worked for several seconds, until his warmth enveloped her, beginning where their thighs touched and spreading through her until she wanted nothing but to lean into him. Instead, she kept as much distance as she could, and cast about for something to say that was not *Kiss me again, please, if you don't mind so very much.*

Although she wondered if he would do just that if she asked very nicely.

She stiffened, as though posture could dispel errant thoughts. "What about your curricle?"

"What about it?" he replied, not looking at her.

"Why not drive that instead of sitting inside this coach?"

"My curricle is dismantled and headed to Lyne Castle."

Her eyes went wide. "Why?" Surely it was not for her benefit. She enjoyed the company, but he should be enjoying his life.

"It lacks proper wheels," he said, dryly.

Of course it did. "I am sorry."

His eyes opened again, surprise in the green depths. "I think you might be."

She nodded. "Is that surprising?"

"People rarely apologize to me," he said, simply. "Even fewer do so without artifice."

She did not know how to reply to that, so she changed the subject, returning to something safer. "I've never seen anyone drive a curricle with such recklessness."

"Did it seem reckless?"

"You tipped onto one wheel. The whole thing could have toppled over."

He looked away. "It's happened before. I survived."

She imagined him tossed on the side of the road, broken and bleeding. She did not like it. Her brow furrowed. "You could have died."

"I didn't." There was something in the words, something darker than she would like. She wished his eyes were open, so she could make more sense of him.

"But you could have."

"That's part of the fun."

"The threat of death is fun?"

"You can't imagine that?"

"Considering I nearly died of a gunshot wound several days ago, I do not."

He did look at her then, and there was no humor in his gaze. "That's not the same."

"Because it was not at my own hand?"

"There are many who would say that, yes." The carriage bounced over a rough patch of road and he gritted his teeth.

"Are you afraid you might die? Now? Is that why you dislike carriages?"

He paused. "This is a very small carriage."

It was a perfectly ordinary-sized carriage. "Why?"

For a moment, his gaze darkened, and she lost him to thought—something that seemed unpleasant. Haunting. She resisted the urge to put her hand on him. To soothe whatever that memory was. She didn't expect him to answer. And he didn't, despite shaking his head and saying, "I don't care for them." He paused. "And I do not wish to discuss it further."

She nodded. "All right, what do you wish to discuss instead?"

"I suppose that I cannot say that I wish to sleep instead?"

"You look as though you might leap from this carriage at any moment," she said. "You are no more going to sleep than I am going to fly."

He narrowed his gaze on her. "If you were a man, I would not care much for you."

Her brows rose. "You do not care much for me, anyway."

He watched her for a long moment. "I was warming to you."

The words sent a thread of excitement through her that came on a wave of memory, the dark hallway behind the Warbling Wren pub, his hands and mouth upon her. The feel of his hair in her fingers.

She had been warming to him, as well.

She cleared her throat. "We can discuss anything you like." He did not reply, and the minutes ticked by in silence, until, finally, she gave up. "You are tremendously antisocial, my lord. Has anyone ever told you that?"

"No," he said.

Obstinate man. Sophie reached into the satchel on the floor of the coach and extracted a book. She opened it, pretending that he was not there, hoping that it was something diverting.

He leaned forward, and she could smell him, clean and with a spice she could not identify. It was lovely.

She cleared her throat and looked down at the book. *A Popular and Practical Treatise on Masonry and Stone-cutting.* Oh, dear. It was not diverting.

Could nothing in the world go her way?

She began to read. Vaguely. She was distracted by the stretch of his trousers over his thighs, which were larger than she could have imagined. Of course, she should have guessed they would be, what with all the curricle racing he did.

Her fingers itched to touch the thigh closest to her. The one touching her. The one that she'd had a leg wrapped around earlier in the day.

It was very warm in the carriage.

"Where did you get a book?"

She started at the words, cheeks flaming. She did not look up. "I thought you did not wish to talk."

"I don't. But that does not mean I do not wish an answer."

"It was at the back of the drawer in the table in my bedchamber." She turned a page with force, as though doing so would make him smaller. Less formidable.

Less intriguing.

It did not.

Of course, anything would be more intriguing than a treatise on masonry and stone-cutting. But one made do. She soldiered on.

The silence stretched between them as the carriage careened up the Great North Road, away from Sprotbrough and toward their futures, and Sophie read, slowly, distracted by every sway of the conveyance and the way it pressed her to him.

King, however, remained unmoved.

On several occasions, she nearly spoke, desperate for conversation, but she refused to break first and, after an age, she was rewarded.

"Is it any good?" he asked.

"Quite," she lied. "I had no idea that masonry was so fascinating."

"Really," he said, voice dry as sand. "Well, I suppose I should not be so surprised that you find it so. What with you being the unfun sister."

She cut him a look, took in the small smirk on his lips, and decided that if he wasn't going to be a decent companion, neither was she. "There's nothing unfun about it, my lord." She took a deep breath and waged her war.

"This book has a comprehensive explanation of hemispheric niches, hemispheric domes, and cylindric groins. There is a great deal to learn."

The smirk grew. "About groins particularly I would imagine."

She ignored the words, punishing him far better than she could ever imagine by reading aloud. "*This is the first and only work in English on the art of stone-cutting, and such a publication has been long and eagerly sought after.*"

"No doubt"—he reached across her to close the book and consider its cover—"Peter Nicholson, Esquire, has convinced himself of such a thing."

She ignored the sliver of pleasure that coursed through her as his hand brushed hers, instead reopening the book. "I think he might be right. There are several full chapters explaining the basic and complex geometry necessary to properly stonework. Isn't that fascinating? Did you know that," she read, "*In preparing stones for walls, nothing more is necessary than to reduce the stone to its dimensions so that each of its eight solid angles may be contained by three right angles?*"

His smirk became a grimace, and Sophie was now quite happy that this was the only book to be found at the

Warbling Wren. She gave herself over to the moment, enjoying how much he hated it. "And listen to this next bit, about Druids and standing stone structures."

"I don't think I will."

"Everyone thinks Druids are interesting."

"Not everyone, I assure you."

"Everyone with taste, of course. This structure is called Tinkinswood."

"It sounds lovely."

The words indicated that the Marquess of Eversley thought Tinkinswood might be nothing short of Hades. Sophie was beginning to enjoy herself. "Doesn't it? Quite quaint. Listen to this fascinating description. *This Welsh dry stone masonry boasts a horned forecourt weighing more than thirty tonnes, and the structure would have required some ten score Druids to lift it into position.* Imagine that!"

"All those white robes in one place," he replied, sounding as though he might perish from boredom.

She turned the page. "Ooh! Henges! Shall we learn about those?"

The henges broke him. "Stop. For God's sake. Stop before I leap from this conveyance not from my own demons but from your eagerness over horned groins."

"Horned forecourts."

"I honestly don't care. Anything but more of the damn masonry."

She closed the book and looked at him, willing herself to seem displeased with his insistence. "Is there something else you'd prefer to discuss?"

Understanding dawned in his green eyes, followed by irritation, and then what Sophie could only define as respect. "You sneaking minx."

She blinked. "I beg your pardon?"

"You did it on purpose."

"I don't know what you mean."

"To get me to choose a topic of discussion."

She widened her eyes until they felt as though they might pop out. "Certainly, if you'd like to choose a topic, my lord . . . I wouldn't deign to eschew conversation."

He gave a little laugh and stretched his legs, propping his feet up on the bench across from them. "I shall choose a topic, then."

She did the same, placing her feet on the bench next to his. She clutched the closed book on her lap. "I imagine it won't be stonework."

"It will not be." His attention moved to their feet. "Are the boots comfortable?"

She followed his gaze, considering his great black Hessians next to her smaller grey shoes, ankle height and designed for function rather than fashion. She should dislike the previously owned footwear, but he'd procured it, and somehow that made the boots rather perfect. "Quite," she replied.

He nodded. "I should have had the doctor look at your feet."

"They're perfectly fine."

"You should have been wearing better shoes."

"I was not planning for an adventure."

He looked down at her then. "So you decided to head for your future husband on a whim?"

Oh, dear.

She did not wish to speak of that. She'd never really meant to lie to him. But now, she would seem ridiculous if she confessed the truth—that Robbie wasn't the purpose of this journey. That the journey had been without purpose until it had begun to seem as though it might be for freedom.

But the Marquess of Eversley would not take well to knowing that he'd rescued her from highwaymen and bounty hunters for the whisper of freedom. So she nodded and lied. "Yes. Sometimes when an idea strikes, you must follow it."

He raised a brow. "You are headed to, what, propose? Woo him?"

She looked down at her lap, toying at the edges of the pages. "What makes you think he has not already been wooed?"

He crossed one black boot over the other, brushing his foot against hers. "Because you aren't headed to Mossband in a beautifully appointed carriage, your mother and sisters in tow."

She couldn't help but chuckle at that image.

"That is amusing?"

"The idea of my mother and sisters choosing to leave London for little Mossband, even if it were for my wedding." She shook her head. "We haven't been back since we left a decade ago."

He watched her for a long while. "You haven't seen Robbie in ten years?"

"No," she said, feeling quite trapped.

"Have you exchanged a lifetime of letters?"

She ignored the question, rather than lie.

He pressed on, his tone softer, knowing. "Why don't you go home?"

And still, she could not bring herself to tell him the truth. "I am going home."

"I mean your London home. The massive town house in Mayfair."

She shook her head. "That's not home."

"But a dusty town filled with farmers is?"

She thought for a long minute about that, about the

quaint honesty of Mossband. About the people who lived and worked there. About the life she had before Father had become an earl. The life she could have again.

Maybe it was the rocking of the carriage, or the way King waited, with the patience of Job, or the close quarters. Whatever it was, she told the truth. "It is the only place I have ever felt free."

Until now.

"What does that mean?"

She did not reply.

He lifted his boots off the bench and let them fall to the floor before moving to sit across from her, to get a better look, knees spread wide, fingers laced between them. "Look at me, Sophie." She looked up to find his gaze on her, glittering in the carriage's fading light. "What does that mean?"

She dropped her own feet to the floor and fiddled with the deckled edge of the book, uncertain of where to begin. "I was ten when my father earned his earldom. He burst through the door of our house, where I had never dreamed of more than I had, and announced, 'My ladies!' with a great, booming laugh. It was such a lark! My mother cried and my sisters screamed and I . . ." She paused. Thought. "They were infectious. Their happiness was infectious. So we packed our things and moved to London. I said good-bye to my life. To my home. To my friends. To my cat."

His brow furrowed. "You couldn't take your cat?"

She shook her head. "She did not travel well."

"Like your sister?"

"She howled."

"Sesily?"

Sophie smiled at the teasing. "Asparagus. Would cling to the back of the seat in the coach and howl. My mother's nerves could not bear it." She grew serious. "I had to leave her."

"You had a cat named Asparagus."

"I know. It's silly. What's asparagus to do with the price of wheat?"

He smiled at that. "That's the second time you've used that phrase."

She smiled, too. "My father," she said simply.

"I've always liked him, you know."

Her brows rose. "Really?"

"You're surprised?"

"He's crass compared to the rest of London."

"He's *honest* compared to the rest of London. The first time we ever met, he told me that he didn't like my father."

She nodded. "That sounds like Papa."

"Go on. You left Asparagus."

She looked out the window again. "I haven't thought about that cat in years. She was black. With little white paws. And a white nose." She shook her head to clear it of the memory. "Anyway, we left and we never came back. There is a country seat in Wales somewhere, but we never go there. My mother was too focused on our making a new, aristocratic life. That meant visiting other, more established country seats filled with aristocratic young women who were supposed to become our friends. Who were to help us find a place for ourselves. To *climb*.

"She swore that in a few years, we'd fit in perfectly. And my sisters do. They somehow realized that their perfect beauty would lead to the gossip pages adoring them, which would lead to the *ton* adoring them. Against its better judgment. They are expert climbers. Except . . ."

She trailed off, and he had to prompt her to finish. "Except?"

"Except I am not. I do not fit in. I am not perfectly

beautiful." She gave him a half smile. "I am not even beautifully perfect. You've said it yourself."

"When did I say it?" he asked, affronted.

"I'm the plain one. The boring one. The unfun one." She waved a hand down at her livery, the clothing that had driven him to call her plump. "Certainly not the beautiful one." He cursed softly, but she raised a hand before he could speak. "Don't apologize. It's true. I've never felt like I belonged there. I've never felt worth the effort. But in Mossband—I felt valued.

"In escaping London, I have become more than I ever was there." She smiled. "And when those men came looking, when you ferreted me out, I've never felt more free." She paused, then added, softly, "Or more valued. You never would have helped me escape before."

"That's nonsense," he said, and the tone brooked no refusal.

"Is it? You left me standing in a hedge with your boot," she pointed out.

"That's not the same. I left you there *because* you had value."

"No, I had a title. Those aren't the same thing."

He opened his mouth to argue, but she stopped him, unable to keep her frustration at bay. "I would not expect you to understand, my lord. You, who have such value to spare. Your name is *King*, for heaven's sake."

Her words circled the carriage, fading into heavy silence. And then he said, "Aloysius."

She blinked. "I beg your pardon?"

"Aloysius Archibald Barnaby Kingscote. Marquess of Eversley. Future Duke of Lyne." He waved his hand in a flourish. "At your service."

He was joking.

But he did not *appear* to be joking.

"No," she whispered, playing the name over in her head, and her hand flew to her mouth, desperate to hold in her response. But it was too much. She couldn't stop herself. She began to laugh.

He raised a brow and leaned back in his seat. "And you are the only person to whom I have ever offered it. This is why, in case you were wondering. Because even I have my limits of supercilious pomposity."

She caught her breath, unable to stop herself from laughing again before she said, "It's so—"

"Horrible? Ridiculous? Inane?"

She removed her hand. "Unnecessary."

He tilted his head in acknowledgment. "That, as well."

She giggled. "Aloysius."

"Be careful, my lady."

"Others don't know?"

"I imagine they do. It's there in black and white, in *Burke's Peerage*, but no one ever brings it up in my company. At least, they haven't since I was in school and made it clear I did not wish to be called such."

"The boys at school simply acceded to your request?"

"They acceded to my boxing training."

She nodded. "I suppose they weren't expecting you to be very good at that, what with being named Aloysius."

He put on his best aristocratic tone. "In some circles, it's very royal."

"Oh? Which circles are those?"

He grinned. "I'm not certain."

She matched his grin. "I confess, I would call myself King, as well."

"You see? Now you should feel sorry for me."

"Oh, I do!" she said so quickly that they both laughed, and Sophie was suddenly, keenly aware that she liked the sound of his laughter. She liked the look of it, as well.

And then they were not laughing anymore. "You are not uncomfortable," she said quietly, leaning forward. The motion of the carriage no longer unsettled him.

He seemed startled by the reminder. "I am not. You are a welcome distraction."

Her cheeks warmed as he, too, leaned forward. She considered retreating, but found she did not wish to. When he lifted his hand to her cheek, she was very grateful for her bravery, his warm hand a welcome temptation. They were so close, his eyes a beautiful green, his lips soft and welcome and just out of reach. She wondered what might happen if she leaned forward. Closed the distance between them. And then he spoke, the words on a whisper. "He doesn't even know you're coming, does he?"

She retreated at that, not pretending to misunderstand. "Why do you ask all the questions?"

"Because you answer them," he replied.

"I should like to ask some."

He nodded. "I'll answer yours if you answer this one. Why the baker? I understand the bookshop and the freedom, but the baker—it's been a decade. Why him, as well?"

She looked away, watching farmland beyond the window, the countryside dotted with sheep and bales of hay. So much simpler than London. So much more free. She opened the book on her lap and closed it. Again and again. And finally, she said, "He was my friend. We made a promise."

"What kind of promise?"

"That we'd marry."

"A decade ago."

What had she done? Where was she going? What would come from this mad adventure? She couldn't ask him any of that. Didn't want him to hear it. And so she lifted her gaze to his and said, "A promise is a promise."

He watched her for a long time, and then said, "You realize that this ends poorly."

"Not necessarily."

He stretched his arm across the back of the seat. "How does it end, then?"

She paused, thinking for a long moment about Mossband. About her childhood. About the world into which she'd been born and the world into which she'd been thrust. And then she answered him. "I hope it ends happily."

He went utterly still, and she had the sudden sense that he was angry with her. When he spoke, there was no mistaking the disdain in his tone. "You think he's been pining away for the earl's daughter who left a decade ago?"

"It's not impossible, you know," she snapped. Must he always make her feel as though she was less than? "And I wasn't an earl's daughter. Well, I was, but not really. I've never really been an earl's daughter. That's the point. We were friends. We made each other happy."

"Happiness," he scoffed. "You haven't any idea what to do with yourself now that you're free, do you?"

She scowled. "I don't care for you."

"Shall we wager on it?"

"On my not caring for you? Oh, let's. Please."

He smirked. "On Robbie's caring for you."

She narrowed her gaze on his smug face, ignoring the sting of his words. "What's the wager?"

"If we get there, and he wants you, you win. I'll buy you your bookshop. As a wedding present."

"What an extravagant gift," she said smartly. "I accept. Though I have a second demand now."

His brows rose. "More than a bookshop?"

She tilted her head. "Be careful, my lord, I might find reason to believe you are not so certain that you will win."

"I never lose."

"Then why not allow a second demand?"

He leaned back, "Go ahead."

"If I win, you must say something nice about me."

His brows snapped together. "What does that mean?"

"Only that you have spent the last week telling me all the ways that I fail. My lack of intelligence, my lack of excitement, my lack of proper figure, my lack of beauty, and now, my inability to land a husband."

"I didn't say—"

She raised her hand. "And you had better make it exceedingly complimentary."

There was a long silence, after which he said, in a tone that could only be described as grumbling, "Fine."

"Excellent. I think I might look forward to that more than to Robbie's proposal."

One black brow rose. "A clear indication that marrying the baker is an excellent idea." He leaned forward, his voice lowering. "But don't forget, Sophie. If we get there, and it's a disaster . . ."

Her heart began to pound. "What then?"

"Then *I* win. And you must say something nice about me."

Before she could retort, the carriage began to slow, and a wild cry came from the coachman. She stiffened, nerves chasing her triumph away. She snapped her gaze to him. "Is it highwaymen?"

"No." King touched her ankle, the warm skin of his hand against that place that had never been touched by another person making her breath catch. "We are at the next posting inn."

Her shoulder ached, and she was happy for the stop. "Will we spend the night?"

He shook his head. "We only change horses, and then

press on. We have to put some distance between you and your pursuers."

And then the door was open and he disappeared into the afternoon's golden sunlight.

Chapter 11

SOPHIE AND EVERSLEY: SEDUCTION OR ABDUCTION?

*T*hank God they'd arrived when they did.

A quarter of an hour longer, and King would not have been held responsible for what happened between them. Lord deliver him from long carriage rides with impossible, infuriating, remarkable women. How was he supposed to keep from kissing her? From touching her?

Every time the woman opened her mouth, he wanted her more.

And then she'd declared herself less than valued. Told him that only now, as she ran, London and her past at her heels, did she feel free. Proclaimed herself existent.

As though he'd needed a proclamation to notice her.

As though he wasn't keenly aware of her every movement. Her every word.

Despite knowing that he shouldn't see her at all.

She had been trouble since the moment he'd met her, at the bottom of the damn trellis at Liverpool House. And still, he seemed to never quite be able to escape her. He was the Minotaur, trapped by her labyrinth.

It was useful to have the break to remind himself of all

the reasons why he didn't want her. Why he didn't even enjoy her.

She was the very opposite of women he enjoyed.

Except she wasn't.

Indeed, he would have no trouble saying something nice about her. When she'd enumerated all the terrible things he'd said until now, he'd felt like a proper ass. He didn't believe any of those things. Not anymore.

Not ever.

He began to unhitch the tired horses, quickly and efficiently, as he remained keenly aware of the fact that the men they'd encountered in Sprotbrough might be stupid enough to believe Sophie had been an ordinary footman on an ordinary carriage, but were also smart enough to realize she'd left the inn—and sooner rather than later. There would be no lingering. Which was for the best, because when she'd asked if they would be sleeping here tonight, his entire body had leapt to answer in the affirmative.

In the same room.

In the same bed.

With as little sleeping as possible.

She wanted to be free—he could show her freedom.

He could show her happiness.

<u>Except he couldn't.</u>

Cursing under his breath, he handed the first of the four horses off to the coachman and made quick work of unhitching the second when she poked her head out of the door. "My lord?" she called, before returning to the shadows of the carriage.

He didn't wish to think of her. He was too busy thinking of her.

"Bollocks," he muttered.

Christ. Now he was swearing like her.

"My lord!" She was sounding more panicked.

He passed the second horse to the coachman and returned to her. "What is it?"

"I must go inside."

"You shouldn't be seen. You stay here."

She pressed her lips into a thin line. "I have *necessary requirements.*"

He sighed. Of course she did.

"And I think perhaps I ought to find other clothes. The livery has become somewhat . . . obvious."

She was right, of course. She looked like a footman who'd been dragged through the muck, shot, and left for dead. Which wasn't an entirely incorrect assessment of her situation. And with her long brown hair coming out of her cap, she would be discovered in a heartbeat. And when her hunters arrived, a girl dressed as a bedraggled footman would certainly count as something unique enough to mention. He hadn't a choice.

"You handle your needs. I shall get you a dress."

He charmed the pub owner with a long-suffering sigh and a handful of coin, and returned to the carriage with a frock and food and a skin of hot water. Opening the door, he found her already returned, and tossed the first two items into the carriage before handing her the water. "For your tea."

He did not give her a chance to thank him, instead closing the door before returning to help the coachman hitch new horses.

"We've two good stretches before we get to Longwood, sir," said the coachman. "We'll need another change of horses in the night."

"And a new coachman. You'll need to sleep," King said, triple checking the leather harnesses.

"I can see you through until then."

King nodded. "Good man, John."

John smiled. "The night is the best time to ride the roads."

King knew it keenly. He also knew it was the worst time to ride inside a carriage—the darkness closing in around him, reminding him of the past, which became more and more difficult to ignore as they drew closer to Cumbria.

He opened the door to the carriage with more force than he'd planned, and she squeaked from her seat, hands clutched to her chest. She was wearing the green dress, festooned in little frills of lace and ribbon. "I'm not ready for you, yet," she said, the words nearly strangling her.

"Why not?"

"Because I am not," she replied, as though it were a legitimate answer to his question.

He raised a brow and did not move.

"I require another five minutes," she said, shooing him out of the carriage. With her foot.

It was the foot that tipped him to her concern. His gaze fell, lingering on the hands at her breast, white laces crisscrossing up the bodice of the dress. "Are you having trouble lacing yourself into it?" he asked.

She went crimson, and he had his answer. "Not at all!" she squeaked.

"You're a terrible liar."

She scowled at him. "I don't typically have cause to lie, sir. It is rare that men ask me such . . . ungentlemanly questions."

"Don't you mean rapscallionesque?"

"That, as well. Yes."

He smiled. "Do you require my assistance, my lady?"

"I most certainly do not," she replied. "It's simply that the previous owner of this particular garment was somewhat less . . ."

Close the door, he willed himself. *Don't let her finish that thought.*

Sadly, his arms forgot how to work.

And then she finished the sentence and his brain did the same.

". . . ample."

Christ.

"You have five minutes," he said, "and then we leave, laced or no."

He closed the door and returned to the horses, checking the cinches again as he counted to three hundred. By thirty-six, he was imagining her ample breasts. At ninety-four, he was cursing himself for not having a good look at the breasts in question when he had Sophie in hand earlier in the day. By one hundred and seventy, he'd relived the events of earlier in the day, much to the twin emotions of pleasure and guilt. By two hundred twenty-five, he was cursing himself the worst kind of scoundrel, but, truthfully, she was the one who had brought up breasts.

You are the one who is acting like a boy in short pants.

No. Boys in short pants were much more appropriately behaved.

Two hundred ninety-nine.

Three hundred.

He opened the door and climbed in, working very hard not to look at her. She did not squeak, so he supposed that meant she'd finished the task at hand. He rapped on the roof, and the carriage took off.

They traveled in silence for long minutes—twenty or so—before she broke the silence. "Do you remember me?"

He looked at her then.

Mistake.

She was beautiful. The dress was shabby and too small for her, and he could see why she'd had trouble. It had to be laced as tightly as possible up her midline to cage her breasts, which spilled out of the top, as though they were desperate to be free.

Just as he was quite desperate to free them.

He dragged his gaze to meet her eyes. "I was not gone very long."

She smiled at that, and he warmed at the sign of her entertainment. Good God. It felt like he *was* a boy in short pants, eager for her approval. "I did not mean from earlier today. I meant from earlier in our life."

"Remember you from where?"

The smile faltered a touch. "We danced once. At a ball."

His brows rose. "I would remember that."

"It was a quadrille. At the Beaufetheringstone Ball."

He shook his head. "You're mistaken."

She gave a little huff of laughter. "My lord, I believe that I would remember you more than you would remember me."

She was doing it again. "Stop it."

"Stop what?"

"Stop believing whatever everyone has said about you for all these years. There's nothing about you that is unmemorable. The last week has been the most memorable of my life, for Chrissakes. Because of you. Stop imagining that you're something you're not."

Her eyes went wide, and King immediately felt like an idiot.

"What does that mean?" she asked quietly.

He didn't want to answer. He'd made enough of a fool of himself. So instead he said, "I'm simply saying that I should remember that we danced." She went silent, and for a long moment, he thought she might be hurt that he didn't remember. "I will remember you now."

It was an understatement in the extreme.

And then she said, "May I still have my question?"

The question he'd promised her before they stopped. Before he'd almost kissed her. Before he'd noticed her breasts. Well. Before he'd noticed her breasts, today.

This evening.

"Yes."

"You said you were going to your father to tell him something before he died."

"I did."

"When was the last time you saw him?"

The feel of the carriage returned, as did his awareness of the waning light. Darkness was coming, and with it, memory. And demons. And this woman was not going to let him ignore them. "Fifteen years ago."

"How old were you?"

"Eighteen."

"And why haven't you ever come back?"

He exhaled on a long breath and leaned back against the seat, wishing she were next to him again. He'd liked that, the time when she'd been next to him, her thigh against his, as she'd read her excruciating book on stones. "I don't wish to see him."

"Was he very cruel?"

He did not answer, and she eventually added, "I apologize. I should not have asked such a thing."

Silence fell once more, and he reached down to the basket he'd placed on the floor of the carriage when they'd stopped to change the horses. Opening it, he extracted a bottle of wine, bread, and cheese. He tore her a piece of bread and offered it with some of the cheese. She took it with a quiet "Thank you."

The Duke of Lyne had been as good a father as an aristocrat could be. Where other fathers had spent their time in London, machinating at their clubs and pretending their families did not exist, King's had prioritized the country estate and his time with King.

"He was not cruel. Not with me."

"Then why—?" She stopped, clearly aware that she trod a strange, fine line.

King drank deep of the wine, willing it to stay the memories she awakened. "How is your shoulder?"

"Tolerably sore," she said before taking a deep breath and diving in. "Why don't you wish to see him?"

He should have known she wouldn't be able to stop herself. "You're like a dog with a bone."

"You're calling me a dog again?"

He smiled, but with little humor. "Cruelty is not the only way fathers ruin their sons. Expectations can do the same damage."

"What did yours expect?"

"For me to marry well."

She cut him a look and spoke dryly. "What a horrible thing for a father to desire." When he did not reply, she continued, "Why not marry one of the women you've ruined?"

None of them had wanted to marry him, but he didn't tell her that. Instead, he told her the truth. "I'll never marry."

"You're a man with a title. Isn't that your only purpose?"

He cut her a look. "Is that what women think?"

She smiled, small and clever. "Isn't that what men think of women?"

"It's not my purpose. Despite my father's keen desire. The Dukedom of Lyne has passed from generation to generation of pure, unadulterated aristocracy. Every Duchess of Lyne has been perfectly bred to be just that, a duchess. Blue blood, pristine manners, and beauty beyond the pale."

"I've never heard anything about your mother," she said. "Not even when we lived in Mossband."

He looked out the window at that, taking in the sky, streaking pink and red in the west, heralding the night. "That's because she died in childbirth. It killed my father."

"Did he love her very much?"

It was so preposterous that King laughed. "No. He was upset because it meant he wouldn't get his spare."

"He could have married again," she said.

"I suppose he could have."

"But he didn't. Perhaps he did love her."

Memories overtook him. "No Duke of Lyne has ever married for love. They've married for duty and for offspring. It's what we're bred to want."

"And you? What do you want?"

No one had ever asked him the question. It had been a long time since he'd thought on it. Since it had been possible. And then it hadn't been possible any longer, because of his father's arrogance and his own recklessness.

Because of the vow he'd made in the dead of night on a road much like this one.

Later, he would blame it on the darkness when he told her the truth. "I want to look my father in the eye and take away everything he ever wanted."

The line ends with me.

How many times had he written the words to his father? How many times had he said them to himself? And somehow, now, they ached in a way they hadn't for years.

"I'm sorry," she said, softly.

He didn't want her pity. He drank again. Offering her the bottle, he asked, "Do your parents love each other?"

"Oh, quite desperately," she said, taking the wine. She looked to the basket on the floor. "Is there a glass?"

He shook his head and she wiped the top of the bottle with her skirts. For a moment, King considered reminding her that they'd done a great deal more than share a wine bottle, but he refrained when she resumed speaking. "My father is crass and disinterested in anything but coal, and my mother is—crass in her own way, I suppose—but very eager to be accepted by Society. One without the other, however—it would not be possible. That is why my sisters and I are unmarried. Because we know what we might have."

Happiness.

He heard the word without her speaking it.

"Except Seraphina . . . she's different."

"She caught a duke," he reminded her as she drank. "Love didn't seem to be her goal."

Sophie shook her head and passed the wine back. "I will never understand what happened. Sera, more than any of us . . . she was waiting for love."

"And you?" He didn't know why he asked. It didn't matter.

She opened the book, then closed it. Again and again. "That's part of the freedom, isn't it?" He didn't reply, so she added, "I've never imagined anything as freeing as love must be." She smiled, and he saw the sadness in the fading light. "I hope to experience it, of course. All the bits and pieces."

"With your baker." He disliked the taste of the words.

She did not hesitate. "In our bookshop, gifted to us by a losing marquess, who was positively obsequious with his compliments."

The words made him chuckle. "Do not count your books before they are shelved, my lady." Silence fell for a long moment before he added, "It is not the stuff of poems and fairy tales."

"Bookshop owning?"

"Love. Make no mistake. Love has nothing to do with freedom." Her focus snapped to him as he told her the wicked truth, "It's the most devastating trap there is."

Surprise flashed in her eyes. He was surprised himself, he had to admit. What in hell had him saying such a thing?

"And you would know?" she asked.

"I would, as a matter of fact," he said, wondering if the waning light was addling him to the point of confession.

"I thought the Dukes of Lyne did not marry for love."

"I am not married, am I?"

"Are you in love?" she asked, the words coming on a shocked whisper. "With Marcella?"

"Who is Marcella?"

"Lady Marcella Latham."

"Ah." Memory returned. Lady Marcella from the Liverpool party. "No."

She scowled at him then. "You really should remember the women you ruin, you know."

He drank. "If anything worthy of ruination had happened between Lady Marcella and me, I would remember her."

"You escaped her via rose trellis!"

"Precisely as she asked me to."

"I highly doubt that's the case."

"It's true. The lady and I had an arrangement."

"All the more reason for you to remember her. It's common courtesy." She reached into the basket. "There are pasties in here!" Extracting a pasty, she tore it in half and offered it to him. "Pasties are a glorious food. One I never get in London."

"Why not? You have a cook, don't you?"

She nodded and spoke around her food. King resisted

the urge to smile. Her manners had fled as the sun had set. "But she's French. And pasties aren't good for the waistline."

"There's nothing wrong with your waistline," he replied without thinking. She paused mid-chew. He likely should not have an opinion on her waistline. He shrugged a shoulder. "It's perfectly ordinary."

She began chewing again. Swallowed. "Thank you? I suppose?"

"You are welcome."

She washed down her pasty with more wine. "So, you do not love Lady Marcella."

She'd had enough wine to be nosy, and not nearly enough to forget the conversations they'd been having. "I do not."

"But you are aware of the emotion. In a personal sense."

Enough to know I never want it again.

"Yes."

"Why don't you marry the poor girl?"

He'd tried. He'd wanted to.

He remembered bringing her to meet his father. To show her off. To prove to the great Duke of Lyne that love was not an impossibility. He'd been young and stupid. And his father had ruined it.

I'd rather you never marry at all than marry some cheap trollop in it only for the title, the duke had sneered. And Lorna had run.

He remembered the way his heart had pounded as he'd chased after her, to find her, to marry her. To love her enough to spit in his father's face. And then he stopped remembering, before he could remember the rest. He looked up at Sophie, fairly invisible. Night had fully fallen. "I can't marry her."

"Why not?" It was strange, the way her voice curled around him in the darkness. Curious. Comforting.

"Because she is dead."

She shot forward at the words, and though it was too dark to see, he could hear the movement of her skirts against her legs, feel the heat of her in the small space. "Dear God," she whispered, and then her hands were on him, clumsily searching in the darkness. Landing on his thigh before she snatched them back, as though she'd been burned. He caught them, wishing he could see her face. Grateful that he could not see her face when she repeated the words. "Dear God. King. I am so sorry."

She is dead, and my father killed her.

She is dead, and I killed her.

He shook his head, the darkness making the story easier to tell. "Don't be. It was a long time ago. Truthfully, the only reason why I told you was because you asked why I'd never returned."

"But you return now."

"My father—" he started, then stopped. Instead, he laughed humorlessly. "Suffice to say, I want him to know that his precious line died with her."

There was silence. "Did he—" She did not finish the question.

He answered it anyway. "As though he'd put a pistol to her head."

She paused, considering the horrifying words. "And your happiness? You shall never take it?"

She was a fool, Sophie Talbot. A beautiful fool. A man could have money, a title, or happiness. Never all three. "There is no happiness for men like me," he said.

"Were you ever happy?" she whispered.

Memory flashed, summoned from God knew where by

this woman who had a remarkable way of winning his secrets. "I remember a day when I was a child—I'd just been given my first mount, and my father and I rode out to visit the blacksmith." He could have stopped there, but somehow, it was easy to tell the story in the darkness, and once it had begun, he couldn't stop it. "He was hammering out horseshoes in his little workshop, which was hot as hell.

"My father talked to him for a long while—longer than any young man wants to listen—and I wandered out into the yard, to discover a metal stake in the ground and a half-dozen horseshoes wrapped around it."

"It's a game," she said.

"I knew instinctively that whatever it was, it was not for future dukes."

"I shall show you how it is done," she said fervently in the darkness, making him want to pull her onto his lap and kiss her mad. "Hang rules for future dukes."

"No need. I know how to play."

A pause. "The blacksmith taught you?"

"My father did." Silence followed the pronouncement, until King added, "I was happy that day."

She shifted, and the sound of her skirts brought him out of the memory, back to this place, no longer the boy at the blacksmith's. Now a man who had seen the truth of what his father could do if his expectations weren't met.

Another image flashed, a carriage much like this one, on its side, in the road, and King wanted desperately to be on his curricle, careening up the road with wind whipping around him, drowning out the thoughts that seemed to grow louder as he drew north.

As though she heard the thoughts, Sophie moved again, leaning forward, her hand coming to his knee in a thoroughly inappropriate gesture. Inappropriate, and desperately welcome, as it chased the thoughts away.

He wanted her to chase everything away.

Everything but this moment. Her. Them.

He moved, crossing the dark carriage, filling the bench next to her and threading his fingers through hers, something about the simple touch tempting him more than anything had ever tempted him.

Something about *her* tempting him.

Her breath caught in her throat at the touch, and pleasure shot through him. She wanted him as much as he wanted her. "Sophie," he whispered, her name echoing around them.

"Yes?" she asked, so quietly he barely heard her.

"You said you wished to experience the bits and pieces of it." He spoke close to her ear, where she smelled of honey and spice.

"The bits and pieces of love."

One of his hands slid up to her jaw, his fingers threading into her hair. "Would you like me to show you this bit?" He nipped at the skin on her opposite jaw, scraping his teeth there until she gasped at the pleasure of it. "This piece?"

The darkness made it all better.

His lips found hers, stealing a heartbeat of a kiss before he moved to worship at her throat. "We aren't supposed to like each other." Her words came on a sigh.

"Don't worry. We don't."

What a lie that was.

Chapter 12

ROGUE'S REIGN
OF RAVISHMENT RESURGES

She shouldn't allow it.

The man was a legendary scoundrel. An expert ruiner of young ladies. And he'd never once been punished for it. Perhaps because he was so very good at it. It seemed a shame to punish someone for what was clearly a remarkable skill.

But still, she shouldn't allow it. She should tell him to stop . . . stop the way his fingers threaded through her hair . . . the way they played gently over her skin and the too-tight fabric of her dress . . . the way his lips pressed soft, lingering kisses along her neck as he made his wicked promises to show her the bits and pieces of love.

Of course, it wasn't love he promised. It was the rest—the unsettling, carnal bit. The bit she'd been imagining since the night of her bath, when he'd stood mere feet away from her, his back turned, his shoulders wide, and she'd washed herself, wishing, strangely, that it had been he washing her.

The bit she'd wanted even more once he'd kissed her in false passion in the Warbling Wren. She'd wanted that kiss to last forever and ever.

But he'd never indicated that he desired such a thing—not until tonight, when darkness had fallen and their conversation had become somehow more honest and clandestine. And he'd told her his secrets and she'd accidentally touched him.

It hadn't been an accident, though.

She'd wanted to touch him. She'd wanted him to touch her.

And then he had, and it was *glorious*.

She didn't care that she shouldn't allow it.

He lifted his lips from where they played at the place where her neck met her shoulder and placed them at her ear, speaking, the words low and dark and full of wicked intent. "Tell me."

He sucked the lobe of her ear and made everything worse. Or better. She wasn't sure. It was difficult to form thought. "Tell you?"

"Would you like me to show you this bit?"

Yes. Yes yes yes.

She swallowed, knowing instinctively that if she said no, he would stop. But she did not wish to say no. She wished to say yes. Most definitely. Without question. If ever there were a time when she wanted something, it was now. He scraped his teeth over her skin, sending a shiver of delight through her. She gasped her answer, "Please."

She could hear the grin in his reply. "So polite."

She pulled away from him. "I'm grateful for the offer."

He laughed then, the sound a promise of something wonderful and wicked. "It is I who should be grateful, my lady." And then his lips were on hers once more, and she was lost, the darkness making everything more illicit and somehow more acceptable, as though no one would ever discover their actions. As though this place, this night, this journey was nothing more than a dream that would disappear with the light of day.

And it would. The Marquess of Eversley was not for girls like Sophie. Uninteresting, unbeautiful. But in the darkness, she could pretend otherwise. And this night would keep her in memories for an eternity.

"What bits, in particular, Sophie?" He was at her ear again, his fingers stroking at the edge of her bodice, where her breasts strained for release against the too-tight lacing. "What has you curious?"

Her cheeks should have been flaming at the question, but the darkness made her bold. "All of it," she said.

He laughed at the words. "No," he said, moving his hand away, teasing her. "That's not enough. Tell me, specifically."

"I don't know," she said, the words coming on a wave of frustration. "Touch me again."

"Where?"

Everywhere.

"Sophie," he beckoned, like the devil at the door to hell.

She fought for thought. "A few years ago, I saw . . ." She trailed off, shocked by what she was about to tell him.

He stilled against her. "Don't stop there, darling. What did you see?"

"I stumbled upon a stable hand. And a maid."

"Go on."

She shook her head.

"Where were you?"

"Looking for a place to read."

"Where?"

"It was raining, and cold. And my sisters were talking about balls and gowns and gossip . . . and the mews were warm and quiet."

"What did you find there?" He kissed down her neck, long, lingering sucks that made it difficult to think.

"I was in the hayloft."

"And the stable hand was there? With the maid?" There was something in his tone that she'd never heard in a man's voice before. Something breathless. Like . . . excitement? The thought made her excited, as well. *More* excited. As though such a thing were possible.

"No," she confessed. "They were in a stall."

"And you looked?" His tongue swirled at the crest of her good shoulder.

"I didn't mean to. I was only looking for a quiet place to read."

"I do not judge you." He licked—licked!—the skin between shoulder and dress, and she thought her breasts might break free of their bindings. "I simply want to imagine the full scenario. What did you see?"

"At first nothing," she said. "I didn't know they were there. If I had—"

"You never would have stayed. You're too good a girl."

"But once I heard them . . ."

He filled her silence. "Once you heard them, you couldn't stop yourself."

"Even girls get curious," she defended herself.

"What did you see, Sophie?" His hand was moving now, over her thigh, toward her knee, the sound of it on the fabric of her skirts unsettling.

"I couldn't see much at first. I was looking down over the edge of the hayloft. I saw the tops of their heads. They were kissing."

His lips settled on hers, immediately lifting, leaving her quite desperate. "Like that?"

She shook her head in the darkness. "No."

"How, then?"

"You know how."

"I wasn't there," he said, and the teasing in his tone made her even more aware of him. "Show me."

God knew how she had the courage to do as she was told, but she did, running her hand up his arm, over his shoulder, to the back of his neck, pulling him to her. "Like this." And then she kissed him, letting her tongue slide over his lips and into his mouth, where he tasted like wine, hoping that she was doing it right.

He groaned and gathered her closer, careful of her shoulder, turning her so that her thighs draped over his lap, his hand finding the hem of her skirts and sliding to her ankle, the touch warm and wonderful.

She was doing it right.

After a moment, he broke the kiss. "Is that all you saw?"

No. "It became more . . ." She trailed off, hoping he would fill in the descriptor so that she did not have to. He did not. ". . . erotic."

The sound he made was best described as a growl. "There are few things I like more than that word on your lips."

"Erotic?"

He kissed her quickly, his tongue stroking deep before releasing her and leaving her breathless. "What was so erotic, Sophie?"

She was lost in the memory again, in the hope that she might relive it now. Here. With him. "He opened her dress."

"Christ," King said. "I was hoping he would do that."

And then the bodice of her dress loosened, the too-tight lacing coming easily undone, and her breasts were free. She gasped, the sensation welcome, but somehow not enough. For he did not touch her. His hands were around her hips for some unknown reason. She squirmed, aching for his touch. "King," she whispered.

The growl came again, softer, more breath than sound. "Then what did he do?"

"He touched her."

One finger found the curved underside of her breast, and it was so unexpected and so desired that she nearly leapt from her skin. He ran that single, remarkable finger in a long, slow circle around her breast, leaving fire and aching desire in its wake. "Here?"

"No."

The circle became tighter. Closer to where she wanted him. Closer to where she'd only imagined anyone ever touching her in the dead of night, alone.

It was the dead of night, but she was no longer alone.

"Here?"

She shook her head. He might not have been able to see it, but he knew. The circle tightened, and she thought she might die from the wait. "Here?"

"No."

He stopped moving. "Where? Show me."

She barely believed it when she did as he asked, clasping his hand in hers and placing it where she wanted him. He immediately gave her what she asked for, stroking and plucking at the straining tip until she sighed her pleasure, pressing against him, aching for—

"What did he do next?" The words sounded like carriage wheels on stone.

"He kissed her," she whispered. "There."

"Smart man," he said, and set his lips to where his fingers were, sucking gently, as though he had an eternity to explore her, and perhaps he did. Perhaps she would let him explore her for as long as he wished.

But he did not remain gentle, soon running his teeth across the hardened nipple in a wicked caress that had her crying out and sliding her fingers into his hair to hold him there. But King did not give her what she wished, instead lifting his mouth at her touch and blowing cool air across her flushed skin before lavishing similar attention on her other breast.

It went on and on, back and forth, until she was straining for more of his touch, for more of his lovely mouth, for more of him. And he gave it to her, the hand at her ankle sliding farther beneath her skirts along the length of her leg, higher and higher, until it stilled, at the soft skin of her thigh, fingers stroking softly as he lifted his head and spoke in the sinful dark. "And what did you think of it?"

"I thought—" She stopped, embarrassed of the memory.

He kissed the soft skin of her neck in a long, lingering caress. "Did you wish it was you?"

"No . . ." she said, and it was true. "I wished . . ."

She wished his hand would move.

"I wished I could feel it, though. I wished someone would worship me like that. I wished I could command that kind of attention."

He kissed her again, long and slow and deep. "This kind?"

She sighed. "Yes. And then he—"

In her silence, those fingers stroked and stroked, slow and deliberate, as though he had nothing more to do ever. She couldn't tell him. Could she?

But it was dark, and they were cloaked in secrets anyway, and when they got to Mossband, they would part ways. Why not tell him?

"Then he lifted her skirts."

The fingers stilled for barely any time. A tiny hiccup that she might not have noticed if she weren't so busy noticing him. And suddenly, she felt very, very powerful. And the words broke free. The words she'd never imagined saying out loud. The memory she barely allowed herself to remember. "And then he got to his knees."

His whispered curse came out part blasphemy, part benediction. "And what did he do?"

"I imagine you know," she said, drunk on the way the moment consumed her.

"I know what I would like to do."

And then he was dropping her feet to the floor of the carriage, and lowering himself to his knees, and Sophie was grateful for the darkness of the carriage, because she wasn't certain she would ever be able to look at this man again. Cool air kissed her legs as he raised her skirts, folding them back onto her lap before pulling her to the edge of her seat and spreading her legs wide.

Her cheeks flamed; she wore no undergarments, as they had not fit beneath the livery she'd worn earlier. Belatedly, she tried to close her thighs, but he held her open. "Sophie?" he asked, and the world was wrapped up in her name.

"Yes?"

He pressed a kiss to the inside of her knee, and she jumped at the unexpected touch. He laughed, low and liquid in the space, then spoke to the sensitive skin there. "Do you want me to show you this bit?"

All the bits and pieces.

"I can smell you, and I want quite desperately to taste you. To show you just what that stable hand did to that maid." His fingers moved, and she stiffened as they touched her, barely, a whisper of him over the hair at the apex of her thighs. "You're so warm. And I'm betting wet, as well. But I won't do it until you tell me yes. Until you give me permission."

Yes. Yes.

"Do you . . ." She trailed off. Regrouped. "Do you wish to? Show me?"

He exhaled, hot and lovely against her. "I am not certain I have ever wanted to do anything in my life so much as I want to do this." Her stomach clenched, along with somewhere lower, deeper, more secret.

"He made her scream," Sophie whispered, the story helping to keep her wits about her.

That lovely laugh again. "I hope he did. And I would very much like to do the same to you. But you must stay quiet, love, lest we give the coachman a show." He inhaled, long and deep, and exhaled before he said, "You are slowly torturing me. Tell me you want it, and I'll give it to you. Everything you desire. More."

Yes. Yes.

She stood on a precipice, feeling as though this decision, more than all the others of the past week, would change everything. But there was no question. She wanted this bit. This piece.

And she wanted it from him.

"Yes," she said. And before the word gave way to silence, he was there, his fingers pressing, parting the folds where she wanted him most, exploring in delicious strokes and slides.

He groaned. "So wet," he said in between kisses to the soft skin of her inner thighs. "Were you wet then?" he asked, wickedly. "In the hayloft?"

"I don't know," she replied.

"No?" he said, stilling, torturing her with the lack of his touch. Punishing her for her lie.

"Yes," she said. "I was wet."

He spread her wide and she closed her eyes at the touch—lewd and lascivious and lovely—at once thankful for the darkness and quite desperate for the light. "Did you touch yourself?"

She shook her head, her hands searching for him. Finding his soft hair. "No." He stopped again and her fingers curled against him. "It's true. I didn't. But—"

He blew softly on the exposed center of her. "But?"

She inhaled, the breath ragged and not enough, and though it was he who knelt, it was she who confessed. "But I wanted to."

He rewarded the honesty with his mouth, consuming her like fire, his tongue stroking in long, slow licks, curling in a slick promise at the hard center of her pleasure, and she lifted her hips to meet his remarkable mouth, not caring that the action could be called nothing but wanton. She did want.

She needed.

And he gave without purchase. The fingers of one hand holding her wide as those of the other explored, pressing deep, curling, finding a spot that made her writhe without care for anything but him and his wonderful touch. "King," she whispered, and he lifted his mouth from her.

"Tell me what you like."

She shook her head. "I don't know."

He licked, long and slow and devastating. "You do, though." He set his tongue to the hard bud at the top of her, working until she gasped his name again. "You like that."

"I do," she groaned. "More."

He laughed, the sound like sin in the dark. Like the devil himself. "As you demand, my lady." And he set his mouth to her again.

She soon became a master at telling him what she liked, even as she discovered it herself, using words she'd never thought she'd say—words that would ruin her in polite company forever.

But she did not care about polite company. She cared about *his* company, this glorious man who showed her more in the darkness than she had ever known in the light.

And as he did her bidding, his touch accompanied by a low, rumbling growl, she came closer and closer to the edge he had promised. Her sighs grew louder, and she cried out his name.

He stopped.

She sprang forward, sitting up straight in protest. "No!"

He pressed her back against the seat and whispered, "What did I say about you being quiet?" He lowered his head and kissed her gently, openmouthed, teasing. "You must be quiet, Sophie. We mustn't be heard."

The words had a wicked impact, sending desire flooding through her. He was asking the impossible. "Should we stop?" she asked, hating the question.

"Dear God. No. We shouldn't stop."

Sophie gave a little sigh of relief that became a gasp when he kissed her again. "I quite desperately want you to scream, Sophie," he said between idle, unbearable licks. "I want to stop this carriage, lay you down beneath the stars, and make you scream again, and again, and again."

She stifled a cry at the words and his touch, stiffening. Clenching her fingers in his hair. "Please, King."

"Shhhh." He spoke directly to the core of her, the rush of air making her wild. "Be careful." And then his fingers moved again, joining in her torture, sliding deep, stroking and curling again and again. "He might hear us."

The words did nothing but excite her further, and it grew worse as he teased and tempted with his fingers, reminding her to be quiet in that wicked voice, all enjoyment, as though he knew he was slowly destroying her, making her want him more than she'd ever wanted anything in her twenty-one years.

"He might hear us," he repeated to the core of her, his warm breath making her ache as his fingers worked against her. "He might hear you, your little cries, the way you call my name, like sin and sex in the darkness."

She wasn't sin and sex, though. He was.

But when he set his mouth to her, she widened her thighs and lifted herself to him, proving him right. Biting back the cries that came again and again as he pressed more firmly, rubbed more deliberately, giving her everything she desired.

"Don't stop," she whispered. "Please, King. Don't stop."

He didn't, not even as the tension built with no purchase, with no release, when she fell into the darkness, victim to his tongue and lips and touch, taking everything he offered without hesitation.

She rocked against him as the carriage rocked beneath them. And then the tension released, in glorious, wicked sensation, and she forgot everything but him, his dark growls and his strong grip and his wonderful mouth.

When the pleasure crested, breaking over her, breaking her, it was King who held her together, letting her explore all the corners of pleasure without hesitation. Without embarrassment. Without shame.

Perhaps it was the darkness that kept the shame away. Because she should have been ashamed, shouldn't she? Ladies did not behave in such a manner. But somehow, she did not feel ashamed, even as he lifted his mouth from her, lifted his touch from her. Restored her skirts and resumed his place on the seat beside her.

Somehow, it was easy to be without shame with him.

She yawned as he wrapped her in his arms and whispered, "Did you like them?"

The bits and pieces.

She curled into his heat, ignoring the little twinge

in her shoulder—she hadn't thought of her wound in hours—and told the truth. "Very, very much."

*T*hey changed horses in the dead of night at the next posting inn, and King left Sophie sleeping as he left the carriage to fetch wine, food, and hot water for her tea.

He could not deny the guilt that coursed through him as he crossed the courtyard of the inn; he was keenly aware that he pushed them both, and that forcing her to travel so far and without quarter—her shoulder only just having begun to heal—was ungentlemanly at best and irresponsible at worst.

There were three ways to travel to Cumbria, and he was willing to bet her father's men were taking the straightest path rather than this one, which was the fastest. At this point, he and Sophie were far enough from Sprotbrough that they could have stopped for the night. She could have slept a few hours on a proper bed. Had a proper bath.

But he did not wish to think of her in a bath. The vision was too clear and far too tempting.

And as for a proper bed, after how easily he'd taken advantage her in the furthest possible thing from a proper bed, he should not think of her against crisp sheets, hair spread across white pillows, skirts raised, bodice lowered, his hands on her skin.

Bollocks.

If they moved quickly, they could be at Lyne Castle by morning. Because, of course, he wasn't leaving her in Mossband, baker and silly dreams or no. He was taking her to Lyne, where he would keep her safe until her father came to get her.

But not a moment longer.

He was not a monster, after all, but he was also not in the market for Sophie Talbot. He reminded himself of that as he returned with his spoils, heading for the carriage where she lay asleep, her bodice open and her skirts wrinkled, beckoning him for a repeat of the events immediately prior.

Of course, it would have been significantly more gentlemanly if he'd reminded himself of the fact before he'd nearly had her in his carriage.

But he was only human. Made of flesh, just like her.

What glorious flesh it was. If only he was in the market for it.

He set the food and water inside the door quietly, leaving it ajar to avoid waking her with its closing, and went to assist in hitching the new horses. No, he was in the market for facing his father and telling him the truth—that when King died, the dukedom died with him. That he'd never marry. Never carry on the name.

He had spent more than a decade imagining his father's response—the way the promise would break him.

The duke had asked for it, had he not? He'd said the words himself—proclaiming a preference for the death of his line than King's marriage for love. And that's what the duke would get. The end of the dukedom.

He would die with it on his head, and finally, King would win.

Were you ever happy?

Sophie's words echoed through him.

There was something charming in her naiveté, even as she knew that happiness was no guarantee. Her sister was in the most loveless marriage of them all, and still Sophie seemed to believe in the fairy tale—that love might, in fact, triumph.

That she held even a sliver of wistful memory for the baker boy she'd last seen a decade ago was proof that he should be rid of Lady Sophie Talbot, and quickly.

Then why didn't he leave her?

He was saved from having to consider the question fully by an unwelcome greeting. "I must say, even without your curricle, you've made terrible time."

King stiffened, quickly counting the days before turning to face the smug Duke of Warnick, sauntering across the courtyard, cheroot in his hand, gleam in his eye. King scowled. "You were supposed to be here three nights ago," King said. "You should be at your drafty keep by now."

"I found I liked it here," the duke said.

"You found you liked a woman here, if I had to wager."

The Scot grinned, spreading his hands wide. "She likes me, and who am I to disappoint the lassies? And you? What's kept you?"

King did not answer, instead accepting the harness for a second horse from the new coachman and focusing on hitching the beast to the coach.

"Secret reasons?"

King tightened the cinch.

Warnick pressed on. "Did you find you liked a woman, as well?"

"No." The word was out before King could stop himself.

"Well," the duke drawled, "that sounds like a lie."

King shot him a look. "You question my honor?"

"I do, rather, but I'm not in the market for a duel, so don't be throwing your glove to the ground or whatever it is you English idiots do."

There was nothing in the wide world worse than an arrogant Scot.

"This isn't your coach," Warnick said.

"You're very perceptive."

"Why are you in a coach that's not your own?"

King sighed and turned to face the duke, feet away,

arms crossed, one shoulder leaning against the vehicle. "When did you become a Bow Street Runner?"

Warnick raised a brow and took a long drag on his cheroot before dropping it to the ground and stomping it with his massive black boot. "I don't suppose you'd have room to hie me home?"

"I do not," King said through clenched teeth, knowing that Warnick had no interest in passage over the border.

"Och," scoffed the Scot. "It's a few hours. You shan't even require new horses to do it."

"No room," King said.

"Of course there is. I've all your wheels, so you've nothing but space. And I'm wee."

Aside from being irritating as hell, the Scot was twenty stone if he was a pound. "You are nothing like wee."

"Nevertheless . . ." Without warning, Warnick opened the carriage door.

King should have seen it coming. With a wicked curse, he dropped the hitch he was working on and went for him. "Close it."

Warnick did, so quickly that it was almost as though it had never been open to begin with. He turned a knowing smile on King. "So, you did find a woman."

"She's not a woman."

Warnick's brows rose. "No? Because her bodice is undone, and things seem fairly clear on that front."

King looked away for a heartbeat, frustration and fury making it impossible for him not to look back and plant his fist squarely in the center of the arrogant Scot's face. "That's for looking at her bodice."

The duke put a hand to his face, blood spilling freely from his nose. "Dammit, King. Was that really necessary?"

King thought it rather was. He reached into his pocket

and extracted a handkerchief, wiping his hand. He'd need to get a blanket for her. To cover her while she slept. He handed the square of linen to his friend. "I like you better when you're over the border."

"I like *you* better when I'm over the border," the duke said, holding the white linen to his wound. "I've never seen you so wound up. Is it your father? Or the girl?"

It was both, no doubt. "Neither."

Warnick made a sound that indicated he knew better. "There's a curricle here. Buy it. Race me home. Send some of that anger packing before you face your dying father."

He'd never heard an offer he so desperately wanted to take. He ached for the freedom of the curricle. For its promise. He wanted to feel as though he was on the edge of danger, knowing that it was his strength and skill and nothing else that kept him from losing everything. He wanted the reminder that he held his life in his hands. That he controlled it.

But for the first time in all the time he'd raced, it wasn't the past he sought to escape. It wasn't his memories he wished to control. It wasn't the coach he wanted to avoid, but its contents. And the things those contents made him desire. Without realizing it, he looked to the carriage.

The duke realized it. "Send the girl back to where she came from."

"I cannot."

"Why not?"

I can't leave her.

He did not reply.

Warnick watched him carefully. "Ah."

Anger flared. "What's that to mean?"

The duke shrugged a shoulder. "You care for your little footman."

He did no such thing. "How did you know—"

Warnick smiled. "I might have been slow on the discovery, but once it's seen—it can't be unseen."

"Do your best to unsee it, you ass." King turned away, ignoring the other man, returning to the horse.

"Where are you taking her?"

He was taking her to Lyne Castle, until her father turned up to take her back to London. What other choice did he have? If he left her here, she could well end up in the clutches of someone like Warnick.

King thought of her at the castle, at the base of the ancient stone façade in her ridiculous borrowed frock, looking nothing like the lady she was.

I'd rather you never marry at all than marry some cheap trollop in it only for the money.

He stilled.

"Who is she?" Warnick asked.

She's the youngest of the Dangerous Daughters.

"Because she's too clever by half for you. Which means that she's more trouble than anything else," Warnick continued, oblivious to the fact that King was lost in his own thoughts, his own words echoing through him. "You shouldn't dally with clever women. You'll never outsmart them, and before you know where you are, you're married to them."

King looked up at the words.

You shan't trap me into marriage, he'd promised her when he'd believed she wanted nothing but his title. He no longer believed it. It wasn't in her to connive. But she remained a Talbot sister.

And others would have no trouble believing it.

His father would have no trouble believing it.

It would mean he had to win his wager with Sophie—prove that her perfect baker was nothing more than fantasy. And then he would have to keep her close. He ignored the thread of pleasure that curled through him at the thought.

Keeping Sophie close was not ideal. They did not even enjoy each other's company.

You enjoyed her company a great deal over the last few hours.

He pushed the thought away, tested the strength of the harness, and turned to his new coachman. "Mossband, as quickly as we can get there."

The coachman climbed up and took the reins.

Warnick was gingerly exploring the bridge of his nose. "I'm fairly certain it's broken," the Scot said.

"I wouldn't worry. It can only be an improvement for your craggy face."

The duke scowled at him. "I rarely get complaints."

"Because women are scared silent at the look of you." King put a hand to the door. "Will you linger here?"

The duke looked up to the second story of the inn, before shrugging his shoulders. "A day or two. She's a welcoming piece." He tilted his head in the direction of the carriage. "You don't think I ought to have another look?" King scowled and the Scot laughed, big and burly, before he grew serious. "Take some advice, King. Be rid of her, before you find you can't be."

King nodded, even as something in the words did not set correctly. "I shall be," he replied, opening the door with renewed vigor. "Just as soon as she's served her purpose."

Chapter 13

BAKER'S DOZEN?
OR BAKER DOESN'T?

*T*he carriage smelled like fresh-baked bread.

The scent curled through her, hunger and desire coming on its heels. It felt like it had been an age since she'd eaten a full, warm meal, and perhaps it had been. Between her escape from the Liverpool estate, the gunshot wound, and the running from her father's pursuers, eating well had not been paramount.

And last night, when King had delivered a basket of hearty food to the dark interior of the carriage, she hadn't had much time to enjoy it, as she'd been too distracted by its messenger. Memory of the evening's events had her sitting up in her seat, keenly aware of her state of disarray, a blanket she did not remember pulling to her chin falling to her lap.

King must have covered her. She ignored the warmth that came with the thought and sat up, quickly pulling the laces on her borrowed frock tight, covering herself as well as she could with the too-small dress. Once the most pressing task was complete, she looked up, simultaneously noticing three things: the whisper of grey light that filled the carriage, indicating that it was barely dawn;

the fact that King was not on the seat opposite her; and the fact that the carriage was not moving.

She peered out the window, somehow already knowing the truth, but the little brick buildings all in a row, mere feet away, confirmed it.

They were in Mossband.

It was all still there, the haberdasher, the butcher, and, yes, the baker.

Already awake. Already baking.

Opening the door to the carriage, Sophie stepped out onto the block that was already there, sitting as though it had been waiting for her along with this little town and all the memories that came with it. She faced the little greensward at the center of town, marked by a massive stone, bigger than a small house and unable to be moved, and so left as a marker, moss climbing its north side, giving the town its name.

She took a deep breath, inhaling the light and the air and the early morning.

"Is it all you remembered?" The words were quiet in the predawn silence. She turned to find him close to her, leaning against the coach, closer than she expected. Close enough to smell him, to see the dark stubble that shadowed his chin. They'd been traveling without quarter, and he hadn't shaved. Her fingers itched to touch it.

It's not yours to touch.

Not by the light of day. Not here, at the end of their journey, when they were about to end their acquaintance. An acquaintance that had become far too close than any acquaintance should be.

She cleared her throat and found speech. "It is exactly the same." She looked down the row of buildings, drinking in this place she'd dreamed of for years; there was a tea room now where there hadn't been when she was younger, just on the crest of the little slope that curved round behind the pub. "Except for the tea shop."

He was looking at the pub. "The Weasel and the Woodpecker? Really?"

She laughed at his surprise. "I think it's creative."

"I think it's ridiculous."

She shook her head, pointing to the rock at the center of the greensward. "Seleste climbed that once." She noticed the question in his gaze. "My sister."

"The one we haven't discussed."

He did not mention her suitor, and Sophie noticed. She nodded. "She climbed up—couldn't have been older than eight or ten—and once up there, she became terrified. She couldn't get herself down."

"What happened?"

"My father came to save her," she said, the long-forgotten memory returned with utter clarity. "He told her to jump into his arms."

"Did she?"

Sophie couldn't hold back the laugh. "She toppled them both to the ground."

He laughed with her, the sound deep and soft in the early-morning light. "Did she learn her lesson?"

Sophie shook her head. "No. In fact, we all wanted to climb the rock and play with Papa after that."

The words came on a thread of sadness, something she didn't entirely understand, and she shook her head, willing the emotion away. Turning, she found King staring at her. "Did you climb the rock?"

She pushed past him, rounding the corner of the carriage. "Yes."

He followed. "And did you jump?"

She stopped. Looked down at her feet. "No."

"Why not?"

"Because . . ." She paused, not wanting to say the words out loud. Not wanting him to hear them. Not that it mattered what he thought of her. They were through today. After this, they'd never see each other again.

"Sophie?"

She turned, loving the sound of her name on his lips. The way it wrapped around her in the cool, grey morning air. The way it made her remember the night before. The way he'd sounded in the dark.

She shouldn't think of that. Of course, she would, but she shouldn't think of it here in public. In daylight. In the presence of him, and all of Mossband.

"Sophie."

She shook her head, staring over his shoulder at the rock in question. "I was too afraid to jump."

Silence fell and she imagined him judging her. She wasn't much different now, was she? Still afraid. Still uninteresting. Still unfun. She braced herself for his retort.

"Until now."

She blinked, returning her gaze to his, beautiful and green and unwavering. "I beg your pardon?"

"You're not afraid to jump now. Isn't that why we're here? Why you stowed away in my carriage? Why you stole my wheels and got yourself shot? Isn't that why we escaped your father's men? All so that you could be here, now? So you could jump?"

She didn't know what to say, his words so pointed they almost goaded. And then they did goad. "So you could win your wager? With happiness?"

She looked to the bakery, its chimney spouting happy smoke, keenly aware of the fact that the wager was ridiculous. She'd never win it. But he was driving her to its logical conclusion. She would enter the bakery, see

Robbie, and return to Mossband. She would be free of London.

Everything would change.

It would begin again.

She would be free.

"Or do you forfeit?"

She was grateful for the teasing in the words. The way they brought her back to the moment. The way they reminded her of the woman she had promised herself she would become. The life she had promised herself she would have.

Without titles or pretension.

Without London.

Without him.

Not that she wanted him. She didn't even like him. And he certainly didn't like her.

Now was the time. She was here, in this place where she knew no one, had nothing. She'd found her way here. She'd made her wager and she would follow it through. Yes, she might fail, but she could not return to London. And she could not rely on King's help forever.

He wasn't for her.

I was too afraid to jump.

Until now.

It was not the seeing of Robbie that mattered, but the proving to herself that she was brave enough to do this. Alone. The proving to King. Because he would leave her, and she wanted him to think her brave.

To value her.

To see her. One final time.

She pasted a bright smile on her face. "Why would I forfeit when I am so very close to my bookshop?" Triumph flared at his surprise. He didn't think she would do it, and so she returned to the open door of the carriage, reaching in to collect her paltry things.

Setting her basket at her feet, she smoothed her skirts, asking, "How do I look?"

"As though you've been riding in that carriage for twenty-four hours."

She scowled up at him before collecting the basket and standing straight. "I shouldn't have asked you."

He stepped forward and raised a hand to her face, pushing a lock of hair behind her ear, the touch sending a thrill through her. A thrill she tried to ignore, even when his thumb stroked over her cheek, wiping away some invisible mark. The tips of his fingers lingered at her jaw, tilting her face up to his, and she felt her cheeks warm under his unwavering gaze.

They stood that way for a long moment, long enough for her to wonder if he might kiss her again. Long enough for her to wish he would kiss her again. There, next to the Mossband town greensward in full view of anyone who cared to look.

"Do not forget to keep your wound clean."

If she'd wagered a thousand pounds, she would not have guessed that he'd say that. Her breath caught in her chest at the strange, caring instruction. "I shan't." She lifted the basket as unnecessary proof. He nodded and stepped away, and she felt the loss of his touch keenly. Disliked it. Grasped for something else to say, unready to be rid of him.

"I never intended to trap you into marriage, you know." It was an odd thing to say, but true, and that was what mattered, she supposed.

"I know that now," he said, a little smile on his handsome face. There was a dimple there, in the dark stubble of his unshaved beard. She itched to touch it.

Instead, she said, "Thank you. For everything."

"You're welcome, Sophie."

And that was that. She nodded once. "Good-bye, then," she said, disliking the words.

"Good luck," he replied. She disliked those words more.

With a deep breath, she crossed the street to the bakery, telling herself that the discomfort in her stomach was nothing more than nerves. Nothing at all to do with turning her back on Kingscote, Marquess of Eversley. The man with whom she'd spent the better part of the last week.

After all, they didn't even like each other.

She pushed the door to the bakery open, a little bell above the door tinkling happily, announcing the heat of the ovens, and the smell of cinnamon and honey making her mouth water. The counters were empty of food, as it was too early for passersby, and it took her a moment in the dim light.

"I'm sorry, miss, we haven't anything for sale just yet—" Robbie began, coming to his full height at the great mouth of the brick oven that sat at the center of the room. He met her eyes, his already warm and kind and gentle—exactly as she remembered. "Sophie?"

He remembered her.

Her chest constricted with an emotion she could not immediately identify. She smiled. "Robbie." The name felt strange on her tongue. Unfamiliar. Incorrect.

He came out from around the counter, tall and broad in his shirtsleeves, his still-blond hair tied back in a queue, his brown eyes filled with laughter. "We didn't know what became of you! I mean, we read the papers, but you never returned!"

He reached for her then, and she stepped back, surprised by his forwardness. He stilled, sensing the awkwardness. "I'm sorry," he said. "I forget that you're a lady now."

The words placed distance between them. Immediately setting her apart. She shook her head. "No," she said. "It's only—you surprised me."

"I'm the one who is surprised, I assure you." He looked around the shop, searching for something and not finding it. "I don't have a coat."

He was embarrassed of his shirtsleeves, and she hated herself for making him feel that way. She lifted a hand. "No, don't worry about that."

He looked away, and silence fell between them. "It's the crack of dawn," he said.

"I just arrived."

"From London?"

She nodded.

"Are your sisters here, as well?"

"No. I came alone."

His brow furrowed. "Why?"

She thought for a long moment, and then settled on, "I wanted to come home." She paused, and when he did not speak, she said, "To a place I knew. To people I cared for."

I wanted to be happy.

He shook his head. "I don't understand."

She searched for more, settling on "I hate London."

He nodded as though the words made sense, but she had the distinct impression that they did not. "All right." He shoved his hands in his pockets, his suspenders pulling tight, and he rocked up on his toes, then back, peering about the room before his attention finally settled on the basket on one table. "Buns are still cooling, but are you hungry? Would you like a biscuit? They're from yesterday, but still good."

And that's when she knew.

This ends poorly.

King had said those very words to her, before they'd made their foolish wager. And she'd known they were true, even as she'd denied it. This did end poorly. And not because Robbie Lander was not to be her husband.

It ended poorly because ten years had made this place different.

Or perhaps it had made her different.

But, either way, Mossband was not her home.

The universe underscored her thoughts with the ringing of the bell above the door. "Papa!"

A little girl pushed past her, and Robbie bent down to catch her in his large arms, lifting her high. "Good morning, moppet. Give me a kiss."

Sophie watched as the child did just that, pressing her face to Robbie's without hesitation before pulling back and saying, "Mama said I could have two buns today."

"Did she?" Robbie replied, his gaze sliding past Sophie to the door. "Two?"

"One promises what one must to make little girls wear shoes." The words came from behind Sophie, and she spun to find a pretty, brown-haired, pink-cheeked woman there, dandling a baby on one hip. The baby had Robbie's brown eyes and a fat, happy look that Sophie recognized from their childhood.

This was his family.

You think he's been pining away for the earl's daughter who left a decade ago?

She hadn't, of course. But still, staring at this woman, this baby, Sophie couldn't help but feel . . . *envious.*

He had a home here. He'd stayed in Mossband, and here he was with his happy life. His happy wife. His happy family.

And it was all so foreign to Sophie.

His wife met Sophie's gaze with a welcoming smile. "Good morning."

Sophie found a matching smile despite her wild thoughts. "Good morning."

"Jane, this is Lady Sophie, daughter of the Earl of Wight," Robbie said, setting his daughter down and moving a tray of sticky buns to the counter.

Jane's eyes widened and she dropped into a curtsy, the baby laughing at the surprising change in altitude. "My lady, welcome!"

"Oh, please don't, Mrs. Lander," Sophie said, hating the honorific. "Please call me Sophie. I've known your husband since we were"—she looked to the little girl—"your age." She leaned down. "What is your name?"

"Alice," said the little girl, riveted by the tray of sweets. Her little throat moved as she swallowed in anticipation.

"I remember those buns from when I was a little girl," Sophie said, the memory coming swift and sad, her throat closing around the words. When she'd been sure of herself. She stood quickly, willing away the tears that threatened without warning. Willing away the sadness that this little girl, this little family wrought.

She'd imagined many things about returning to Mossband, but never sadness. Never this sense of loneliness. "What a fine family, Robbie." She corrected herself. "Mr. Lander."

"It is, isn't it?" He laughed.

It was perfect. A perfect life.

"Lady Sophie and I were playmates when we were young," he explained to his wife, who turned an interested gaze on Sophie.

"Oh?"

Sophie nodded, the weight of the moment heavy in the room. "It's true."

Silence fell, awkward, and Sophie wondered how quickly she might leave. Where she might go. What came next.

"Papa," said the little girl, unaffected by the arrival of the newcomer. "Mama promised buns."

Robbie looked to his daughter. "Well. A promise is a promise."

A promise is a promise.

She'd said those words to King days ago, hated the memory of his smug assurance that this situation would never end happily. She'd known she wouldn't leave it as Robbie's wife. But she'd never imagined she'd leave it with such doubt for her own future.

Her heart began to pound. She clutched her basket to her skirts and took a deep breath. "You've things to do. I must . . . take my leave."

Robbie met her gaze as he lifted a hot bun from a tray by the oven. "Will we see you again?"

The simple question threatened to break her, reminding her that there was nothing for her here in Mossband—just as there was nothing for her in London.

She shook her head. "I don't know."

Jane's brow furrowed. "Are you in town?"

"I am . . ." She trailed off, realizing that she did not know where she was. Where she would be.

"Are you in rooms at the pub?" Robbie's brilliant wife offered.

"Yes," Sophie lied, grasping at the solution. She had to sleep somewhere. "At the pub."

"Excellent," Robbie said. "Then we will see you again."

"For buns," Sophie replied.

"Take one now? For breakfast?" Jane offered, holding one out to Sophie.

She hated those buns then, their warm temptation.

Their promise of happiness and memory and restoration. She didn't want the bun. She didn't want the strange emotions that came with it. Or the strange emotions that came with not accepting it.

And so she stood there in the center of the bakery, staring at that outstretched pastry, wondering just how on earth it was that the smartest of the Talbot sisters had become such a proper imbecile, and what, precisely, she was going to do with the rest of her life—the life that would begin when she left this place and faced a great, yawning future.

How does it end?

King's question echoed through her on a wave of uncertainty.

She had no idea how it ended. But not here.

What had she done?

"Any chance we might leave with two?"

The words were punctuated by the happy bell above the door, and then King was inside the bakery, and Sophie knew that something could, in fact, make matters worse. The Marquess of Eversley, all smiles, playing smug, arrogant witness to her uncertainty.

Jane's eyes widened and her mouth turned into a perfect O. Sophie could not blame her, as King seemed to overtake every space he entered—taprooms, bedchambers, carriages. Why not bakeries?

"We don't need two," Sophie said.

"Of course we do, darling."

The *darling* attracted her attention. And Jane's. And Robbie's, for that matter. Sophie turned to him. "We don't."

He ignored her, turning his brilliant, beautiful smile on Jane. "My lady adores these buns. She's done nothing but talk about them since we left London."

Good Lord. He was ruining her all over again. She was not Mrs. Matthew to these people, she was Lady Sophie Talbot. They knew her. And they would not hesitate to gossip about her.

"My lord," she began, not entirely certain of what she would say.

He ignored her, instead reaching a hand to Robbie. "You must be the famous Robbie."

Robbie looked terribly confused. "I am."

King grinned. "Eversley. Marquess of."

Robbie's eyes were round as plates. "Marquess!" He looked to Sophie. "Are you—"

"Not yet," King laughed, answering the question before it was finished. "Sadly, she wanted to return to Cumbria before she married me. But she swears it will be done just as soon as we've seen my father, the Duke of Lyne." He lifted her hand to his lips, staring deeply into her eyes as he kissed her knuckles. "I didn't need her to stand on such ceremony, frankly. I'd have married her in a hedge on the day we met. Isn't that right, love?"

Sophie ignored the flip of her heart at his outrageously romantic words. He was an actor worthy of the London stage. But what was he doing? What would happen to her when they didn't marry? When she was left in discarded ruin—unwanted by the Marquess of Eversley?

She was not one of the other ladies, with copious offers of marriage. Her only other option for marriage was here. And it was married to Jane. Making sugar buns.

It hadn't been an option at all, if she was honest with herself.

She should be more honest with herself.

She supposed he thought she would be grateful for his arrival. But instead, it embarrassed her quite thoroughly. She didn't want him to see that this had turned into such a disaster. She didn't want him to see that she was alone. Without a home. Without a purpose.

She didn't want him to gloat.

She didn't want him to judge her.

Embarrassment flared hot and unwelcome.

She wanted him to leave.

He stayed, sadly, turning back to starry-eyed Jane, and said, "But she was so eager to see her old friend"—he leaned in conspiratorially—"and, between us, to have one of these legendary buns, that she forgot to ask for one for me." He looked to Robbie. "Of course, we've been traveling for days, so I forgive her. Exhaustion takes a toll on such a delicate lady." Sophie resisted the urge to roll her eyes.

"Of course, my lord," Robbie said, reaching for a second bun and a length of cotton in which to wrap them.

"Are you a lord?" Alice asked, the arrival of an aristocrat apparently more interesting than breakfast.

"I am indeed." King bent down to meet her. "How do you do, Miss—"

Alice did not understand the prompt, so Sophie interjected. "Alice."

"Alice is a lovely name. For a lovely young lady."

Alice laughed. "I'm not a lady." She looked to Sophie. "But she is."

"She is," Jane replied. "She's to be a marchioness. And then a duchess."

Alice's eyes went wide. "Cor!"

"Alice!" Jane hushed her, turning an apologetic gaze on Sophie. "She doesn't meet many aristocrats."

Sophie smiled down at King, hating the way seeing him with little Alice made her feel as though she'd like to see him with other children. With his own. She pushed the thought out of her mind. "I rather wish I met fewer aristocrats myself."

King laughed and stood, looking to all the world like a doting suitor.

Sophie wanted to kick him in the shin, and might have if Robbie hadn't interrupted, extending a package of pastry to King. "Two buns, my lord."

"Thank you. Is there any way you might spare a third?" King asked, smiling down at Sophie, obviously enjoying the part he played, "The coachman will no doubt be peckish."

"No doubt." Sophie said, barely containing her irritation. Was he never planning to leave this place? "You are very kind."

He leaned close, his words whispering at her ear, loud enough for the whole town to overhear. "Only when I am with you."

Still, she blushed, hating herself for it. For wishing it was true.

Hating him for it.

He was making everything worse.

"Thank you," he said to Jane as she packed the buns and finished the transaction, slathering on the outrageous. "You both must come to the wedding brunch. As Sophie's friends and my guests."

Embarrassment and uncertainty were instantly replaced with fury. It was one thing to tease her, quite another to extravagantly, boldly lie. There would be no wedding brunch. Indeed, in minutes, they would part ways. Forever.

"We really must take our leave, my lord. Mr. and Mrs. Lander are just starting their day."

"And me!" Alice said.

"Alice, as well," Sophie said, grateful for the additional assist.

King crouched down to speak to Alice, as though it were thoroughly normal for a marquess to attend to a child. "I apologize for interrupting your very busy day, Miss Alice."

The little girl nodded. "Mama said I could have two buns."

He smiled, and Sophie hated the way her heart constricted. Surely, she would respond to any man's kindness to children. It was a lovely tableau.

Made lovelier by him.

Nonsense.

"My lord," she said.

He stood. "Lead the way, my lady."

And so it was that she did lead the way, across the street and around to the far side of the carriage, before she turned and found him immediately behind her. She drew closer, toe to toe, nose to nose. Narrowing her gaze, she said, "I suppose you think that was amusing?"

His brows rose in feigned innocence. "I don't know what you mean."

She narrowed her gaze and spoke in a low whisper, keenly aware of the coachman halfway across the greensward. "You know precisely what I mean. You marched yourself into that bakery and saw me thoroughly humiliated."

"Humiliated? I saw you engaged to a marquess. I saw you made a future duchess!"

She blinked. He was mad. It was the only explanation. Either that, or he was simply cruel. "Except I am no such thing! What will happen when you don't marry me? When I am nothing but the woman the Marquess of Eversley tossed over? I realize you've ruined a fair number of women in your day, you scoundrel, but that doesn't give you the right to ruin me, as well."

"If we want to be specific, you were ruined the moment you donned livery and stowed away in my carriage."

He was right of course. "I don't want to be specific."

He smirked. "I don't suppose you do."

"I imagine you are enjoying this? Your perfect win—one more to add to a lifetime of successes?" He opened his mouth to reply, but she continued, furious. "Of course you are enjoying it, because you have enjoyed every one of my errors since the beginning of our acquaintance. You have spent the last few days mocking me, so why not add another, final opportunity?" She stepped away, spreading her arms wide. "Don't stop now, *Your Highness*. Isn't this what you live for? To tell me how wrong I've been from the start? How right you've been? To make me feel a dozen times a fool?"

"No."

She didn't care about the reply. "You needn't have worked so hard, charming the child, smiling your handsome smile for the wife, chumming about with Robbie. I was already feeling the fool. You think I do not realize that I have been wrong? That I should have stayed in Mayfair? That Society's censure was at least a known outcome? Or is it that you wish me to say it? You won," she spat. "You get your forfeit. Congratulations. Sadly, I've nothing nice to say about you. Not today. Not ever. I renege."

With a huff of anger, she turned to leave, to find the pub. To rent a room. To be rid of him forever.

"Don't blame me for this," he said, and she stopped in her tracks, turning back as he continued. "I've done nothing but follow your directives as long as we've been together." He approached. "You are the one who wanted to leave London. Who wanted to come to Mossband, as though this were a life you would ever be able to have again, as though a decade in London wealthy and titled could be erased with a damn sticky bun."

"You don't know anything about me," she lied.

"I know you fabricated that boy."

Her brows shot up. "Fabricated him! You saw him, my lord, flesh and blood."

"You fabricated everything about him, your perfect baker, pining away for you. And for what I don't know, because he was never for you and you knew it. Hell, I knew it, and I didn't even know the boy."

"I wanted—" She stopped herself.

He came closer, and they were toe to toe. "Finish it. What did you want, Sophie?"

"Nothing."

He watched her for a long moment, so close that she could see the little specks of silver grey in his brilliant green eyes. And then he said, "Liar."

"Better a liar than an ass," she said. "You simply had to prove yourself right. Couldn't leave well enough alone. Couldn't leave me alone. You had to prove that I was wrong. That I wouldn't find the home I thought I would."

"I wanted to be sure you were all right," he said, the words clipped and irritated. "I thought you might be grateful for the chance to show Robbie that your life turned out well. Better than expected."

"Oh, yes. Very well indeed. I'm stuck in Mossband with no money and absolutely no idea of what I'm going to do with myself." She paused, then said, softly, "I thought I would be welcomed. I thought I would be . . ."

She trailed off, and he wouldn't allow it. "What?"

"I thought I would be happy." Except, instead of happy, she felt more alone than she'd ever felt in her life. "I thought

I would finally be home. And I would be free." She shook her head. "But it's not home. I'm not sure what is."

"I'm sorry, Sophie."

She snapped her gaze to his. "Don't. Don't lie to me. I may be rash and I may be stupid, but you haven't lied to me yet, and at least there's that." The tears came then, and without hesitation, he reached for her, pulling her into his arms, not seeming to care than they stood on a public road in the center of a public town.

She didn't care, either.

She leaned into his warmth and let the tears come, filled with disappointment and frustration and the knowledge that she'd ruined everything and she might never be able to right it.

He let her cry, murmuring softly, soothing her, promising her all would be well. And she let herself believe, for a heartbeat of time, that his comfort was more than fleeting. He was so warm. So warm and so welcome, if she didn't know better, she'd think he felt like home.

Until she remembered that he wasn't. That he'd never be.

She pulled back, straightening and wiping the tears from her eyes. When she looked up at him, it was to discover that he looked as uncomfortable as she felt. "I've relied too much upon you, my lord. You've really been a remarkable guard through this adventure. But it is over now. I shall rent a room at the inn. When my father's men find me, I'll return with them. This entire journey was a mistake."

"Bollocks," he said softly, surprising her. "This was a dream. It was the life you thought you'd have. And now it's not the life you will have. But that doesn't mean you can't still have the freedom." He watched her for a long moment before he shook his head. "You're not staying at the inn."

"I don't have a choice."

"You are coming to Lyne Castle. With me."

Confusion flared, along with something else—
something like desire. Not that she'd ever admit it.
"Why?"

He shoved his hands in his pockets and rocked back on
his heels. "I can think of two good reasons. First, because
if you come with me, I can keep you safe until you decide
your next path. We didn't run from your father's men
so you could change your mind once things go slightly
amiss."

It didn't feel slightly amiss. It felt as though she'd made
a terrible mistake. "And the second reason?"

"Because I've a proposition for you," he said. "One
that won't take long, but will pay handsomely." Her brow
furrowed, and he continued. "Give me a few days, and
I'll give you enough money to buy that happiness you so
desperately want."

She blinked, the promise exceedingly tempting. "That
seems like a great deal of money."

"Lucky for you, I have a great deal of money. And I'm
about to have more."

"Enough for me to never have to return to London?"

He inclined his head. "If that's what you like. Enough
for your bookshop. Wherever you want it to be."

Desire and doubt warred within her. "Why would you
help me?"

For a long moment, she thought he might say something lovely. Something that revealed that he was coming
to like her. Hope flared, quick and dangerous. But when
he replied, he said no such thing. "Because you are my
perfect revenge."

She narrowed her gaze on his, dread pooling. "What
do you want from me?"

"It's quite simple, really." He opened the door to the

coach and indicated she should enter, not knowing how much his next words stung. "I'm going to present you to my father. As my soon-to-be wife."

She stilled. "You are serious."

"Quite. We've been fabricating a marriage for the last week; an engagement shouldn't be so very difficult. We've already started."

"You didn't tell Robbie we were engaged for me. You did it for you."

He shook his head. "For *us*. It works for both of us."

She ignored the pang in her chest at the words. "You're asking me to lie to a duke."

"To my father."

She blinked. "I thought you planned to convince him that you'd never marry."

"And I won't," King replied. "I've no intention of marrying you."

He said it as though it wouldn't hurt. And it shouldn't, she realized. There was never a moment when he'd given any implication that they were more than traveling companions.

Except for last night, in the carriage.

She pushed the thought away. It wasn't as though she would marry him, anyway. But still. "It's a wonder any woman in Christendom finds you charming."

He added, as though it would help, "I've no intention of marrying anyone, Sophie. You know that."

"Have you changed your mind then? Do you wish to make a dying man feel better?" She asked the questions even though she knew the answers.

"No."

You're my perfect revenge.

"Because I am a Dangerous Daughter. God forbid anyone with fortune and title marry a Talbot sister."

He stilled at the words, and she wondered if her frustration was clear. If her hurt was. "Sophie—"

She cut him off. "No, no. Of course. Your great, aristocratic father will no doubt be horrified that you've stooped to marry me. I lack breeding, bloodline, and class. My father won his title at cards—making us at best usurpers of title and privilege."

"He believes those things."

"Just as his son does."

His eyes went wide, and then narrowed with anger. "You know not what you speak of."

"No?" she asked, suddenly feeling very brave. "I think I know precisely that of which I speak. You didn't linger here out of concern for my future. You didn't sally into the bakeshop to rescue me out of the goodness of your heart. You don't offer me this arrangement because you wish for me to have freedom."

"That's not true."

"Really? So if I were another woman, with sounder reputation, with bluer blood, you would have proposed this?" She paused and he did not speak. "Of course you wouldn't have, because those women wouldn't anger your father so much."

"Sophie—" King had the grace to look chagrined.

She was having none of it. "But those women also wouldn't have the opportunity I have. I wasn't raised to marry well, Lord Eversley. I wasn't born with the silver spoon that allows you to be so utterly deplorable. So, fine. You want a Soiled S to trot before your father? You get one."

She took hold of the edge of the coach and hoisted herself in without his help.

Chapter 14

ROYAL ROGUE AND SOILED SOPHIE—
WAR? OR MORE?

*H*e followed her into the carriage without hesitation, closing them into the tight, small space, and waiting for the vehicle to move before he spoke, frustration and anger and no small amount of embarrassment driving his words.

"It seems, my lady"—he drawled the honorific, knowing she would loathe it—"that you have forgotten how very much I have done for you in the past week."

Her gaze shot to his, furious. "Do edify me."

"I had plans of my own, you might consider. I was hieing north on a rather time-sensitive matter."

She raised a brow. "Oh, yes. To find one final way to punish your father on death's door. Very noble."

"If you knew my father—"

"I don't," she said, all casualness, reaching into the basket on the seat next to her and extracting a book. "But frankly, my lord, I am not feeling very kind toward you at this particular moment, so if you're angling for my sympathy, perhaps save your stories for another time."

She was the most infuriating woman he'd ever met. "I gave you everything you wished. I brought you to damn Mossband instead of packing you back to London, as I should have the moment I discovered you, like the baggage you are. I protected you from your father's damn hunters. Oh, yes. And *I saved your damn life*."

"It's hard to believe that a Dangerous Daughter's life was worth the trouble, honestly." She opened the book calmly. "My apologies for your wasted time."

He sat back on the seat, watching her. *Shit.* It wasn't a waste. None of it. Indeed, he wouldn't give up a moment of the last week for anything. Even though she was the most difficult woman in Christendom. "Sophie," he said, trying to change tack.

She wasn't having it. Turning a page, she said calmly, "Do not worry, my lord. Your ailing father will loathe me. I shall make him wish death would come sooner. And when you get your *perfect revenge*, we'll be through with each other. Blessedly."

King watched her for a long moment before he said, quietly, "I don't think less of you, you know."

She turned another page. "For being too common for your perfect life? For being so common the mind will boggle at the possibility that I might make a decent wife? For being so common that you can hardly deign to breath the same air I breathe?"

Damn. That wasn't what he meant at all. "I don't think you are common."

She turned pages more quickly now. "It's difficult to believe that, I must admit, as you have spent the entirety of our acquaintance reminding me of my common appearance." *Flip.* "My common background." *Flip.* "My common past." *Flip.* "My common family." *Flip.* "My *most* common character." *Flip. Flip. Flip.* "Indeed, my lord, you have been very clear on the matter. Clear enough for me to think you're something of an ass."

He stilled. "What did you call me?"

"I feel confident that your hearing is in full working order."

Flip.

He reached across and snatched the book from her hands.

She scowled at him, then sat back, crossed her arms over her chest, and spat, "I shall be very happy to see the end of this carriage."

"I cannot imagine why," he retorted. "As I rather adore it."

The words weren't as sarcastic as he wished. Indeed, when he thought of this carriage, it gave him a great deal of pleasure. More than any carriage he'd ridden in since the last time he was here, in Cumbria. More than any carriage he'd been in since he was a young man.

Except it wasn't the carriage.

It was her.

The realization came with no small amount of discomfort—he did not wish for her to give him pleasure. This journey was not for pleasure, it was for pain. For his father's pain. He came to watch the old man die. Came to ensure that, finally, he was punished for the way he had manipulated and machinated King's life.

Sophie was a means to that end, and nothing else.

She couldn't be anything more than that.

He didn't have room for her in his life.

She wasn't his problem.

Even if he wished her to be.

He sighed, leaning back against the seat, frustration and anger coursing through him. He had been an ass. He'd insulted her from the start. She didn't deserve it. She deserved better than him. The thoughts echoed around him as the carriage began to move, and they drew closer and closer to Lyne Castle.

She deserved better than this.

He looked to her, sitting stick-straight on the opposite seat. Minutes crept by as he considered her, wearing that abomination of a gown. He'd summon a seamstress from somewhere. He'd buy her a wardrobe full of frocks.

Not that there was any kind of seamstress for miles.

He'd send to Edinburgh. To London if he had to.

And boots. He'd have a half-dozen pairs made for her. In leather and suede, in all the latest fashions. He'd have a pair made that laced high up her calf.

He'd like that.

He shifted in his seat, thinking of unlacing such a boot, and put the thought from his mind. He hadn't seen her in anything but livery and ill-fitting dresses since they'd met. He imagined that she'd been wearing a legitimate gown when they'd first encountered each other at the Liverpool party, but he'd been so committed to descending the trellis and escaping the events of the afternoon that he hadn't had a decent look.

His shifted his attention to the place where her breasts rose over the line of her dress, lifting to trace the long column of her neck, the curve of her jaw, the pink swell of her lips.

He'd been a fool.

And apparently more than once. They'd danced at a ball before that, one he could not remember. But it was difficult to imagine that he wouldn't remember her. That he wouldn't remember the feel of her, lush and tempting in his arms. That he wouldn't remember the scent of her, soap and summer sunshine. That he wouldn't remember *her*, all clever remarks and cutting retorts and a brave, bold way of facing the world.

Christ. He'd remember her after this.

Even after she'd long put him out of her mind and built

a new life, all her own. Even after he gave her all the happiness she desired.

He'd never forget her.

I am sorry.

He wanted quite desperately to say the words to her. To begin again. To embrace this wild journey as not a man and a stowaway, a lady and her aide. But as King and Sophie, and whoever . . . whatever . . . they might be.

It was impossible, of course.

She hated everything he was, and he would never be good enough for her.

There was nothing common about her.

He should tell her that, here. Now. Before they turned down the drive to Lyne Castle and he lost the chance.

But she was so livid with him, he had no doubt she wouldn't believe him. And perhaps that was best. Perhaps it was best that he so infuriated her. That she look forward to leaving him. That she desire to put him behind her.

The carriage turned off the main thoroughfare, and he looked up, keenly aware that they drew ever closer to Lyne Castle, where his past and future held sway.

Where his father might already be dead.

He returned his attention to Sophie, suddenly a port in a very turbulent storm. "We are nearly there."

She smoothed her skirts. "I shall require a bath and a change of clothes before I meet your father. While I appreciate that this dress might well-suit your desire to infuriate him, I will not meet him in an ill-fitting frock looking like I've been driving for hours on end. Even a Talbot daughter knows how to behave around aging dukes."

He nodded. "I hope you will sleep as well. You are past due for your herbs." If he wasn't so thoroughly transfixed by her, he might not have noticed the way her breath caught. He did, however, and would have offered a small fortune to know what she was thinking. Instead, she turned back to the window as though he wasn't there.

The carriage turned once, twice, and Lyne Castle rose from the horizon, setting his heart beating faster and harder as the great grey stones loomed and the coach pulled to a stop in front of the home he'd known for his entire childhood.

Something edged through him. Something like sadness.

Tearing his gaze away, he looked to Sophie, wanting to say something. Wanting to tell her that he was sorry.

Instead, he opened the door, stepping out to face the great behemoth, memories of his time here assaulting him: the scent of the green hills of Cumbria, rolling to the River Esk on one side and to the Scottish border on the other; the remains of Hadrian's Wall that made his mountain as a child; the warm food and kind words of Agnes, the castle's housekeeper, the closest thing it had to a mistress and the closest thing he had to a mother; his father, stern and cautious, with a single goal—to raise a future duke.

And Lorna. Golden-haired and pale skinned, filled with promise. The promise of love. Of a future. Of a life beyond name and propriety.

Of happiness.

They'd been so young. Too young for him to realize that none of those things were for him.

He pushed the memories away, turning to help Sophie down, his hands at her waist. When she was on solid ground, she looked up at the stone walls of the castle and then to him, a question in her eyes. "Are you well?"

Even now, the echo of her frustration around them, she found room for concern. He released a breath he had not known he held, considering her big blue eyes, the color on her cheeks, the way she thought of him. For a moment, he wondered what would happen if he leaned down and took those full pink lips for the kiss he'd wanted to give her since day had broken. He'd linger there, at the soft skin, reminding himself of her taste. Replacing the memories of his youth here with something else.

But he knew better than to kiss her here, in this place where memories seemed to etch themselves into the ancient stones.

Instead, he released her. "As well as can be expected."

A shout punctuated the words and King turned to see a great grey horse in the distance, followed by a pack of dogs. He squinted at the rider, tall and grey-haired, ruddy-cheeked and filled with vitality.

It couldn't be.

"Shit," he whispered.

"Who is that?" Sophie asked, and her soft words at his shoulder might have pleased him at another time, the way they curled around him, making him a partner in her curiosity.

He was too livid to find pleasure in anything, however. "That is the Duke of Lyne."

"Your father?"

"The very one."

"He doesn't look to be at death's door to me," she said, and he was almost certain he heard pleasure in the observation.

"The duke requests your company at the evening meal."

Sophie stood at the far corner of the room to which she had been assigned, considering the extravagant view. She'd bathed and slept much of the day in the massive, deliciously comfortable bed, and she'd woken to a collection of no doubt borrowed gowns, several of which actually fit.

A maid helped her dress before leaving her alone to wait there, in the window, considering the labyrinth in the foreground and the rolling green hills of a North Country summer beyond, wondering what was to come next before King rapped on the door and entered without summons. She turned to face him, still full of the anger she'd felt earlier in the day, when he'd made it clear that she was nothing but scandal to him.

Still attempting not to be hurt by it.

Still trying to put the evening before—the way he'd touched her and kissed her and whispered her name in the darkness—out of her mind.

She met his gaze, hating the way his presence had her breath quickening. "Mine alone?"

He leaned against the jamb. "Sadly, no. Ours, together." His gaze lowered to her bad shoulder. "Are you feeling well?"

She smiled, a brilliant, false expression that would have made her sisters proud. "I am about to sup with two men who disdain me, so I have, in fact, felt better."

He cut her a look. "I meant your shoulder. And I don't disdain you."

She ignored the last. "The herbs and honey are working well."

"Did you bathe?"

Her cheeks warmed. "Not that it is your business, but yes."

"It's my business."

"Because if I die you'll be out your revenge?"

He narrowed his gaze on her. "I don't care for your smart mouth."

Another smile. "And here I was working so very hard

to make you care." She approached. "Have you told him that you've returned with a Dangerous Daughter on your arm?"

He looked over his shoulder into the hallway and stepped inside the room, quickly closing the door. "I haven't," he said quietly, "But he'll know soon enough."

"Do I look enough the part for you?" she asked, knowing she looked as much of a Dangerous Daughter as she could without her sisters' belongings nearby.

"You look fine."

She made a show of furrowing her brow. "Are you sure? Women like me, we don't know much about dining with dukes. What with our background."

He cursed beneath his breath. "Stop that."

She blinked. "Stop what?"

"Stop condescending to me."

"I wouldn't dream of it."

"You would, and you are. You no more think of yourself as less than me than you think you can sprout wings and fly. You know you're better than all of us."

She opened her mouth to reply, but closed it, stunned by the unexpected words. Who was this man who so easily insulted her, and at the same time seemed to do the opposite?

"You deserve better than us, as well," he grumbled.

"That, at least, is true." If only she could convince herself of it. "I have been considering our agreement," she continued, turning for the looking glass, making a show of pinching her cheeks as she'd watched Sesily do in preparation for her suitors. *Men like to feel as though you've been dreaming of them*, her sister liked to say by way of explanation.

Ironic, that, as Sophie would do anything to keep King from knowing how she dreamed of him.

He watched her from the door, his gaze on her in the mirror. She made a show of straightening her neckline, drawing attention to her ample breasts, already near bursting from the gown. He'd asked for a Soiled S. And here she was.

"Don't tell me you're reneging," he said.

"I wouldn't dare," she said. "A Talbot keeps her word. But it occurs that what with my father's funds, I don't require your money so much as something else."

His brow furrowed so quickly that she might not have seen it if she weren't so thoroughly focused on him. "And what is that?"

She bit her lips once, twice, hard enough for them to go red and slightly swollen. Yes. Sesily would be very proud. "I want you to ruin me."

"What in hell does that mean?"

"You're such an expert, my lord, I can't imagine you don't already know."

He came toward her, his voice suddenly lower, darker. "How, precisely, do you wish me to ruin you?"

"How do you ruin all the others?" She waved a hand when his eyes widened. "It doesn't matter. We've spent the better part of a week together without a chaperone, and last night—"

"Don't," he said.

She looked to him. Finally looked, for the first time since Mossband. Something in his gaze made her not want to finish her thought about the night before. Made her want to believe it had meant something to him. As it had to her. "Well, the point is, I would appreciate it if you would render me fully unmarriageable. Then I will be able to find myself a new life. I shall get my bookshop somewhere quiet, and live a life. Free."

"Free of what?" he asked.

"Of all of it," she said, unable to keep the truth from her tone. "Of the gossip. The aristocracy. Of all the things I loathe."

"Of me."

No.

She forced a smile. "You know better than anyone how we truly feel about each other."

He was silent for a long moment, and Sophie found herself wondering what he was thinking.

We don't even like each other, she wanted to remind him.

To remind herself.

He broke the silence and did the reminding himself. "Done. I'll see you publicly ruined if that's what you want."

"It is. I want the freedom that comes with it."

He nodded. "Play this game well, Lady Sophie, and we'll be rid of each other before you even realize we were together."

Except she had realized it. She'd realized it the day prior, when they'd raced from the Warbling Wren, and the night prior, when he'd kissed her until she thought she'd go mad from the pleasure. And this morning, when he'd hurt her so thoroughly, and without thought.

They were together, and somehow, she adored and loathed it all at the same time.

She shook out her skirts. "Is it time for supper?"

His gaze flickered to the deep blue fabric, bordering on purple. "That color is beautiful on you."

She willed herself not to blush under his compliment. Failed. She looked away. "They call it royal blue."

Fit for a King.

When she returned her attention to him, it was to find him watching her thoughtfully. "It's beautiful. If slightly too short."

Leave it to him to insult her again. "Yes, well, once again, I haven't much of a choice. And I'm not precisely looking to impress my dinner companions."

"I should like to see you in a dress that fits you. You deserve one that fits. That's all I meant." There was legitimate surprise in the words, and she hated that he hadn't meant to hurt her. Hated that the fact warmed her. Hated the words.

Crossing the room, careful to keep her posture perfect, she faced him, mere inches between them. "You haven't any idea what I deserve."

There was a beat, and he said, "I know you deserve better than this."

Her breath caught at the echo of the words, no longer a taunt, now an honest, quiet observation. She willed herself not to allow him access to the part of her that cared what he thought. The part of her that could too easily imagine that he cared for her. That he thought highly of her. He didn't. The morning had proved it. This afternoon proved it. *Now* proved it. She pushed past him and opened the door. "The faster we begin our charade, the faster it is complete."

He turned, but did not approach, watching her for a long moment before he said, "Full cooperation, Sophie, or no ruination."

She smiled her most brilliant smile and agreed. "Full cooperation."

They walked through the long, dark hallways of the castle, down several flights of stairs and through a brightly lit landing before they arrived at the dining room, a massive stone space decorated with ancient suits of armor and medieval tapestries, enormous chandeliers lowered over a table that stretched farther than any table Sophie had ever seen. It could seat forty or fifty easily, in the high-backed mahogany chairs that sat heavy and imposing. It was a room designed to overwhelm, and it did. She stilled just inside the door.

King was there instantly, his fingers on her elbow. Understanding her. "He chose this room for a reason," he whispered, so softly she barely heard him. "To intimidate. Don't allow it."

For a moment, she imagined that he wished to comfort her. To make her feel valued in this massive, imposing space. But she knew better. He simply didn't wish his father to win. And he would do whatever it took to ensure that happened, including flattery.

She smiled and stiffened her shoulders, not caring a bit about what the duke saw—caring only that her discomfort was invisible to King. Softly, she said, "Talbots don't intimidate easily."

At the far end of the table stood the Duke of Lyne, tall and handsome despite the hair that shot silver at his temples and the lines that marked the edges of his eyes. Those eyes, the same brilliant green as King's, saw everything. He indicated the place settings halfway down the table, where matching footmen held chairs. The duke's gaze was unwavering. "Welcome. Please sit."

There was no request in the words, only command. No ceremonial introduction. Nothing approximating politeness.

Despite a keen desire to ignore it and leave the house, Sophie approached the table.

King spoke up. "You've no interest in meeting Lady Sophie?"

"I imagine we will have met after a meal, don't you?"

Sophie was already at the chair closest to the door when the duke spoke, his words cool and, at best, unmoved by her presence. At worst, he was rude. Irritation flared, and she swerved around the footman proffering the seat, shocking everyone. The duke's gaze widened barely. "But why wait, Your Grace?" She gave him her broadest smile, one she'd learned from Seleste—designed to win the crustiest of aristocrats—and extended a hand to him. He had no choice but to take it, and she sank into a perfect curtsy. "Lady Sophie Talbot. *Enchanté*."

No one can resist French, Seleste liked to say.

It seemed the Duke of Lyne could. He looked down his nose at her. "Well, Aloysius, I imagine you are very proud of the fact that your guest shares your manners."

Sophie straightened, willing away the embarrassment at the words. Talbots were not embarrassed. Not one of her sisters would care in the slightest if this man disliked them.

And besides, nothing about this endeavor had to do with her. It was all to do with King and his father. She was a placeholder. A pawn. She could be invisible and the evening would be no different.

Ignoring both men, she sat.

Soup appeared before her, ladled from a porcelain terrine not by a footman, but by a beautiful older woman who, from her dress, appeared to be a housekeeper of sorts.

The duke turned on his heel and took the seat at the head of the table, his cool gaze falling to Sophie. "Talbot. I suppose I knew your father."

"Many in Cumbria did," she said.

The woman had made her way to the other side of the table, where she served King.

"Hello, Agnes," he said to her.

She smiled warmly at him. "Welcome home, my lord."

King matched the smile, the expression one of the few honest ones Sophie had seen in the last day. "You, at least, have the feel of home."

She put her hand to his shoulder so quickly that Sophie wasn't entirely certain the touch had happened.

"He has a knack for finding coal," the duke said sharply, drawing Sophie's attention. He spoke of her father still.

"I'm not certain it is a knack," she said. "He simply works harder than most men I have known."

Not that hard work was a worthy endeavor for aristocrats—something she'd witnessed again and again as a child. A memory flashed, of her father at a ball several years earlier, a group of aristocratic ladies tittering at his "crass hands," weathered and calloused. "He should wear gloves when in London," one woman had protested. "He shouldn't be anywhere near London, with or without gloves," someone had replied, and the whole group had laughed.

Sophie had hated them for the words. For their insult. For the way they valued appearance over work. For the way they valued snobbery over honor.

"He has a knack for coal," the duke repeated. "And a knack for climbing." He paused. "As do his daughters, apparently." Sophie looked to King, finding his gaze on her as the duke added, "You could have sent word that you were not coming alone."

King drank deep from his wineglass. "You could have sent word that you weren't dying."

The duke turned a cool gaze on him. "And disappoint you?"

Sophie looked from one man to the other, noting the resemblance in the stubborn set of their jaws as King gave a little huff of laughter. "I should have known, of course. Disappointment has ever been part and parcel of being heir to your throne."

Sophie's gaze widened at the stinging words.

The duke remained unmoved. "I imagined that if you were told I was near the end, you would return. We've things to discuss. It's time for that, at least."

King toasted his father. "Well, I have returned. Prodigal son." He looked to Sophie. "And daughter."

A gasp sounded in the darkness behind Sophie, and she looked back to find the housekeeper watching the meal wide-eyed.

The duke sat back in his chair. "So you are married."

"Betrothed," Sophie corrected immediately. There was no way she would allow these two men to send her farther down this garden path.

King turned a winning smile on Sophie. "For now."

The duke drank, savoring the wine for a long moment. "So this is your plan, is it? To return home with a Soiled S in tow?"

Sophie set down her soup spoon. She should not have been surprised by the words, by the moniker, and still she was. This duke seemed not to stand on the same ceremony as the rest of the aristocracy. And despite her loathing the man's words, and the man himself, she had to admit that there was something rather refreshing about them spoken aloud, in public, without shame.

Or, rather, with shame, but lacking in the secret pleasure that so often accompanied the name.

King stiffened on the other side of the table, no doubt surprised and irritated that his idiot plan was discovered within minutes of his return. Sophie would be lying if she were to say she did not find a modicum of pleasure in his failure, for certainly someone with as much arrogance as the Marquess of Eversley deserved to be taken down a notch now and then. If they were discovered, she'd no longer be beholden to their agreement, and she could go on her way. She'd happily bear the weight of her sisters and their reputation if it meant being able to witness the demise of King's plan.

He slammed one hand onto the table, the force of it sending the plates rattling. Her attention flew to him, unprepared for him to redouble his efforts to present her as a woman for whom he cared. "Call her that again and I will not be responsible for what I do." She certainly had not been prepared for *that*. "I won't let you do it again," he said. "I won't let you drive another away."

Another.

Sophie inhaled sharply.

"And we get to the heart of it," the duke said, waving a footman forward for more wine. "Your precious love." He turned to her. "Not you, of course."

She did not look away from King who, despite his silence, revealed more than he should have. She wondered at the way he'd spoken of love a few evenings earlier: *It is not the stuff of poems and fairy tales.*

And while she'd kept from asking if the duke had hurt the girl he'd once loved, he'd answered her nonetheless. *As though he'd held a pistol to her head.*

Good Lord.

Oblivious to her thoughts, the duke continued, goading his son. "And this one?" he prompted, waving a hand in Sophie's direction, "Do you love her as well?"

This was a mistake.

She stiffened with silent realization. She didn't want this. Any of it. She didn't want him to fabricate a love, didn't want to playact it. She looked to King, recognizing the silent fury on his face, knowing that he cared not a bit for her. Knowing that this entire journey, all the little moments of laughter and caring and strange, undeniable interest, paled in comparison to his interest in another, long gone.

Knowing that his desire for Sophie paled in comparison to his desire for vengeance.

She willed him to tell the truth.

To release them both from the lies that bound them.

To let her free.

Perhaps if he let her go, she might still find happiness.

But she knew he would not and, somehow, she couldn't
entirely blame him. This place must be filled with memories of that horrible past. She hated him for what he'd
done to her, for forcing her to be a part of this mad play,
but at the same time . . . she understood him.

Sophie knew better than most what desperation drove
one to do.

"Don't leave the poor girl wondering, Aloysius," the
Duke of Lyne fairly drawled.

King looked to her and time seemed to slow. Sophie
could hear her heart beating, knowing that she could not
believe the words he said, whatever they might be. She
did not want him to say he loved her. She didn't think she
could bear hearing the words for the first time and know
they weren't true.

And, somehow, strangely, she did not want him to *not*
say that he loved her.

She didn't wish to be the means to his end.

She wanted to be more than that.

She wanted to be more than he offered.

"Lady Sophie knows precisely how I feel about her."

It was the faintest praise she'd ever received, and it
stung more harshly than all the aristocratic scorn she'd
ever heard. With those simple words, Sophie was through.
She no longer cared about the agreement—not in the face
of this moment. Not in the face of her desire for something else. For more.

She didn't want to be a part of this back-and-forth, this

battle between powerful men who didn't know a thing about what was really important in the world.

And so it was that Sophie Talbot lived up to her reputation as a Talbot sister, ignoring what was correct, and instead doing what was right.

She folded her napkin into a perfect square and stood. Both men stood with her, their ridiculous manners seeming to somehow matter in this, but not in the rest of the evening. Sophie bit back a laugh at that, instead turning to the Duke of Lyne and inclining her head. "I find I've lost my appetite, Your Grace."

"No doubt," he replied in a voice devoid of surprise.

"I shall take my leave," she replied.

"I shall come with you," King said, already moving around the table. "We needn't dine with the duke. Not if he cannot accept you."

Of course, he must be positively gleeful that his father could not accept her. That was the entire point.

She wasn't acceptable. Not to father or son.

"No," she said, the single word sounding like gunshot in the room.

King stopped, halfway around the foot of the table.

"I shall take my leave," she repeated. "Alone."

He moved once more, his long legs disappearing the distance between them with speed and purpose. "You needn't be alone," he said, the words firm and strangely forthright before he added, softly, "He needn't come between us, love."

The endearment did her in.

What a terrible lie he told.

What a terrible mistake she'd made.

She lifted one hand, staying him again. "He's not between us," she said, her voice calm and cool and filled with truth. "He is not the problem."

"It certainly isn't you who is the problem."

"I'm quite aware of who the problem is."

He looked as though he'd been struck with a soup ladle, just on top of his handsome head, but she took no pleasure in the moment. She was too busy keeping her back straight and her tears at bay as she turned and left the room.

Chapter 15

SAD SOPHIE SEEKS
SOLACE IN SWEETS

$\mathcal{S}$ophie was turning out to be very good at making scandalous exits and absolute rubbish at knowing what to do next.

She couldn't return to her rooms, as she did not wish to be found, and she couldn't leave the house, because it was the dead of night and she had nowhere to go. She did not think the Duke of Lyne would take well to her appropriating one of his carriages, either way. He'd likely consider it stealing.

And so Sophie followed her nose and her appetite, and went to the only place she ever felt comfortable in massive houses like this one. The kitchens.

The room was warm and well-lit and welcoming, just as all kitchens seemed to be. There were two large tables at its center, one set with massive platters of beautiful food: a perfectly golden roast goose, a platter of young asparagus greener than she'd ever seen, a towering pyramid of perfectly matched rosemary potatoes, a rack of lamb on a bed of herbs, a pot of mint jelly, and a tower of strawberry tarts that she was fairly certain she could smell from the doorway.

As it had been days since she'd had a proper meal, the food should have captured all her attention, but in these kitchens, the heavy-laden table was not the most compelling feature. No, it was the second table that drew her attention, filled with servants all eating their own evening meal—a meal that looked nothing like the elaborate plates waiting to be served to the now and future dukes she'd left behind.

The servants' laughter drew her through the doorway, the smell of the warm food making her mouth water. She edged up onto her toes to see what they were eating, envy flaring when she identified the food. Pasties.

The little pouches of meat and vegetable and potato were piled high on several platters at the center of the servants' table, and the chatter reached a fever pitch as they ate. She heard the gossip, about the angry duke, about the returned marquess, about the girl who had arrived with him. About her.

"Are they very much in love?"

"He must be. He's come home with her. As though it's done."

"She doesn't even have a chaperone," someone whispered.

"I've no doubt they're in love."

Sophie hoped the young woman was not planning to wager on it.

"And you are such an expert, Katie." The last was spoken by the woman who had been in the dining room, as she set a pitcher of ale on the table. Agnes.

Katie shrugged. "That's what I'm told." She turned to the housekeeper. "You've been here for a lifetime, Mrs. Graycote, has there ever even been a peep about a wife for the marquess?"

"Never," a girl who was not Agnes replied.

"Only what we see in the gossip pages," a third piped in. "He's more likely to end a marriage than to start one."

Laughter rang around the table, and Agnes shook her head as a footman entered the kitchens from the opposite end of the room. The housekeeper lifted her chin in his direction. "Are they ready for the next course?"

He nodded. "The lady left, and the men aren't speaking."

Agnes pointed to the goose. "Silence makes eating easier."

"Eating makes not murdering each other easier, I think you mean."

Sophie thought he made an excellent point, but Agnes, apparently, did not. The housekeeper looked sharply at the footman. "When I wish to know what you think I mean, I shall ask, Peter."

The footman put his head down and went for the goose, as told. When he lifted the heavy platter to his shoulder and left, Agnes's gaze found Sophie, shrouded in the dim light of the doorway. Sophie made to leave, but was stayed when the older woman noticed her, her eyes going wide in surprise before she offered a kind smile.

The conversation at the table continued, unaware of the silent exchange. "She *left* the table?"

"You wouldn't want to do just that?"

Sophie nearly laughed. Most assuredly, anyone in their right mind would want to leave the table. "Of course I would," came the reply, "But even I know you don't leave a meal with a duke."

"Two dukes, technically."

There was a quiet pause, and then *"Who is she?"*

A young man replied. "The marquess introduced her as his future wife. Some lady nob."

Of course, she was neither of those things. Not really.

"I helped her dress for dinner," Sophie heard the maid

whom she'd met earlier. "She don't seem a nob. She's wounded in the shoulder. And very tall."

"Being tall don't mean anything," someone else piped up.

"Being wounded in the shoulder does, though. Does she have a name?"

Sophie had spent much of the last decade being disdainfully discussed as though she were an insect under glass, but always by aristocrats. It was a new experience entirely to be discussed by servants, and she was immediately aware that she belonged neither above nor below-stairs.

Her stomach growled.

Here, at least, she could eat pasties while being gossiped about.

"As a matter of fact, she does have a name," she said, stepping into the light. Silence immediately fell and she would have laughed at the wide eyes around the table if she weren't so hopeful that she would be welcome here, in this kitchen, with these people, who seemed more honest than anyone she'd known in recent years. "And since she left dinner without even finishing her soup, she'll share it for the price of a pasty."

There was a beat, during which the whole kitchen seemed to still, as though the words had come from up on high instead of from a woman wearing an ill-fitting dress. And then, they came unstuck en masse, moving and shuffling left and right, making room for her. She took her seat, a plate appearing before her, a warm pastry at its center. "It's chicken and veg," the maid to her right explained. "There's also pork and veg."

"This is lovely," Sophie said, tearing the pasty in two, releasing a lovely whisper of steam alongside the magnificent scent of pie. Her mouth began to water, but she resisted taking a bite just long enough to say to the assembly, "I am Sophie Talbot."

She almost did not hear the gasp of recognition from a collection of girls at the end of the table over her own sigh of enjoyment once the food was on her tongue. But she couldn't not hear the excited "You're a Soiled S!"

She stopped chewing.

"Ginny, you don't just *call* her that," another girl said. "It's not *flattering*."

The girl called Ginny had the grace to look mortified.

Sophie swallowed and pointed to the cask of ale at the end of the table. "May I?"

A gentleman nearby immediately filled a pewter mug and slid it toward her, golden liquid sloshing over the edge when she caught it. She drank. And brazened it through. "Some do refer to me as a Soiled S."

"For your father," said Ginny. "In coal."

"How do you know that?" a young man across from her asked.

Ginny blushed. "I read the papers."

"The scandal sheets are not the *papers*," Agnes said.

The table laughed and Ginny dipped her head in embarrassment. Sophie took pity on the girl, taking another bite of pasty. "They're more interesting than the papers, aren't they, though?" She smiled when Ginny's head snapped up. "I'm the youngest of the five."

"The young ladies Talbot," the girl explained to the table. "Daughters of Jack Talbot, who grew up 'ere, in Cumbria. Like us!"

"Except she's a lady, so not at all like us," the man at the end of the table said. What a strange world this was, where in one moment she could be too cheap for a duke, and in the next, too expensive for anyone else.

Without home.

She ignored the thought. "Actually," Sophie said, "I am not very different. My father knows his way around a coal mine, as did my grandfather, and my great-grandfather."

"My brother works in the mines," someone piped up.

Sophie nodded. "Just like your brother, then. The only difference is that my father was lucky and bought a plot of land that eventually became the mouth to one of the richest mines in Britain." Eyes widened around the table, as her carefully bred London accent gave way to her North Country brogue, and she relaxed into the tale, having heard it a thousand times as a child. "He dug and struck for days before he hit on something he could use. Something nobs in London could use."

"See? She ain't a nob!" crowed the maid from earlier that day.

Sophie shook her head. "I'm not. I spent my childhood in Mossband."

"Except ye are," the man at the end of the table said. "Because we're callin' you milady and yer to marry the duke's son."

Not really. She pushed the disappointment aside and drank before smiling down the table at him. "My father isn't only good at coal; he's good at cards, too."

"They say Prinny lost a round of faro and gained himself an earl!" Ginny whispered loudly enough for the whole castle to hear.

Sophie winked, feeling more the Soiled S than ever before here, at this table. Enjoying it. Just as her sisters would. "That is, indeed, what they say."

The questions came quickly then, questions about her life, and her sisters, and their suitors, and her father and how they'd become aristocrats. And she answered them all, her plate and tankard always full. The food and the ale made her warm and chatty, and she realized that for

the first time in what felt like years, she felt free to respond to questions with the truth instead of carefully
crafted replies.

And then the next question came, from Ginny, who
seemed to know everything about her sisters and their
lives. "So you pushed the Duke of Haven into the Countess of Liverpool's pond, and now you're being courted by
the Marquess of Eversley—you're so very lucky to be so
very famous!"

Sophie's brow furrowed. "That paper arrived quickly."

Ginny smiled. "Today. I read it before supper."

"It wasn't a pond. It was a pool. Barely reached his
knees."

"Still! You're the star of the scandal sheets!" Ginny
sighed. "You're so very lucky."

She didn't feel lucky. She felt as though she could never
go home. She didn't even know where home was.

If it was.

"How does it feel to be a girl from Mossband, now
courted by a marquess?"

"A *handsome* marquess," one of the other girls piped
in, setting them to tittering and the men at the table to
groaning.

But Sophie was stuck on the question. How did it feel?
It didn't feel like anything, because it wasn't really court-
ing. Because it was nothing but an arrangement. Not even
a fantasy. She'd never really been headed to live out her
days in Mossband. She'd never really expected Robbie
to be waiting for her, and if he had, she wouldn't have
wanted him to marry her. And King . . . he'd never been
her husband. Never her betrothed. And now, after the di-
sastrous meal they'd barely had . . .

They didn't even like each other.

How many times had they said the words to each other?

How many times had she tried to convince herself it was true?

It didn't matter that there were moments when she came very close to liking him. It didn't matter that she liked him when he kissed her. When he stood by her side and defended her, even when she knew it was for his own gain. Or that she liked him very much when he'd held her, bleeding, in his carriage. Or when he'd ferreted her away from her father's men. Or when he'd come through the door at the bakery.

What mattered was that they weren't betrothed, and they'd never be married.

No matter how much she might wish it.

The thought startled her. She didn't wish it. Did she? She looked up, grasping on to the part of the question she could answer with certainty. "He is very handsome."

"Well, at least I have that."

Sophie closed her eyes at the words, wishing that the floor of the Lyne kitchens would open wide and swallow her whole. Of course he was there. Of course he had heard her. She looked down at her lap, embarrassed beyond measure.

"I'm sorry to interrupt what looks like a lovely meal," King said to the assembly, who immediately leapt to their feet, reassuring him that no, he hadn't interrupted at all, and could they fetch him anything at all? Ale? Food?

"No, thank you," he said, all grace. "I'm simply hoping for some time with Lady Sophie. May I?"

She looked up then, finding his handsome face open and amused. She wasn't certain she should give him time. He certainly didn't deserve it. He must have sensed her trepidation, because instead of saying more, he turned away to investigate the table of food nearby. He selected two tarts from the top of the tower and set them on a little plate, topping them with fresh cream before turning back, licking his thumb and forefinger.

"That's not really behavior befitting an aristocrat," she said, immediately wondering if, perhaps, the ale was talking.

One side of his mouth lifted in a small, sheepish smile. "Neither was my behavior earlier in the evening. Forgive me?"

As apologies went, it wasn't perfect.

Nevertheless, her cheeks warmed at the words, even before he extended the plate to her. "These people are not the only ones who can feed you. I have tarts. Can I tempt you to come with me?"

One of the maids behind her sighed.

Sophie resisted the urge to do the same.

She watched the plate of tarts for a long moment. They looked glorious. "I suppose." She stood and smoothed her skirts. "For the tarts."

He smiled and placed a hand to his chest. "Of course. I would imagine nothing more."

She took the plate as he guided her to the door, where she remembered to turn back. "Thank you all for a lovely dinner."

The servants were surprised by her gratitude, but Agnes replied, "Thank you, my lady. You are welcome at our table any time you like."

She followed King through the door. "I like you smiling," he said quietly, when they were outside the room in the dimly lit corridor. "You don't do it enough with me."

She looked up at him, "I haven't had much reason to smile since we met."

"I should like to change that."

She lifted the plate. "Strawberry tarts are a good beginning."

His gaze did not leave hers. "I think I can do better."
He turned on one heel and was off, through the darkened
maze of hallways, up a flight of stairs and through the
massive doors to one of the wings of the castle.

She followed him, despite not wishing to.

Or possibly wishing to very much.

Everything about this man was a confusion.

"Where are we going?"

He paused in front of a great set of doors, his back to
them. "To have dessert."

There was something in the words, in the look in his
eyes as he said them, that had Sophie's heart pounding.
This was not the King she'd known.

"There's a library here. Would you let me show it to
you?"

She scowled. "You're bribing me with books."

"Is it working?"

She let her gaze linger on the door behind his shoulder.
"Perhaps."

His lips lifted in a crooked smile, the dimple in his
cheek showing. "Let's see, shall we?" And he opened the
door to reveal the largest, most beautiful library she'd
ever seen. The room was cavernous, taking up two stories
on all sides, with a glorious wrought-iron balcony that ran
the perimeter of the room. In front of them, there were
several chaise longues and a massive fireplace a dozen
feet high by two dozen wide.

And all that before the books, stretching for what
seemed like miles, shelves and shelves from floor to ceiling, in deep reds and greens and browns and blues. More
books than a person could read in a lifetime.

But she could try.

She stepped into the room, turning in a slow circle, already wondering how long he would require her attention

before he would release her into the room, free to explore. "This is . . ." She trailed off, astounded.

After a long moment, he prodded. "It is . . . ?"

She looked to him and grinned. "It is working."

He laughed. "Excellent." He pulled the door closed behind them and moved to sit in a large leather chair at the center of the room, next to a pile of oversized books. Balancing the plate of strawberry tarts on one wide arm of the chair, he waved a hand to indicate the room. "I know you are desperate to explore, love. Feel free."

She was off like a shot, climbing the iron staircase without hesitation. "I've always wanted a library," she said, fingers itching to touch the unblemished spines of the books far above.

"I thought you wanted a bookshop," he said from below.

"That, as well. I could imagine my father supporting a bookshop," she said. "After all, they are an investment."

"But a library is not?"

She shook her head, running her finger over the gold, embossed volume of Milton she'd found. "A library is a luxury,"

"Your father is rich beyond measure. I should think he could spare you the bookshop and the library."

"He's always happily bought me books, but my mother . . ." She trailed off, then finished with a little shrug. "She doesn't care for them."

"What does that mean?"

She looked down at him, and for a moment she forgot about the library, drawn to the way his green eyes focused on her, unwavering. "She made me hide them."

"Why?"

"No one likes a female with ideas," she replied, echoing the words she'd heard dozens of times from her mother. "I suppose she imagined books make for thoughts."

"They do. Intelligent ones."

"I'm not sure she'd agree with you. Despite all the books I've read, I am the only one of her daughters stranded in the North Country with an unmarried marquess, bullet wound in my shoulder."

"Nothing about your current circumstance has to do with reading about henges."

Sophie laughed, trailing one hand along the long line of leather bindings. "Are you sure about that?"

"Absolutely. You are better for every book you've read."

She curled her hands around the lintel of the iron balustrade, leaning over to look down at him. "If you were a Dangerous Daughter, my mother would despair of you. It would be a miracle if we ever saw you married."

"What nonsense," he said, looking up at her. "You're easily the most marriageable female I've ever met."

She stilled. "You think so?"

"Certainly." He took a bite of tart, as though the statement were utterly normal.

"Once one learns that I'm not attempting to dupe him into marriage, you mean."

"Once that happens, yes," he said with a smile.

Something had her feeling slightly light-headed. The ale. Most definitely the ale.

Not him.

"Why?"

And it was the ale that had her asking that, the ale and the distance between them, which somehow made her more courageous than she had ever been.

"Why aren't you marriageable?" She didn't reply. "You're intelligent, clever, brave, and honorable."

Excellent, Sophie thought. *Like a horse. Or a dog.*

And then he said it. "Not to mention beautiful."

"I'm not beautiful," she said before she could take it back, instead wishing that she could disappear, simply fade into the books behind her and never be seen again.

No luck. "Yes, you are."

She shook her head, hating the way her chest tightened with hot embarrassment at the question. She didn't want to discuss her beauty or lack thereof. No plain woman wanted to, especially not with a man who was so very handsome.

Dear God. He'd heard her call him handsome.

She swallowed, desperate for an end to the moment.

"Sophie?"

She looked to him.

Don't make me answer.

Don't make me think about why you would never be for me.

It was the ale that had her thinking that. She didn't care to have him.

Except, now and then, she thought about it. When he offered her strawberry tarts. And showed her his magical library. And called her beautiful.

And made her want to believe it.

Then she cared very much.

"These tarts are getting eaten. I feel honor-bound to tell you as much."

Relief flared, replaced quickly with something much more dangerous. Something that made her wish that they were somewhere else. That they were someone else. That jests about strawberry tarts were all they had to think on.

She looked down at him sprawled in the leather armchair, lifting the plate up to her like an offering.

Perhaps tonight strawberry tarts could be enough.

Her eyes went wide. "You've eaten mine!"

"You didn't seem to want it."

"Of course I wanted it, you tart thief!"

He smirked. "Then why are you all the way up there?"

Why indeed.

She was down the steps in seconds, snatching the plate from his hand. "This is a half-eaten tart."

"Better than all-eaten," he said, making a show of opening the book on the table next to him.

"Stop!" she gasped.

He did, turning shocked eyes on her. "What is it?"

"Your fingers. They're covered in tart. Don't touch that book."

"One might have thought I were about to murder someone."

"Some*thing*," she said. "The book would be tarted forever."

He held his hands wide. "Fair enough. God forbid we should tart it."

She sat in the chair across from him and took a bite of her remaining dessert, sighing her pleasure at the delicious fruit, cut perfectly with fresh cream. "This is exquisite," she said, her gaze riveted on the sweet.

"It is, isn't it?" His voice was lower than it had been, quieter. Darker.

She looked up to find him staring at her mouth, and gastronomic pleasure turned to a different kind of pleasure entirely. "Would you like it?"

"Very much."

She was no longer certain that they were discussing dessert. She extended the plate to him, and he shook his head.

"You're sure?"

"Why books?"

Her brows rose. "I beg your pardon?"

"Why are they your vice?"

She set her plate down and wiped her hand on her skirts before reaching for the top volume on a stack of small, leather-bound books nearby and extending it to him. "Go on."

He took it. "Now what?"

"Smell it." He tilted his head. She couldn't help but smile. "Do it."

He lifted it to his nose. Inhaled.

"Not like that," she said. "Really give it a smell."

He raised one brow, but did as he was told.

"What do you smell?" Sophie asked.

"Leather and ink?"

She shook her head. "Happiness. That's what books smell like. Happiness. That's why I always wanted to have a bookshop. What better life than to trade in happiness?"

He watched her for a long moment, longer than she was comfortable, until she returned to her tart. Once she had, he said, quietly, "You didn't tell me if you forgive me."

The change in topic startled her. "I—beg your pardon?"

"For the way I treated you. At dinner."

She picked at the tart, selecting a strawberry and eating it alone, buying herself time to think about her answer.

He continued in the silence. "For the way I've treated you since Mossband. Since last night. In the carriage."

She looked up at him. "You did nothing wrong in the carriage."

He laughed, the sound humorless. "I did a hundred wrong things in the carriage, Sophie."

"Yes, but those weren't the things that made me sad." The words were out before she could think, before she could alter them. Before she could make herself seem less delicate. She set down her plate and stood. "I'm sorry."

He shot forward in his chair. "Don't you dare apologize. I think that's the first time someone has told me the honest truth in years. I—" He hesitated. "Christ, Sophie. I am sorry."

"It's not—" She shook her head.

"Stop. It is." He stood, approaching her. "I'm an ass. You told me so, remember?"

"I shouldn't have said that."

"Was I an ass?"

She met his eyes, grassy green and focused on her. "You were. Quite."

He nodded. "I was."

"And tonight, you were even worse."

"I know. I wish I wasn't."

"I wanted to throw my soup at you."

He raised a brow. "You're getting the hang of telling me the truth."

She smiled. "It's quite freeing."

He laughed, then grew serious. "Forgive me?"

She watched him for a long while. "Yes."

He exhaled, as though he'd been holding his breath for an age, and reached for her surprising them both, his fingertips brushing along her jaw, pushing a lock of hair behind her ear. "I never wanted to hurt you."

She swallowed at the feel of him, the heat of his touch.

"I should never have brought you here," he said softly, and she hated the way the words felt until he added, "you're too good for this place. The men it makes."

She caught her breath at the words. "I don't think that's true."

"You don't know who I am," he said.

"Show me," she offered, wanting desperately for him to agree, to tell her about this place. About the men it made.

He didn't, his gaze falling to her mouth instead, his thumb stroking along her jaw. "You've cream on your lip."

From the tarts. She lifted her hand, but he predicted her move, capturing her wrist before she could brush away the remains of the tart. "No," he whispered, close, the scent of him overwhelming her, soap and spice. "Let me."

She stilled, not quite understanding, but wanting it, whatever he offered. And then he was there, his lips on hers, his tongue licking out to taste the errant cream.

She'd never in her life experienced anything so scandalous.

Anything so . . .

"Mmm," he murmured, the sound low and soft as he lifted his head. "Exquisite."

He hadn't been talking about the tart earlier.

She couldn't stop herself from lifting her hand to his neck, holding him the way he held her, her fingers tangling in his dark hair. "Show me," she repeated, only this time, she didn't want him to talk. She wanted him to take.

Or perhaps it was she who did the taking, turning her face up to his, and capturing his lips with hers.

Chapter 16

LYNE LIBRARY LASCIVIOUSNESS!

*S*he kissed him.

He might have been able to stop himself from anything more than the single kiss, just enough to remind him of her taste without causing more scandal, if she hadn't kissed him, lifting her face, drawing his head down, tempting him with her little, quiet whisper.

But he was a man, after all.

And no man on earth could resist this woman.

And so he'd kissed her back, deepening the caress, his arms coming around her, lifting her high against him, and she wrapped her arms around his neck and leaned into the caress.

The first time he'd kissed her, it had been with one ear on the damn taproom at the Warbling Wren. The second time, he hadn't been able to see her.

He'd be damned if he was going to miss a moment of the third time.

She was soft and sweet and she gasped against him, eyes wide, when he lifted her in his arms without breaking the kiss and returned to the large leather chair where he'd been sitting earlier, watching her high above, trying not to catch a glimpse up her too-short skirts. Trying desperately to catch a glimpse. Trying not to notice her too much, unable to resist noticing her as he told her she was beautiful and she— Christ. She didn't believe him.

Suddenly, it was critical she believe him. He sat, gathering her in his lap, and broke the kiss. Sophie sighed her disappointment, and King stole another kiss. She matched him perfectly, following his lead, opening for him, sliding and stroking and proving that she wanted this as much as he did.

He wanted this with everything he had.

But there was something else. Something more important than what he wanted. He tore his lips from hers. "Sophie . . ."

She opened her eyes, their blue deeper and darker than it had been earlier in the evening. Changed by his touch. His kiss. *Him.*

She made him feel more powerful than he'd ever felt, no longer a title, a fortune, an heir. She made him feel more. He wasn't gong to make love to her. He couldn't. He wouldn't ruin her. She deserved a better man. A man who could love. A man who would marry her.

For once in his life, King would do the right thing.

For this woman who had done so many right things herself.

"You're so beautiful," he said, knowing the words revealed too much. That they were too reverent. He sounded like a schoolboy. He felt like one. She made him feel that way.

What was she doing to him?

She stiffened in his arms, pulling away from him, and he captured her, blocking her escape. "Where are you going, love? We're not done here."

She shook her head and pushed him away. "Stop."

He released her, and she stood. He captured her hand,

and she let him, despite keeping her head down, averting her gaze. "Sophie—" he started, wanting to say the right thing.

"I'm not one of the other women you've had. I'm not like them," she said.

"The other women?" He didn't like those words. Not at all.

She stared down at their hands, fingers entwined. "You needn't lie to me."

Except it hadn't been a lie. He didn't want to lie to her. He wanted her to hear the truth. "It's not—"

She sighed. "Stop. King. You think I do not hear the things they say about me? That the beauty ran out by the time I was born? That my sisters are the pretty ones? The pleasant ones? The talented ones?" She looked to him. "I'm not beautiful. You know it. You've said it before."

What an ass he'd been then. What a blind, horrid ass.

She continued. "You're kind to say so now, and I suppose I understand the impulse, but lying about it won't make me enjoy"—she waved one hand between them—"this more. In fact, it will make me enjoy it less." She released his hand. "It makes me enjoy it less."

He didn't know what to say. It wasn't an impulse designed to make her more likely to climb into his bed. It was the truth. He wanted to grab her by the shoulders and shake sense into her. He wanted to tell her again and again, until she believed him. Until she saw it herself. But it wasn't what she wanted.

And he wanted her to have everything she wanted. Forever.

Good God. *Forever.*

The word curled around him, settling strangely in his chest as he watched her, and he reached for her hand, taking it once more. She allowed it. "Look at me, Sophie."

She did, and he could see the wariness in her eyes.

One day, he'd have the head of the person who made her feel anything less than the beauty she was. "I'm not going to tell you you're beautiful."

Wariness turned to relief and something else that looked like sadness; there, then gone so quickly that he couldn't be sure.

He lifted her hand to his lips, pressing a kiss to her knuckles. "Let me be clear. That doesn't mean that I don't fully intend for you to leave Lyne Castle believing that you are quite beautiful."

She blushed and looked away.

"There will come a day when I tell you that and you don't look away."

She looked back. "You plan to do quick work, then?"

"Why quick?"

"I am leaving when my father arrives," she replied, and the words had more impact than he would have imagined. "You should be happy with that, frankly, as they'd have you at the altar faster than you could imagine if they knew our arrangement."

He didn't want her leaving. He wanted her here.

Forever.

Not forever. Forever was impossible. Forever with Sophie would mean love. She wouldn't be happy without it. Without all its bits and pieces. And love was not in his cards.

Not ever.

Not even with this woman, who somehow grew more perfect each day with her smart mouth and her smarter mind and her laugh that made him want to spend the rest of his life hearing it. More perfect, despite his being an utter ass around her.

"I've treated you abominably," he said.

She shook her head, and he pulled her back to his lap. "You saved my life," she said softly, letting him gather her close.

"I made you sad," he whispered at her temple, to the wisps of brown hair that had come loose there. *Sad* was such a simple, damaging word. It meant so much more than its elaborate cousins. He'd hurt her, and she'd soldiered through.

"I have been sad before, my lord. I will be sad again."

He hated that. "I wish I could take it all back."

She smiled. "You cannot. We are here. Your father and the staff believe we are betrothed, as does the entire population of Mossband. And that does not include the people strewn about the countryside who believe we are married. And named Matthew."

He'd made a hash of it, hadn't he?

"If you think on it," she continued, "if I *were* attempting to land you in the parson's noose, I've done a remarkable job of it."

He laughed at the old-fashioned phrase. "The parson's noose?"

"Very ominous."

"Not ominous," he said. "Simply not for me."

His words shifted the mood, and they both grew serious. He could see the question in her eyes, unspoken. *Why?*

Show me, she'd asked him earlier, when he'd told her she was too good for this place. And he ached to do just that. To tell someone why he was the man he was. To share his past.

He could tell her.

He could show her.

He tangled his fingers in hers, his thumb stroking across her soft skin, his gaze on a collection of little brown freckles that marked the base of her hand. "I left when I was eighteen."

𝒮he stilled in his lap, but did not speak. Did not rush him for fear that he would change his mind, and there was nothing in the world she wanted more in that moment than for him to continue.

He did. "I was home from school for the summer. Like any boy of my age, I hated being here in the quiet. I wanted to spend the summer drinking and—"

She smiled. "You don't need to hide what eighteen-year-old boys wish they were doing."

The dimple in his right cheek flashed. "What do you know about eighteen-year-old boys?"

"Enough to know that drinking isn't the worst thing you wished to do that summer."

"I was too old to fish in the river and while away the days."

She imagined him younger, leaner, his long body not quite what it was now, his face freer of the character it held now. Handsome, but nothing like he was now. The bones of the man he would become. Her smile widened as she settled into his arms. "I should like to have fished with you."

He looked at her, surprised. "I'll take you."

"Aren't you too old for it, now?" she teased.

He shook his head. "Now I'm old enough to know that whiling away the days is not such a horrible way to spend one's time." He paused. "Particularly with the right companion."

Did he refer to her? She'd like to fish with him. She'd like him to build a fire on the banks of the river and spend the evening telling her about his life as it grew dark around them.

She warmed at the impossible thought.

"She was a milkmaid," he said with a little disbeliev-ing laugh, lost in thought. "A *milkmaid.* As though we all lived in a painting by a Dutch master. Her father ran the dairy on the estate to the east, and she worked with the cows."

Sophie didn't laugh. "How old was she?"

"Sixteen."

"And how did you . . ."

She trailed off, but he knew her question. He brought her hand to his lips, kissing her knuckles, sending little shocking threads of pleasure through her. When he stopped, he held her hand to his mouth and answered, "One of the cows escaped. Ended up on Lyne land. She came looking for it." He paused, then said, quietly, "It was Shakespearean. She was the most beautiful thing I'd ever seen."

Sophie inhaled at the words. It was amazing how easy it was to believe them when it was so difficult to believe them when he spoke them about her. "What did she look like?"

"Blond, with perfect pink skin as smooth as cream," he replied, and Sophie could see the woman, young and doe-eyed. "The moment she looked up at me, dirt on her face, skirts muddy from her search, I wanted to protect her."

She believed that, as well, thinking back on his at-tacking the man who'd shot her, the way he immediately threw himself into the fray. "Did she require protect-ing?"

"It felt that way," he said, lost in the memory. "There was something precious about her. Something that felt nearly breakable." He met her gaze. "I wanted to marry her from the start."

She wasn't prepared for the hot thread of jealousy that

wove through her at the words. Nor was she prepared for the flood of questions that came on their heels. "And?"

"We spent the summer together, meeting in secret, hiding everything from our respective fathers. We passed messages through the stable boys, one in particular, whom I paid handsomely for his trouble. She was terrified her father would discover us." Sophie nodded, but did not speak. "Terrified enough that she began to beg me to marry her in secret. She wanted us to run, over the border, to find the nearest blacksmith and have an anvil marriage. Get it done." He stopped. "I should have."

"Why didn't you?"

"Because I didn't want it to be secret. When I took a wife, I wanted it to be in front of all the world. All of Britain. I'd make her a marchioness. She'd be a duchess. There was no shame in that, and I wouldn't allow us to be a scandal. I loved her."

"You'd make her your wife," Sophie said softly. The titles were nothing of import compared to that. Compared to the idea of living with him, as his partner, forever.

Forever.

Sophie's heart ached at the words, with sorrow for what she knew was to come, and with jealousy of this girl who had stolen his heart so long ago, making it impossible for Sophie to do it now.

Not that she had the skill to do it, anyway.

He laughed humorlessly. "Of course, I was young and stupid. And tilting at windmills."

Sophie could feel the frustration in him, in the stiffness of his chest and the quickness of his breath, in the way the cords of his neck stood prominently, revealing a clenched jaw, a grim mouth. She did the only thing she could think of—she set her palm to his face, her thumb stroking over his high, angled cheekbone.

For a moment it seemed like he didn't notice her touch, and then his eyes met hers, glittering green and so focused, and he lifted his hand to hold hers to him. He turned his face and pressed a kiss to her palm before he continued. "It was 1818 and the King was mad, and the Regent was drinking and gaming and throwing elaborate, scandalous parties, and the war was over, and it was time for my father to put away his stupid thoughts on title and blue blood, and accept that there was a place for love in the world."

Sophie couldn't help her little sad smile at the words, her heart in her throat. Of course there was a place for love in the world. But the aristocracy was a world far beyond normal, and there, milkmaids didn't become duchesses.

It was as though he heard her thoughts. "I was young and I'd never in my life been told no."

Her brows rose. "And the name to prove it."

He did laugh then, a little chuckle that reminded her that, however tragic the tale became, he was here now. Hale and healthy and hers.

Not hers.

Hers for now, she qualified. Hers for this moment.

"No one tells a King no."

Silence fell between them, and she grew cold, knowing instinctively that the tale was about to turn.

"I marched her in here, into that ridiculous dining room, my father at one end of that insanely massive table, Agnes serving her famed roast goose. I presented Lorna to my father like the petulant child I was. I can still feel the tremor in my voice. My heart beating in my chest."

Sophie's heart matched his. It had never occurred to her that he'd recreated the events tonight. That the entire experience had been designed to punish his father for not simply past sins, but past sins in that very room.

"I stood her in front of my father and I introduced her as my future bride."

Good Lord.

At least when he'd done it to Sophie, she'd been prepared for it to turn sour. But poor Lorna. That poor young girl who knew nothing better. Who had no doubt been quaking in her slippers at meeting the imposing duke Sophie had met earlier.

Sophie's hand flew to her chest, as though she could protect herself from the rest. "What happened?"

"He eviscerated her. I've never seen a man treat a woman so poorly, milkmaid or otherwise." King shook his head, his eyes unfocused, staring into the past. "He drove her away, insisting that he'd never approve, that she would never be a duchess, that she was cheap and scraping and willing to do anything to climb."

He has a knack for climbing, the duke had said earlier, about Sophie's father.

"Climbing is his worst sin."

"Unforgivable," King agreed. "A special place in hell for those who do it."

Sophie couldn't stop herself from returning him to the story. "So you left."

"I should have. I should have grabbed Lorna's hand and run. Immediately. Should have taken her across the border and done just what she wished. Gretna Green is *right there*," he said. "But I didn't. I took her home. I left her to sleep in her bed. I wanted a night to gather funds and prepare for a journey that would keep us away from Lyne Castle until my father was dead and I was duke. I needed a plan, and I was going to return to her in the morning with one."

She nodded. "That was sound logic."

He looked to her at the words, and she saw the sadness

in his gaze. The remorse. The regret. "It wasn't, though. I didn't think he'd go to her father."

Sophie's eyes went wide. "What happened?"

"The Duke of Lyne visited his first dairy that night. Told Lorna's father what had happened. Made it clear that if she set foot on Lyne land again, he'd see them both punished for trespassing."

Her mouth fell open. "What did her father do?"

King shook his head. "She arrived, gown torn, lip bleeding. She came to me, terrified." He paused. "Threw herself into my arms and begged me to save her. I can still feel her quaking. I packed her into a coach, her father on our heels. My father at his back, the greatest threat of all."

Dread pooled in Sophie's stomach as she began to see the way the story ended. She captured his hands in hers, clutching him tightly, wishing she could take away what he was about to say.

"I drove the coach. She was inside. It was dark and rainy and the roads . . ." He hesitated. "Well, after this week, you know the roads."

"King," she whispered, clutching his hand.

"I took a corner too fast."

She shook her head. "It wasn't your fault."

"The horses were unmatched. I'd hitched them too quickly, without enough care."

That was why he spent so much time checking the hitches on the carriage. "You were a child," she said, holding his hands tighter and tighter, until her knuckles were white.

It was his turn to shake his head. "I wasn't a child, though. I was eighteen, old enough to inherit an estate. To sit in Parliament. She relied on me. And I did the last thing in the world that would protect her."

She lifted his hands to her lips, raining kisses down

upon them. "No," she whispered between the caresses. "No. No. No."

"The coach toppled, bringing all of us down—the coach, the horses, me—into a ditch not a mile from here. I'm not even certain if we made it over the border." He shook his head. "I don't think we did."

"Were you—"

He looked to her. "I was fine. A few bruises. Nothing to speak of."

"And—" She couldn't say the name.

"She screamed," he said quietly, and she could tell that he was no longer here, in the library, but there, on the rainy road. "I could hear her as we flipped, but by the time we'd stopped, it was silent. She was silent. I climbed back, tore at the coach doors, but—" Sophie pressed a hand to her lips, tears coming as she imagined him screaming for the woman he loved. "—the way the coach fell, the doors were bent shut. There was no way in. She was stuck in there. I couldn't hear her. I broke a window, finally." He looked down at his knuckles, flexing his fingers, as though the wounds from the glass were still there.

Sophie had never heard anything so horrible in her life. Tears streamed down her face as she watched him, as he finished his story.

"She died inside the damn coach, at my hand."

No wonder he hated riding in coaches. "That's why you race the curricles," she said. "You pay your penance. You risk yourself."

He didn't reply to the words, instead saying, "I told you that my father killed her. As though he put a pistol to her head."

She nodded, not knowing what to say.

"It wasn't his hate that put the pistol to her head. It was my love."

She reached for him then, taking his handsome, shadowed face in her hands and turning him to face her, waiting until he met her gaze, until she was certain he was paying attention. "It was an accident."

"I shouldn't have—"

"You were a child, and you were doing what you thought best. What you thought right. You didn't kill her."

"I did." The confession devastated her, and suddenly she understood so much about him. She did the only thing she could think to do ease the ache in her heart. In his.

She drew his face to hers, and kissed him, at first soft and tentative, as though he might push her away at any moment, as though she was intruding. She lifted her lips once, twice, a third time before she deepened the caress, letting her tongue slide over his bottom lip, loving the way he inhaled at the sensation, his mouth opening, his hands coming around her.

And then he was kissing her back, taking and giving, stroking and sampling, groaning as he took over, turning what had begun as a tentative caress into a wicked, wonderful claiming. It was glorious.

He released her lips, pressing warm, wet kisses down the column of her neck as her fingers found purchase in his hair, guiding him to places she did not even know were kissable. He licked at the place where her neck met her shoulder, his hands coming around to the front of her dress, fast and furious, working at the laces there. There was nothing controlled about this moment, nothing thought out. His hands and lips tempted and touched and promised, sending shivers of pleasure through her without thought. Without hesitation.

It was sheer, unadulterated desire.

Desire for another person who understood.

Who did not judge.

Who wanted.

Sophie understood that better than anyone.

And then the laces on her dress were free, and her breasts were spilling into his palms, and his thumbs were sliding over the tips as he lifted them up and he stared down at them. "You're magnificent."

She believed him as he leaned down and sucked one rosy, pebbled tip into his mouth, working with lips and tongue around and around until she was squirming on his lap and he was lifting her to rearrange her until she was on her knees, above him, and he was worshipping her.

It felt like worship every time his tongue worked its slow orbit.

It felt like worship every time his fingers stroked across her skin.

It felt like worship when he opened his green eyes and stared up at her, as though she were his anchor in the storm.

She wanted to be that. Now.

Forever.

"Yes," she whispered.

He released her. "Yes what?"

"Yes anything. Whatever you want."

He blew a long, wonderful line of air over the place where she wanted him. "But what do you want, Sophie?"

She put her fingers in his hair, marveling at its softness. "I want your tongue." Later, she would be shocked and a little embarrassed by the words, ladies did not say *tongue*, she was sure. But now, she didn't care.

He groaned and gave it to her, long, lingering licks that threatened her sanity. "You are dangerous for me."

She smiled. "Dangerous how?"

His fingers slid into her hair, her pins scattering across

the chair, across the floor of the library, her curls falling down around them. He stared deep into her eyes. "You make me want . . ."

She lowered herself to his lap, feeling him hard and strong beneath her. He growled low in his throat, and power thrummed through her. "What do you want?" she asked, repeating his words, shocked at the sound of them on her lips, low and full of desire.

She was a different woman when she was with him.

He took her mouth again, in a deep, shattering kiss, and when he released her, they were both panting. "You make me want," he said simply. "Christ, Sophie. You make me want."

The words shattered her as much as the kiss had.

She nodded. "I want, as well."

Everything he could give her.

All the bits and pieces. Even if they were just bits and pieces. She would take them.

He closed his eyes. "Fuck." The curse came soft and shocking, and Sophie stilled as he sat up, his hands no longer lingering, no longer holding, now pulling her bodice up around her.

What had she done?

"King?" she asked, his hands at the laces of her gown, pulling them tight, making her panic. Had she done something wrong? "What's happened?" Once it was done and she was dressed, he lifted his eyes to hers, and she relaxed, recognizing the desire there, restrained, but clear as the North Country sky. "Why did you stop?"

"I'm sorry," he said, his voice low and dark and full of want.

"For stopping?" She stared down at him, more confused than she'd ever been in her life. "You don't owe me an apology."

"But I do. For all of it," he said. "For the things I've done and said to you. For bringing you here. For this."

"I was quite enjoying it."

He exhaled, the sound harsh in their close quarters. "That's the problem."

Her eyes widened. "It is?"

He stood, guiding her feet to the floor. "No. Of course I want you to enjoy it. But this . . ." He paused and cursed again, low and wicked in the quiet library. "Christ. I was enjoying it, too. Too much. I can't enjoy it, Sophie. I can't enjoy you. And you shouldn't enjoy me."

Too late.

Her brow furrowed. "Why not?" She cast about for a way to protect herself. "You promised you'd ruin me, didn't you? This is it, isn't it?"

He looked at her then, his green eyes glittering with anger and frustration and something near sorrow. And then he broke her heart.

"I've no intention of making love to you, Sophie. Not tonight. Not ever."

Chapter 17

KING ONCE, DUKE TO BE

He spent the next day roaming about the castle, half avoiding Sophie and half hoping he'd find her. Half hoping that seeing her might restore the incredible relief he'd felt once he'd told her the truth about Lorna and she hadn't run screaming from the room—a relief that had been consumed by guilt at her disappointment when he'd told her he wouldn't make love to her.

By afternoon, he'd found himself in the library once more, deep into the scotch, seated in the chair where he'd had her the night before, torturing himself with the memory of her exploring the massive room with exhilarating pleasure, eating her tart with the same. It occurred to him that he would think of her that way now, laughing with the servants, sighing over pasties, facing him in the dining room.

He'd think of her with passion.

She was all passion and strength and perfection, and stopping himself from taking her there, in that chair, on the floor, against the shelves of the library, again and again until neither of them remembered anything but each other, had been one of the hardest things he'd ever done.

But leaving her had been far more difficult.

And that terrified him.

As a gentleman, he should not have felt guilt. He did not ruin her, despite their idiotic agreement. That was the point of it, no? It was his role as a decent man to protect her virtue, was it not? But guilty he was, and it had nothing to do with not taking her to bed.

It had to do with the fact that he could not be what she wanted.

He could not give her the love she desired. The love she deserved. And the best thing in the world he could do for her at this point was to pack her back to the inn in Mossband and pretend as though they'd never met.

As though he would forget her.

He drank deep, guilt turning to frustration. What a damn fool he was to have brought Sophie here, to have introduced her to his demons. To have tempted them both with what could never be.

Because even if he did marry her—he could never love her.

He'd done that once. And look where it had landed him. Alone. Drunk. In the library.

"My lord?"

King turned his attention to the door, where Agnes stood. Agnes, who had been by his side from childhood, more mother than housekeeper, more friend than servant. She was the only person in the world who could look at him with such equal parts adoration and disdain. "Come in, Agnes," he said, waving a hand to the chair opposite. "Sit and tell me tales of the last decade."

She drew closer, but did not sit. "Are you drunk?"

He looked up at her. "I'm working on it."

She considered him for a long moment and then said, "Your father wishes to see you."

"I do not wish to see him."

"You don't have a choice, Aloysius."

"No one calls me that," he said.

"Well, I am most definitely not going to call you King," Agnes said, dry and certain. "I already have one of them."

"And a monarch in London, as well," King quipped.

"That's the drink talking, or I'd take a switch to you for rudeness."

He looked up into her pretty face. The years had been kind to her, despite the fact that he imagined his father was anything but. "I'm too old for switches, Nessie. And I'm well past the age where I mustn't disrespect the pater."

She narrowed her brown eyes on him. "You may disrespect your father all you like. I won't have you disrespecting me. Drunk or otherwise."

The words set him back. For a boy who had grown up without a mother, Agnes had been the best possible companion, always forthright, always caring, always there. She'd been young and pretty when King was a child, always willing to play. It had been Agnes who had shown King the secret nooks and crannies of the castle, always finding time for him. When King had broken his wrist after tripping down the castle stairs, it had been Agnes who had gathered him in her arms and promised him he would be well. And it had been Agnes who had always told King the truth, even when it made him feel like an ass.

Like now.

"I apologize."

The housekeeper nodded. "And while we're at it, why not try your hand at not disrespecting your future wife, either?"

It was too late for that.

"She's not my future wife."

Agnes raised a brow. "Has she come to her senses and left you, then?"

Somehow, she hadn't. But he was through keeping her here, against her wishes, forcing her to tell a story that she didn't want to tell. He was releasing her from their agreement as soon as possible. This afternoon. The moment he next saw her.

And she would leave him.

"She will," he replied, hating the words.

"You know that will be entirely your fault."

He nodded. "I know."

And he did. He'd drive her away, just as he did with every other woman who had ever shown a modicum of interest in him since Lorna. Except, all the other times, it had been easy . . . a smile, a stolen kiss, a promise that they'd find someone even better. More ideal. Perfect for them.

But he didn't want Sophie finding someone more perfect.

He wanted to be someone more perfect for her.

Except he didn't know how to be.

Goddammit.

"I hate this place."

"Why?"

He sighed, leaning his head back on the chair and closing his eyes. "Because it makes me feel like a child. It makes me feel like the child I was when I lived here, clinging to your skirts, uncertain of what to do next. The only difference is that now I could not care less about his opinion of my actions."

She watched him carefully. "I'm not certain that's true."

She was right, of course. He cared deeply about his father's opinion of his actions. He wanted him to loathe them. He stood, irritated by the revelation. "When I inherit, I'm razing the place and its memories." He moved to a low table nearby and filled his glass once more. "Lead on. Take me to the king of the castle, so I may receive my instructions and leave him in peace. If all goes well, we can have it out, and we'll never see each other again."

He would have left already, if not for Sophie.

"He is not the villain you think he is, you know."

He cut her a look. "With due respect, you are not his son."

"No," she said, "but I have run his house since you were born. I was here the night you left. I've been here all the nights since."

"Since he forced my hand and left me to kill the woman I loved."

Agnes stopped short. King had never said the words aloud, and in the last twenty-four hours, he'd said them twice. It was as though telling Sophie had unlocked something in him.

"What is it?" he asked.

She shook her head and began to move again. "I promised your father I'd fetch you."

"I am fetched, Agnes," he said. "I do not require escort."

"I think he is afraid you will leave if you are left to your own devices."

If not for Sophie, he would have already left.

"He isn't wrong. I only came to tell him that the line dies with me."

"You don't think that lovely girl will want children?"

Of course she would. And she'd make a wonderful mother.

But not to his children.

To someone else's children. Someone who loved her as she deserved, her and her damn bookshop stocked with texts no one but she would ever want. That would be his gift to her. The freedom to have that bookshop. To find that happiness. That love.

Just as it had been his gift to all the other women

whose marriages he'd stopped before they happened. The chance to find love.

The chance Lorna had never had.

Sophie would have it.

That he hated the idea of her in love with another man was irrelevant.

"You'll hear what he has to say before you leave," Agnes said, as though it were her bidding that would make him. "You owe it to me."

"For what?"

She looked to him then, and he realized that, though fifteen years had passed and she remained a beautiful woman, this place had aged her. "For all the years I've worried about you."

He was ever disappointing the women around him.

They were at the door to his father's study and as he stared at it, he remembered being a child and standing here, heart in his throat, worried about what the man on the other side would say.

There was none of that youthful trepidation in him now.

Agnes lifted her hand to knock, to announce their arrival.

King stayed her. "No."

He turned the handle, and stepped inside.

The Duke of Lyne was standing at the far end of the study, at the oriel windows that looked out on the vast estate lands. He turned at the sound of the door. His father was impeccably turned out in navy topcoat and buckskin, boots to the knee, and perfectly pressed cravat.

"One would think that you would eschew formal attire this far from London in both distance and time," King said.

The duke leveled him with a long, thorough, disdainful gaze. "One would think you would remember your manners in spite of the distance, and not turn up drunk in the middle of the day."

King did not wait to be told to sit, instead sprawling into a chair nearby, enjoying the way one of his father's grey brows rose in irritation. "I find that alcohol helps with my great distaste for this place."

"You didn't hate it when you were a child."

"I didn't see its truth."

"And what is that?"

King drank. "That it turns us into monsters."

The duke approached and sat in the chair opposite him. King considered his father, still tall and trim, the kind of man women would find handsome even as he aged. And he had aged in the last decade, the silver that had once been the purview of his temples now spread throughout all his hair, lines at his mouth and eyes that King had once heard referred to as signs of good humor.

It was humorous indeed to think of his father as the kind of man who was known for such a thing.

"You look well," the duke said. "Older."

King drank. "Why am I here?"

"It is time we speak."

"You sent word you were dying."

Lyne waved a hand. "We are all dying, are we not?"

King cut him a look. "Some of us not quickly enough."

The duke sat back in his chair. "I suppose you think I deserve that."

"I know you deserve more," King said. There was a pause, and he said, "I won't ask again, Your Grace. You either tell me why I've been summoned here or I leave, and the next time I see this place, I shall bear its name."

"I could follow you to London."

"I have avoided you for fifteen years, your grace. London is a very big city."

"It will be difficult for you to do so if I resume my role as duke."

"To do that, you'd have to take your seat in Parliament. I'm sure the rest of the House of Lords would be thrilled you were at last treating your title with respect." He considered his father. "In fact, for a man who so thoroughly respected the title that he went to such lengths to protect it from being damaged by bad blood, it is a shock that you have eschewed such an important duty. You've been in London, what, a half-dozen times in fifteen years?"

"I had my reasons for staying away."

"I'm sure they were excellent," King scoffed.

"Some better than others." The duke inhaled. "I should never have left you alone for so long."

King raised a brow. "Left me?"

The duke fisted his hands on his knees. "You were young and insolent and you knew nothing of the world. Every time I returned, you refused to see me. A single, petulant message. *The line ends with me.* I should never have allowed it."

"I enjoy the way you think you have *allowed* me to do anything I've done since the night you exiled me."

Lyne leveled him with a cool green gaze that King had used on countless others. He did not like being in its path. "I have allowed you everything. I filled your coffers with funds, I gave you horses, the Mayfair town house, the curricle you drove hell-for-leather for a year before you crashed it, the coach you never used."

King sat forward, loathing the way his father seemed to claim his successes for himself. "That money is now worth twelve times its original value. The house sits empty, right there on Park Lane, entailed to you. The horses are dead. And yes, the carriage is crashed. Just as the coach here was." He narrowed his gaze on his father.

"I lived by your hand until I could live by my own. And I have never asked you for another shilling. One would think you would not have kept such a ledger. One would have thought you would count those funds as penance for killing a girl so far beneath you that you thought her expendable."

"And so we get to it."

"So we do."

The duke sat back in his chair. "I was not the instrument of her death."

It was a strange phrasing, one that King imagined his father used to eschew his responsibility. "No, I was, and thank you very much for clarifying the situation as though I wasn't there."

"You weren't, either."

King held up a hand. "I carried the reins, Your Grace. I heard her scream. I was there when she fell silent. I held her in my arms."

"And that will be your cross to bear. All men have them."

King ran a hand through his hair, barely able to contain his fury and frustration. "*Why am I here?*"

"I offered her money," the duke said. "The milkmaid."

"To leave me." Lorna had never said so, but it was not an enormous surprise.

"I am not proud of it, but I had no other way of ensuring that she wasn't after your title. Your money. That she wasn't trying to climb."

King laughed at that. "I am supposed to believe that you were, what . . . making certain she loved me?"

The duke's gaze flickered over King's shoulder. "Believe it or not, it's the truth."

"It's bollocks and you know it. You've done nothing for your entire life but espouse the importance of blue blood and good name and strong breeding. If you offered her money, you did it to ensure she would leave me. I assume you offered her father the same."

The duke nodded. "I did."

"And he accepted. And she ran to me. Because she loved me. And money wasn't enough to end that."

"Neither accepted it," the duke said, "And money was not enough, you are right. You'd tempted them with something else. Something far more valuable. Something they thought they'd never get, and then . . . it seemed as though they might."

The words unsettled. She'd wanted to run away from the start. Across the border. Into Scotland. King had pushed her to marry in a church. In Britain. In front of all the world. She'd agreed. Hadn't she?

"She didn't tell you about the money," his father said, "because she knew that if she did, you'd come to me, angry. And I'd tell you the truth. She worried you'd believe it. So she told you something else."

King did not believe it.

He shook his head. "It's not true."

"It's true." The words came from the door, where Agnes had apparently stayed, sentinel.

"He even has you lying for him?" he said, betrayal hot and unpleasant in his chest.

"She's not lying," the duke said.

"Her father came to the castle after her death, Aloysius," Agnes said. "After you'd disappeared. He was destroyed. And he told the truth—that they'd been after a title from the start. Together."

King shook his head. "No. She was afraid of him. She told me her father was coming. That he'd kill her if he found her. That he was afraid of you."

"That man wasn't afraid of me," the duke said. "He

had visions of being a Boleyn. He spat in my face and
tore her gown. Backhanded her—and well. Split her lip.
And vowed to me that she'd be the next Marchioness of
Eversley by sunup."

King could still see the gown, torn at the neck. He
could see her lip, bleeding. He pushed memory aside. His
father lied. It was what he did.

"Why didn't you stop them?"

"I went to Rivendel." The neighboring earl, master of
the estate where Lorna and her father lived. The duke
laughed at his stupidity. "I actually thought he would be
able to help. But your girl and her father had been promised a dukedom. And they were willing to risk all. By
the time I returned home, you were gone. With her. And
the coach." The duke paused. "That's when I learned that
against human will, the aristocracy had no power."

King's mind reeled with the images of that night,
burned into his memory. Her tears, her begs, her eyes
filled with fear. Those eyes. She'd have to be the best ac-
tress in Britain. *Or want something badly enough to do
anything.*

But the idea that she'd lied—that everything he'd
thought about that summer, that girl, the life they could
have had, was imagined—it was devastating. And impossible to believe. It did not matter that the doubt was there
now, seeded. Growing. What if the only love he'd ever
believed was a lie?

What if the darkest pain he'd ever felt was the product
of betrayal instead of love?

Who was he if not the man made by that night?

King stood, desperate to leave the room. To be rid of
his father. To be rid of Agnes, whom he'd never thought
would betray him. He leveled his accusation at her.
"You're both lying to me."

"Call her a liar again, and you will no longer be welcome in this house," the duke said, cold fury in his tone. "I will take your insults, but Agnes has been nothing but your champion since the day you were born, and you will not speak ill of her."

At another time, the anger in his father's words would have shocked him, but King hadn't the patience for it now. He rounded on the duke. "This changes nothing. This place still made monsters of us both. The line will end with me, as I have always promised."

"And the wife you presented to me? What of her desires?"

Sophie.

"Don't tell me you believe she loves me. She's a Dangerous Daughter."

The duke's gaze did not waver. "After witnessing last night, I think the girl might well care for you. Your milkmaid would never have left you the way the Talbot girl did."

Perfect, untouched Sophie, who wanted a home full of happiness and honesty. Sophie, whom he would return to the life she desired as soon as possible. King hated the thought of her here, in this place, with this man and his revelations.

There had been a time when he'd believed in love. When he'd desired it. But he'd lost the only thing he ever loved, and now even that truth was clouded with lies. "Then her desires shall suffer along with mine."

There was only one thing he could ensure remained true.

This place. This line. It ended with him.

Even if it meant leaving Sophie.

Even if leaving Sophie had somehow become the last thing in the world he wanted to do.

His jaw clenched with anger and disbelief and something far more complicated. "Why am I here?" he asked a final time, the words harsh and unpleasant on his tongue.

"You're my son," the duke said, simply, something in his eyes that King did not wish to identify. "You're my son, and there was a time when you were my joy. You deserve to know the truth. And more than that, you deserve to know happiness." The duke paused, looking older. "Pride be damned."

The words were the worst kind of blow, and King responded the only way he could. He left the room without a word, going to the only place he could think of to find solace. The labyrinth.

Anger and frustration propelled him through the complex maze, every turn bringing back another memory of his youth, of his mistakes. Of the past he'd been escaping for a dozen years. He followed the path without hesitation, the memory of the route to the center innate. He was Theseus, headed for the Minotaur, the battle already raging in his mind and heart.

But at the center of the labyrinth, he did not find a monster.

He found Sophie.

The Lyne labyrinth was as magnificent as she remembered.

Sophie sat on the edge of the extravagant marble fountain at the heart of the maze, book forgotten in her lap, shoring up her courage to leave the estate.

She'd spent much of the day exploring its twists and turns, the search for the fountain at the center occupying her thoughts just enough to keep her from going mad thinking of King. Of course, she thought plenty of King, of his childhood here, in what he'd confessed was his favorite place on the estate. Of the things he must have avoided when he was hidden away inside this labyrinth.

As one who was avoiding things herself, she could attest to the benefits of this particular location.

He'd escorted her to her bedchamber the previous evening, separated from his own by a wall and an adjoining door, and she'd kept herself from protesting his decision to leave her untouched. She had been masterful at hiding her emotions from him, if she were to offer her own opinion on the matter.

Of course, once her bedchamber door was shut and the candles beside the bed were snuffed, she'd let the tears come, along with the desire—not just for his touch and his words, but for the rest. The story he'd told, the love he'd had for Lorna—she ached for him, and for the girl he'd lost.

And then she'd ached for herself.

She'd ached at the unbearable knowledge that she wanted him. That she wanted his confessions and his desires and his truth. And it didn't matter. Because she could want him forever, and he would never risk his heart again.

So it was best that she was here, inside this complicated maze, invisible to the world. Here, she could find courage to ignore what she felt for him. And to leave, head high, and find herself another life.

But never another man.

She knew that now. There was no other man for Sophie Talbot, youngest daughter of a North Country coal miner, than the Marquess of Eversley. And the Marquess of Eversley was not for her.

So she was leaving.

Just as soon as she found him, she'd tell him as much.

She dangled her fingers in the cool water, staring up

at the magnificent marble battle at the center of the fountain. The Minotaur, head-to-head with Theseus, water cascading around them as they battled hand-to-hand, each as strong as the other. There was something in the fine detail of the sculpture that made her feel for the monster in battle—he'd been a pawn in another's game, born a monster as punishment to his mother. It didn't seem fair that his whole life had been spent in solitude, even if the labyrinth of myth was as beautiful as this one.

"You remembered the way in."

She snatched her hand from the water. He'd found her, first.

Her breath quickened at the words, and she turned to face King at the entrance to her secret hideaway. "I was—"

"Hiding from me."

She smiled, hating the ache that came at the sight of him. Even with the shadow of an afternoon beard, with his hair in a state of disarray, in shirtsleeves, rolled to the elbow, he unsettled her. Perhaps those things unsettled her more, giving her a taste of the man he was outside of London's view. Of the man she might have had, at another time, in another place.

She looked away, back to the water. "More from the idea of you than from the actuality of you, if that helps."

His lips lifted in a small smile. "They are different?"

"The idea of you is much more unsettling."

"That's a pity," he said. "I should like to be unsettling in person."

Except he was terribly unsettling. Indeed, if he were any more unsettling, she'd have run screaming from this place. As it was, she stood, drying her hand on her skirts. "If you are here to hide from me, my lord, I am happy to leave you in peace."

She was surprised when, for a moment, he appeared

to consider the offer. Surprised, and somewhat affronted. After all, it was he who had insulted her, was it not? It was he who'd made it clear that they were never meant to be. So why would she be the one who left?

She'd been here first, had she not?

She did not imagine that he subscribed to the rules of siblings.

But he seemed to change his mind. "Stay," he said, quietly. "Stay, and keep me company."

Something in the soft words had her sitting, turning to him, wishing she were closer. Wishing she could see the glittering green of his gaze. That she could read the emotions there.

And then he added, a soft, unbearable "Please."

Something had happened.

"My lord," she said, "is all well?"

He ignored the question and sat on a low stone bench a few yards away, facing her and the fountain, stretching his long legs out and crossing them at the ankle as he crossed his arms over his chest, revealing wide bronzed forearms that she had difficulty ignoring. He lifted his chin, nodding at her lap. "Still reading about henges?"

It took a moment for her to remember that she was holding a book. She clutched it more tightly and said with a forced smile, "Do you care for another reading?"

He didn't return the expression. "Believe it or not, not even henges could capture my attention at this moment."

She looked down at her book. "It's not about henges."

"What is it?"

She couldn't remember. She looked down. "It's the Greek myths."

"Is it interesting?"

"It's filled with rakes and cads and every sort of scoundrel."

"Sounds fascinating."

"If you enjoy ruiners of women."

"And do you?"

Yes.

She paused, considering the question. Its answer. She met his gaze. "Well, I like you."

"I thought we did not like each other?"

She shook her head. "I find that I've changed my mind." He stood then, moving toward her, and she finished. "Even though I shouldn't."

He sat next to her on the edge of the fountain, raising a hand and tucking one long lock behind her ear. "You shouldn't," he agreed softly. "I won't ruin you, Sophie."

"That was the arrangement," she said.

"So we have both reneged."

"You take excellent care of me," she replied, and his brow furrowed in confusion before she clarified. "Something nice about you," she said. "As agreed. I have not reneged."

He closed his eyes for a long moment. When he opened them, they glittered brilliant green. "I still renege. I won't destroy your reputation."

Her brow furrowed. "Why not? You don't hesitate with the others." He paused, and she pressed him. "You didn't hesitate with Marcella." Something bothered her about his silence, something that had bothered her that afternoon at the Liverpool soiree. Marcella waving happily from the window above, as though she were perfectly satisfied with King leaving her to pick up the pieces of her ruination.

"You don't ruin them, do you?"

He raised a brow. "Why would you think that?"

She was flooded with memories. "Because I saw Marcella's face when you left. When she looked out the window and thanked you."

He looked down to the water, dragging his fingers across the surface. "Perhaps she enjoyed our tryst."

Sophie's gaze narrowed. "I don't think so."

"Well. That's a bit hurtful."

She ignored the attempt to dodge the point. "I don't think there was a tryst. Was there?"

He inclined his head. "There was not."

Her brow furrowed. "Then why the mad escape? Why enrage the earl?" She paused, realization dawning. "I see. Marcella will marry another."

He nodded. "The owner of Hoff and Chawton menswear, if I recall. He's promised me cravats any time I require them."

"Marcella's father won't be able to argue the match."

"I imagine he'll be grateful for someone to happily marry his daughter. And Mr. Hoff is very wealthy."

Sophie laughed. "You gave her the marriage she'd never have been able to have."

"She swore it was a love match."

"And the others?" Sophie asked. "Did they vow love matches as well?"

"Every one."

She thought back on the other women, the ones she'd envied during their discussion in the carriage. "You ruin them so they can be happy."

She would be happy, ruined by him.

"I give them the push they require."

"I should have seen it," she said. "If there was something between you, they wouldn't have—" She stopped. She couldn't tell him that.

"Wouldn't have been what?"

"Nothing."

"Oh, no, Lady Sophie," he said. "It was just becoming interesting."

She exhaled sharply, tired of lying. So she told him the truth. "If there were something between you, they wouldn't have been so quick to tell you good-bye." He stilled at the words. "Marcella wouldn't have been able to do it so easily." He lifted his hand from the fountain, touching her cheek with his cool, wet fingertips. She closed her eyes at the sensation. "It's very difficult to tell you good-bye," she whispered.

Silence fell for a yawning stretch of time before he said, quietly, "Is that what you want? To tell me good-bye?"

No.

Never.

King looked to the statue behind them. "What do you know about the Minotaur?"

The question set her back. She followed his gaze to the beautiful stretch of marble—a naked man with the head of a bull. "I know he was trapped in the labyrinth."

"He was kept at the center of an impossible labyrinth, the solution to which was known only by one person."

"Ariadne," she said.

He raised a brow.

She blushed. "I know some of it."

He took her hand in his, turning it so her palm was open to the air. He dipped a finger into the water and painted the center of her hand with cool drops, the sensations thrumming through her with visceral pleasure. "As the only one who knew the secrets to the labyrinth, Ariadne was tasked with leading the virgin sacrifices to the Minotaur each year to keep the gods happy."

"That sounds like a terrible task," Sophie said.

"Her father gave it to her because she was too precious for anything else," King said, tracing the lines on her palm as though learning her own secret labyrinth. "Making her so essential to the process kept her close to home. It had the added bonus of convincing her that she was not worthy of what was beyond the maze walls."

Sophie raised a brow. "And was she? Worthy?"

He leveled her with his green gaze. "More than she could ever know. Beautiful beyond imagination, brilliant, and kind." Her breath caught at the words as he continued. "The Minotaur never attacked her. It was said that he loved her."

He was not talking about her. She was going mad. Sophie cleared her throat. "Alternatively, he was intelligent enough to know that she was his line to dinner."

One dark brow rose. "Are you going to let me tell you the story? Or make jokes?"

She put a hand to her breast. "My apologies, my lord. Of course. Do go on."

"On the third year, as the sacrifice approached, Theseus came to the labyrinth."

She looked up at the statue. "It seems as though he'll be trouble."

"He vowed to slay the Minotaur, and Ariadne agreed to help him navigate the maze."

She snatched her hand back from him, the swirling touch unsettling. "That seems rather cruel, considering the Minotaur's feelings."

"Love makes us do strange things."

She knew that better than anyone. "She'd fallen in love with Theseus?" At King's nod, Sophie added, "He was most definitely trouble. The worst kind."

King continued with the story. "Ariadne led her love to the center of the maze, where he and the Minotaur fought."

"For their lives," she offered.

"You see? You're not paying close enough attention. Theseus fought for his life," He shook his head. "But the Minotaur, he fought for Ariadne."

At the words, Sophie went still, her gaze finding King's, watching as he continued. "He fought to be with her in that world he could not escape, willing to take the years of solitude if it meant that he could see her, however fleetingly. She was the reason he lived; and if he could not have her, he did not care if he died. She was the only person in the world who understood him." Sophie's breath came faster and faster, and she leaned forward, listening intently. "The only person he'd ever loved."

"How tragic," she whispered.

"But Theseus didn't have a lock on the fight—the Minotaur was stronger than ten men," King said, watching her intently. "Theseus had brought the sword of Aegeus with him, the only weapon that could kill the Minotaur, but he lost it mid-fight." He pointed to the feet of the statue and Sophie looked to find a sword discarded there, in marble. "The Minotaur would have won, if not for Ariadne. She entered the fray and returned the fallen sword to Theseus."

Sophie shook her head. "The poor beast."

"Betrayed," King said, the word rough on his tongue. "By the woman he loved. It's said that when he saw her choose Theseus, he laid himself down and submitted to the blow." He paused. "Though I always thought the blow of the sword could not possibly have been as bad as the blow Ariadne dealt."

She shook her head, tears on her cheeks. "What a terrible story."

He reached up and brushed away her tears. "Death was likely the best outcome—he'd never have been free of the labyrinth, anyway." There was a long, silent moment before he let her go. "Suffice to say, I have always been partial to the Minotaur."

Knowing she shouldn't, knowing it was a mistake, she reached for him, putting her hand on his warm arm, willing him to look at her. When he didn't, she came to stand directly in front of him, her skirts brushing against his knees. He did not look up, his gaze locked on her body, staring through it, at the tale he told. At something else.

"King," she whispered, and he met her gaze, the sadness in his eyes overwhelming her. Without hesitation, she put one hand to his dark hair, loving the feel of it, silk between her fingers. "What has happened?"

He closed his eyes at the question, then did the unthinkable, putting his hands to her waist and pulling her closer, pressing his face into her midriff and inhaling, holding her as tight to him as he could.

Her free hand joined the first, fingers threading through his hair, holding him as well, wanting him, wanting to hear everything he thought, wanting to tell him everything she felt.

She should tell him she wanted to leave.

Except here, in this moment, with his hands on her and his breath against her, she didn't want to leave. She wanted to stay forever.

"King," she whispered.

He shook his head at his name. "I want you quite desperately, Sophie."

Her heart stopped at the words. "You do?"

He looked up at her, handsome and devastating. "I do," he said. "I've wanted you from the start, you know. From the moment I nearly hit you in the head with a boot."

She smiled, small and sad. "No, you didn't."

He tilted his head. "Maybe not just then. But definitely

by the time I found you drinking with Warnick in the stables."

"In your footman's livery?"

"Ah," he said. "So you admit he is *my* footman."

"Never." She laughed, loving the feel of him. Loving the look of him.

Loving him.

She took a deep breath. "King, what—"

"She didn't love me," he said softly.

Her brow furrowed. "Who?"

"Lorna. She wanted the title and nothing else."

She couldn't believe it, not after the way he'd spoken about her. "How do you know that?"

"Because I do." He released her and stood putting distance between them. "The line ends with me," he whispered, and she ached at the words even as he continued. "It was so much more than revenge. It was penance. I swore off marriage because I couldn't bear the thought of betraying the girl I'd once loved." Sophie ached at the words, tears threatening as he continued, devastating betrayal in his tone. "But now . . . she wanted to marry me for money. For title. For security. She lied to me."

He turned away from Sophie, making his way to the labyrinth's path. He turned back before he entered the maze and looked at her for a long while, anger and frustration and disappointment in his gaze. "I thought she was the only person who had ever wanted me for me. And now I know the truth. She wanted me for my title and my fortune. Not for me. There's never been anyone who wanted me."

Sophie did not hesitate, a desperate need for him to hear the truth propelling her closer to him. "That's not true." She wanted him. Desperately.

He understood, his gaze turning predatorial. He, the hunter. She, the prey. And then he said, "I can't love you."

A single tear slipped down her cheek as she nodded. "I know."

"I don't want you to leave. I want you to stay here. I want to keep you here, at the center of this labyrinth. Even though it's the worst possible thing I can think to do to you."

"I don't think I can survive your betrayal."

He came to her then, quick and purposeful, lifting her face to his, staring deep into her eyes. "I don't want you to go," he said. "I want you to stay."

"And what happens if I do? What is my life if I stay?" Her throat ached with the words. Because she knew the answer. She knew he'd never be able to give her what she wanted. What she'd always wanted and somehow had never realized she wanted.

He would never love her. He would never marry her. They would never have children, despite her ability to see them quite clearly, little dark-haired cherubs, with his beautiful green eyes and dimples that showed when they smiled.

He didn't ask her what she saw. What she wanted. He already knew. "Sophie . . ." he started, and she heard the knowledge. Heard the denial. She didn't want to hear the words.

Instead, she reached for him, her fingers trailing down his cheek, drawing him closer to her. "Tomorrow," she whispered, so close to his lips that it felt as though he had spoken instead. "What if we return to the world tomorrow?"

"Yes," he replied, the word somehow a vow and a

prayer and a curse all at once. "Yes," he said again. "To-morrow."

And then he lifted her in his arms and carried her back to the fountain.

And she knew, this place, this man—he would always be home.

Chapter 18

LYNE LABYRINTH LOVERS!

*H*e knew it was a mistake, that he was the worst kind of scoundrel, taking what she offered. He didn't deserve her. And she deserved infinitely better.

But the knowledge didn't stop him.

Instead, it pushed him forward, the knowing that he shouldn't touch her. The wanting her in spite of his keen awareness that he couldn't have her. His path had been set out for him, a long, straight road without room for diversion. No place for the emotions she tempted, no place for the beauty she brought with her, for the promises she made.

She called to him from beyond his labyrinth, tempting him with the promise of something more, making him forget—almost—what his life was to be.

What is my life if I stay?

The question had been rhetorical when she'd asked it; she'd known the truth, that he couldn't give her what she wished.

He couldn't give her love.

And Sophie would want love. She'd want it pure and unfettered, given freely, along with all its trappings. She'd want the marriage and children and happiness and promise that came with it.

He could see it, the life she wanted. The line of little girls, blue-eyed and brown-haired, in love with books and strawberry tarts. For a moment, he imagined them smiling at him the way their mother did, filled with happiness and hope.

For a moment, he let himself believe he might be able to give it to her.

But she would want love, and he would never be able to give it.

He didn't have it to give anymore. And those children, they would never be his.

He set her down on the edge of the fountain, coming to his knees, as though she was Ariadne and he the Minotaur, worshipping at her feet, adoring her even as he knew she could not survive in the labyrinth, and he could not survive beyond it.

"Tell me about last night," he said softly, looking up at her, his hands at the hem of her skirts.

"What—" She caught her breath as his fingers explored the skin of her ankles. "What about it?"

"I hated it," he said. "I hated stopping."

She pressed her lips into a thin, straight line. "I hated that you stopped."

His hands were beneath her skirts, pushing them back, farther and farther, up and over her knees. He pressed his lips to the inside of her knee, swirling his tongue there, loving the little gasp of surprised pleasure that came at the touch. "I hate that I will have to stop today, as well," he whispered at her skin.

One of her hands came to his head, fingers threading into his hair as he began to kiss over her thighs, pushing her skirts higher, bunching the fabric on her lap as he bent over her, pressing long, hot kisses to soft, undiscovered skin—skin no one but he had ever touched. "King." She sighed. "I won't stop you."

He closed his eyes at the words even as he pressed her thighs apart, making room for himself between them. He pressed a long, lingering kiss to the soft skin of her inner thigh, drawing a little cry from her as her fingers clenched in his hair and held him to her.

She was perfect.

He smiled against her skin, scraping his teeth there at that private, untouched place. "You won't stop me from kissing you here?"

She opened her thighs wider, gloriously. "No," she whispered.

He stroked higher with one hand, his fingers finding soft curls that he'd touched before but never seen. "Wider," he said, and the word came like a demand. "I want you open to this place."

She did as she was told, opening herself to his touch and his gaze, and he sat back on his heels, unable to stop himself from marveling at her, perfect and pink and his for the taking.

His, full stop.

He looked up at her, loving the flames in her cheeks—loving that even embarrassment was not enough to keep her from him. "Wider," he said, letting the demand curl between them.

Damned if she didn't obey, making his mouth water.

"Christ," he whispered, reaching for her, running his fingers softly through those curls until they found the wet heat of her. "You're the most beautiful thing I've ever seen."

She looked away. "It's not true."

He hated that she didn't believe him.

"I know I said I wouldn't tell you that. I know I said I would do as you asked, and find another way to compliment you, but I can't." He came up on his knees again, reaching for her, lifting her gaze to his. "You are beautiful, Sophie. More beautiful than you can imagine."

Before she could deny it, he took her mouth in a long, wicked kiss, as though they had an eternity to explore each other. As though time did not pass in the labyrinth. And it was an exploration, a long, lingering journey of tongue and teeth and lips, of sighs and cries and growls that promised more than they could ever deliver.

Because he would not ruin her.

If it killed him, he would not ruin her.

He broke the kiss and ran his lips over her cheek, finding the soft skin beneath her ear, where he lingered before saying, "It's true."

She sighed, but he could tell she did not believe him. "I want you naked here, in this place, on this grass open to nothing but the sun and the sky and this statue and my mouth. I want to explore every inch of you, and learn the sounds you make when you come, hard and fast and yes, love, beautiful."

He sucked on the lobe of one ear, long and lingering until she groaned her pleasure, her hands stroking across his chest, down his torso. "King," she whispered.

He grasped one of her hands and guided it to where he strained, hard and desperate, against the fabric of his trousers. "Feel what you do to me," he whispered. "You make me ache for you. You make me want to lay you down and take you until there is nothing left but us and the labyrinth."

Her eager fingers explored. "Yes," she said without hesitation, flattening her palm against him and making him want to show her precisely how to make him wild.

Instead, he shook his head and pulled her away from him. "No. I won't ruin you, Sophie."

Her brow furrowed. "But . . ."

"This is not for me, love. This is for you."

She shook her head. "I want it to be for us both."

He couldn't let it be for them both. If he did, he might never let her leave.

Hating the thought, King returned his touch to her core, parting the folds there, baring her to the sun and air, loving her heat, her softness, her scent. "You're so wet," he marveled, dipping a single finger inside her, adoring the way she responded, rocking toward him, eager for more of him. And he was so eager to give her more.

"I can't," he said. "I can't not taste you."

He pressed her thighs wide and leaned in, painting her pretty pink center with his tongue, adoring the feel of her against him, the way she sighed and moved and guided him without even knowing what she did. He lifted his lips from her and blew a long stream of air directly on the center of her, adoring her cry of pleasure.

Her fingers slid into his hair, clutching him close, pressing him to the open, aching center of her, using him as he tasted her again and again, losing himself in her. He licked and sucked and stroked with tongue and fingers until she rocked against him, her breath coming faster and faster, her hips working to find that magnificent purchase that would give her release.

And just before she found it, he stopped, lifting his mouth from her, knowing he was the worst kind of ass when she cried his name in frustration. He pressed his lips to the silk of her inner thigh once, twice, as she settled before looking up at her, finding her blue eyes glittering with desire and something more primitive. Something like need.

"Poor love," he said, the taste of her on his lips, teasing him as much as the feel of his words against the hot center of her teased her.

"King," she groaned. "What are you doing?"

"I want you to talk."

Her eyes went wide. "Talk?"

"I want you to tell me all the things you desire."

"I desire . . ."

"What?"

She shook her head. "I can't."

He leaned in and licked, long and slow, and she sighed her pleasure. "Please."

He lingered over the place where she strained for his touch. "I like it when you beg, love. What more do you desire?"

"*That.*"

He blew a long stream of air across her aching skin. "What, precisely?"

"Don't make me say it," she said.

"Why?" he teased. "Because ladies don't say such things?"

She laughed at that, a little huff of air that made him adore her even more. "Ladies most definitely do not say such things."

"Try."

"I desire—" For a long moment, he thought she might not say anything, even as he hovered there, a hairsbreadth from where she wanted him. From where he wanted to be. And then she did speak, and in four words, she destroyed him. "I desire your pleasure."

He pulled back, meeting her gaze at the words, seeing the truth there. He couldn't find the words to speak.

She reached for him, lifting his face to hers. "Whatever you want, King. I want it, as well." She pressed her lips to his, long and lingering, before lifting her head and saying, "Don't you see? My pleasure is yours. I am yours."

And that was it.

The kiss they shared then was nothing short of a claiming, wicked and full of promise. "You're mine," he said, as though her words had unlocked him, and perhaps they had. They'd certainly threatened his control. His desire. His need. "You're mine," he repeated, taking her mouth even as she took his. "You're mine."

"Yours," she whispered as he released her lips and returned his attention to the core of her.

"You gave yourself to me," he whispered, desperate for her.

Her fingers guided him to her. "I did," she whispered. "I am yours."

And then his mouth was on her, his tongue working at her, and he was pouring everything into the caress— desire and need and frustration and adoration and yes, anger. Anger that he couldn't have her like this forever, here, open to him. Anger that he hadn't met her years earlier. Anger that her love was not enough to heal him now.

He kissed her again and again, making wild love to her with his mouth, wanting to reward her for her honesty and punish her for it, as well—for the way she seemed to know that what he wanted was in concert with her own desire. For the way she used him.

For the way he loved it.

His tongue and fingers played over her and she cried out gloriously to the fountain and the labyrinth and the sun and the sky, first his name, and then a single word, again and again, like a litany and a weapon, at once blessing him and destroying him.

"Yours."

His.

He gave her no purchase, remaining there at the throbbing, aching place where she wanted him most, making love to her until she came apart, crying her pleasure on that one word.

Yours.

He stayed with her until she returned to earth, to the labyrinth, Ariadne to his Minotaur, somehow able to destroy him with her touch.

Yours.

He would hear that word, spoken in her voice, for the rest of his life.

Yours.

Truth and utter lie all at once.

She couldn't be his, of course. She couldn't be his, because it would require him to be hers. It would require him to love her the way she deserved. And that would never happen. It was impossible.

He lifted his head to tell her so, finding her sleepy, sated smile above him, tempting him more than he could ever imagine. And then she spoke, shattering his intentions. "What of your pleasure?" she said, the soft words a blow as hard and harsh as anything he'd ever received in the boxing ring. A blow he'd never wanted so much in his life. "Don't you wish to take it?"

He did, of course. Rather more desperately than he ever had. But he couldn't. *He wouldn't.*

She deserved better.

"No," he lied, working hard to keep his words calm and collected, hating himself for saying them. "I don't."

If she'd had all the money in Britain, Sophie would have wagered it on his laying her down and taking her there, at the base of the fountain, with only the Cumbria sky to witness it.

She would have lost the wager.

The disappointment that rioted through her was to be expected, of course. She'd been hoping he would agree to make love to her fully, and his refusal was no kind of positive experience. She'd found a magnificent pleasure in his arms, and she wanted more. She wanted to share it with him.

What she had not expected was the desolation. The sense that without him, she was alone in the world. That without his touch, without his companionship, she might not survive the day.

The sense that without him, she might not exist.

The thought terrified her.

She had not planned for this moment. Ever. She'd never planned to want someone so much, or to wish that her future entwined with his, or to wish to see his face every day, for the rest of time.

She'd planned to be happy, yes. To marry, to have a family, to live a quiet, peaceful life. But she'd never planned to want someone so much that his refusal actually pained her.

She'd never planned for a single, inaccessible path to be the only one she could imagine having.

She'd never planned to love.

Vaguely, it occurred to her that other people found love to be a pleasurable experience, filled with roses and doves and sweets and whatever else. Those people were obviously cabbageheads. Because she loved the Marquess of Eversley quite desperately, and there wasn't anything remotely pleasurable about it.

She cleared her throat and straightened, pushing her skirts down her legs, trapping his hands beneath them for one excruciating moment as she tried to escape his touch. "I see."

His fingers trailed along her ankle and she shot to her feet at the sensation, the touch breaking something inside her, making her at once wish to leap into the fountain to wash it from her and toss herself into his arms and beg him to continue. She did neither, thankfully, stepping away from him as though the events of the afternoon were perfectly ordinary. As though she weren't rushing to protect herself from the pain he seemed to be able to exact without so much as a thought. "I see," she said again, hating the repetition. Willing herself to remain silent.

She backed away from him. Why was he still kneeling on the ground? Why wasn't he on his feet? Why was he still here?

Why hadn't the statue of the Minotaur sprung to life and gobbled them both up?

He rose, spreading his hands wide and coming toward her. She put one hand up. Oh, dear. He on his feet was worse by far. "Sophie, let me explain."

Dear God. The very last thing she wanted him to do was explain why he did not wish to make love to her. She backed away from him, eyeing the exit to the maze, beyond his shoulder.

And then he was close enough to block it from her view, forcing her to consider that shoulder in entirety. That broad, beautiful shoulder.

Enough, she admonished herself. Normal women do not care about gentlemen's shoulders.

Normal women were in the wrong.

"Sophie, I won't ruin you," he said, approaching, giving her nowhere to go but backward.

"I see," she said, fairly tripping over herself to get away from him. "I see."

Good Lord. Could she say nothing else?

"I don't think you do see," he said. "You don't see that you deserve more." Her back came up against the hedge, prickly and uncomfortable and damn inconvenient. And still he drew closer. Close enough to raise his hand and tuck a lock of her hair behind her ear and make her quite desperate for him when he spoke, soft and lovely. "You don't see that you deserve someone who will marry you."

She closed her eyes at the words, as though if she couldn't see him, he hadn't said them. She'd known he wouldn't marry her. She wasn't a fool. But still, the words smarted.

He didn't have to point it out. Did he?

"I see," she said.

Apparently, that was all she would ever say again. Excellent. He'd turned her into an imbecile.

He swore roundly, making her wish that she'd been left with a fouler phrase than the one she seemed doomed to repeat for eternity. "Christ, Sophie. Stop saying that. You deserve someone who can love you."

She had to leave this labyrinth. This estate. This man. Now.

Before she said, "I see" one more time.

Or worse, before she couldn't even say that anymore.

She nodded, crossing her arms, and pushed past him, heading for the path of the maze without a word. At another time, she might have been proud of her straight shoulders and purposeful walk. At this time, however, she couldn't see past the tears to think about such trivial matters as posture.

He swore again, this time at her back.

She stopped, but did not turn back. She couldn't. Not without risking telling him everything and making a wretched fool of herself. So she gathered the last shred of her pride and said, "I should like to return to Mossband."

There was a long pause before he spoke. "When?"

"As soon as possible," she said.

He nodded. "We shall purchase your bookshop tomorrow. I'll connect you with my father's solicitor. You'll have all the money you require to live happily here."

She didn't care about the bookshop. She didn't care about Mossband. Indeed, Mossband was absolutely not her future. She couldn't be so near to this place and its memories. She couldn't be so near to him. She took a deep breath. "I don't think I can wait until tomorrow."

"Sophie," he said softly, closer than she would like, and she hated the sound of her name on his lips. "Look at me."

She turned to face him, unable to deny him. He was the most beautiful thing she'd ever seen, his dark hair and his green eyes and his lips, firm and magnificent. He was far too beautiful for her. Far too perfect.

She swallowed around the thought. "I must leave. Now," she said. "Today."

He watched her for a long moment, and she thought he might kiss her again. She wanted him to kiss her again. She loathed the idea of him kissing her again.

Instead, he reached out, offering her his hand, warm and bronzed from the sun.

She stared at that hand for a long moment, unable to keep the tears from brimming over, hating them and then somehow loving them when he lifted that strong, perfect hand to brush them away. She let him touch her, adoring the feel of him, memorizing it until she couldn't bear it and she moved to push him away.

The moment she touched him, however, he captured her, threading her fingers in his. She tugged at her hand, quite desperate for him to release her even as she reveled in the feel of him.

He refused to give her up, instead leading her through the maze, his warm hand wrapped around hers. They walked in silence, through the twists and turns, to the exit, where he stopped, just inside the hedge, and turned to her, pulling her close, holding her face in his hands. "I'm sorry," he said. "I'm so sorry I cannot be the man you wish me to be."

Tears threatened again and she shook her head. No more of that. "It's you who don't see. I only ever wished you to be the man you are."

He did kiss her then, one final, lush moment, and she clung to him, pouring all her emotion into the caress. Desire, sorrow, passion.

Love.

But he'd never know that.

He lifted his lips from hers and gestured to the exit, letting her leave the maze first. Letting her choose real life instead of this magic, mythic place.

She did, stepping out into the world once more, King at her back, already threatening to become a long-ago memory.

The only memory that would matter.

She heard the horses almost immediately, the wicked thunder that came from a coach and six tearing up the main drive to the castle at full gallop. Together, she and King turned to face the new arrivals, hands shielding their eyes from the gleam of the late-afternoon sun on the carriage.

On the *gilded* carriage.

On the gilded carriage with cherub outriders.

"Bollocks," Sophie whispered, filled with desolation and no small amount of uncertainty.

The conveyance stopped in the round drive of Lyne Castle, and an outrider immediately leapt down to open the door and release the inhabitants, who piled out like lambs released into pasture.

Exceedingly well-appointed lambs. In lovely silk dresses and outrageous coifs festooned with arrows and feathers and—was that a birdcage? The last of them cried out, "Let me through!" and rushed to a nearby rosebush to promptly cast up her accounts.

"Let me guess," he said, in a tone dry as sand. Only a fool would see the outrageous carriage and not divine its inhabitants. "That one is Sesily."

"It's all ruined!"

Sophie had barely closed the door to the receiving room at Lyne Castle when her mother's dramatic pronouncement loosed a tide of panicked cries.

"Every invitation to the country has been *rescinded*!" the countess announced.

"Derek won't even speak to me," Sesily said matter-of-factly, opening her reticule and extracting a tube of smelling salts. "He disappeared before the end of the Liverpool garden party, the bastard."

"Sesily! Language! You see? *Everything is ruined!*" the Countess of Wight cried, falling into a chair. Sesily passed the salts to the countess, who inhaled deeply. "Literally *everything*!"

"We've been exiled!" Seleste collapsed into a nearby chair, her elaborate pink skirts cascading over the arms. "We're in *Cumbria*, for heaven's sake! Could there be anything worse?" She leaned back, only to catch one of the arrows in her coif in the gold brocade of the seat. She snapped forward with a little squeak, and yanked the arrow out of her hair, tossing it to her feet.

Remarkably, not even stowing away in a footman's livery, being shot on the Great North Road, and faking an engagement with a man who would never marry her was as fraught with difficulty as an afternoon with the Talbot ladies.

And it hadn't even been an afternoon. It had been thirty seconds.

"And let's not even *discuss* what's happened to Seraphina," Sesily said, unstrapping her birdcage hat from atop her head.

Sophie might have questioned the millinery if not for the pronouncement, and instead turned to her older sister, the only arrival who had remained silent. Seraphina stood by the large window, staring out at the estate beyond. "What's happened with you?"

Sera waved a hand. "Nothing more than you already know."

"Of course more!" their mother cried, standing once more. "The duke won't even allow her in the house! He says that after *your* actions, he wants nothing to do with her or with any of us! And she's to have his child!"

Sophie did not look away from her sister. "Is this true? Bollocks."

"Sophie, language!"

Sera waved that hand again. "It's not you, Sophie. If it hadn't been you, it would have been something else." She met Sophie's gaze. "What of you? Are you well?"

"I am," she lied. She might be heartbroken, but she was not exiled by her husband and increasing, so there was that, was there not?

Sera watched her for a long moment, seeing more than the others did. She always could see Sophie's truth. "You mustn't worry, Sophie. This is not on you."

"It damn well is," Sesily protested.

"Sesily," their mother spoke up. "Language."

"If ever there was a time to curse, Mother, it's this!"

She turned on Sophie. "You certainly should worry about *the rest of us*. Derek won't even speak to me! He says he requires the support of the aristocracy. And thanks to you, now he won't get it." She sighed. "He'll never marry me."

Sophie didn't think a missed marriage to Derek Hawkins was such a trial, but she was attempting to be supportive.

"The same is true of Lord Clare—he hasn't called in a week," Seleste said, sounding quite desolate at the loss of her earl, reaching into her bosom to extract a well-folded square of paper. "We've resorted to love letters." She paused. "It's quite romantic, actually, assuming the situation will be rectified."

"Consider the silver lining," Seline teased. "It's difficult for you to argue in print."

Sesily snorted a laugh. "If anyone can find a way to argue in print, it's Seleste and Clare." She looked to their sister. "Have you ever gone more than twenty-four hours without an argument?"

"Of course," Seleste said. "This week."

Seline smirked. "And there is the proof. Perhaps you ought to avoid each other as a matter of course."

"We can't all have Landry scaling our trellises like weeds," Seleste retorted.

Seline laughed at the mention of her paramour. "That's Mark being careful," she explained to Sophie, pouring scotch from a bottle on a nearby sideboard and passing the glasses around. "He won't use the front door."

"Why does he care what people think?" Sophie asked. Mark Landry had more money than most of London combined, and not an ounce of interest in Society. She would never have imagined he'd worry about reputation.

"Haven has power," Sesily said, accepting the drink from Seline. "More than we would have imagined. And he's furious. The aristocracy is shunning Landry's for Tattersall's. They won't buy horseflesh from anyone close to you. Presumably, Derek had similar threats, but unlike Landry, he's a goddamn coward."

"Sesily!" the countess barked.

"Well, he is," Sesily said. "See if he gets back into my graces after this. What a betrayal." She toasted Seline. "You should keep Mark, though. He's a poppet."

"I should like to," Seline said before turning to Sophie, "but he's waiting for you to fix it."

"You must fix it!" their mother cried.

Sophie looked from one to the next. "How am I to do that?"

No one seemed to have an immediate answer.

"Who would have imagined that you would be the scandal?" Sesily opined, taking the chair by the fireplace, "Landing Haven in a fishpond and running off with Eversley?"

"I did not *run off* with Eversley," Sophie said.

"You most certainly did," their mother cried.

"It wasn't running off! I landed myself in the wrong carriage!"

"Oh, well, let's tell the scandal sheets. I'm sure they'll scramble to get it right," Sesily said. "They do work so terribly hard to check their facts."

"You needn't be unkind, Sesily," Seraphina said.

"We're all in a state," Sesily replied. "None more so than you. Or must we remind you that you and your child are currently without a home?"

"Of course that's not true," Sophie interjected.

"No?" Seline asked, "Then you've a plan to marry the marquess and rescue us all?"

The casual question reminded Sophie of earlier in the afternoon, when she'd faced the truth about King—that he'd never love her. That he was never to be hers. That she was going to leave him, and spend the rest of her life wishing that their future would be different.

She shook her head, swallowing around the knot in her throat. "I'm not marrying him."

"Then why are you here?" Seleste asked. "Are you taking up residence as his mistress?"

"That won't help at all," Seline pointed out.

"We need discretion!" the countess cried.

Sophie ignored the willingness that flared at the suggestion. If he'd offered her the role of mistress, she would take it. She would take whatever she could get of him. Whatever time he might give her.

She'd take him here or in London, forever or for an afternoon.

She loved him.

Surely, of all the emotions the human heart could explore, love was the worst.

She looked away from her family. "I was returning to Mossband when you arrived. He was returning me to the inn."

Sesily groaned. "We're *ruined*!"

The countess collapsed to her settee once more, dramatic as ever. "I knew all those books would eventually do you in!"

None of the other Talbot girls appeared to mind the accusation in the countess's words, so Sophie did not linger on it, either. "To be fair, our reputations weren't the most welcome to begin with."

"At least we received invitations!" the countess protested. "Your sisters were all being courted!"

Seline's brow furrowed for the first time since they arrived. "Mark won't have me, will he?"

Sophie's frustration could not be kept at bay. "Oh, for

heaven's sake," she said. "It's not as though I did anything truly scandalous. The Duchess of Lamont faked her death and married the man thought to have killed her, and the *ton* can't get enough of her."

"She didn't publicly malign the aristocracy!"

"Oh, yes. That's quite worse than *ruining a man's life*. Whatever will the rich and titled do now that I've insulted them?"

"They will ruin *our* lives!" Sesily said firmly, her trademark dry wit replaced with cool honesty. "Why do you think we're here? Every one of us has lost our suitor! Because of you!"

"Every one of you has been mistreated by men who could not find their spine if they were kicked directly in it!"

"Those men were willing to *have* them!" her mother cried. "And they were willing to take *you* on, as well, Sophie, a welcome spinster!"

"That's what I was? A future old aunt? Destined to rooms in the castle turret? Hidden away from life?"

"What kind of life could you have possibly planned on?" Sesily asked.

"Well. That was unkind," Sophie replied.

The room grew quiet. "I apologize. But you must understand, Sophie, this is painful for everyone."

"I didn't mean for you all to suffer the residual effects of my . . ."

"Mistake." Seleste again.

Except it wasn't a mistake. For all the emotion since the Liverpool summer soiree, Sophie had lived more in the past ten days than ever before. She looked from one sister to the next. "I didn't ever wish to be your burden. Not before this, and certainly not now."

"You must have seen that it was a possibility, though,"

said the countess, her tone softening the sting of the words. "You're not the most . . ."

Sesily picked up where she left off. "Marketable."

"Of us." Seline finished.

Not beautiful. Not charming. Not exciting.

Unfun.

Except, in these recent days, she'd been all those things. And not because she'd been shot. Not because she'd dressed as a footman. Not because she'd sold away a carriage full of curricle wheels and run from her father's henchmen. Not even because she'd nearly lost her virtue in a hedge maze.

Because she'd fallen in love with King.

Because he'd fed her strawberry tarts and kissed her senseless and tempted her with a glimpse of a life that was more than she'd ever imagined. Because he'd teased her with the idea that she was more than Sophie Talbot, the youngest and least interesting of the Soiled S's.

And then her family had arrived, and reality threatened. But she would not return to it without telling them the truth. She looked from one sister to the next. "If they will not have you because of me, they were not worth having."

"Oh?" Seline said, quick to defend her suitor, "And your Eversley—who will not have you—he's worth nothing, I assume?"

It wasn't the same thing at all. He wasn't turning her out because she'd knocked the Duke of Haven into a fishpond. Indeed, he'd remained at her side after discovering what she'd done.

He was worth everything.

"You did this on purpose," Sesily was saying. "You never wanted to be an aristocrat. And now you've dragged the rest of us back into the muck with you. Look at us, faded and wrinkled after days in a carriage. *In Cumbria.*"

"It's beautiful here," Sophie said.

"If you like sheep," replied Sesily.

"And *green*," added Seleste.

"It's not London." Seline sighed.

"Honestly, we should be called the Spoiled S's."

"None more than you, Sophie." The retort was from Seraphina, and Sophie turned to her, shocked by the words. Her eldest sister spoke quietly, the words somehow firm and kind. "Do you know how we responded when we returned home after the Liverpool party to discover that you'd left with nothing more than the word of an alleged footman dressed in stableboy's clothing? We were so *proud* of you. You'd turned your back on a world for which you'd never cared. I thought it was quite wonderful." She tilted her chin toward the other Talbot sisters. "As did they, though they won't admit it."

"I'll admit it," Sesily said. "You've always been the first to defend us. I was very happy to defend you."

"And I," Seline said. "Mark thought you were damn fantastic."

"Seline, language."

"It was Mark's language, Mother."

"Well, I am unable to admonish him."

Sophie smiled. She'd missed her sisters. Her mother. The whole wild family.

"But it wasn't so easy to be proud of you when London turned on us. We didn't expect the aristocracy to simply exile us," Seline added. "Which I'm sure sounds like heaven to you, Sophie. But . . ."

"It's not for us," Seleste finished.

Of course, Sophie knew that. She didn't wish them the life she wanted. She wished them all the life they wanted for themselves. Happiness in the shape of garden parties and titles and invitations to Windsor Castle.

She sighed. "I am sorry that I have caused such trouble," she began. "But if the scandal sheets have taught us anything, it is this: when the summer is over and you've all returned to London—without me—Society will forget you ever had a youngest sister, and your gentlemen will return. And, if they do not, you're all young, beautiful, and outrageously wealthy," she pointed out. "The three most important qualities in a future bride. You'll find other gentlemen. Who deserve you more."

Silence fell.

"You deny it?" she said, looking from one to the next. "I assure you, you all remain beautiful, despite my scandalous behavior. I shall ask Papa for my dowry, and fade away. All will be well." She turned to Seline. "It's you who always says we're like cats. You'll survive this. Easily."

"Even cats have a limit on their lives," the Countess said, the sad words strangely familiar. An echo of the Liverpool Summer Soiree.

When everything had changed.

"It's not beauty that's the problem," Sera spoke quietly from her place on the edge of the tableau. "Sophie—"

"It's the blunt." The words came from the door, which Sophie hadn't heard open. Her breath caught as she turned to her father, crop still in hand, trousers still covered in dust and horse sweat.

"Papa." She paused. "You came."

And that's when she knew that something terrible must have happened. Jack Talbot did not hie across Britain with his wife and four daughters for a lark. A sense of wild foreboding threaded through Sophie, and she had the keen realization that this day would be the most important of her life. It was the day she said good-bye to King. And the day that her father changed everything.

Her father looked to the rest of the girls. "Find your rooms, girlies."

They did as they were told, leaving in a squawking gaggle, along with the countess, to find rooms that were no doubt being aired for the first time in an age. If she weren't so shocked by her father's arrival, she would have been amused by the idea of the Duke of Lyne coming face-to-face with the Dangerous Daughters.

Once alone with her father, she asked, "Why are you here, Papa?"

"I came," he said, "because I can't take care of this."

She blinked. "Papa, you know as well as I do, Society will find another thing to loathe in less than a week. It likely has already."

"But Haven won't."

"Haven is an ass," she said.

"That's never been more true, kitten, but he's a duke. He holds the purse strings."

Her brows snapped together. "You're Jack Talbot. You're richer than all of them combined."

Her father went silent. "Not without them, Sophie. That was the deal I struck for the title your mother wanted so badly. They invest, I mine. And you all become ladies. I can't make money without the nobs. And you've done an excellent job of running them off. Calling Haven a whore did it better than I ever could've."

Fear gripped her at the words. It made sense, of course. Titles weren't simply doled out, not without requirements. "I thought it was a wager?"

He smiled. "It was. But Prinny made the terms. And I accepted them."

"They've stopped investing?"

"Pulled their funds to a man. Haven took great glee in making it so. I received notice from thirteen of them by sundown after your excitement. The rest came in the morning." He paused for a long moment before he approached her, and for the first time in her life, she saw Jack Talbot's age. His worry. "You want your dowry? Your freedom?" He shook his head. "I want to give it to you. But there ain't no dowry to be had, kitten. I can't keep your mother and sisters in new clothes and gilded carriages and—" He looked to a nearby table. "Now why in hell do they need birdcages on their heads?"

She smiled, halfheartedly. "At least there's no bird in it."

"Don't say that in front of Sesily, or I'll have to find funds for birdfeed."

She shook her head. "Papa. I thought we were—"

"You'd be surprised how quickly blunt flows out the door, kitten. Especially when the nobs want you gone." He reached for her, and she went into the embrace. He smelled of leather and horseflesh, the scent wrapping her in memories of her childhood, when what was right was all that mattered. Jack Talbot had always been larger than life—a hero in every sense. He'd fostered Sophie's love of books, embraced her desire for more than the aristocracy. And in all her life, he'd never once asked her for help. Perhaps she could have found a way to deny her sisters what they wished, but her father—he hadn't an ounce of the dramatic in him. And if he was concerned for their future, so, too, was she.

He kissed the top of her head. "I was so proud of you for standing up for your sister. For yourself," he whispered there. "But now . . . they have us by the bollocks."

She pulled back, staring into his clear brown eyes. "Haven behaved abominably."

"And I'd have beaten him blue, love. Don't you doubt it. But the world was watching you. His world. You embarrassed him in front of it."

I shall destroy you.

Her brother-in-law's words, from the Liverpool greenhouse, echoed through her. And she'd taunted him for them.

I'd like to see you try.

He'd done it. Without hesitation. His name and title making him more powerful than they would ever be.

She shook her head. "I didn't think."

"You think now," he said.

Jack Talbot might have been given the Earldom of Wight, but he'd never been given a son, and therefore, his five daughters had no future without marriage. They had no future. Not now that Sophie had ruined it.

She blinked up at her father. "What have I done?"

He offered her a little smile. "You acted rashly, my girl. You defended your sister in the moment without thinking of the long game. And we pay the price."

She knew what came next before he suggested it. And later, when she faced the dark truth of what she had to do, she would admit her most private secret.

That she'd never in her life wanted anything more.

"How do we survive it?" she asked.

There was a long silence before her father answered. "Eversley."

Chapter 19

***

BEYOND THE BEDPOST—CUMBRIA CASTLE CONFESSIONS!

That night, long after the house quieted, Sophie waited for her thoughts to do the same.

She sat straight up on the edge of her bed, clad in one of Sesily's dressing gowns, a beautiful grass green satin covered in pearls and feathers, with a matching silk nightdress and slippers.

It was a costume more than anything else—a uniform. She was to use it to do what countless other women had done in similar frocks. Land herself a husband.

Willing away the distaste that came at the thought, she stared at the door between her rooms and King's. She'd done all she could to put off approaching him, bathed and changed the bandage on her shoulder, dried her hair by the fire, combed it until it gleamed. It was late enough that he was no doubt abed, no doubt asleep, without thought of her.

They'd barely spoken in the hours since her family had arrived. He'd taken his leave immediately, no doubt grateful that his responsibility to her was complete. They'd dined with him, his father nowhere to be found, her sisters more than willing to fill whatever awkward silences arose with their chatter about London and Society.

King had remained quiet, answering only those questions that came directly to him.

Her sisters had known better than to engage him.

There'd been a moment when her mother had inquired after their journey—why it had taken such a long time. King had looked to Sophie in the aftermath of the question, surprised that the countess seemed not to know that she'd been shot and convalesced in Sprotbrough.

There hadn't been a time to tell her family what had happened, strangely, as a bullet wound had seemed trivial when compared to the wound her family suffered. The one she would cause for King.

She'd watched him throughout dinner, memorizing his face, his eyes, the way his lips curved around his words. She wanted to remember all the little moments she could amass before tonight. Before she knocked on that door and changed their lives forever.

If she could find the courage to do it.

If she could find the willingness to do it.

Perhaps he would refuse her.

Relief flared at the idea. If he refused her, her family would have to try another way. If he refused her, she could leave, and find another life. She'd never have to return to London. To Mossband. She could disappear, and they could live their lives without her.

He could live his life without her.

She would have to live her life without him.

The thought ached in her chest, her heart somehow beating there, in spite of it, and she exhaled, standing and crossing to the adjoining door. She could end this now. She would knock; he would refuse her; she would leave.

Even though she desperately wanted him to accept her.

Not like this.

No, not like this. But the idea that she would never

see him again, never touch him again, never be near him again . . .

It was torture.

She put her hand to the door, palm flat against the cool mahogany, and she lowered her forehead to the door. Breathing deep, imagining that she could smell him there, on the other side, soap and spice and King.

How much she wanted him, and how little she wanted this.

She straightened and lifted her hand, preparing to announce herself, when a knock sounded on the main door to her chamber.

She pulled her hand back from its task as though she'd been burned, immediately putting distance between her and the entrance to his rooms. She crossed to the door and opened it to reveal Seraphina, her hands at her stomach.

The eldest Talbot sister was out of breath. "I was afraid I had missed you."

Sophie stood back and waved Sera into the room. "I have been . . . postponing."

Sera crossed to the center of the bedchamber and turned to face Sophie as she closed the door, locking them both inside. "Do you love him?"

The question surprised Sophie, and it was a moment before she found her reply. "Does it matter?"

Sera sat on the edge of the bed, catching her breath. "It does, rather."

Sophie crossed and poured her sister a glass of water, watching as she drank deep before saying, "Why?"

"If you don't, you shouldn't do this."

Sophie shook her head. "You think I'll find another who loves me?"

"I think you shouldn't marry a man who doesn't care for you."

It was too late for that. "It is easy for you to say such a thing. Nothing about my actions will change your future." Sophie sat next to Seraphina. "I'm so sorry, Sera. If I hadn't—"

Sera reached over and took Sophie's hand, clutching tight. "You defended me. No one else would have." They were both lost in the memory before Sera chuckled. "And he deserved it."

"He deserved much worse," Sophie said.

The chuckle became a laugh. "Right on his backside in that pool!"

Sophie joined her sister in laughter. "Poor fish!"

"Oh, I hope he's put off fish forever!" Sera giggled. "The cook is French, with a particular skill for *poisson*!"

They laughed together for an age, brushing tears from their eyes before reality returned, and they grew serious once more. Sophie turned to her sister. "I would do it again," she confessed. The events of the Liverpool soiree had brought her to King. And she wouldn't ever change that.

Sera squeezed Sophie's hand and nodded, then repeated her question. "Do you love him?"

The tears returned, this time without a hint of laughter, pricking the backs of Sophie's eyes with honesty. "I do," she whispered. "I love him quite desperately."

More than she'd ever thought possible.

She lied to me. How broken he'd been when he confessed that. How devastated.

She couldn't do this.

She couldn't lie to him. What a monster that would make her. Ariadne in the labyrinth, undeserving of him.

And she desperately wanted to deserve him. She'd never deserve him like this.

Sera turned to her then, taking both her hands in hers

and giving voice to Sophie's thoughts. "You mustn't do this."

"But if I don't—what of you? What of Sesily and Seleste and Seline? What of Papa?"

Sera smiled. "We climb like ivy. Think you one harsh winter will end our journey?"

"You can say it . . ."

Seraphina nodded. "I can. Because my life is cast in stone. I am Duchess of Haven. And I carry the future duke inside me." Sophie watched as her sister's gaze grew sad. "Because of that, I can tell you that if you love him, you should tell him." She shook her head. "I never told Haven. And look at the mess I've made." She lifted Sophie's hands to her lips and spoke to them. "Tell him, Sophie. Give yourself a chance at happiness."

I can't love you.

Sophie shook her head. "He doesn't want love."

"Perhaps he doesn't know he already has it." Sera's eyes swam with unshed tears. "I never told him, Sophie. And by the time I thought to . . . I'd already lost him." She took a deep breath. "What Father asks . . . it's so much. Yes, it might save him. Might save Sesily and Seleste and Seline. You'll be a marchioness and a duchess and that title might help us all. But Eversley—he'll hate you for it."

She couldn't bear the idea of King hating her. But what of the family she loved?

"You cannot protect us all, Sophie. Not forever."

She looked to Seraphina, her eldest sister, whom Sophie had always considered her most kindred sister. "I love you."

Sera pulled her close, wrapping her in a tight embrace. "I know. We know. Why do you think we came to you? But you love him as well. And love does not come in half measures—you shall hate yourself forever if you trap him. I know it better than any."

She didn't want him trapped.

She wanted him to want her. As desperately as she wanted him.

She couldn't do it. Not even for the family she loved. There had to be another way.

"Sophie . . . please. Tell him you love him and see what comes of it."

Sophie looked to the door beyond which he slept, hope and terror warring for position in her chest. "What if he laughs?"

"I'll toss him in the nearest fishpond," Seraphina vowed.

Sophie gave a little huff of humorless laughter at that. "What if . . ."

I can't love you.

"What if he doesn't love me?"

Sera was quiet for a long time, and then said, "What if he does?"

Sophie nodded. "If he doesn't . . . I must leave. Mother and Papa—"

"*I* shall help you."

"With what money?"

"There are benefits to being the Duchess of Haven," Sera said with a little smile. "I shall help you. Wherever you wish to go. Wales. The Outer Hebrides. America. Wherever."

Far from here. Far from him.

Free from him.

As though she would ever be free of him.

Sophie nodded. "Tomorrow."

"Tomorrow."

She nodded and stood, knowing that she could not have him forever. Wishing that she could at least have him tonight. She tightened the belt on her extravagant dressing gown, festooned with feathers and brocade. "This is a ridiculous gown."

Sera chuckled. "Sesily would tell you it makes your bosom look wonderful." She reached up and pulled the pins from Sophie's hair, loosing it around her shoulders and arranging it this way and that. When she was satisfied with the work, she met Sophie's gaze. "He shan't know what's struck him."

Sophie took a deep breath, eyeing the adjoining door as Sera moved to leave the room.

"Sera," Sophie called, staying her sister as she opened the door.

Seraphina turned back.

Sophie did not know what to say, but the eldest Talbot seemed to understand nonetheless. Her hand moved to her swelling midsection, stroking over it. Protecting it. "Tell him. And let the road roll out before you."

Sophie nodded.

She would. For her sister.

For herself.

The door closed behind Seraphina with a soft click, and the sound propelled Sophie across the room, to where she'd been standing before her sister had arrived. Her heart pounded nearly unbearably; she'd never been so nervous in all her life.

If she did not knock now, she would lose her nerve.

She'd promised Seraphina she'd knock.

What if he doesn't love me?

What if he does?

She lifted her hand, willing herself to knock.

Perhaps he wasn't even in the room.

Perhaps he was a sound sleeper.

She wouldn't like to wake him.

Stop being a cabbagehead and knock on the ruddy door.

Sophie took a deep breath, willing her heart to stop its racing, and knocked.

The door opened instantly, as though he'd been standing on the other side, waiting for her. She gave a little yelp of surprise at the instantaneous response, and he raised a brow. "Did I scare you?"

"A bit, yes," she said, taking him in, his dark curls fallen haphazardly over his brow, his shirtsleeves rolled up to his elbow, boots off, feet bare. So desperately handsome, it was difficult to look at him.

He was too much for her.

She was not enough for him.

"You do know that the normal response to knocking is for one to open the door?" His casual teasing made her immediately more comfortable. She knew this man. She'd spent days on end with him.

She smirked. "You do know that most people don't linger on one side of a door and wait for knocking?"

"Most people don't share a door with you." Her heart skipped a beat and he used her surprise to take her in, top to toe. "Christ. I know I'm not supposed to say it, Sophie, but you are beautiful."

This time, she believed him. Somehow. She looked down at the dressing gown. "It's Sesily's."

"I'm not talking about the gown."

She didn't know what to say, so she asked, "Were you waiting for me?"

"Hoping more than waiting."

Her brow furrowed. For what could he be hoping? He'd said good-bye to her earlier in the day. He'd made it clear that they were not to be. "But this afternoon you said—"

"I know what I said." He paused. "Why did you knock?"

There were a half-dozen reasons, and only one that mattered.

Tell him.

"I . . ." She couldn't. ". . . am leaving tomorrow."

He nodded. "I assumed your family was not planning to take up residence."

"I don't imagine your father would like that."

"The idea does have its charms."

Silence stretched between them, the thought of his father reinforcing everything she knew about this man and their nonexistent future. He wouldn't marry. He wouldn't have children. The line ended with him.

Whether or not she loved him.

Tell him.

She took a deep breath. "I wished to say . . ."

Good Lord. It was difficult.

"What is it?" She couldn't meet his eyes, her gaze falling to his hand, where it was fisted at his thigh, knuckles white, as though he was holding something tightly.

She spoke to that hand, beginning again. "I wished to say . . ."

I wished to say that I am not sure I can live without you.

I wished to say that I will always be yours.

I wished to say . . .

"Sophie . . ." Her name was more than a prompt and less than a question.

She looked up at him then, his green eyes utterly focused on her. "I wished to say that I love you."

For a moment, the universe stilled. He did not speak. He did not move. He did not look away from her. Sophie's heart stopped beating. Indeed, the only evidence that she'd spoken at all was the heat that flooded her cheeks in the aftermath of her confession.

When she could not bear the silence a moment longer,

she added in a flood of words, "I'm leaving tomorrow. And I'm not going back to London. I'm going to find my freedom. And earlier . . . we agreed that tonight might be ours." She paused. "I know I said I couldn't bear to be with you any longer . . ." She looked down at that hand again. "But I changed my mind. I should like to be with you. Tonight. Just this once. I should like you to ruin me. Because you've ruined me anyway, really. For all others. You once asked me how all this ended. And I don't know, honestly. I don't know that happily is viable anymore. But I know that tonight . . . with you . . ." She trailed off, then whispered, "I could be happy tonight."

He remained still, but when he spoke, the words came like gravel, pulled from somewhere deep and dark inside him. "Say it again."

She shuffled her feet, feeling like a child on display, suddenly uncertain of her words.

"Please, Sophie," he begged. "Again."

As though she could resist him. "I love you," she whispered.

And then that fist released, and he moved, reaching for her, tangling his hand in her hair, pulling her to him for a long, wicked, wonderful kiss, stealing her breath and her sanity until he pulled back and pressed his forehead to hers, his thumb raking over her jaw as he met her gaze. "Again."

"I love you," she said, the words lost in another wild kiss, this one accompanied by his hands stroking down her back, pulling her tight against him and lifting her high off the ground, encouraging her to wrap her legs around him as he backed away from the door and kicked it closed with one long, muscled leg.

He carried her to his bed, following her down, pressing her into the soft mattress, the weight of him welcome between her thighs. She gasped at the sensation, the pleasure of him there, where she'd wanted him for days. He rained kisses over her face and neck, speaking as he went. "Christ, Sophie . . . I shouldn't want this . . . I shouldn't take it . . . I can't be what you desire."

Except he was what she desired.

He was the only thing she'd ever desired in her life.

"I shouldn't accept your love," he said between soft, drugging kisses, his fingers working at the sash of her dressing gown, his lips on the soft skin of her neck. "I'll never be good enough for it." He paused, lifting his head, meeting her eyes. "But Christ, I want it."

"It's yours," she said, leaning up and catching his bottom lip in her teeth, sucking at it until he groaned his pleasure and gave her the kiss she desired. "As am I."

He cursed, the word a benediction in this, and released the belt of her dressing gown. "I've never seen you naked," he said, working at the pearls of the nightgown beneath. "I want that. I want that before you leave. Before you go and find a life more perfect than what I can give you. I'll spend an eternity in hell for it," he vowed, "But I don't care. I want to see you naked. I want to worship you until you remember nothing but my name. But my touch. But this place.

"I want to worship you until I can't close my eyes without seeing you. I want the memory of you, Sophie. Forever. So when another man loves you and gives you the life you deserve, I can torture myself with it."

Tears threatened at the words. *There would be no other men. No other love*, she wanted to scream at him— she was his alone. Forever.

She wanted it, too, and she loved the feel of the silk sliding off her, baring her skin to the candlelight and his gaze. He pulled back, lifting off her, sitting up, and she was instantly nervous at the loss of him, moving to sit up herself, to cover her nudity.

"No," he said, pressing her back down to the bed flat against the crisp linen sheets, open to his gaze and his touch. His attention lingered on her shoulder. "How does it feel?"

She smiled at his care. "I barely notice it."

"Liar," he said. "Let's see if we can make it truth." His hands spread over her skin, down the sides of her torso, over the swell of her belly, down her thighs, and she forgot she even had a shoulder, let alone one that had been shot. "You're so beautiful," he said again. "So beautiful."

His hands ran down her legs to her slippers, and he slid off the bed to kneel there, at her bare feet. He took one in his hands, running his thumbs over the sole, sending waves of unexpected pleasure through her. "I still think of you in slippers on that road," he said softly, pressing a kiss to her ankle as he made her wild with decadent pleasure. "I hated that you mistreated yourself."

He switched to her other foot and offered the same treatment as she shook her head. "They don't hurt now."

"No?" he asked, kissing at her ankle, his tongue slipping out to find the sensitive skin there.

She sighed her pleasure. "You feel wonderful."

"Good," he whispered. "I want you to always feel wonderful."

She loved his touch, but she wanted him, too. Wanted to explore him as he had explored her. If tonight was all they would have, then she would take her pleasure as well. She sat up, her fingers finding his soft hair, urging him up, over her, until she could reach his long, muscled thighs, tracing up to the waist of his trousers, to work at his shirttails.

He grasped her wrists, and she resisted his touch. "No," she whispered. "Tonight is for me, as well."

He watched her for a long moment, his green eyes darkening with each passing second. "I'm not sure I can bear it."

"You shall have to," she replied. "I want my exploration."

He released her, rising up on his knees over her, pulling the shirt out of his trousers and over his head, revealing his chest and torso, defined like a statue from a Renaissance master. She couldn't stop herself from running her fingers over the muscle there, loving the catch of his breath. "You're like Michelangelo's David," she marveled, exploring the dips and rises of hard muscle. "You're perfect."

He watched her as she touched him, his breath ragged and glorious. "I'm not at all perfect," he said. "But Christ if you don't make me feel so."

She sat up then, wanting to get closer to him, to feel his warmth, to explore him. She flattened her palms against his chest, loving his heat and strength, and couldn't resist leaning in and pressing a kiss there, glorying in the feel of crisp hair. At the caress, his hands threaded into her hair, tilting her face up to him. "I don't think I can take much of this, love."

She smiled, adoring the power that rioted through her at the words. "Surely you can, my lord. Need I remind you of your reputation?"

He gave a little huff of laughter that turned into a groan as she sought out the falls of his trousers. "I thought we discussed the fact that my reputation is more tale than truth?" Her fingers fumbled at his buttons, betraying her own inexperience, and he cursed, stopping her movement. "Sophie. I don't think it's a good idea for us to—"

"I do," she said, surprising herself with her bravery. "I think it's my turn."

He raised a brow, watching her. "More mine than yours, it seems."

She smiled. "We'll see."

He leaned down and took her lips in a wild kiss, releasing her after a long moment to whisper, "You are unbearably perfect."

She blushed, then found her courage. "Trousers, please," she whispered. "I've wanted them off since I saw you that first night—in leather breeches, standing tall on your curricle."

"You liked those?" He laughed, and lifted himself from the bed to remove them.

She remembered the way the leather of his breeches had revealed the thick muscles of his thighs. "Very much." The grey wool slid to the floor, revealing long, muscled legs, and she realized that the leather had not done him justice.

And then she saw the scar.

Long and thick and brutal, white with years of healing, it ran nearly the full length of his left thigh. She couldn't help but gasp at it, at the pain it must have caused him. She reached for it, and he stepped back. "I forget that it is there," he said.

It was a lie, of course. No one could forget such a thing. "What happened?"

"The carriage accident."

The one that killed his love.

No. Not his love. The one that killed the woman who betrayed him.

The woman who made him swear off love. The woman who made it impossible for Sophie to have the only thing she desired.

She reached for him, eager to will away the pain from the accident. But she knew without asking that he would take any more attention to the scar as pity. And he would deny her the rest. Instead, she moved toward him, coming to the edge of the bed, where he stood, one hand covering the most critical part of him, and she let her gaze fall to that mysterious place. "I wish to see you."

He watched her for a long moment, and then moved his hand, revealing the hard length of himself, throbbing high against his stomach. Her gaze did not waver, not even when she said the only thing that came to mind. "In this, you do not look like David."

He laughed and reached for her. "I shall take that as a compliment," he growled, pulling her closer, brushing the edges of her dressing gown over her shoulders and down her arms until she, too, was naked.

"I don't suppose you would lie down for me? It would make everything much easier," she said, and he did, re-markably, stretching out on his back and lifting her to straddle him, her knees on either side of his hips.

She stared down at him, taking in his sheer masculine beauty. "You are . . ." She trailed off.

He reached up to cup her breasts, playing at the hard tips until she sighed and rocked against him, making him groan.

She would never get her exploration this way. She clasped his hands. "Stop. It's my turn."

He raised a brow. "You don't want me to touch you?"

"Of course I do. But I wish to touch you more."

He exhaled, long and graveled before he stretched his arms up, stacking them beneath his head. "I am yours to explore, my lady."

And he allowed it, allowed her to stroke and discover, over his arms and chest, leaning over to kiss the corded muscles of his shoulders, to suck at the skin of his neck, to kiss down the slope of his chest until his breath came in quick pants and he groaned her name. "You're the worst kind of tease," he whispered. "I can feel you there, hot and wet above me."

She pressed against him, reveling in him, hard and hot. "Does it hurt?"

"Yes," he said. "In the best kind of way."

"How?"

He reached for her, pulling her down for a kiss. "You're so curious."

"If this is the only time—" She stopped. She wouldn't think about this being the only time. She collected herself. "How does it hurt?"

"It aches. For you."

She scooted back, revealing the hard length of him. "May I touch it?"

He gritted his teeth. "I shouldn't let you," he said. "I should pack you into that pretty green gown and send you back to bed. Before it's too late."

She shook her head. "I wish you wouldn't." And she touched him anyway, stroking him in a long, lingering touch, reveling in the way he sucked in a breath of air and closed his eyes. "Does that help?"

"Do it again." The command sent wicked pleasure through her.

She obeyed. "Like this?"

King's green eyes opened, and he leveled her with the most glorious look she'd ever seen, his hands coming to hers, showing her how to touch him, how to stroke. He grew under her ministrations, somehow harder, longer. More handsome.

She could not stop staring at him, even when she said, "What you did to me . . . with your mouth."

He groaned, harsh and unsettling in the quiet room. "Yes?"

"I'd like to . . ." She didn't finish the sentence, instead scooting back, leaning down to press a kiss to the hard, hot tip of him, straining above their hands. He growled at the touch, and she lifted her head. "Is this . . ."

"It's fucking perfect," he said. "Christ, Sophie."

Somehow, the foul language made the entire moment more perfect, and she lowered her lips again, taking him into her mouth, licking at him, sucking tentatively, glorying in the way he moved against her, showing her what he liked, chanting her name like a prayer. "Sophie . . . love . . . yes . . ."

She continued, learning the taste and feel of him, loving the pleasure she gave him. Loving the fact that she could give him this pleasure, here, now, once, before she left. She put all her love into the caress, wanting him to know the truth—that there would never be anyone else for her.

After too short a time, he thrust his hands into her hair and lifted her from him. "Stop," he said, sitting up, his strong arms pulling her up to straddle him as he stole her lips in a long, wicked kiss. He released her with a gasping breath and repeated himself. "Stop."

"Did you not . . ."

He rolled her down onto her back, finding his way between her thighs, his hands coming to her hair, holding her still for another kiss. "I did. Christ. I've never enjoyed anything like I did that." He pressed his forehead to hers, his eyes closed. "You must go back to your room, love. We cannot do this."

No.

She didn't want to leave him.

She put her hand to his cheek. "King."

He shook his head. "I stood on this side of the damn door for an age, trying to convince myself that you are not mine. That I can't have you. If we do this, Sophie . . ."

He trailed off, and she heard a myriad of finishes of the sentence.

If we do this, I'll never forgive myself.

If we do this, you'll be ruined.

If we do this, you'll still be alone tomorrow.

She reached up and kissed him softly. "I don't care. I want it."

"You want me."

"I love you," she vowed. "I'll only ever love you."

"How am I to deny you anything after that?"

She lifted her hips against his, testing the power of her movement, loving the way his eyes darkened at her touch. "You aren't to deny me."

"Sophie," he whispered, shifting, the hard length of him finding the wet heart of her, the tip of him teasing at the place where she wanted him quite desperately. Pleasure shot through her.

He repeated the motion.

Good Lord.

"King, don't stop."

He didn't, instead pressing deeper, rocking into her, stretching her gently before he stopped and said her name. Her gaze flew to his. "You're so tight, love. Is it all right?"

It was strange and unsettling, and somehow wicked and wonderful. She nodded. "Is there more?"

He laughed, catching her lips in a long kiss. "There is."

"More, please."

And he gave it to her, rocking deeper and deeper until she was filled beyond anything she'd ever experienced. And he was so close to her. They were together for this one moment, for this one night. She'd never forget this moment. When she took her last breath, it would be this moment she remembered. The moment when King was hers. Forever.

Tears came, unbidden, and he stilled. "No. Christ. No." He began to pull out of her. "Sophie, love. I'm sorry."

"No!" she cried, tightening her thighs around him. "No. Don't stop."

"I'm hurting you."

"You're not." There was nothing near pain in the way he touched her. Nothing close to it.

"Love, I can see it," he said. "I can see the tears."

She shook her head. "You're not hurting me. It feels rather wonderful."

He kissed her, holding her still, staring deep into her eyes. "What then?"

This hurts me. This moment. The truth of it.
That this is all I'll ever have of you.

She couldn't tell him any of that, of course. So, instead, she told him the only thing that mattered. "I love you."

He kissed her again, reaching between them, stroking the tender, sensitive spot above the place where they were joined. "I could listen to you say that forever," he said, running his thumb around and around the straining part of her. "I am going to make you say it tonight, again and again. I am going to make you say it when you come. I am going to watch the words on your lips as you fall apart in my arms, and as I put you back together."

She would tell him whenever he liked. The words had freed her, and she whispered them over and over like a prayer as he lifted himself over her, rocking against her, long and slow, wreaking havoc on her body and mind. His thumb moved faster and faster in small tight circles, playing over that glorious place, sensation building, making good on all his promises. She was drawn tight as a bow, desperate for release, and she opened her eyes, meeting his, aching for the pleasure only he could give her.

"I love you," she whispered, and the words rocketed through them both, tipping her over the edge as his movements came deeper, faster, more powerful, making her forget everything but his name, but the feel of him against her, but the way she loved him.

"Look at me, Sophie. I want to see it."

She did, crying out as the crest came again, and she threw herself into the pleasure, the sound of her name on his lips, as he tumbled into it with her.

It was magnificent.

He rolled away from her, clutching her to him, careful of her bandage, his fingers trailing over her good shoulder. "Sophie . . ." he said, letting her name trail off, curl around them in this warm, dark room.

He was magnificent.

She sighed, curling closer to him, and he kissed the top of her head, the soft caress tempting her nearly as much as the rest of the interlude had.

They were magnificent together.

But they would never be together.

And with that insidious thought, she was returned to reality, to the arms of the man she loved, who would never love her. Who had another plan for his life. A plan that did not include love.

Perhaps she could have lived without love before tonight. Before her confession. Before knowing that she'd never be able to be with him without quite desperately wanting him to love her in return.

But she couldn't. And so she would leave. Tonight. Escape in the dark, and hang her family and their wild plan to trap the Marquess of Eversley into marriage. She didn't want him trapped.

The only way she wanted to marry the Marquess of Eversley was in a love match. And that would never happen. So she would find her way away from here and spend her life with the memory of tonight.

With the memory of his pleasure when she told him the truth.

When she confessed her love.

The memory would be enough.

What a lie that was.

She slid out of his arms, to the edge of the bed.

It would be enough, she told herself, ignoring the truth.

It had to be.

Chapter 20

KING CONQUERED!

*H*e was going to marry her.

Indeed, he likely should have told her so before he made love to her, here in his bed. Before he ruined her, quite thoroughly. But there was something tremendous about making love to her, knowing that she was willing to give everything to him, without the promise of a title.

Knowing she didn't care about the promise of a title.

Knowing she wanted him for him, and not his name, and not his fortune.

Knowing she loved him.

She loved him.

The moment she'd said it, he'd known their fate. He'd known that he would take her here, in this bed, against the cool linen sheets where he'd fought to find sleep and instead found visions of her. He'd known he'd take her virginity, and with it, her future.

He'd known they would marry.

She loved him.

He wanted her to say it again, as though she hadn't said it a dozen times already. He didn't think he'd ever tire of hearing her say the words. Of knowing the truth of them. Sophie Talbot loved him.

Her love made him want her thoroughly, without hesitation.

Even if he could never find a way to love her in return. He knew it was selfish and arrogant and the worst kind of greed, but he'd tasted the honesty in her words, and seen it in her eyes, and felt it in her touch.

And he wanted it for himself.

Forever.

So he'd taken her without hesitation. Without telling her the truth—that if she let him take her, they would marry. He'd been afraid she'd stop him if she'd known, afraid she would demand his love in return for her hand in marriage.

And so he'd resorted to the worst kind of trick.

She'd have to marry him now, as she was well and truly ruined. And, despite the fact that her ruination had been part of their ever-evolving agreement, there was no way on earth he was allowing her to leave him.

Ever.

It occurred to him, as they lay quietly in his bed, drenched in candlelight and shadows, her skin soft against his touch, her breath slowing, pleasure threading through them both, her profession of love still lingering in the heavy air, that he should tell her what was to come next.

He should propose.

She deserved a proposal.

He could manage a proposal—a summer fair in the Mossband town square, a masquerade ball, jewels, and public declarations of his intention.

Except Sophie wouldn't want anything so extravagant.

She sighed in his arms, cuddling closer to him, and he kissed the top of her head.

He'd take her to the center of the labyrinth again. With a plateful of Agnes's strawberry tarts and a soft wool blanket. He'd go to Mossband and fetch a basketful of sugar buns from Robbie the baker. King smiled in the darkness. His lady had a sweet tooth. He'd feed it for the rest of his life, with pleasure.

Just as soon as he took her to the labyrinth and told her the truth—that even as his past made it impossible for him to promise her love, he wished to promise her the rest. That he would do his best to make her happy.

As meager an offer it was, she loved him, and she would say yes. She would say yes, and they would eat sweets, and then he would lower her to the blanket and strip her bare and lick the sugar from her lips with only the sky and the sun as witness.

It wasn't a fair in the Mossband town square, but it had the benefit of being quick. He'd take her over the border and marry her in Scotland. They could be wed by this time tomorrow.

And she'd be his. Forever.

She stiffened in his arms, pulling away from him, moving to the edge of the bed. Where was she going? It was the man who was destined to skulk off in the dead of night, was it not? He had plans for her. They involved more kissing. More touching. More of her telling him she loved him.

And she was leaving him.

He reached for her, catching her hand before she could escape. "Where are you going?"

She reached down for her dressing gown, lifting it up and covering herself. "I . . ."

"You don't need the gown, Sophie," he said, letting all his desire into his tone. "I shall keep you warm."

She dipped her head, embarrassed by the words. He'd take great joy in teaching her not to be ashamed of desire. Someday, she'd come naked to his bed. The thought had him instantly hard again.

"Sophie," he said, "come back to bed."

"I cannot," she said, standing and pulling the gown back on, tying the belt haphazardly. "We mustn't be caught."

"We shan't be caught," he said, moving across the bed, reaching for her, pulling her back to him as he knelt before her. It didn't matter if they were caught, anyway. He was going to marry her.

He tucked a strand of glorious brown hair behind her ear, running his thumb over the high arc of one cheek. She was the most beautiful thing he'd ever seen.

"Stay," he whispered, leaning in and stealing a kiss, long and lush, reveling in the way her tongue matched his stroke for stroke until they were both gasping for breath. He pulled her close, worrying the soft skin of her ear with his teeth and tongue. "Stay, love. There's so much more to explore."

She sighed at the words, but stepped back nonetheless. "I cannot," she said, the words catching in her throat as she backed away. "We agreed—one night."

That was before, of course. Before she'd loved him.

Before he'd made love to her.

She couldn't imagine he'd let her go now—she couldn't imagine one night would ever be enough. And yet, she was leaving him. Cold realization threaded through him. "Where are you going?"

She met his gaze. "Away. Away from here."

Away from him.

"And if I wish you to stay? What then?"

She shook her head. "I can't. It's too much."

There was something in the words, something soft and raw and sad, and he realized that she was leaving him because she wanted to stay. Because she thought he wouldn't give her what she desired.

And perhaps he wouldn't, in the long run.

Perhaps he'd never be the man she deserved.

But damned if he wasn't going to try.

Damned if he didn't want to spend his whole life trying to make her happy.

He came off the bed then, following her as she made for the adjoining door. "Sophie," he said. "Wait."

She shook her head, and he could have sworn there were tears there, in her eyes, as she turned away, making a run for the door. His plans changed. He wasn't going to propose tomorrow. He was going to propose now. He couldn't bear her sadness, even for a moment.

He loved her.

Good Lord.

He stopped short at the realization, so clear as he considered the possibility that he might have hurt her. *He loved her.* He never wanted her hurt again. He'd do anything to stop it. He'd do anything for her.

Forever.

And he wanted her to know it. Immediately.

"Sophie, wait," he said, unable to keep the laughter from his tone as she tore the door open, desperate to be rid of him. He was going to catch her and take her back to bed and tell her how much he loved her. Again and again, until he'd professed it as much as she had.

Until she believed him as he believed her.

He was going to propose to her, and capture her pretty agreement with his lips and make love to her until the sun rose and painted her with gold.

She loved him.

Except she'd gone still, her gaze fixated on something in her bedchamber, horror on her face. King stopped as well, dread twisting in his gut as she shook her head. "No," she whispered, her hand clutching the edge of the door. "No," she said again, louder. "I changed my mind."

Changed her mind.

Jack Talbot stepped through the doorway, his gaze finding the bed and sliding back to where King stood. Naked.

The earl's brow rose. "Eversley."

King looked only at Sophie. "You changed your mind about what?"

"You've ruined her," her father said.

Understanding flared, clear and angry, on a wave of pain he would not acknowledge. King spat his reply. "Except it seems she had quite a hand in the ruination."

Pain flashed in her blue eyes, and he almost believed it. "King—I don't want this."

"You did, though, didn't you? You wanted to trap me."

Betrayed by the woman he loved.

She shook her head. "I didn't. I swear."

"You wanted to trap me," he repeated, hating the way his throat tightened around the words. They way they reminded him of another woman. Another time. Another love that wasn't love at all. "You wanted to be a duchess."

"No," she said. "I was leaving." He could hear the distress in her voice. It sounded so honest. "I told you, I was leaving!"

"You were leaving to be caught," he said. "So *I* could be caught."

"No!" she cried.

"You lied to me."

She wasn't leaving.

She hadn't planned one final night.

She didn't love him.

It was the last that destroyed him. He met her gaze. "You lied to me."

Her eyes went wide at the words, at the anger in them. "I didn't," she said, coming toward him, reaching for him.

He stepped back. If she touched him he did not know what he would do. He'd never felt so broken. Not even the night Lorna had died.

He'd never loved Lorna like he loved Sophie.

The realization stung worse than any blow.

"You wanted to marry me."

She swallowed. "No," she said.

He heard the lie and it wrecked him. He was unable to keep himself from thundering, "Stop lying to me!"

Her father stepped between them. "Shout at her again and you won't be alive to marry her."

"You arrange to trap *another* duke using your daughter as bait, and now you rush to protect her?" King did not have a chance to punctuate the question with a fist into his future father-in-law's face, however, as Sophie was shouting herself, now.

"Fine! I did want to marry you!"

He shouldn't have been shocked, but he was.

He shouldn't have been devastated, but he was.

Even as he'd heard the lie, he'd hoped it was true.

I wished to say that I love you.

What an idiot he'd been. He'd never in his life wanted to believe something as much as he wanted to believe that she did love him. But he couldn't. She'd betrayed him, Ariadne and the Minotaur in the labyrinth. And like the goddamn monster, he never saw it coming.

"I wanted to marry you. Yes. No woman in her right mind wouldn't want to marry you. You're . . ." She paused, her eyes glistening with unshed tears. "You're perfect." She was destroying him with her simple words, with the way she spoke them, her voice rising just slightly, as though she couldn't quite believe them herself. "You don't have to marry me. Think of all the others—you never married them."

He hadn't ruined the others. He'd never touched them. He'd never known the feel of their soft skin or the way their hair fell across his bedsheets or the way their lips looked, red and lush, covered in strawberry tart and kisses.

He hadn't loved the others.

He considered her for a long moment, hating her for her tears, for the way they clawed at him even as he dealt with her lies. Hating her for making him love again. For making him love her. For making him hate loving her.

"You might not be the prettiest or the most interesting, but you're the most dangerous of all the daughters, aren't you, Sophie?" he said, hating himself for the words as she went rail straight.

He imagined he'd be hating himself a great deal over the course of this marriage.

He wanted to punish her as she had punished him. To give her everything she'd ever wanted, and then snatch it all away.

King looked to his future father-in-law. "You'll have your wedding," he said, before turning away, stalking to his desk, extracting paper and pen. "Now get out."

King summoned her to the drive of Lyne Castle the next afternoon.

Sophie arrived coiffed and dressed in a deep, beautiful purple that Seleste had provided—her sister had sworn that the gown—tighter than Sophie might like—would be flattering enough to draw King's attention. It was a stunning gown, all lush satin skirts and low necklines, with slippers to match.

They, too, were too tight, but Sophie was willing to do anything necessary for a chance to convince King that she hadn't lied, so it seemed that being trussed into a new frock and uncomfortable shoes was a small price to pay for it. Perhaps, if he found the dress attractive, he'd allow her to explain what had happened. Why she'd come to him in the night. Why she'd left.

Perhaps he'd let her go.

Let her walk away, and free him of her. Give him a chance to find another woman. One whom he believed.

He waited for her on the riding block of his curricle, two perfectly matched handsome black horses stomping in the dirt. She looked up at him, jaw set, hat low over his brow, reins in hand. "Your curricle is returned."

"Not the wheels," he replied without looking at her.

Guilt flared. "I am sorry."

"I find your apologies rather vacant, Lady Sophie," he said casually, setting the reins for driving. "Come on then, we haven't much daylight."

It was three in the afternoon. "Where are we going?"

He turned to her then, his gaze cool and unmoved and . . . un-King-like. "In, my lady."

This man, this tone, none of it was familiar. Sadness consumed her, along with no small amount of frustration, She looked for a block to climb up. There wasn't one. He did not reach over to help her in.

She met his gaze, and he raised a brow in challenge.

She wouldn't back down. Not now. Instead, she lifted her skirts high—higher than any proper lady should—revealing her legs and knees, and taking hold of the massive curricle wheel, hauling herself up next to him.

He said nothing about her movement, instead flicking the reins expertly and setting them on course. After long minutes of silence, Sophie decided that this was a perfectly reasonable time to explain herself. "I'm sorry."

He did not reply.

"I never intended for this to happen. I didn't care that

you were a marquess. Or that you were to be a duke." She paused, but he gave no indication that he had even heard her. "I realize you don't believe me, but everything I told you was the truth. I never wanted to return to London. I never wanted to marry an aristocrat."

And then I fell in love with you.

She wanted to say that to him. But she couldn't bear his disbelief.

She couldn't blame him for not believing her, either.

"I ruined my family," she said. "Seraphina has been exiled from Haven's house, with child. None of my other sisters has a suitor worth his salt. My father's lost the titled investors for his mines. Because I acted rashly. Yes. For a moment, I considered trapping you into marriage. But only because I wanted you so desperately. It never had to do with the title. Never with my family. Never for any reason but that I wanted you." She paused, and whispered the last. "Forever."

"Don't ever say that word to me again." The reply was cold and angry. "We do not have a forever. Neither of us deserves it."

The words stung, but she refused to cry. Instead, she watched the road, rising and falling before them. "When I knocked on the door last night—"

I only wished to tell you I love you.

She didn't say it. "—I'd already changed my mind. I don't wish to marry you," she said, instead, not knowing if the words were true or false. "I don't wish for you to be saddled with me."

"I shan't be," he said, the words cold and distant. "You needn't worry."

She did not care for the certainty in his words. "Where are we going?"

He did not reply, instead turning off the road and onto

a smaller road, and then a drive that wound up to a great stone castle that rose up out of the landscape like something out of the Knights of the Round Table.

Outside the keep was a coach and six, hitched and ready, as though someone had just arrived. King pulled the curricle to a stop behind the coach and leapt down to bang on the door to the keep. Seconds later, the door opened to reveal the Duke of Warnick and a young woman draped in a green and black plaid.

Warnick stepped out of the keep with a smile, clapping King on the back heartily before turning to her. "Lady Sophie," he said, coming forward to help her down, "Your husband-to-be is already neglecting you, I see."

Sophie blinked. "Husband-to-be?"

Warnick tilted his head to one side, watching her with curiosity before turning back to King. "You haven't asked her? A little late for that, no?"

King did not look at her. "She knows we're to be married. She's simply playing coy."

Sophie forced a smile at the words. "Of course," she said, attempting to hide her confusion. "I simply did not know that *you* knew, Your Grace."

He laughed. "We have lax rules in Scotland, my lady, but the ones governing witnesses to weddings are fairly firm. I know, as your officiant."

Sophie blinked. "Our officiant."

"Yes! Don't worry, I've been to several weddings. I shall take today seriously."

"Today," she said.

"Yes."

"We're to be married, *today*."

"Aye," the massive Scot said with a smile. "Else why would King have ferreted you away to Scotland?"

"Of course," she said. "Why else?"

But she wanted to scream.

"You make a beautiful bride, if I may say so," the duke continued as though all was perfectly normal. "Of course, the last time I saw you, you were much more . . . interestingly . . . dressed."

"Shut up, Warnick," King growled.

Sophie blinked, unable to be embarrassed of her footman's garb as all her affront was taken up with the fact that she was about to be wed. "We're to be married here. In your house."

Warnick looked back at the massive keep. "One of them. Unfortunately, it's not the nicest."

"We won't be going in," King said. "If nothing else, the Scots understand marital expediency." He looked to the plaid-covered girl. "I assume you are our second witness?"

"Aye, m'lord," she said.

"And what's your name?" he asked, the words an octave lower than his usual voice.

"Catherine."

He smiled at her, and Sophie couldn't help the way her heart pounded at the dimples that flashed there, in his handsome face. "Well, Catherine, you may call me King."

The girl returned his smile warmly, and Sophie wanted to hit him. Hard.

King turned to Warnick, who was watching the scene carefully. "Let's have this done."

Warnick nodded. "I suppose we can skip the dearly beloved bit."

"Indeed," said King.

"I don't know," snapped Sophie. "Catherine seems fairly beloved."

Warnick's black brows rose and he looked to King. "Dearly beloved, then."

King smirked. "Whatever my betrothed wishes."

"Dearly beloved," the duke intoned, "we are gathered here today to join this man"—he indicated King—"and this woman"—he waved to Sophie—"in holy matrimony."

"Wait," Sophie said.

"My lady?" asked the duke, all solicitousness.

"We're doing this now?"

"Yes," said King.

"In the drive of the Duke of Warnick's castle?"

"Och. You see? She doesn't like the castle." Warnick pointed out before leaning in. "My highland keep is much nicer."

"No no. It's not the castle. The castle is lovely. But the drive—we couldn't do it in a place more . . . authentic?"

King stared at her for a long moment and then said, "If I were marrying a more authentic bride, I might be troubled to find somewhere better."

She gasped at the words. "You're horrid."

"Indeed, it seems I am. Aren't we a sound match."

"Perhaps we should wait and finish the ceremony another time," the duke said, looking from King to Sophie.

"Perhaps so," she said. She wasn't going to marry him. Not like this. Not with him furious. She turned for the curricle and took several steps before landing herself on a particularly jagged rock. She gasped her pain and reached down to inspect her slipper. "Perhaps never is a good time for Lord Eversley."

"You should be more careful about where you walk," King said, his gaze on her foot. For the first time since she'd met him in the drive at Lyne Castle, he revealed emotion. He was livid.

"Well I'm sorry if I wasn't prepared for a craggy-drived wedding. *You* should be more careful about where *you take me*," she retorted. "Now you've torn my slipper."

Warnick snorted his laughter.

"We're to be married. In this place. At this time," King said, looking away from her, the words cold and certain. He glowered at the duke. "Do it."

She stopped and turned back. "I don't think you understand," she began. "I'm not—"

Catherine interrupted her, speaking from her place in the doorway to the castle. "It's done."

Everyone looked at her.

"I beg your pardon?" Sophie asked.

"I said it's done." Catherine pointed at her. "You said, *We're to be married here.*" She pointed to King. "And he said, *We're to be married in this place, at this time.* I witnessed it, as did Alec." She looked to the duke. "You heard it, didn't you?"

"I did," Warnick said, surprise in the words. "It's that simple? No dearly beloved required?"

Catherine shrugged one shoulder. "It's the marriage that's important, not how you get to it." She looked to Sophie and King. "It's done. We've witnessed your intent to be married, and so, you're married." She smiled. "Congratulations."

It couldn't be true.

Warnick's brows rose and he nodded. "Fair enough."

"That was significantly less painful than I expected it to be," King said.

"No!" she said. If she was to marry him, she wanted something to feel like marriage. They couldn't be. This couldn't be it.

The duke looked to her. "You don't wish to marry him?"

"Not like this," she said.

"This is the only way it happens," King replied. "I want it over and done."

Sophie met his gaze, hating him. Loving him.

"My lady, do you wish to marry him?" Warnick asked again, serious this time.

She didn't look away from King. Couldn't. And she told the truth. Made the vow there in that mad place. "I do."

Fury flashed in King's eyes before he looked away.

He collected a box from the floor of the curricle and left to deliver it to the floor of the coach.

As Sophie saw it, she had two options. She could watch him leave her there, in the drive belonging to the Duke of Warnick and whoever Catherine was, or she could tell him the truth. Every bit of it. And let him decide what came next.

One month earlier, she might have chosen the first option.

But she was a different Sophie now, and so she followed him, not caring that their first argument as husband and wife was going to be immediately following their wedding, which she seemed to have missed, anyway.

"I didn't want this," she said. "Not like this."

"I'm afraid I was not in the market for half the *ton* at St. George's," he said.

"You needn't have been in the market for any of it," she said. "I never asked for you to marry me."

"You are correct. There wasn't a moment of asking."

She closed her eyes, hating the words. "I thought you did not intend to be saddled with me."

He moved to the front of the coach and six, inspecting the perfectly matched chestnuts, and testing the harnesses for each of the great beasts. "I shan't be," he said, unhitching one of the horses and reconnecting it to the coach. "We may be married, but there's no reason for us to ever interact again."

The words made her ache. The thought of having him so close, and yet impossibly far away, made her want to scream her frustration. She'd never intended for any of this. "It's that simple?"

"It is, rather," he said, moving to the next horse. "I've a half-dozen houses throughout Britain. Choose one."

She watched him. "I choose the one where you are."

His hands hesitated on the harness, briefly, barely enough to be noticed. "You want Lyne Castle?" He laughed humorlessly. "By all means. My father will no doubt adore having you in residence. What with you being everything he's always dreaded in a daughter-in-law."

She ignored the pain that came with the cold words. "I don't choose Lyne Castle. I choose wherever you are. The castle today, the town house in Mayfair tomorrow. I choose to live with my husband, whom I—" *Love.*

She trailed off, but he heard her nonetheless. "You needn't lie any longer, Sophie. You got the marriage you were hoping for. I've no need for your professions of love. And you lost the chance to live with me when you lied to me and trapped me into marriage."

She did her best to suffer the blow. "I had plans to leave."

"And be found by your father. I'm aware of those plans. They worked well."

"No," she said. "I had plans to leave the *castle*. To leave Cumbria. I never wanted anything from you but the one thing I knew you couldn't give me."

"And yet, somehow, you managed to require it of me," he said, the words filled with ire. "Lady Eversley," he fairly spat, moving to the next horse, checking its harness. "Marchioness. Future duchess. Well played."

"Not the title, King. Not the marriage." She paused. "I didn't wish to marry you. I only wished to love you."

He looked back at the harness, securing it carefully before coming around the horses to face her. "Never say those words to me again. I'm tired of hearing them. I'm tired of believing them. Love is nothing but the worst kind of lie."

"Not from me," she said. "Never from me."

"Your lie was the worst of them all," he said, and she heard the pain in the words. "Even as I struggled with the truth of the past—with the knowledge that Lorna betrayed me, with the knowledge that she'd never cared for more than my title—you gave me a new truth. You tempted me with a future."

Tears came at the words, at the confession that she had not expected. That she could not bear. "King—"

He stopped her from speaking. "You threatened to heal me," he said. "You tempted me with your pretty vows." He paused. "You made me think I could love again."

She reached for him, but he backed away from her touch, opening the door to the coach. "Get in."

She did, grateful for the privacy, eager for the journey back to Lyne Castle, for the chance to convince him that they could try again. Once seated, she looked to him, framed in the door. He did not join her, however.

He wasn't coming with her. Uncertainty unfurled through her. "Where are you sending me?"

"To London," he said, matter-of-factly. "Isn't that what you wanted all along? To return to the aristocracy the conquering heroine? The next Duchess of Lyne?"

Her stomach dropped. It was nothing like what she wanted. "I never wanted any of that and you know it."

"Well, Sophie, it seems that we all must make do with not getting what we want today." He met her gaze, his eyes glittering green and furious. "The irony of it is this—I would have given you whatever you asked. I would have begged you for forever if you hadn't been so quick to steal it."

The words were more damaging than any blow.

Before she could recover, he closed the door, and the carriage began to move.

*K*ing watched the coach trundle down the long drive, twisting and turning until it was out of sight. Until she was out of sight.

Until he was alone in Scotland, newly married, and filled with anger and something far, far more dangerous. Something like sorrow.

"Well. That was the strangest wedding I've ever witnessed." Warnick leaned against the low stone wall that marked the long-ago filled-in moat of the castle, cheroot in hand, watching him.

"You don't seem to have witnessed many weddings," King said, "Considering what a hash you made of it."

"I was trying to give you some pomp and circumstance. To remember the occasion."

King did not think he'd ever forget this occasion.

What a fucking nightmare.

He'd married her. She was his wife.

Christ. What had he done?

"I'll say this—" Warnick began.

"Please don't," King replied, unable to take his gaze from the crest where the carriage had finally disappeared. "I am not interested in what you wish to say."

"I'm afraid you're on my land, mate," the Scot drawled. "At your own request, I arranged a wedding for you. I gave you a coach and six of my finest horses."

"They weren't hitched correctly," King said, thinking of her in that carriage, careening down the Great North Road. Had he checked all six horses?

"They were hitched fine," Warnick said. "You're just mad."

"Was there food in the carriage? And water?"

"Everything you asked," the duke replied.

"Boiled water?" King asked. She'd need it for her tea, which she would find in the box he'd brought from Lyne Castle. "Clean bandages?"

She might need them.

"And honey, just as requested," Warnick said. "A strange collection of items, but every one in there. She's all the comforts of home."

Home.

The word brought an image of Sophie, leaning over the upper walkway of the library at Lyne Castle, laughing down at him. Of her in the kitchens, eating pasties with the staff. Of her at the edge of the labyrinth fountain, book in hand.

In his bed, pleasure in her eyes.

Pleasure, and her pretty lies.

He shoved a hand through his hair, hating the way she consumed his thoughts. She was gone. He looked to Warnick. "I'm ready for the next race."

Warnick raised a black brow. "After your wife?"

King swore at him, low and wicked. "North. Let's for Inverness."

"That's a long race. The roads are dangerous."

Perfect. Something to keep him from thinking of her. "Are you not up for it?"

"I'm always up for it," Warnick boasted. "And with you so distracted, I might actually win this one. I'll send notice to the lads. When would you like to leave?"

"Tomorrow," King said. As soon as he could be rid of this place and its memories.

Warnick looked to the curricle. "I see your darling is repaired."

King followed his friend's gaze, hating the look of the

carriage he'd once loved so dearly, now rife with memories of her. "No thanks to you."

The duke smiled. "She was a clever girl, selling your wheels."

"They weren't hers to sell. She's a thief."

"You think I didn't know that? She's very convincing."

I wished to say that I love you.

He'd never been so convinced of anything in his life.

He'd never wanted something to be more true.

The damn curricle was full of her. Of wagered carriage wheels and her glorious defiance earlier, when she lifted her skirts high and climbed up on the seat.

He'd been an ass, not helping her up.

And now as he faced a drive back to Lyne Castle, those memories marred the perfection of his curricle—no longer a place of safety, empty of all but thoughts of speed and competition. Instead, it was filled with thoughts of her. With her pretty lies.

I wanted you. Forever.

"I'll sell it to you," he said.

Warnick blinked. "The curricle?"

"Right now," King said.

The duke watched him for a long moment. "How much?"

It was worth a fortune, the custom box, the high, special wheels, the perfectly balanced springs, designed to keep the seat as light and comfortable as possible on long races. It was several stones lighter than other curricles. Built to King's exact specifications by the finest craftsmen in Britain.

But he couldn't look at it any longer.

She'd ruined it.

He shook his head. "Nothing. I don't want it any longer." He considered the horses and turned back to the duke. "I require a saddle."

"You are giving me your curricle," Warnick said. "For a saddle."

"If you don't want it—" King said.

"Oh, no. I want it," Warnick replied, shock in his Scots burr, moving to the door to send a servant for a saddle.

"Good," King said, moving to unhitch one of the blacks. "You can return the other horse when you've time."

The two men stood in silence for the long minutes it took for a saddle to arrive from Warnick's stables, until the duke spoke. "If I may . . ."

"I thought I made it clear that I wish you wouldn't."

Warnick did not seem to care for King's wishes. "I've never seen a man brought so low by love."

"I don't love her," he snapped.

And what a lie that was.

"It's too bad, that," Warnick said, crushing the remainder of his cheroot beneath his boot. "As she seemed to love you quite a bit."

She'd betrayed him. For his title. Which he would have given her freely. Without hesitation. Along with his love.

"Love is not everything."

The saddle arrived then, and King made quick work of fitting it to his horse. Warnick was quiet for a long time, watching him work before replying. "That may be the case, but with the way you look, I wouldn't believe it. And with the way you look, I'm damn grateful I've escaped it myself."

"That, you should be," King said, pulling himself into the saddle.

"She'll want children, you know," Warnick said. "They all want children."

The words brought back the vision of those little, blue-eyed girls. The ones he'd been sure he'd never know.

He'd been right all along.

The line ended with him.

"She should have thought of that before she married me."

Chapter 21

MISERABLE MARQUESS
MAKES MASSIVE MISTAKE

*H*e returned to Lyne Castle as darkness fell, the dwindling light having already seen the house and its residents to their chambers—sun set late during a North Country summer. He was happy for the quiet and the dark—the best conditions for getting drunk. He would leave on the morrow, to his house in Yorkshire.

The library was obviously out of the question, as it was filled with her memory, and so he took himself to the only place he knew there was decent scotch. His father's study.

He did not expect to find his father in residence.

And he certainly did not expect to find Agnes in his father's arms.

They broke apart the moment the door opened, Agnes immediately turning away from the door. Good Lord— she was relacing her bodice.

Good Lord.

King turned his back on the tableau as quickly as he could. "I— Christ. I beg your pardon." And then he realized just what he'd seen. His father, in flagrante, with *Agnes*.

His father, *the duke*, in the arms of his housekeeper.

"You may look, Aloysius," she said quietly.

He turned back to them both, standing at separate ends of the great window at the far end of the study. He considered the duo, his father silver-haired and distinguished, and Agnes, as beautiful as she'd ever been.

He glared at his father. "What in hell are you doing?"

The duke raised a black brow, a smirk on his lips. "I imagine you're well able to divine it."

Agnes blushed. "George," she admonished.

King couldn't believe he'd heard it correctly. He'd never heard anyone refer to his father as anything other than his title. In honesty, it would have taken King a moment to remember his father's given name.

Agnes did not even hesitate over it.

His father turned and winked at her. "We aren't children, Nessie. He needn't be so shocked."

"I am, indeed, shocked," King said, "How long has this—" He shook his head and looked to Agnes. "How long has he been taking advantage of you?"

They both laughed at that, as though King had told a wonderful joke.

As though he did not want to kill someone.

As though this day were not the single worst of his life.

"I do not jest," he said. "What in hell is going on?"

"What is going on is that we've a houseful of visitors, and Agnes insists on our skulking about rather than telling the truth." His father moved to a sideboard and poured two tumblers of scotch. He looked up at King. "Drink?"

King nodded, watching, flabbergasted, as the duke poured a third glass and delivered it to Agnes with a warm, unfamiliar smile before crossing to offer the remaining scotch to him. "What is the truth, Father?"

The Duke of Lyne met King's gaze. "I love Agnes."

If his father had sprouted wings and flown about the

room, King could not have been more shocked. "Since when?"

"Since forever."

Forever.

God, how he hated that word.

"How long is that?" King drank, hoping the spirits would bring reason.

Agnes replied. "Nearly fifteen years." As though it were the most ordinary thing in the world.

He looked to his father. "Fifteen years."

The duke met his gaze, all seriousness. "Since you left."

Anger flared. And frustration. And not a small amount of jealousy. His father had had Agnes. He'd had no one. "You didn't marry her."

"I've asked her every day for the lion's share of that time," the duke said, looking to Agnes, and damned if King didn't see the truth in that look. They loved each other. "She won't say yes."

King turned to Agnes. "Why in hell not?"

The duke put up his hands. "Perhaps you will understand it."

Agnes ignored his father. "I'm a housekeeper."

"Oh, yes. That's much better than being a duchess," King said.

"It is, rather," she said.

And in her words, he heard Sophie, in her slippers, nose to nose with him on the Great North Road, lambasting the aristocracy and him with it. *Arrogant, vapid, without purpose, and altogether too reliant on your title and fortune, which you have come by without any effort of your own. And somehow I am looking to trap you into marriage?*

Agnes explained. "I don't want the whole world thinking I trapped him. Thinking he's saddled with me for some idiotic reason. I don't want the aristocracy in our business."

"Hang the aristocracy, Nessie," his father said, going to her.

"Easier said than done," Agnes replied, lifting her hand to his face, stroking his cheek. "I don't wish to marry you. I wish to love you. And that will just have to be enough."

The words crashed over him. He stilled. "What did you say?"

I didn't wish to marry you. I only wished to love you.
I don't wish for you to be saddled with me.

"Aloysius?"

How many times had she said it? That she didn't want the marriage. That she wouldn't go through with it.

How many times had he told her she no longer had a choice?

He'd made a terrible mistake.

He looked to his father. "But Lorna. You drove her away. You didn't wish me to marry for love."

"I drove her away because she was after your money. Your title." His father took a deep breath, and said, "I never expected it to go the way it did. I never intended the girl's death. I never intended your desertion." Lyne drank deep before looking into his glass. "You had the anger of youth and I had the imperfection of age. I let you go," he said to the amber liquid. "I never imagined you'd be so . . ." He trailed off.

Agnes finished the sentence. ". . . so like him. The two of you, so proud, so obstinate, so unwilling to listen."

King watched his father, finally seeing the cracks in the great Duke of Lyne. Recognizing them, the way they broke the cool, unmoved façade, and made a man.

The duke looked to him. "You brought Lady Sophie

to anger me. So I gave you what you wished. Because it is easier to be the man you wish me to be than the man I wish to attempt to be." He looked to Agnes. "But I don't think she's after your title."

Agnes smiled. "I'd wager all I have on her being after something much more valuable."

I only wished to love you.

And he'd packed her in a carriage and sent her away.

He looked to his father. "I married her."

His father nodded. "I spoke to the father today. He told me the girl had lost him quite a bit of investment. Something about Haven and a lake?"

"It was a fishpond."

"Either way. He said he forced the marriage."

Except he hadn't. Not really. Sophie had said it herself; King could have refused. They were scandalous enough—*she* was scandalous enough—for no one to have questioned his decision.

But he'd wanted to marry her.

Even as he'd wanted to punish her, he'd wanted her for himself.

Forever.

"She didn't want it."

"Smart girl," Agnes said, looking to his father.

She was smart. He didn't deserve her. And she deserved infinitely better. "I forced it."

"Smart boy," his father said, meeting her gaze. "Perhaps I should post banns without your approval. Then you'd have to marry me."

King set his glass down. "Scotland is faster."

The duke raised a brow. "Gretna Green?"

"Warnick's drive." He closed his eyes. "We didn't even say vows."

It wasn't true. She'd said them. She'd looked him

straight in the eye, proud and strong and braver than he by half. And she'd said, loud enough for all to hear, "I do."

And he'd never been so angry in all his life. What an ass he'd been.

His father grew serious. "Have you made a mess of it?"

She was alone in a carriage on her wedding night. When she should be with him. "I have."

"Does she love you?"

"Yes." He'd closed the door on the words, too busy pretending he could live a life without her now that he'd lived it with her. Pretending he could live a day without her. He looked to his father, and said the only thing that mattered. "I love her."

The Duke of Lyne nodded to the door. "Then you'd best go repair what you've broken."

King was already moving.

He tore through the empty night roads, stopping at inn after inn, finding no sign of Sophie. With each successive stop, he grew more frustrated, hope dwindling as he considered the mistakes he had made, desperate to find her and put them right.

How does it end?

I hope it ends happily.

It would. He'd make it end so. He'd find her. He'd sent her away, crying, and he would not stop until he found her, and made certain she never cried again. He'd ride straight to London without stopping if he had to. He'd meet her in Mayfair.

He'd do anything he could to make sure she never cried again.

He leaned into his steed and allowed himself, for the first time since he realized he loved her, to imagine what it would be to have her. Fully.

Forever.

He imagined her in his arms and in his bed and in his home, filling it with books and banter and babies. *With babies.* The line would not end with him any longer. He'd give her children—sweet-faced little girls with a penchant for adventure, just like their mother, who was the most adventurous woman he'd ever known.

From the moment he'd climbed down the Liverpool trellis, Sophie Talbot had led him on an adventure.

Sophie Talbot no longer.

Sophie, Marchioness of Eversley.

His wife.

His love.

Goddammit, would he never catch up to her?

The thought had barely formed when he came upon a sharp turn in the road and saw a coach several hundred yards ahead, exterior lanterns swinging in the dark. It was large enough to be the one he sought, and as he drew closer, he heard the thundering of hoofbeats, loud enough to be from six matched horses.

It was she.

He nudged his mount on, eager to reach her. To win her back.

To love her.

He'd get her a cat. Black. With white paws and a white nose. Perhaps then she'd forgive him.

Two hundred yards halved, and halved again, and again, and he could see that it was the right carriage as it approached the next turn in the road. Sophie's carriage, emblazoned with the crest of Warnick's clan on the back.

He couldn't stop himself from calling out her name as the coach turned, "Sophie!" he called, pushing his horse harder, faster. He'd be alongside it in no time, and then he'd have her again.

If she'd have him.

The thought stung.

She would have him. He'd do whatever it took to win her back. He'd resort to any actions—he'd stop this carriage and hie her away on his horse, like a highwayman of yore. He'd take her somewhere beautiful and secluded, and right all his wrongs. He'd prove to her how well he could love her—better than anyone ever could.

He would spend the rest of his life proving it to her. "Lady Eversley!" he called this time, as though her married name could convince the universe that he deserved her.

He'd had enough of being away from her.

Now he wanted to be with her.

Forever.

The coach took the curve in the road, and King used the turn to draw closer. Close enough to hear the telltale pop as the inside front wheel strained. He'd heard that precise sound before, only that time, that night, he hadn't understood what it heralded.

Fear overcame everything else.

"Stop!" he shouted, pushing his horse to its limits. Begging the steed to go faster even as he yelled, "Slow that carriage!"

It was too late.

The turn was too sharp and the carriage too large, and the wheel popped again. He screamed, "No!" desperate for the driver to hear him, but the word was lost in a mighty crack, followed by the screech of horses as the coach tipped, sending the coachman flying from the block before the vehicle toppled onto its side and was pulled along the road for a dozen yards before the terrified horses came to a stop.

"Sophie!" he screamed, leaping from his still-moving steed, desperate to get to her. "No! No no no," he repeated again and again as he ran toward the carriage, unhooking a lantern and scaling it without pause, tearing open the door to find her.

Let her be alive.

Dear God, just let her live.

I'll do anything for her to live.

"You must be alive, love. I've so much to tell you," he said into the darkness, willing her to hear him. "I won't lose you, Sophie. Not just as I found you. You're not done with me, yet."

It was dark inside, and he held the lantern high, searching for her.

"Live," he said. "Live, please, God. Live."

The words were a litany as he found the pile of silk—that beautiful purple gown she'd been wearing earlier in the day.

She wasn't in it the dress.

She wasn't in the carriage.

Relief slammed through him, blessed and welcome, his heart beating once more.

She was alive.

And on the heels of that realization came another, devastating one.

She'd left him.

Chapter 22

HAPPY NEVER AFTER?

Sophie spent the first few hours on the ride from Scotland in tears.

They'd flown freely as she recounted every minute they'd spent together, every conversation, every touch. The anger he hadn't hidden from her the night her father had found them, as King had stood, naked and furious, the Minotaur betrayed.

Except she hadn't betrayed him.

She would have done anything to stay with him there, at the center of that impossible maze. Forever.

But neither of them deserved forever.

He'd said it himself, before he'd packed her into Warnick's coach, with those final, devastating words.

I would have given you forever if you hadn't been so quick to steal it.

Her tears had eventually dried, and then she'd spent what seemed like an endless time staring at the countryside, sheep and cows and bales of hay over and over, until night had fallen, and she couldn't stare at anything.

And all she could think was that he had ruined her, in the end. For all others.

Forever.

And in the darkness, she'd found strength. And made her decision.

He'd left her with a purse full of coin, bandages, and salve, and an unimpeachable understanding that he didn't wish to see her ever again. And so he wouldn't.

When her coach had stopped to change horses, the mail coach had blocked the drive, in the midst of its own change of horses and coachmen. And it had left with a new passenger, dressed as a stable boy.

After all, she couldn't very well start a new life in one of her sister's frivolous gowns. Warnick's coachman hadn't even noticed that she'd left.

Dawn crept into the mail coach, turning the inside of the vehicle silver grey, revealing the other travelers in various states of slumber. Sophie wondered at their destinations. Wondered at her own. Perhaps she'd return to Sprotbrough.

The thought of the town brought thoughts of King.

Of his lifting her from the bath.

Of his kissing her behind the taproom.

Of his hiding her from her father's men.

Tears threatened, unbidden.

No. Sprotbrough would not do.

The coach began to slow, and Sophie closed her eyes, willing away the memories that consumed her, of his welcome touch, of his teasing laugh, of his deep, wonderful voice, whispering her name.

She would never be free of that voice.

"Sophie!"

She shot up at the words. It couldn't be.

The other passengers in the coach began to wake, and the man closest to the window pushed back the curtain to find the source of the noise. He sat up. "We ain't at an inn."

She closed her eyes as the coach stopped.

"Is it highwaymen?" the woman next to her asked, panic in her voice.

"I don't think so," replied the first. "Looks like a madman."

Sophie craned to look out the window.

Her heart began to pound.

He didn't look like a madman. He looked rather perfect.

But he sounded rather furious. "Sophie Talbot, come out of that damn coach now before I come in and fetch you!"

The man by the window nudged the woman next to him. "You called Talbot?"

She shook her head.

He asked the other women in the coach one by one, ignoring Sophie altogether. When they'd received denials from all wearing frocks, the man lowered the window and shouted, "There ain't no miss named Talbot in this coach." He turned back and said to the now rapt audience, "He don't believe me."

Sophie shrank back against the seat and lowered her cap, willing herself invisible. The door burst open, heralding early-morning light and her husband, whose gaze immediately found her, then scanned her clothing. "Does no one in the goddamn country look at footwear?"

She looked down at her too-tight slippers. "There were no boots that fit."

The man at the window started back. "He's a girl!"

"He is, indeed," King said dryly, clearly unamused. "What have I said about mail coaches, Sophie?"

She scowled. "As you packed me off to London mere hours ago, with a promise never to see me again, I'm not terribly interested in what you have to say about my means of travel."

"Ah. Lovers' quarrel," explained the woman next to her, sounding rather gleeful.

"We're not lovers," Sophie snapped.

"If he's chasing after the mail coach to fetch you, you will be," said the man by the window, lowering his cap over his eyes and leaning back in his seat.

Except they wouldn't.

"Little do you know. He doesn't even like me."

"Get out of the coach, Sophie."

"Go on, Sophie, we've all places to be," said another passenger.

"As do I!" she insisted.

King raised a brow. "Oh? Where are you headed?"

She didn't know that bit. Not yet. Still, she wasn't about to say as much to him. "Sprotbrough. Perhaps you remember it. Handsome doctor?"

"I remember it, love. Every minute of it."

"Don't call me that."

"Why not? I love you."

She caught her breath at the words. He was a beast. "Get out," she said softly, hating him for saying them. For making her wish they were true.

"In or out, my lord," the coachman said from King's shoulder. "I've a schedule to meet."

He didn't look away from her when he said, softly, "Shall I get in? Or will you come out?"

"I'll go if she won't," said another woman in the carriage.

"Go, girlie," said the man at the window.

She ignored him. "You sent me away."

"I was an ass."

"You were, rather."

"That's it, lass," her neighbor said. "You stand for yourself."

King reached in, one strong hand extended to her. "Please, Sophie. I've so much to say. Come out and hear me?"

To the immense gratitude of the driver, the mixed feelings of the passengers, and her own significant doubt, Sophie exited the coach. The coach was in motion in seconds, leaving her and King alone on the Great North Road, with none but his mount as witness.

She turned to him as the sound of the mail faded into the distance. "What—"

He stopped the question with a kiss, deep and long and with an urgency that unsettled even as it tempted, his hands cupping her face. She lost herself in the caress almost instantly, devastated by it, by the fact that she'd never imagined he'd kiss her again.

She shouldn't let him kiss her.

It wasn't fair that she so desperately wanted him to kiss her.

As he released her, leaving them both gasping for air, she realized his hands were trembling. She clasped them with her own. "King?"

"I thought you were dead," he whispered before taking her lips again, equally as urgently.

She pulled away. "What? I wasn't dead. I was on a mail coach."

"The carriage crashed."

Her eyes went wide as she remembered how he so carefully checked the horses' harnesses whenever he was preparing for a journey—a vestige of the drive with Lorna. "How?"

"The wheel broke," he said. "I watched it fall." He shook his head. "I couldn't stop it. You could have died."

She took his hands in hers, holding them tightly, knowing he relived the moment—his worst nightmare. "The coachman?"

"Well. Miraculously well."

"Thank God."

"But you could have been killed," he repeated.

She pressed his hands to her cheeks. "I am quite alive."

"I nearly lost you," he said, the words quiet and devastating. "And then, just as I discovered you weren't in the coach—that you were alive, I lost you again."

She released him and took a deep breath, stepping away from the words. From their truth. "You sent me away."

He reached for her. "Sophie—"

She stepped back. "I told you that I loved you, and you sent me away."

He cursed, running his hands through his hair, "I know. I was wrong. Christ."

"I didn't wish to marry you," she said, hating the sadness in her words. The weakness there. "Not like that."

"I know," he said.

"I'm not sure you do," she said, and she couldn't bear to look at him any longer. She turned, looking down the road, where the mail coach had disappeared.

She was trapped.

Just as he was.

"I can't be married to you, King. Not like this. That's why I left the carriage." She paused and looked back to him, meeting his beautiful green eyes. She loved him too much to be married to him without trust. Without love. "I told you everything. I bared myself. My love. And it wasn't enough. You deserve better than to be trapped in a marriage you don't want." She shook her head and added, "And I deserve more."

She turned her back to walk away, not knowing where she was going, but knowing she could not stay with him.

He called after her. "I want it."

She closed her eyes but did not stop.

"God knows that you do deserve more, but I'm sorry, Sophie, you can't have it. You're my wife. And I want you. Every bit of you. I love you. More than you could possibly know. And I was a proper ass. I should have listened to you. I should have believed you."

She turned back to face him, unable to stop herself. He was coming for her, the words pouring out of him.

"I should have proposed to you last night. Before I made love to you. But like an imbecile, I wanted to propose properly. I was going to take you to the labyrinth, love. With strawberry tarts. Would you have liked that?" He stopped in front of her. "Please, Sophie."

"I would have liked that," she said softly.

"I'll do it," he vowed. "As soon as we're home. I'll take you there. I'll do it."

"I don't need it. We're already married."

"I do," he said. "Christ. I do. Give me your hands."

She did, marveling as he lowered himself to his knees in front of her. "No. King."

He kissed her hands, first one, then the other. "We don't have witnesses, but this will have to do. I love you, Sophie Talbot. I love your beauty and your brilliance and I swear here before you and God and the Great North Road that I wanted to marry you yesterday and I want to marry you today, and I fully intend to want to marry you for all the days for the rest of our lives."

She stared down at the top of his head, marveling at those beautiful curls, unable to believe that he was here, and that he wanted her.

"You believe me? I did not wish to trap you."

He stood, pressing his forehead to hers. "I was an ass. I was angry and shocked and I . . ." He paused. "I wanted to trap you, I think. And then, like a fool, I sent you away."

He closed his eyes. "I saw the carriage topple and—" He opened them. "Christ, Sophie. I died in that moment. I don't know what I would have—"

"I am alive." She pressed his hand to her breast, where her heart beat strong and true. "King. I am alive." She smiled. "You seem to have made a career of rescuing me."

He slid that hand up to her jaw, tilting her face to his, staring deeply into her eyes. "I will always rescue you." He kissed her again before continuing, "I sent you away because I was terrified of you. Terrified of how you made me feel. Terrified of the life you made me want to live. I sent you away because I was afraid I would never be the kind of man who deserved you.

"I want to be that man, Sophie. I need to love you. I need you to love me again. I need you to teach our children how to love." *Children.* "I hope you don't mind, but I'd quite like a collection of brown-haired, blue-eyed, book-loving daughters."

"You love me?"

He threaded his fingers through hers, bringing her hand to his lips. "Quite desperately."

She shook her head. "I never thought I would have it," she said softly. "I never thought I was interesting enough. I never thought anyone would love me. To be honest, I never really worried about it. I had my family, and I was happy. And then I met you." She paused. "And you turned my life upside down."

"I believe it was you who turned my life upside down."

She smiled. "All I wanted was a lift to Mayfair."

"Do you regret that Mayfair wasn't in my plans?"

She shook her head. "Not a bit. Though I could have done without all the excitement on the road."

"Too much excitement." He stole another kiss. "You are never traveling by coach again."

"I was never exciting before I met you," she said.

"I don't believe it," he said.

"It's true." Her fingers stole into his hair, pulling him to her. "I never once stole a footman before you." She kissed him then, long and lingering.

When the caress broke, he nipped at her lip. "Thief." Another kiss. "This ends happily," he vowed softly. And she believed him. "Say it again," he said, "I want to be certain that I haven't lost you."

"I love you. My husband. My King." She paused, then whispered, "Now you say it again."

And he did, again and again, until she couldn't remember a time when it wasn't true.

Epilogue

―――――――― ✑ ――――――――

SOPHIE'S ST. JAMES SURPRISE

November 1833

"This is deeply embarrassing," Sophie said from her place high atop her husband's curricle. "Are we able to be seen by a great deal of people?"

"As it is midday on a Tuesday," he replied, the words deep and dry and lovely, "Yes. We are."

She blushed. "This is absurd."

"Shall I tell you some news that I think will take your mind from it?"

She turned to him, loving the way he laughed. She smiled. "Do I look ridiculous?"

"You look perfect." He took one of her gloved hands and lifted it for a kiss. "I received news from the idyllic Sprotbrough this morning."

She straightened. Mary, John, and Bess had ultimately chosen to settle in Sprotbrough. "And?"

"Your doctor reports that Mary is the best nurse this side of the channel, and that John has a particular head for anatomy. The doctor has hopes that such a head, combined with nimble fingers, will make him a brilliant surgeon someday. Bess is running her governess ragged."

Sophie smiled. "And the doctor?"

"I'm sure the madman enjoys every bit of the mayhem."

She smiled at that. "I think it's wonderful. Everyone received their happy ever after." She had high hopes for Mary becoming more than the doctor's nurse.

The carriage made a left turn, and Sophie lifted her hands to remove her blindfold. "Is the blindfold entirely necessary?"

King caught her hands before she could achieve her goal. "You're not being a very good Soiled S, you know."

"Not even my sisters would allow themselves to be blindfolded in full view of all of London."

"Not even Sesily?"

"Perhaps Sesily," she allowed.

Once Eversley and the Duke of Lyne had combined forces to restore Jack Talbot to the ranks of the aristocratically worthy, Sophie's sisters had returned triumphantly to London. While the Earl of Clare and Mark Landry had been received happily by their respective Dangerous Daughters, Derek Hawkins had not been so lucky.

Sesily had fairly pushed the footman out of the way when Derek had arrived at the front door of the Talbot house and, in front of all Mayfair, given him the thorough set-down that the pompous, arrogant man deserved.

Since then, Sesily had become the most talked-about Talbot in London.

Until now. "This will be in the gossip columns tomorrow," she said. "I can see the headlines now."

"Sophie Sans Sight?"

She laughed. "That's not really salacious enough."

"Blindfolded Beyond Bedroom?"

She blushed again, the image delightfully scandalous. "That's too salacious."

He lowered his voice. "I am happy to show you how perfectly salacious it is this evening."

She turned toward him, and matched his tone. "Now I really do wish that we were not in public."

He growled, and she was suddenly quite warm beneath the traveling blanket. "You shan't distract me from my surprise," he said, bringing the carriage to a stop. "We're here."

She reached for the blindfold. "May I—"

"Not yet," he said, and the curricle moved as he descended.

"King!" she squeaked, "Don't you dare leave me here in front of the whole world!"

And then the vehicle moved again, and he was leaning over her, whispering low and dark, "Never. I shall never leave you."

She turned toward the words as he untied the blindfold, and she found him close enough to touch. To kiss. Her gaze fell to his lips and he smiled, then promised, "When we get inside, love."

She raised her eyes to his. "You are a rogue."

"And you aren't?"

Before she could answer, he backed away and helped her down onto the street where a collection of bystanders watched her, no doubt calculating the speed with which they could deliver this tale to the scandal sheets. The Marchioness of Eversley, delivered blindfolded and by curricle to a perfectly ordinary location in St. James by her possibly mad and most definitely madly-in-love husband.

But Sophie didn't care a bit about them now that she could see the excitement in his gaze. She shook her head. "I don't understand. Where are we?" She looked away to the storefront. "A bookshop?"

"Not just any bookshop," he said, and the look he gave her was full of arrogant pride.

She looked up to the shingle, hanging above. "Matthew and Sons Bookshop." She stilled, then turned to him, surprise and glee overwhelming her. "Matthew?"

He grinned. "The first name we ever shared."

She raised a brow. "The name we shared with my footman."

"I think you mean *my* footman, but yes."

Matthew was *their* footman now, happily employed in their Mayfair home.

Sophie laughed. "A bookshop."

That smile again. The one that made her love him more every day. "Would you like to go inside?"

She was at the door before the question was finished.

He slipped a key from his pocket and put a hand to the door. "You should know it's empty. I thought you would like to stock it yourself." He opened the door, letting it swing open into the dark, quiet room that she was already planning to fill with books from all corners of the world.

She didn't enter, instead stepping into the jamb and turning to face him in full view of all of St. James. "It's perfect."

Happy confusion flooded his face. "You haven't seen it."

She shook her head. "I don't have to. It's perfect."

He leaned in close. "You're perfect."

She lifted her hand to his face, not caring that ladies did not touch their lords in public. Not caring for anything but him. "Matthew and Sons." She tilted her head. "It might not be the right name."

"We can change it," he said quickly. "If you don't like it. Matthew doesn't mind—I think he's rather chuffed to call it his namesake—but it could certainly be something else."

"It's not that."

He shook his head, and she could see that he was becoming frustrated with her. "Sophie, it doesn't matter. Don't you wish to see inside?"

She did, quite desperately, but the moment was too perfect. "I do," she said, feigning doubt, "But I think it's important to note that we won't know for sure what the name of the shop is for a few months."

"Who cares about the damn—" He stopped. "Months?"

It was her turn to grin.

He stepped closer, and if she were more of a lady, she would have put distance between them. There were benefits, however, to being a Soiled S.

"What might the name be, Sophie?"

She did love that growl.

"Well," she said, "I cannot be certain, but do you have an aversion to the possibility of Matthew and Daughters?"

When the scandal sheets reported the events of that afternoon, it was not the blindfolded marchioness that dominated the headlines. Indeed, it was the deeply in love marquess, who, in a fit of unbridled adoration, eschewed propriety and kissed his wife in broad daylight, in the doorway of a new bookshop in front of all St. James.

All that before he lifted her in his arms, carried her over the threshold, and slammed the door with one great black boot.

Author's Note

~~~~~~

*T*he inspiration for this and all Scandal & Scoundrel books is modern celebrity gossip, something that readers who—like me—have a secret love for *US Weekly*, Defamer.com, and the *Tattler* will notice right away. Indeed, it's hard to imagine a more similar time to ours than the early 1800s, when gossip rags were as plentiful and as powerful as they are today. While *Scandal & Scoundrel* is my creation, there were dozens of scandal sheets during Sophie and King's time, many of which were just as scintillating then as they are now. I'm indebted to the vast, fascinating collections of the New York Public Library and the British Library. In less scintillating reading, Peter Nicholson, Esq. was real and did publish *A Popular and Practical Treatise on Masonry and Stone-cutting* in 1828—the perfect text with which Sophie could tease King on their travels.

When I began this book, I had no intention of anyone being shot. But Sophie is, after all, a Dangerous Daughter. I'm indebted to Dr. Daniel Medel for many reasons this year, not the least of which is his willingness to answer my panicked calls about nineteenth-century medicine and only sometimes tell me that Sophie was going to die. As always, errors are entirely my own.

This book is nothing without my tremendous editor, Carrie Feron, the wonderful Nicole Fischer, and the remarkable team at Avon Books, including Liate Stehlik, Shawn Nicholls, Pam Jaffee, Caroline Perny, Tobly McSmith, Carla Parker, Brian Grogan, Frank Albanese, Eileen DeWald, and Eleanor Mikucki. I'm so grateful to this team, and to my agent, Steven Axelrod, for making Sophie and King happen.

Thanks to Ally Carter for a long-ago bequeathal of the title *The Rogue Not Taken*, and to Lily Everett, Carrie Ryan, Sophie Jordan, and Linda Francis Lee for faith and cheerleading on this one. You'll never know how much it meant, or how much I treasure your friendship.

And, as ever, thank you to Eric—the finest tart thief I know.

Scandal & SCOUNDREL

Vol 2 / Iss 1   *Sunday, 13 October 1833*

WARNICK'S WILD WARD

WE HAVE IT on *excellent authority* that the oddsmakers on St. James's are wagering that *a certain duke* has returned to London to remind his *not-so-young ward* that **her gossip** is not **his gain.** As the air turns brisk, ***The Duke of Warnick*** dons the *mantle of matchmaker* for **Miss Lillian Harwood,** now known as MISS MUSE to those who have heard of (or, better, seen!) the *promiscuous painting* that has scandalized society and summoned the SCOTTISH SCOUNDREL south! Excitement is expected, as we await the arrival of the *Highland Devil* (and Halfhearted Duke). All that can be assured is that *autumn will bring more tartan to town . . . and ton.*

MORE TO COME.

A Scot in the Dark
SCANDAL & SCOUNDREL, BOOK II

Coming Autumn 2016

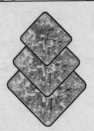